*Praise for the books by Dean Whitlock,*
*First Place winner in the Young Adult category for*
*the 2019 Writer's Digest Self-Published Ebook Awards!*

[Finn's Clock is] a delightful adventure with a street-smart narrator with a heart of gold. . . . overall, a spirited story with a lot of heart . . .
*–Judge, 2019 Writer's Digest Self-Published eBook Awards*

The *Arrow Rune* is a thrilling, world-traveling fantasy novel and Ed Lewis is a sympathetic and worthy hero. Readers will love learning about runeology and imagining themselves in the dangerous and mysterious world of this must-read tale! *–S.S. Taylor, author of The Expeditioners series*

Kudos to Dean Whitlock on another highly readable and highly entertaining work of fantasy. I couldn't put *The Arrow Rune* down, stayed up way too late to finish it. His characters, human and magical, are well-drawn and believable, the pace of the story is compelling, and his understanding and narration of the world of re-enactment and Renaissance Faires is marvelous. Even his explanation of the process of making bows and arrows was enlightening! *–Scott R. Russell, retired language teacher, beer and mead brewer/writer, author of "North American Clone Brews*

In *Sky Carver*, Dean Whitlock gives us a unique world of his own creation – a true world, deeply perceived and fully realized. As Carver, the young artist, begins his journey upriver, we can only wish for other journeys to come. – *Lloyd Alexander, Author*

The vivid characters in this novel bring it to life, giving it great depth and making it hard for the reader to put it down. Raven, with her curses and fighting spirit, and Carver with his gentle determination, carry the story forward to a dramatic climax and a most unexpected conclusion. – *Through the Looking Glass Children's Book Review*

# THE ARROW RUNE

## Dean Whitlock

**BOATMAN PRESS**
Thetford, Vermont

Cover illustration ©2019 by Maurizio Manzieri
Cover design ©2019 by Maurizio Manzieri

*Published by Boatman Press, LLC, Thetford Center, Vermont*

*This is a work of fiction. It represents many months of thought, writing, and rewriting. If you like it, please tell your friends. Thank you.*

Ed Lewis is sick of being dragged to Medieval Faires, sick of helping his uncle make bows, of minding the store, of translating his mute mother's sign language as she reads runes for the faire-goers. Only one thing makes him come this time, a chance to impress a certain young woman by winning the archery tournament. Then he discovers an ancient, rune-marked arrowhead tucked in his bedroll. Embarrassed by losing the tournament, he buries himself in making an arrow for his find. What he creates is a gate-key to another world locked in battle between his mother's people and a Briton war chief and druid witch. It's the world where his father was lost, where mad harpers pluck illusions from their tunes, and Beowulf's saga is fresh and real. Facing magic and war, Ed finds that skill, wit, friendship, and a healthy dose of fear will solve riddles that reveal the true nature of life and death. Young adult, Fantasy, Adventure

ISBN-13: 978-0-578- 59915-1

## Other books by Dean Whitlock

Finn's Clock

*The Carver's World Series:*
    Sky Carver
    Raven
    Fireboy

Iridescence and other stories
The Man Who Loved Kites *(a chapbook of the novelette, also in Iridescence)*

For Rufus the beggar
And the Bonnie Weaver

Tiw

# Chapter 1

*Gif þu wilt wyrcan godne boga   þu þearft ðrie ðing:*
*druge wudu, stranglic twin,   ond scearpe ecge.*
*Gif þu wilt wyrcan rihtan boga   þu þearft run-cræft.*

That's what Uncle Alf always said whenever he finished a new bow. "If you would make a good bow, you need three things: seasoned wood, stout linen, and a keen blade. To make the right bow you need rune-craft."

Then he would take it to my mother. She would cast her runes, point to one or two, and Uncle Alf would carefully carve them on the grip. Then he would cover the grip with leather or linen twine, whichever the customer had asked for. Most of the time, the guy didn't even know the runes were there. Or the woman. There are a lot of lady archers at the faires, particularly the SCA events. That's the Society for Creative Anachronism, the hard-core medieval re-enactor scene. They gave Uncle Alf a lot of good business. They wanted The Right Bow.

Uncle Alf never said anything about The Right Arrow. I mean, he knew that a good arrow had to be made just right – an arrow was the first thing he taught me how to make – but he never went to Mom for runes to put on an arrow. It never occurred to me on my own, either. If it had, you can be sure I would have asked for a few before the archery tournament at the Scarborough Medieval Faire.

You see, there was this girl I wanted to impress, Lady

Margaritte du Troyes. That's her character name; her real name is Gail Silverton, and she was ... What she was was way beyond my reach. We went to the same school, but I was seventeen and just finished my junior year; she was nineteen, just graduated and off to college somewhere in a couple of months. She was like five-ten; I was five-eight. And still growing, I liked to think. She had honey-colored hair and blue eyes and looked like the kind of girl who would get elected prom queen, except she could kick the ass off any guy on the football team. She was a swordswoman. Even more, she was a jouster. As in, knock someone off a horse with a big spear while riding your own huge horse. Jousting is very cool. For sure, me knocking her off her horse would've gotten her attention, but you have to be pretty rich to own a horse and buy the armor and lances and all. No way was I rich. But Gail Silverton was also a judge for the archery tournament, so I had this last, minuscule chance to get her to notice me.

It seemed like a question of life or death at the time. I had no idea.

I started planning my strategy as soon as Uncle Alf and Dennis decided we would go back to the Scarborough Faire. The organizers had hired Dennis and the Gay Blades, his sword-fighting trio, and he'd agreed as long as they also hired him on as Beorhtscyld, the *scop* – that's an Anglo-Saxon bard – to entertain at the big feast on the closing day. That guaranteed he and Uncle Alf and Mom would be going.

I was trying to think of how to *not* go. The fact is, I was getting sick of the faires – the medieval festivals, the renaissance faires, the SCA events, all the stuff I'd been doing almost every weekend, May through October, since I'd been seven. It just seemed like a really lame thing to still be doing. There was school, with college visits coming up. And friends. Music. Girls. Well, girl. Okay, that part was mostly fantasy, but it was a whole world that didn't have much to do with make-believe medieval stuff. So I hadn't been practicing my archery. I'd been avoiding it, to be honest, that and working with Uncle Alf. Your wannabe modern medieval archer would pay a lot for one of his bows, and that was really the reason Uncle Alf went to the faires. He didn't care about the costumes or the shows or the pageantry. He hadn't entered an archery tournament in years. He just liked to make bows and sell them to people who would really appreciate them. And I was supposed to feel the same way, to be happy spending all of my spare time splitting rough bow staves out of logs or making arrows and bowstrings and rubbing layers and layers of wax and oil on everything. He had me make bows, too, sometimes, like he was doing me a favor.

"You could be a skilled bowyer if you didn't let your mind wander so much," he would growl whenever I broke a stave or turned out a bow that drew a few pounds under weight. He'd burned more bows of mine than he'd sold. But he still thought I should be a bowyer, and that I should *want* to be a bowyer. There was a time when I thought I did, but not anymore. I was about to tell him so, and no way was I was going to that faire, but Dennis cut in.

"There's going to be jousting, too, Ed," he announced. "That lithesome Valkyrie, Margaritte du Troyes, will be in the lists, fighting for the honor of God and Queen against the old and loathsome Sir Gerard du Sangrise, etcetera, etcetera. I'm sure you know the pitch by heart."

I did, but I shrugged like I couldn't care less.

"There will also be an archery tournament, and our dear Lady Margaritte will bestow the honors on the victor."

"She will?" I said.

"Aha! A palpable hit!" Dennis thrust an imaginary rapier at my heart. "What say you, Egili, my pet? Methinks young Eadgar has a liking for the gel."

Egili popped his head out of his hammock and blinked at me.

Most medieval re-enactors are a little nuts, which is okay. It's just that some of them are certifiably insane. Take Dennis. He was an associate professor of Medieval Studies at Cornell. Egili was a ferret. Dennis was athletic and wore a clipped beard. Egili was a white sable male with a brown mask. Dennis could read and speak Old English (and French, Latin, and a little Greek). Egili could *dook*, hiss, and sleep a lot. Dennis loved to dress up like a courtier from the days of Queen Elizabeth, or maybe a crusader, or Beorhtscyld the *scop*, and run around the country sword fighting, reciting ancient poetry, and dragging me, Mom, Uncle Alf, and Egili with him. Dennis was really into the whole culture: the clothes, the food, the music, the epic poems. His *Beowulf* was a big hit with the dark-age Anglo-Saxon bunch. The old Anglo-Saxon riddles, too, especially the sort of dirty ones. Dennis was even a vendor. He made period hats and capes. Accessories for the best-dressed medievalists, he called them. But his real love was the Gay Blades. He said swordfighting was like chess and ballet, all in one. It was also acting, and he loved to act, even when he wasn't on stage.

Uncle Alf didn't act, he just frowned.

"Don't expect Eadgar to win," he growled. "He hasn't loosed an arrow since the fall."

"Then it's time to brace your bow and loose a few at the right target, young swain," Dennis told me. "The way to that woman's heart is through the bull's eye."

He was right, but even then I almost said I wanted to stay home, because I knew Dennis had only told me about Gail to make me want to go. I suppose he thought he was doing me a favor, but it still felt like he was using her to get at me. So I didn't practice, not when he and Uncle Alf were home, and not even much when they weren't. Okay, I did practice once, but I convinced myself I was shooting just fine and there were other things I needed to do more, even when you didn't count homework or feeding the chickens or checking the beehives or helping Uncle Alf or translating for Mom. And then it was June, school was out, and it was too late anyway.

But I had it all planned, right up to how gracious I'd be when I accepted the "honors." And the first thing I did when we got to the faire, after we had set up our tents and

Uncle Alf had his back turned for a second, was to run down the line of vendors to Cloaks and Dags and buy a jerkin I'd seen on their on-line store. A jerkin's a kind of vest. This one was leather, and it looked really cool, even if it didn't go with the rest of my gear. I thought it made me look older; maybe not taller, but stronger. More important, it was high fashion in 1350, which was the time period Gail had chosen for Margaritte du Troyes.

You can be anything you want at the faires. You invent your own character and build your own outfit. You could run into anything from Vikings to Crusaders to pirates, with belly dancers and fairies thrown in for good measure. Dennis had as many characters as he had swords, and could play each part to the hilt: Anglo-Saxon *scop*, Arthurian knight, Elizabethan courtier, Spanish soldier-of-fortune, Swiss mercenary, even a buccaneer. Mom always dressed Uncle Alf and me for the Dark Ages, 500 AD or so: plain wool pants, tunics, and cloaks. She made everything herself, even wove the cloth. And it looked it. We were commoners in real life and at the faires.

But I wanted something better for the archery tournament, and the jerkin was on sale – a faire special – so, like an idiot, I spent everything I had for Gail.

I managed to slip into the tent and hide the jerkin with my other clothes before Uncle Alf spotted it. He'd have given me hell for spending so much on a piece of clothing that Mom could have made. He'd have started by telling me I should have made it myself. But he'd noticed I was gone, so I spent the rest of the day paying for my purchase all over again by working twice as hard setting up the shop and Mom's tent and Dennis's stall, and making bows and arrows, which always fascinated the faire-goers. And there were a couple of hours translating for Mom, and Dennis's shop to cover when he went off to perform with the Gay Blades. We were straight-out busy all day, with barely time to take a breather until dinner. I didn't even get a chance to go watch Gail ride in the jousts.

The Scarborough Faire ran across three weekends, and

there was a joust each morning and afternoon. Dennis and the Gay Blades performed twice each day, too, and there were other entertainments and vendors, food halls, *jongleurs*, demonstrations of weaving, black-smithing, wandering minstrels, and lots more. Me, I didn't get one chance to wander.

I was pretty tired by the time we got to bed that night, but I hardly slept. I kept thinking about the archery tournament the next morning. About Gail. About how she would reward the victor. It would probably be a chaste kiss on both cheeks – she played a French damsel when she wasn't jousting – but I imagined a lot more. I finally dozed off listening to Uncle Alf's snoring, which was enough to drown out even the hottest romantic thoughts.

The next morning, I woke up late, to a nudge from Mom.

"What?" I groaned, then sat bolt upright when I remembered what day it was. "What time is it?" I snapped. "You didn't let me sleep in, did you? How soon is—?"

She held a hand to her lips and the other to mine, smiling. Then she signed *Calm* and *Seven. Come eat.*

Mom didn't talk. She used signs, her own made-up language that Uncle Alf and I had learned, so I was her translator at the faires. It was ironic, because I was shy and she was not. Not at all. Of course, languages were her thing. Runes. She was named for them: *Alrun*. All runes.

She had heated up leftovers for breakfast as usual: the stew and bread from the night before, plus some apples. I didn't have much of an appetite and she noticed. Mom may have been dumb, but she wasn't stupid. She caught my eye with raised eyebrows and the upward-inward turn of her wrist that meant, *Are you okay?* Sort of like she was touching her heart. I nodded but didn't say anything. She nodded back and slid her flat hand out and over, palm down. *Smooth.* In other words, *You'll do fine.*

Then she made a double-sign that translated literally to *Little Smiling*, followed by *Come Soon.*

Little Smiling was Josie Mayer's sign-name, because

she'd been so small when we met her and she never stopped smiling. Josie had been my best friend every summer since Dennis brought us to our first faire. Her mom and dad were regulars, friends of Dennis, and she was my age. Luckily for me, she didn't care that I was shy. She had enough personality for both of us. Her family hadn't been able to come this weekend, but they'd arranged a ride for Josie to be with us. When she was with her dad, Josie performed with his troupe of mud beggars, but she had become a fill-in translator for Mom and was even learning Mom's rune craft.

That was part of my plan: I didn't want Mom watching the archery tournament. Or Uncle Alf or Dennis either. It was bad enough they all knew I had a thing for Gail Silverton. I didn't need them there watching me try to win a kiss. With Josie on hand, Uncle Alf couldn't say I had to stay and work, and none of them had an excuse to close shop. I didn't say any of that to Mom, of course. You know how moms are: always wanting to know everything about your life. My mother couldn't talk, but she sure knew how to pry.

While we were eating, she reached into her rune pouch and pulled out a single rune stick. I grabbed her hand before she could open it and show the rune.

"No, don't!" I said.

She raised her eyebrows, but I couldn't explain how I felt. Almost panicked that the rune would show a bad ending.

"I just want to let it happen, okay? Whatever it is."

She nodded and put the rune away, and I mumbled, "Thanks."

She smiled, signed *Smooth* again, then reached up and brushed my hair back off my forehead, studying my face so closely, like she was trying to absorb every detail. Or read my thoughts. I felt half naked. But then she rubbed her hand hard through my hair and gave me a light slap on the cheek. Now she was just teasing me.

"Mo-om," I moaned, playing along. She flicked her

fingers at me, took my dishes, and shooed me into the tent to help Uncle Alf.

Josie arrived just as the gates were opening, blowing into the tent like a noisy gust of wind. She wasn't small anymore, but she still smiled more than most people would find humanly possible. I heard her yell *hi* to Dennis as she passed his tent and then she was inside giving Uncle Alf a big hug. She was the only person who could ever get away with it. He hardly ever hugged Mom even, his own sister. But Josie never asked permission, and it probably helped that she was one of the few people who could say a few words in his own language. She let go of him and ran over and threw her arms around me before I could dodge. We were best friends, but not hugging friends. Hugs can get misunderstood.

"Hey, Ed! You're looking good," she said, stepping back with a huge grin. "I bet you've grown an inch since March." She squeezed my biceps. "Beefing up, too."

I blushed. Josie could always get me to blush. I muttered something about her growing, too, and blushed again, because she was growing more curvy than tall. She was wearing one of Mom's old outfits, hemmed up because Mom's taller, but Josie filled out the width just fine. She laughed and slapped my cheek, mimicking Mom. "Any spare damsels better watch out." Then she was off though the flap into Mom's half of the tent.

Mom used the back half of the tent, where it was more private. People could come in, ask her any kind of question, and watch her cast the runes while sunlight played against the canvas and outlined the linen and wool weavings she had hanging around. A lot of faire-goers really get into that stuff: the show, the mystery, the linen screen between them and the real world. Mom's silence only added to the mood. The customers would guess at her signs and gasp if they got it right, even if it meant something awful was supposed to happen. They would moan or squeal. One woman even fainted once. It used to be funny, but I was so tired of being the middleman.

An hour later, Dennis still hadn't come back, and I needed to leave for the tournament. Mom didn't have any customers right then, and Uncle Alf was deep in conversation with a couple of guys dressed like Robin Hood, so I figured it would be a good time to slip off. I peeked in on Mom to make sure it was okay with her. She was studying a spread of runes scattered on her white cloth, frowning as though they'd just insulted her somehow. I probably shouldn't have interrupted, but the tournament was the only thing on my mind.

I said, "Mom? I've got to leave now, okay?"

She jerked upright, glaring at me so fiercely I almost ducked back behind the canvas flap. But her face cleared and she forced a smile, folding the cloth over the rune sticks so I couldn't see them. Suddenly my stomach felt awful. I didn't really believe she could see the future in her runes, but it was hard not to wonder. I mean, she *did* believe. And she must have read my expression. She shook her head and signed, *Not you. Smooth. Go now.*

I should have asked *If not me, who? And what? What's so awful?*

But I didn't. I just gave her half a nod and scooted to the corner of the bow shop, where my new jerkin was rolled up in my bedding. I shoved my hand in to grab it, and something sharp jabbed me in the finger. I cursed and yanked open my bedroll. My jerkin fell out, along with an arrowhead, its tip dark with a spot of blood. I cursed again and stuck my finger in my mouth. All I needed was a sore finger when I was about to draw a bowstring a few dozen times in quick order. Luckily, it was just a prick. I stared at the arrowhead, wondering how the hell it had gotten into my bedroll. And where the hell it had come from. It wasn't like any arrowhead I'd seen before. It was hand wrought, I could tell that right away. Just as I bent to pick it up, a trumpet fanfare sounded the call to the tournament.

I cursed Dennis and Josie for being late, dropped the arrowhead into my pouch, grabbed my bow and quiver, and raced out of the tent. Being late was really going to impress Gail.

Our tent was always down at the far end of Vendor's Close, a healthy distance away from the nearest vendor, so we could set up a safe target for people to try Uncle Alf's bows. The archery range was set up on the far side of the grandstand and riding ring, all the way on the other side of everything. By the time I got there, I was really late. I ran up to the judging booth just as the first archers were stepping into the stands. That's when I found out I was supposed to have pre-registered. My heart almost stopped, but Gail Silverton herself stepped in, leaning over the sign-up guy and telling him to go ahead and register me.

"Just do it quietly," she whispered. She smiled at me and my heart almost stopped again. "It's Louis, right?"

"Um, yeah," I muttered. "That's my last name. Ed Lewis. With a double-u."

"Of course, I remember now." She smiled again. "You're Eadwine. Sign in with your character name." And she strode off to watch the shooting. She looked gorgeous in a long, slender gown, kind of open at the top, with swooping sleeves, what they call a *bliaud*. But she always looked great in plate armor, too.

I signed in as Eadgar, promised to pay the fee afterward – another thing I didn't know about – and then waited for my turn. When it came, I stepped up to the stand alongside three other archers, set out five arrows, nocked a sixth, and waited. My heart was pounding.

Then Gail called, "Clear down range, *gentilhommes. Tirez!*"

The French threw me for a moment. Then I realized she meant shoot. I drew, aimed, and loosed my first arrow.

There's this thing about archery, at least the way Uncle Alf taught me: You don't aim, not really. You get the stance right, you get the draw right, but then you just see the target. Only the target. Only the bull's-eye. So it's the only place your arrow can go. If you can do that shot after shot, you're a great archer. If you can't, you suck.

That day I sucked. I looked at the target, and all I saw was Lady Margaritte du Troyes. Actually, I saw Gail Silverton. Forget the *bliaud* or the armor, I was seeing tight shorts and a tank top, hair all loose and wavy. So I blew it, shot after shot. The only thing I did halfway decent were the timed rounds, when you had to shoot as many arrows as you could in just thirty seconds. I didn't have time to think then and I did okay. But that was only one part of the score.

It didn't help that, in between my rounds, when the other groups of archers were shooting, I made the mistake of looking at the crowd. A bad idea. Doubly bad, I was pretty sure I spotted Mom and Josie hiding in the back. At the end, I waited for the scores, too shy to just leave, but not too shy to split before Gail went to kiss the winner. I threw the jerkin to a wandering beggar.

Uncle Alf gave me a look when I got back to our tent. I just shrugged and walked through into Mom's half. She and Josie were both there. They glanced up at me with blank faces, then quickly turned away. I could feel their pity. Obviously, I did see them at the tournament, and they had rushed back ahead of me. Sure, they already had a pair of chubby fairies sitting across from them on the blanket, but Mom was just getting out her runes.

I had gone in to see if she needed any help, and mostly so I wouldn't have to talk to Uncle Alf about the tournament. But Josie was here, along with the two fairy ladies, complete with wings. More like Junebugs than damselflies. They gave me twin wide-eyed stares, then giggled in harmony and looked down at the runes, as if I could read their impure thoughts. I swore that if I never had to translate Mom's silence for another bugged-out faire-goer again it'd be too soon. Josie could have it. I just wished she could translate Mom to me. Or Gail Silverton. Or life in general. *Josie? How do you translate suck?*

I mumbled *sorry* and backed out.

Uncle Alf was still giving me a dark glower. It didn't help that he is like six-four, with these really thick, pale eyebrows and a huge mustache. It made me want to hunch.

"Customers," I said, jerking my head at the tent flap. "Josie's with her."

"You could be making arrows," he said. "We need another dozen, maybe two."

"Now? I just—"

"—wasted two hours. Where your mother and I come from, a boy works as soon as he can walk. At twelve—"

"I know, I know," I told him, "I would work a full day, like any other man." *And we aren't where you come from*, I added silently. He and Mom were immigrants. I'd once said, "If it was so great there, why don't you go back?" He almost hit me then but Mom stepped between us.

"You know nothing!" he'd growled, and worked me till I dropped.

This time I just pretended I didn't know why he was being so uptight. He already knew I hadn't won; I could tell that. He was just waiting for me to tell him why. And I couldn't blame it on the bow, of course. It was The Right Bow. I'd made it myself. Uncle Alf had given it his official grunt of approval, and Mom's runes were etched under the grip. But there was no way I was going to tell him about Gail Silverton in short-shorts.

Instead, I just said, "Okay, arrows it is." And then I got my phone. Most of the fairs have rules about not using devices except for things like swiping credit cards. On top of that, Uncle Alf can't work when there's music playing, and he refuses to believe I can. I did it to bug him. I went to the arrow bench, sat down, made a show of putting in the earbuds, bringing up some tunes, adjusting the volume. But he was back at work on a bow and didn't even notice. I turned down the music, picked up an arrow blank, and clamped it in the jig.

Then I remembered the arrowhead. I fumbled in my pouch to find it, and jabbed my finger again. When I pulled out the arrowhead, there was a fresh drop of blood on the point. Uncle Alf said blacksmiths in his homeland blooded their sword blades to help temper the steel. To give them life, teach them to know their prey. Maybe it worked with arrowheads, too, and I would never lose a tournament again.

Yeah, right.

I wiped off the blood and studied the arrowhead. It had a good feel: slick, cool to the touch, a slight ripple in the surface from the blacksmith's hammer. It was beautiful really, a graceful, leaf-shaped point, sharpened all the way down both edges. But the pile – the vein between the blades – was hefty, squarish, more like a bodkin point, made to punch through chain mail, even armor. Instead of a socket to take the arrow shaft, the pile narrowed to a tang. I had never seen an arrowhead like it. I turned it over in my hand. The rippled steel had been pattern welded, which means it was forged by combining hard and mild iron rods, folding and pounding them in on themselves again and again. Arrowheads were never made like that, not as far as I knew. Only the best sword blades and maybe some spearheads. The snaking patterns in the metal seemed to move as I turned it in the light. They tricked the eyes, but my fingertips felt what I couldn't see – something etched into the steel.

I held the arrowhead closer and shifted it to catch the light from a different angle. Three straight lines appeared on the tang. It was a rune shaped like an arrowhead itself: ↑. An Anglo-Saxon rune that meant the sound of the letter T. But it also stood for an ancient battle god, *Tiw*. Warriors had it etched onto their spearheads or sword guards or pommels. It was a rune of power and protection. My heart skipped. This was very cool.

Then my fingers found another pattern on the opposite side of the tang. I turned it over, angled it to the light, and there was a second rune: ▷. *Wyn*, which was W and also *Joy*. Tiw's Joy? It sounded like a typical pagan warrior kind of thought. I turned the arrowhead over again, caressing the patterned surface. I wondered who had stuck it into my bedroll, Mom or Uncle Alf. Or Dennis? Or Josie? I knew I should ask. I should at least ask Mom about the runes. But first I was going to put it on an arrow.

I picked out an arrow shaft with a heavier spine. This arrowhead needed a stout shaft with perfect grain. It needed The Right Arrow. And I knew Uncle Alf wouldn't bother me as long as I was working. He was only a pain when I tried to enjoy myself.

I never noticed when the fairy beetles buzzed off, so when Mom came out and put her hand on my shoulder, I jumped. She was so freaking quiet. I pulled the earbuds out to let her know I was paying attention, but she gave me a really intense look, not at all like Uncle Alf's. She could glare, but she never glowered. She was tall like him, and just as blond, but pretty. I got my size and brown hair and plain face from my dad.

Mom noticed the arrowhead lying on the bench and smiled. Suddenly I didn't feel like asking her about it. She probably would have wanted to cast some runes or say something about the archery tournament. I wanted to work on the arrow. I had a good feeling about how it was going to come out, and I needed something good right then. Mom just patted my shoulder and went behind her screen. That was weird, even for her, but I was glad to be off the hook.

Josie covered for me all day, with not even a joke to try to cheer me up. That was weird, too, but fine by me. She was much better with the customers than I was. She went out front and juggled some knives until she had a crowd, then made a pitch about the bows. I just kept working. By mid afternoon I had finished the dozen arrows – I don't think I'd ever made a sheaf so quickly before – and was on the final steps on the special arrow. Everything just went Right. I was putting a spot of hide glue on the linen thread that secured the fletching, when a trumpet fanfare sounded from the grandstand.

A second later, Dennis poked his head in. "That's the call to the joust, Ed," he said.

"Yeah, I know," I mumbled. I didn't look up from the

arrow. "I'm kind of busy."

"What!" Dennis exclaimed. "Have your affections proven so flighty? Has another damsel already supplanted your sweet Margaritte? Where's your chivalry, my young squire? Where's your—" He drew his sword and waggled it. "—*force majeure?*"

I pulled out an earbud but glared at him. "Stick it, Dennis," I said.

"God's wounds! Can it be your love is unrequited? What think you, Egili? Do you smell the scent of sorrow on dolorous Eadgar?"

Dennis opened the flap on his pouch and Egili looked out, nose twitching. He yawned.

"Alas!" Dennis cried. "'Tis true then. My deepest sympathies."

I kept dabbing on glue. "I don't really want to talk about it, Dennis," I said. "Okay?"

He cut the act. "Sorry about that, Ed. She really hurt you, eh?"

I shrugged. "It's nothing she did."

Uncle Alf gave a grunt.

"Ah, yes," Dennis said. "The tournament. Major suckage, or whatever the current slang might be. For what it's worth, Ed, I have been ignored, rebuffed, rejected, and outright stomped on more than once in my inglorious youth. *Þæs ofereode, þisses swa mæg.*" That passed away, this also may.

"Yeah, thanks."

Sometimes Dennis didn't know when to stop. Uncle Alf was almost the opposite; usually he never knew what to say, so he just gave me more work to do. I put the earbud back in and tried to ignore them both. Dennis went back to his tent. Uncle Alf grunted again, then went back to work on his bow. By then the hide glue was dry, so before Uncle Alf could think of some new job for me, I pulled out the earbuds, grabbed my bow, and took the arrow outside to our little target range. I put the arrow into the rack, braced my bowstring, and tested it. Nocked the arrow.

That was when the second call to the joust sounded, and Oswald came trotting by.

"To the joust! To the joust!" he yelled, waving his arm and pointing, as if we wouldn't know where the grandstand was. Oswald, like Dennis, lived for the faires. Unlike Dennis, he was a jerk about it. He always played a court dandy, and he always volunteered to be an organizer. He liked to tell people what to do and when, convinced that he, and only he, knew the right way to do it. If he'd kept running by, we could have ignored him. Unfortunately, he glanced into Dennis's tent and saw Egili.

Oswald skidded to a stop. "Hey, you! Yes, you, Palmer. You can't have that ferret here!" He waved his hands as if he'd caught Dennis exposing himself to a busload of nuns.

No one likes to be scolded, especially by a jerk. Dennis stepped out of the tent, arms crossed. "Is there a problem, sirrah?" he said.

Oswald jabbed a sharp finger at Egili, who was perched on a shelf full of caps, staring back at him. "No pets allowed, you know that," Oswald declared.

Dennis glanced at Egili, gave a theatrical start, and turned back, acting offended. "That, sirrah, is not a pet. That is Egili, and he is very much his own ferret." As if to prove it, Egili bounded off the table, across the grass, and up Dennis's leg, to perch on his pouch.

Oswald jumped back, as if Egili had poisoned fangs. "He's an animal," he snapped.

"As are we all," Dennis replied, tucking Egili into the pouch. "Yet, unlike some of us, Egili is quiet, unobtrusive, amiable, and knows his true worth."

"Very funny," Oswald replied. "You—"

"I don't find it funny at all," Dennis said. He sighed. "In fact, I find you very tiresome."

"You cannot keep that ferret here. No dogs, no cats, and that goes for ferrets, too. It's completely against the event regulations. No animals!"

The joust fanfare sounded a third time.

"What about horses?" Dennis asked.

"That's not the—" Oswald threw up his hands and huffed. "Remove that ferret or I will have you expelled from the faire!"

Dennis smiled brightly and laid his hand on his sword hilt. "I have a better idea: let's settle it in the lists in proper medieval fashion. Ælfweard, will you second me? Alrun?" They'd both come out to watch, and Josie, too. "How about you, Eadgar? I'll need a squire."

Oswald looked very nervous. He started to shuffle off. "I'm warning you, Palmer, if the ferret is still here by the end of the joust, I'll—"

Dennis flicked his fingers at him. "Oh, begone, you lackey, you suck-joy, you pinch-faced, mewling, soft-handed, rule-bound spawn of a cleric."

Oswald could only sputter. He gave a final shake of his fist and scurried off. Right beside our target range. Dennis, Uncle Alf, and Josie were laughing at him. Even Mom was grinning. And I had an arrow nocked on my string. It was totally unsafe, but I couldn't resist: I drew and let fly just as he reached the target.

The arrow struck the bulls-eye, dead center.

The target seemed to bow inward, to ripple, like water struck by a stone.

Then it exploded.

# *Chapter 2*

Oswald yelped like a kicked puppy and tumbled to the ground. I was hit by a gust of cold wind that smelled like bitter smoke. The target was gone, and the piece of sky behind it had split open in a dark gash. The edges curled to the sides, like burning paper. Then it tore to shoulder width, all in the few heartbeats since I'd loosed the arrow. A thin, sharp wail blew out with the fading wind, as though the sky itself was crying.

A man stepped through the gash, broad-shouldered but lean, and tanned almost as dark as Josie. He was a wearing a bronze helmet, sort of Roman-looking, and he had a scowl on his face that could melt iron. He was also carrying a sword. He glanced around quickly, then turned back to us. He shouted. I didn't know the language, but it was obviously a command. Two more men hurried through the slot to stand beside him. One had a sword, the other a spear, and they both carried gray oval shields with the black outline of a raven in the center. They were dark-haired, like their leader, with black beards and tight leather helmets. Just as tanned, but their faces were streaked with blue lines. They could have been really done-up re-enactors except for the way they'd appeared. The gash was pulsing behind them. Still wailing. There was someone else in there, singing. I could just make out a figure, wild hair, a glint of metal. I stood there gawking, too stunned to think.

Mom walked past me, right toward them. And I stood there like a stick, mouth open.

The two sidemen – bodyguards, soldiers, whatever – they came forward, weapons ready. Mom didn't stop. She just lifted her hand, palm out, and kept walking. They hesitated. The one with the spear even stepped back. The leader said something harsh and pushed between them, sheathed his sword, grabbed Mom by the arm. She slapped his face. He shook her like she was a child.

That finally woke me up. I yelled *Mom!* and started to run toward her.

Dennis was faster. He had drawn his rapier and was racing over the grass.

"Let her go!" he yelled. The big guy just lifted her off the ground and hauled her back toward the gash. "Alrun, kick his balls!"

He was on them before I was halfway there. The spearman drew back his arm. Did I have an arrow? No, I had left my quiver in the tent. So I threw the bow at him. He just bounced it off his shield, then stabbed the spear at Dennis. Dennis parried quickly and bulled his shoulder right into the spearman's shield. The man stumbled back. Dennis lunged forward with a deep, low thrust. Even off balance, the spearman managed to dip his shield. Dennis's rapier stabbed into it and stuck. The swordsman moved in and struck down at him. Dennis twisted to the side, and the blade missed him by inches. Before the swordsman could strike again, one of Josie's juggling knives bounced off his shield with a clang. They aren't sharp, but he couldn't know that. He jumped back, looking around wildly for the threat. Another knife spun past him. The spearman, still off balance from the weight of the rapier in his shield, tried a jab at Dennis. Dennis yanked on his hilt, jerking the shield this way and that, dodging the spear. The swordsman blocked Josie's third knife with his shield and came at Dennis again, then stopped in mid stride. An arrow had struck his shoulder. Uncle Alf could always see the bull's-eye.

But it was only a target arrow. It had gone in deep, but just made a small hole. The swordsman stumbled to one knee, dropped his shield, and groped at the arrow. Blood was staining his tunic, but he switched sword hands and stood back up. A second arrow glanced off his arm, just below the first one. It tore his thick woolen sleeve and some flesh. He swore. I think. Whatever the word was, he was angry and in pain. Dennis drew his dagger and used it to parry another spear thrust, then jabbed it at the swordsman. He kept yanking on his rapier. I drew my knife, all I had left for a weapon, a pitiful thing meant for whittling and cutting food. I looked for an opening, waving the little knife, trying to distract the guy at least. Josie ran up beside me. Now she had her juggling clubs and was throwing them hard. She caught the spearman right in the face. He stepped back and cocked his arm, spear high, ready to throw. An arrow punched deep through his shield, but not far enough to reach him.

At that moment, Egili popped out of Dennis's pouch, bounded under the shield, and up the spearman's leg. The guy had on tight, checked trousers, a perfect ladder, but Egili tried to dig his way beneath them. Maybe he was just trying to find a better place to hide. It was too much for the spearman. He shrieked, dropped his shield, and danced away, kicking wildly.

The leader called them off. He was standing in the gash, clutching Mom in both arms. She wasn't struggling any more. She was looking right at me. I took a step toward her, but she shook her head sharply, once. I had no idea what she meant. She made a hand sign: *Wait.*

The leader barked another command and backed into the darkness beyond the gash, past the wild-haired, wailing shadow. The spearman gave a last kick that sent Egili soaring and ran for the opening. The swordsman took a weak swing, just to keep us back, and stumbled after his companions, gripping the arrow in his shoulder. Dennis gave up on his rapier and went after them with just the dagger. Uncle Alf loosed another arrow. Both too late. The wailing stopped. The gash snapped shut with a crash. The tail-end of the arrow dropped to the ground, chopped right off. My ears rang in the silence.

I ran to the spot, but there was nothing but air. And Oswald, crouching on the ground. His cod piece was soaked and he stank of piss. He stared at me, wide-eyed, pulled a cell phone out of his pouch, and keyed 911.

Dennis came up, cradling Egili in the crook of his arm. "What's this, Oswald? A cell phone? I thought they weren't allowed."

"What happened?" I demanded. "What the hell happened, Dennis? Where did they go? Where did they take —"

Uncle Alf grabbed my arm and pulled me away. "Quiet," he muttered.

"What do you mean *quiet*?" I snapped. "They kidnapped Mo—"

He slapped me hard. "I said quiet!"

I blinked back tears, stunned. Uncle Alf could be rough – he'd swatted my butt more than once – but he'd never hit me like that. I jerked my arm free. I almost tried to punch him, I was that close to losing it. "What's the matter with you? Mom's gone!"

Dennis put a hand on my shoulder. "Ed, please, there's nothing we can do until we're alone." He lowered his voice. "Don't admit that anyone is gone. You neither, Josie."

"But the police—"

"Can't help. This is something we'll have to deal with ourselves. Look, here comes faire security. Follow my lead. If they ask, say your mother went to the joust."

"They would not believe us anyway," Uncle Alf muttered.

Then the security crew arrived, followed quickly by the cop on duty, along with two or three people from the Vendors Close. By then, Josie had gone over to Oswald and calmed him down a little. Josie could do that when shit hit the fan, stay calm and talk to you in a quiet, sensible kind of way that shared it. Not at all what she was like when she was juggling or acting in a mud show. She'd worked the calm voice on me more than once when I was ready to blow up at Mom or Uncle Alf or whoever. I could have used it then. I felt like screaming.

The cop – his name badge said Quincy – asked who had made the call, and Josie stepped right in.

"It was Sir Oswald here," she said. "He was knocked down and roughed up by some tough guys dressed up like dark-age warriors, only more like Goths – anyway, very rough." She put on her big, brown puppy eyes and looked so very concerned for poor old Oswald. I knew she was acting and it just made me more angry. She should have been yelling about Mom.

Oswald cut her off and tried to tell it his way, but he was babbling so fast he got it all mixed up. You'd have thought Egili and Dennis were with the bad guys and had tried to slit his throat. Josie cut back in and gently corrected him. She said the warriors had come from behind the tent after Oswald had told off Dennis (her words) and started walking away.

"They charged the archery target and hacked it up with their swords," she said, pointing out the mess of hay and canvas scattered at our feet. "That's when they knocked Sir Oswald down. Then, when Mr. Palmer and Eadgar tried to stop them, they began to threaten all of us with their swords."

"And spears," Dennis put in. "One of them had a spear."

"One had a spear," Josie agreed. "He kept jabbing it at Mr. Palmer."

"I admit, Officer Quincy, I drew my own sword to try to parry it," Dennis said, shaking his head and looking down, acting all ashamed. "It only made them more belligerent. They must have been drunk. Luckily one of them wasn't totally blasted. He called them off when he saw Oswald pull out his phone, and they ran off that way, back around the archery tent."

"He fought with them!" Oswald cried, pointing at Dennis. "He stabbed one!"

"Don't I wish," Dennis said. "One of them rushed me with his shield, and I just held my hands up." He lifted his hands dramatically, like he was startled and afraid. "Instinctively, I guess, only I was holding my sword. What a dummy. It stuck in his shield, and when we both tried to jerk it free, he lost his grip." He pointed to the shield, lying a few yards away.

"Nice bit of gear," one of the faire security guys said. He went over to the shield and bent to pick it up.

"Don't touch the handle," Quincy ordered. "We may need to fingerprint it."

"There's another one over there, officer," Dennis said, pointing to the one the swordsman had dropped. "The guy completely forgot about it when they ran off. They had to be high on something to do that."

"They were really well costumed," Josie said, cutting off Oswald again. She started describing exactly what the three guys were wearing, with Dennis joining in on the details. The vendors who'd come over backed them up. They were the only witnesses to the whole thing, and the Vendors Close is a ways away, and it was like, whatever Josie said, they agreed to. Uncle Alf was right, no one would have believed the truth. Even the people who saw it didn't want to. Only Oswald kept going on about how they'd appeared in a clap of thunder and disappeared into thin air, and that Uncle Alf had shot arrows at them – Josie said it was just me shooting at the target before the bad guys arrived – and that they had grabbed my mom. Josie said she was the one they tried to grab, which was totally unbelievable. If you'd ever seen my tall, blonde mother next to Josie, with her chocolate hair and Hispanic skin, you'd have known she was lying. But not even the vendors picked up on it. Dennis quickly put in that Mom was at the joust with everyone else. Uncle Alf gave me a warning look. I stayed quiet, cursing him inside.

Finally, one of the vendors came right out and told the cop that Oswald had been covering his head on the ground most of the time. Josie and Dennis made such a show of ignoring the remark that you just knew it had to be true.

"I'll call in a description," Quincy said, and told the security guys to search the fairgrounds before they made any more trouble. "First bring those shields to my cruiser," he added. "Use gloves." He shook his head. "Swords and spears. And probably drunk." You could almost hear him thinking, *What a bunch of idiots. Why did I have to draw this duty?* "If you find them, call me right away. Don't try to sword fight with them. And you, Mr. Palmer, would be smart to leave that sword of yours in your tent if you don't have the sense to leave it in its sheath."

"Scabbard," a faire security guy said.

"Whatever! Go on, start looking for them. And please escort Mr. Oswald to the medical tent to make sure he's all right."

"Yes," Dennis said. "It would be simply terrible if anything permanent happened to him."

Oswald almost started in again, but two of the security guys took him by the arms and led him away, still muttering. Quincy and the other guy collected the shields and headed back to the front gate, where his cruiser was parked.

Right away I started to say something, but Uncle Alf and Dennis took me by the arms, like I was another Oswald, and marched me toward the tent.

As soon as we were inside, I jerked loose and blew.

"What the hell is going on? Who were those guys? Where's Mom? Where did they take her?" I guess I was like Oswald, hysterical. But you have to understand, my dad disappeared when I was four. No explanation. They told me he'd gone on a dig over in England – he was an archaeologist – and he'd disappeared. No one ever found him, not even a body. I had nightmares about it, about someone hauling him off and murdering him, somehow because of me. About Mom disappearing, too. I thought I'd gotten over it. It had been thirteen years, after all. I was seventeen now. But the nightmare was back, like nothing I'd ever imagined, only it was real. And I was raving. Uncle Alf raised his hand.

"Don't you dare hit me!" I shouted, fists up and ready. "Tell me what is going on here! You know! I can tell!"

"We'll tell you as soon as you calm down and stop shouting," Dennis said quietly, "Come on, Ed, take a couple of deep breaths. Lower your hands, unclench. You, too, Ælfweard."

Uncle Alf and I glared at each other. He dropped his hand. I took the two breaths and lowered mine. "Tell me," I said.

"They have taken her back," he said.

"Back? Back where?"

"Back to our homeland."

"Through a hole in the sky? That's a pile of crap!"

"Breathe, Ed," Dennis said. "Yes, through a hole in the sky."

"That's . . . that's crazy." I looked at Uncle Alf, at Dennis. I had seen it happen, but I was like the vendors: I just couldn't believe it. "How? *Why?*"

Uncle Alf shook his head. I realized there were tears in his eyes. "I don't know how."

"I do," Josie said.

She had come into the tent behind me. Holding the arrow.

# *Chapter 3*

Uncle Alf growled. That's just what it sounded like, an angry dog. He grabbed the arrow from her, glared at it, then thrust it under my nose.

"Where did you get this?" His voice was tight as his fist.

"I made it, where do you think?" I was just as angry as he was.

"The head," he said, shaking the arrow. "Where?"

"Nowhere. I found it in my bedroll this morning."

"You just found it?"

"Yeah, I just found it."

"And the feathers? You just found them, too?"

"They were on the workbench. What about it? What do they have to do with—" I stopped, remembering. We kept feathers in a box until we needed them. The ones I'd used to fletch the arrow – raven for the cock feather, white swan for the hens – they'd been lying on the bench, right where I'd find them.

"It was Alrun," Josie said. "I saw her put the feathers there when she brought your lunch. You were so busy working you didn't even notice."

"Why?" Uncle Alf said. "Why this? Why now?" It wasn't a question for us. He was glaring at the arrowhead again.

Josie answered him anyway. "The runes," she said. "She's thrown the same set of runes three times since I got here. The last time, she said, 'It's now.'"

"She said it?" Dennis asked. "Out loud?"

"No, like this." Josie slapped the back of her right hand into the palm of her left, Mom's sign for *Get going. Do it. Stop shirking. It's time.*

I'd seen that one a lot, but now I thought, *Time for what? Another nightmare?* Mom stopped talking when Dad disappeared. She didn't speak, sing, hum; she didn't even say ouch when she got hurt. Not just around me, with everyone. I didn't realize that at first. I thought I'd done something really awful, that she was mad and it was my fault. She had a beautiful voice. She and Dad used to sing together when they put me to bed. It's one of my best memories; just about the only thing I remember of him is them singing. Silence was part of my nightmares: her gone, too – into thin air, just like Dad, just like today – and nobody would speak to me.

But Mom did figure out how to speak using signs. By the time Dennis had met Uncle Alf, moved in, and started taking us to the faires, she was ready to cast the runes for anyone. Glory-twigs, they're called, or god-twigs, because God is the origin of all speech. ᚠ *byth ordtuma ælcre spræce.* ᚠ is *Os*, which means god, only this god is Woden. Mom would cut fresh branches from an apple or a pear or a cherry tree each spring to make new glory twigs. She cast the runes on a shawl of bone-white linen that she made herself from raw flax, and then she made her predictions or answered questions for her customers.

"What runes were they?" I asked.

"Tiw and Wyn and Ear," Josie said.

Ear was death, but it also translated to the sound *ea*. As in ᛠᚪᛞᚷᚪᚱ. Eadgar. Me.

"Did she say what they meant?"

"No," Josie replied.

"Tiw and Wyn are etched on the arrowhead," Uncle Alf said.

"How did you know?" I asked.

"It was made by our mother's mother's uncle," he said. "The wives kept it all the years. I watched our mother give it to Alrun."

"And now she's handed it on to Eadgar, whose name begins with Ear," Dennis said. He almost chanted it, like a prophecy or something. The knot in my stomached tightened.

"Will you all stop talking in riddles and tell me what's going on?" I demanded.

"*Wyrd*," Uncle Alf muttered.

That's Old English. Even older, before English. It looks like weird, but it's pronounced *woord*. It starts with Wyn, and it means fate.

Before I could ask whose fate, he said, "It opened the gate for Urien and the *dry-wicce*. Alrun knew it would."

"That's not any clearer!" I shouted. "What do you mean 'opened the gate'? What druid? Who's Urien? What does he want with Mom? Where did he take her?"

"He is from the old world," Uncle Alf said. He struggled for more words.

Dennis put a hand on his shoulder. He glanced at Josie, then said, "Considering what Alrun has done, I guess she thinks you're both ready for this." He took a deep breath. "Ælfweard and Alrun are not from here," he said.

"I know that, Dennis," I replied. "You've only got to listen to Uncle Alf to know it. And they're not legal immigrants, either. I figured that out years ago. Well, maybe Mom is; I mean, if she and Dad really did get married."

"She married him," Uncle Alf said, as if I'd insulted her.

"But no one married you, and that's why you only do odd jobs for cash. Why you're so frigging careful not to get noticed. Why Dennis always does the shopping and everything else that's out in public. You don't have a green card, not even a passport from your so-called Old Country. What is it today: Scotland? Freisland? Denmark? I've heard you claim all three."

"It's none of them," Dennis said.

"I don't care! It doesn't matter! Why are we standing here even talking about it! We've got to go there and help Mom, wherever it is!"

Uncle Alf raised his hand to slap me, but Dennis grabbed his wrist.

"Ed, will you please shut up and listen to me. I'm trying to answer your questions so you'll know what we're up against. It's not the Old World, it's *another* world. Another *Earth*. A parallel Earth, like this one, but . . . Well, different."

I stared at him. I opened my mouth, but couldn't come up with a single sane thing to say. I looked at Uncle Alf. He nodded slowly, totally serious. I looked at Josie. Her eyes were huge. She was as lost as I was.

"Okay," I said finally. "I've heard of that. It's a sci-fi thing?"

"It's completely real, Ed," Dennis said.

"Okay. And this Urien guy, he broke through somehow and grabbed Mom. Took her back through with him."

"Not Urien," Uncle Alf said. "This opened the gate." He held up the arrow. The arrowhead was dull gray, the ripples in the steel hidden by shadow. There was nothing magical about it. Except that the target had exploded.

"This blew a hole between . . . ?" I just couldn't say it out loud. It was too impossible.

"Not blew," Uncle Alf said. "Unlocked. Like a gatekey, a latch-lifter."

"And Urien just happened to be waiting on the other side?" Josie asked. "Ready to push the gate open as soon as the latch clicked?"

"Not alone," Uncle Alf said. "Morgwydd was there. She it is who knows how to use the key. She has a matching key and knows a charm. She waits always, watching for sign of your mother."

Dennis jumped in again. "Morgwydd is the dry-wicce, the sorceress – stay with me on this, Ed. You, too, Josie. I know I'm sounding even crazier than usual, but I swear this is the truth. Morgwydd and Urien are working together. He is a warrior chief, a warlord. His people are fighting with your people – your mother's and Alf's people, I mean. If they were on this world, we'd call them Angles, and Urien's people are Otadini, Celtic Britons. Your mother has some knowledge that Morgwydd wants to use against the Angles. This isn't the first time she's tried to take her."

"Wait a minute," I said. "You've known all along that this could happen? That this Morgwydd was just waiting for a chance? Why didn't you do something?"

"What?" Dennis asked. "Tell the police?"

"Okay, they wouldn't believe you. And Uncle Alf isn't legal anyway. Okay. But you could have set her up, ambushed this Morgwydd, hit her first. I mean, Mom had the key, right?"

"You think like your father," Uncle Alf said, "but where is he now?"

That stopped me cold again. I swallowed. "He's dead. Isn't he?"

"Most likely dead, yes. Maybe a slave. Better dead." He looked at Dennis for help.

"They did try an ambush, Ed" Dennis said. "Your father's idea. But it didn't work. In fact, it failed miserably."

"My father's idea?" I looked at Uncle Alf. "What happened?"

He just shrugged.

Dennis answered. "I wasn't there, Ed. I never knew your father, you know that. He was gone before I met Alf, or even moved to Ithaca. But what Alf told me – and your mother backed him up – was that Morgwydd was ready with Urien and a band of his men. There was a fight. Your father sacrificed himself to save your mother."

Uncle Alf finally spoke up. "Eadwine threw himself past them, charged Morgwydd with only his song. He broke through the men, broke her spell, shut the gate on the middle world." He chanted it in his own language, the language of Mom's runes. I had grown up with it. *Anglisc.*

"Alrun tried to reopen the gate and follow him, but Alf stopped her," Dennis said. "Morgwydd would have had them all otherwise. Alf told her to wait till they had the upper hand, and I think it was the right thing to do. But that's why your mother stopped singing. She cried, she mourned, but she hasn't sung a note or said a single word since."

This was all too much, and also not enough. A dozen whys and hows crowded my mind, but I could hardly sort them out. I couldn't handle any more revelations then. I stuck with the one important question.

"What do we do now? She gave me the arrowhead and the feathers, knowing I'd make an arrow and use it. She wanted the gate open, and now she's gone through. I mean, she walked right up to him and just about threw herself in his arms. She had to know we'd follow. Right?"

"Yes," Uncle Alf said. "We will follow."

"But not like this," Dennis added, gesturing at his Elizabethan costume.

"Jesus, Dennis!" I cried. "Do you think they're gonna care what you're wearing when they try to kill you!"

"We're going to need to blend in, Ed," he replied firmly. "And Alf needs his own weapons. Believe it or not, we have been thinking about this. We just weren't expecting it yet."

↑

So Josie stayed to take care of Egili and guard the tent, and Dennis drove Uncle Alf and me the two hours home to Ithaca in the van. It was a tense ride. Uncle Alf was in a black mood, silent as a rock. Even Dennis was quieter than usual. And I was even more angry, because they hadn't told me any of this until now.

"You were not ready," Uncle Alf muttered when I demanded to know why.

"Mom seems to think I'm ready!" I pointed out.

"Your words show she was wrong!" he snapped back.

"Ed, we talked about it a lot," Dennis said, "but we couldn't risk having you tell anyone else, not even Josie."

"It looks like even Josie knew more than me." Then I realized how whiney I was sounding and shut up.

Back at the house, I went right to my room and tried to decide what to take with me. My outfit was okay; Mom had made it for my last birthday – linen undershirt, wool pants and tunic, a plain wool cloak – and I realized that she must have been thinking of this day when she made them. Or a day like it, a day when I would need to fit into her world. I felt cold and then hot again. I considered taking one of Dennis's swords, but I wasn't really good enough. So I strapped on my hunting knife, a *seax* in *Anglisc*, with an eight-inch blade. Then I went out to the workshop to fill my quiver with hunting arrows.

When I came back in, Dennis and Uncle Alf were still in their room. I could hear them arguing through the door.

"No! He is not ready!" Uncle Alf said.

"She meant him to come with us, Ælfweard," Dennis replied. "She gave the arrowhead to him, not you."

"They will kill him in the first moment."

"You don't know that."

"He is foolish. His mind wanders, soft. This place is no place to become a warrior."

"He can shoot a bow, and she's his mother."

I threw open the door. "That's right! She's my mother and I'm going with you, and even if they kill me, a bunch of them are going down first!"

They were standing beside their bed, dressed like me, only Dennis had a long sword at his side and Uncle Alf was holding a spear that almost stabbed the ceiling. Two round shields lay on the bed behind them. Uncle Alf turned toward me, glaring.

"You hear him? He watches TV and computer when he should practice bow and spear. He thinks a hero learns by watching. He knows nothing of what we face."

"I work for you every spare minute," I told him. "I make arrows and strings. I split staves from piles of logs so you can make your bows. I try and try to make them myself. I clean feathers and sweep out the shop and whatever else you tell me to do. And I go to school and do my homework and follow you to faires all over the frigging countryside to help you sell bows and translate for Mom, and that gives me what? A half hour every couple of days to do something for myself? At most? You tell me how I'm supposed to learn to be a hero, because I don't even have time to take a crap!"

"You talk like a child," he growled.

"I'm seventeen, and every day you tell me to work harder, because back where you come from, a boy is a man at twelve and works like one and fights like one. Well, we're going where you come from, Uncle, and I'm going with you."

"He's right, Ælfweard," Dennis said, "he's old enough. He has the right, and the duty to his mother and father, too."

"And I made the key," I said. The arrow was lying on Uncle Alf's pillow. I grabbed it and held it up. "You don't go anywhere without me."

"You have it," he said. "Can you use it?"

# *Chapter 4*

"Of course I can use it," I snapped. I hoped. All I knew was that I'd shot it into the target. Had that done it? There was only one way to find out.

Uncle Alf and Dennis pulled haversacks from their closet and filled them with food from the kitchen and pantry: cheese, hazelnuts, some hard rolls, a few small apples, beef jerky. They moved quickly, as though they knew exactly what they wanted. I realized they'd had it all planned out, everything waiting for this moment. And they'd never told me. I was so angry I could hardly talk to them. When they were finally ready, I led them out back and set up a target. I paced off twenty yards, braced my bow, and took the arrow from my quiver. The gatekey. It didn't feel like a key, just an arrow. I nocked it, drew, aimed, and loosed. The arrow hit the target.

And nothing happened.

"You're in the red," Dennis remarked.

He was right, the arrow was in the red ring. I had missed the bull's-eye by a couple of inches. I walked over, pulled out the arrow, walked back, shot again. And missed again. Uncle Alf leaned on his spear, glowering at me. I got the arrow. Again. In all, it took five shots before I could stop trying to aim and just see the frigging bull's-eye clearly enough to hit it. And still nothing happened.

"Okay," I said, swallowing a lump of anger, "You've made your point. You do it. But I'm still coming."

"I don't know how," Uncle Alf muttered.

"You what?" Now it was me glowering at him.

"I am no *hagtesse* or *wicca*. Alrun knows the charms. There was a charm, a song, that's all I know."

"And you let me stand here and make a fool of myse —"

"She taught your father!" he snapped. "She sang to you, she taught you runes! I thought you would know!"

I almost threw my bow at him.

"Calm down, both of you," Dennis said. "Maybe this isn't the right place. Maybe we have to be at the fairgrounds."

"Like that's going to make a difference?" I said.

"It might," Dennis replied. "There might be a piece of sky iron there."

I just stared at him, wondering what else they hadn't told me about.

He explained on the drive back to Scarborough. The iron in the arrowhead was taken from a meteorite. It was one way to get good iron before they figured out how to mass-produce the stuff. Makes sense, right? The next part doesn't. When a meteorite strikes our world, its twin or match or whatever you want to call it strikes another one of the other worlds. Actually, there are lots of those worlds and the ones most like ours get hit, too. Not always in the same place, but as long as there are matching meteorites – *dopplegängers* Dennis called them – there's a link between the worlds. The arrowhead was made on their world, but it was in sync with the matching meteorite on our world. This earth. It brought them here, and it could follow the link home.

"It's keyed to something in the atomic structure of its original rock," Dennis said. "At least, I think that's what's going on. Alf believes Thunor has something to do with it. His hammer was a stone. Maybe it was a meteorite."

"Then why will going back to the fairground make a difference?" I asked again, a little more nicely. I had calmed down some now that he was telling me things.

"The *doppelgänger* might be buried beneath the fairground, still there millennia after striking the Earth. Which might amplify the effect."

"How could they make an arrowhead from it if it's buried here?"

"On their earth, it's in Northumbria."

"Where?"

"Northumbria, in England. Here, it's called Northumberland now. That's where your father first found a matching piece of sky iron, on one of his digs."

Dad met my mom on one of his digs, too. At least, that's what they had told me. I wondered how much of anything they'd ever said had been true. It shouldn't have mattered so much, I guess. A part of me could understand why they'd kept such crazy stuff secret. Crazy and dangerous, considering what had happened to Dad, and now to Mom. But the other part of me, the biggest part, felt hurt. Insulted. It was my birth story they were talking about. They should have told me.

It was after dark by the time we got back to the faire, and the spectators had all left. Only the vendors were still there. They all slept in their tents, like we did, to guard their wares. There was a group gathered around a small fire in the center of the green, but Josie was sitting at our tent. She had a kettle going on the camp stove. There was a white cloth on the ground at her feet, with a few glorytwigs scattered on it. She scooped them into her bag as we came up.

"Hi," she said, folding the cloth and tucking it under her belt. "Help yourselves to coffee and tea. There's leftover dinner inside if you're hungry." It was like she'd been expecting us.

Before we could answer, Egili poked his head out of his pouch, *dooking* quietly. Dennis scooped him up.

"What ho, furry brave friend," he said. "You saved us dinner? There's a good beast."

Egili nipped the end of his nose.

Josie made a *tchking* noise, and Egili looked at her with an expression that clearly said, "What? What'd I do?"

Dennis laughed. "He minds you better than he does me, Josefina. You are his true love."

"No, Alrun is. Egili's mad at you for going off to rescue her without him. What happened?" she asked, looking at me.

"I couldn't make the arrow work," I muttered. "Like a key, I mean."

"He doesn't know the charm," Uncle Alf said.

"Neither does he," I added.

"And I suggested we come back here, where the gate opened before," Dennis put in, before Uncle Alf or I could say anything else. He explained about the meteorite, the sky iron, and the *doppelgänger* idea. Josie didn't bat an eye.

"Makes sense," she said, "and I think I can help you with the charm." She pulled a folded slip of paper from beside the white cloth under her sash. "I found this on your work bench beside the other arrows." She handed it to me. "Alrun must have put it there. No one else writes like that."

Josie was right, the paper held a few lines of Old English mixed in with some runes. Mom had learned to write Old English from Dennis. She'd asked him to teach both of us when I was in third or fourth grade. It was fun for a while, because Josie joined us whenever she was around and Dennis was a good teacher. He was funny, using the old riddles and poems as examples, and making up new ones. I lost interest after a couple of years – I mean, none of my friends talked like that, and I was trying really hard to sound like everyone else – but I could still read and speak it. Mom never let me give it up completely. And now, looking at the three lines she'd carefully printed on that slip of paper, it occurred to me that this was the language Uncle Alf had always spoken to her before Dennis came. Old English was *Anglisc*. Their native tongue.

"What does it say?" Uncle Alf asked, peering over my

shoulder. He had never learned to write, even American English. Just his name and the numbers, and he could only read a little more. I couldn't believe I had never made any of the connections. Idiot. But what connections? They couldn't really be Angles or Saxons if they were from a different world.

"Read it, Dennis," he demanded.

"I can do it!" I snapped. I forced the anger and confusion out of my head and focused on reading the text. It was written like a poem or song, but I was used to that, thanks to Dennis. Literally translated, it went:

*Thunor's stone and Tiw's ax, fill the hole in Woden's gate*
*Sunwise thrice and moonwise back, Egil's kin work well the lock*
*Open sky-gate, open path, open world-road, Wyn's key*

Yeah, I know it doesn't rhyme. Old English poems don't, even in Old English. And Mom had used runes for all the names; sometimes just one, like ↑ for Tiw, sometimes all of them, like ᛗᚷᛁᛚ for Egil, so it didn't look like any poem you'd be used to. But the meaning seemed clear enough, except for the parts that weren't. *Thunor's stone and Tiw's ax* had to mean the arrowhead, or maybe the whole arrow. But *Fill the hole in Woden's gate*? It could mean that the arrowhead or arrow would fit the keyhole in Woden's gate. Or it could mean, *Hey, you! Put that thing into the keyhole in Woden's gate.* Or put yourself into the latch. Assuming you could figure out what Woden's gate was. And who were Egil's kin? Who was Wyn? I'd never heard of an old god named Joy.

I ranted on like this, feeling more and more frustrated every second. Uncle Alf shut me up with an answer.

"We are Egil's kin," he said. "Alrun and I. And you. He was my mother's mother's father. The arrowhead was made for him. For his children and his children's children down to this day."

"Why an arrowhead?" Josie asked. "Why not a key?"

"He was the greatest bowman ever to live. He would have such an arrowhead. No one else would know it for what it really was."

"Okay, that's all very clever," I said, "but where's the frigging keyhole?"

"There is none!" Uncle Alf growled. "There is no key! There is the sky-iron and there is the charm! That is what we must use!"

Dennis laid a hand on his arm. "Ælfweard, please, not so loud. The walls are thin."

Josie elbowed me in the ribs. She could tell I was about to snap back. "Let's all go outside where the target was and try to work the charm," she said. "Okay?"

I stomped outside. Josie had cleaned up the wreckage of the target, but I knew exactly where I'd set it up. I planted my feet, pulled the arrow from my quiver, and stuck it straight up, pointed at the sky. Nothing happened, of course.

"Now what?" I demanded. "Turn the arrow? Turn myself?"

"Walk a circle," Uncle Alf said. "Sunwise, like this." He swung his arm clockwise.

"I know sunwise!" I snapped. I started walking.

"*Gesingan!*"

"I don't know the tune!" I yelled.

"Remember!" he yelled back. "They sang it to you to sleep!"

I stared at him. "The lullaby? But these aren't the words."

"They would not use those words," Alf said. "Too dangerous. I told them not to use the song at all, but they didn't listen. You remember it. You must."

I didn't, even though I'd dreamed it so many times. It always vanished as soon as I woke up. I closed my eyes and tried to hear it. I could hear someone talking over near the campfire, cars on the highway, a plane far off and way up. No song. I shook my head.

"Remember," Uncle Alf whispered, almost begging.

"Quiet!" I took a deep breath. "Please." I started humming, trying to find the notes. There was something there, right at the edge of my hearing. I thought maybe I could coax it out if I just gave it a few real notes to play with. A couple of notes clicked. I tried the combination again and a few more fell into place. A whole phrase came back, and an image came back with it: Mom and Dad, sitting on opposite sides of my bed, singing. My throat tightened and almost choked the song, but I swallowed the knot and hummed louder.

"*Þæs is god,*" Uncle Alf whispered. "*Gesingaþ wordes eac.*" Sing the words now.

I swallowed, held the arrow up again, and started singing the charm.

"Wait," Dennis said. He gave Egili to Josie. "Call your parents in the morning. Tell them as much as you think they'll believe and ask them to come help you pack up. We'll be back as soon as possible, but don't wait here for us." He came and stood by Uncle Alf. "All right, Eadgar, sing on. We'll be right behind you. Um, we do walk behind him, Alf, right?"

"When he turns moonwise," Uncle Alf muttered. "First he walks around us. We must stay very close. Do not lose sight." He looked as grim as I'd ever seen him.

Dennis noticed, too. "Right. Don't go too fast, Ed."

I nodded. My lips were suddenly dry as ashes. I licked them, swallowed, and began to sing. I took the first step sunwise, then the next, and the next. Circling Uncle Alf and Dennis. I finished the charm by the end of the first circle and hesitated.

"*Gesingaþ,*" Uncle Alf whispered.

I repeated the circle and the song and kept going. Halfway through the next circle, the steps got harder, like walking in loose sand. I pushed on, and it got like wading in water. At each word, the water got deeper. The arrow got heavier. I began to worry that maybe the tune wasn't right. Maybe the memory was bad. I ended the third circle and turned back moonwise. I was in thigh deep, and the water was cold, thick, and getting thicker. I was half aware of Uncle Alf stepping in behind me, Dennis beside him. Their hands were clenched together. I stumbled but caught myself. Dennis took hold of my belt.

"We've got your back, Ed," he murmured.

I pushed on, but the weight of the arrow was too much. It was all I could do to keep walking and singing. My arm drooped more and more with each note, until it was pointing forward. And the weight went away. The air thinned a little. I could move more easily. At the end of the verse, the stars began to waver. There was a crack, and a dark line formed in the air at the tip of the arrow, with a smell of bitter smoke. The iron began to glow a faint blue-green. I kept singing and took another step, pushing against the strange gravity that fought to hold me back. The arrow tip touched the slit and the glow brightened. The patterns in the wrought sky-iron began to writhe like snakes. The slit tore open, a sound like a raging fire, and folded back like the halves of a double gate.

There were stars in there, wavering in an indigo sky. I hesitated, surprised by how many there were, how bright. And different, not a single constellation I knew. It freaked me, and my voice wavered. But I shook it off and sang louder, went toward them, step by step, note by note. It seemed a straight line, though I'm pretty sure I was still turning moonwise. The pressure didn't let up, it gusted in my face. And it was colder now, numbingly cold, pressing in so hard my eyes began to tear. Cold mist swirled around my knees. The blue-green sheen of the arrowhead was a ball of ice, leading onward. I wasn't aware of anything else but that and the stars, ahead, behind, above, below. And the cold all through me.

The stars were pulsing, some bright, some dim. I took aim at one, a bright one that seemed the closest, but the nearer I came to it, the harder it was to walk. I forced myself against the pressure, the freezing wind. The point of the arrow touched something hard. I leaned into it, hardly able to move my foot. A slit formed in the dark indigo ahead of me. I pushed harder, and it opened a crack, just a crack, and inside was a swirl of fire, a billow of reeking, hot wind that jetted through the crack, singeing my chilled face. I stumbled back against Dennis, lurched sideways, and the slit squeezed shut instantly, cutting off the flame.

I turned toward another star, but that was even harder. I hesitated again, and the cold became so thick it hurt to inhale. I tried swinging the arrow from one side to the other, till I felt the pressure ease again. I went that way till one small, yellow star came into view, brightened, till it was the only star I could see. The arrow twitched, like the nose of a hunting dog. The point of the iron touched the point of light, and now there was an edge there, the outline of another slit in the indigo sky. It widened, and other stars shone inside the slit, with a crescent moon. They looked familiar. I took one, careful step through.

"Thunor's stones, keep moving!" Uncle Alf growled.

He pushed, and I stumbled forward a few more paces, fell to my knees. My legs were shaking, like I'd climbed a mountain. I gasped in a lungful of air. It was cool, but not cold. Sweet on my lungs. Sweet to smell. Damp. Quiet. So very quiet; no plane, no cars, not a single voice. I hoped that was a good thing, because I couldn't go another step.

"Are we there yet?" Josie asked. She gave a faint laugh, but her voice was shaking.

It took a moment to sink in: Josie wasn't supposed to follow us. But there she was, a dim outline behind Dennis.

# *Chapter 5*

"What in all the hells are you doing here?" Dennis demanded.

As if in answer, Egili squirmed out of her grip, bounded over the coarse grass, and scrambled up Dennis's leg.

"He ran after you," Josie said. She tried to laugh again, but it was more like a sob. "By the time I managed to catch him, we were through the hole. Then it snapped shut behind us. I couldn't see you, but then I saw the light moving, the arrowhead. I yelled, but the wind . . . And the fog was . . . like hands." She shivered. "I just ran as fast as I could against it. Thank god that first star didn't open. I was afraid you were going to leave me out . . . there. Wherever."

"Little fool!" Uncle Alf growled. "You should have let the beast go."

Josie wiped her eyes. "Dennis would never have forgiven me."

"I'd have been upset, Josie," Dennis said, "but you're more important." He stroked Egili's back and muttered, "Sorry, little friend." Egili squirmed, trying to jump free. "Oh, so now you want to go back to her? Fickle as ever. Into the pouch with him, Josie, and tie it shut. If he runs off again, you're on your own."

"Wait a minute," I said. "She's coming with us now?"

"Unless you want to take her back," Dennis replied.

He had me. No way was I trying that path again until

after we'd rescued Mom. "Okay, what now? This is the place, right?"

"It is," Uncle Alf replied. He took a deep breath and looked around. We were inside some kind of enclosure, surrounded by low, grass-topped buildings and a sagging earthen wall.

"What's this, a village?" I whispered.

"*Ad Gefrin*," Dennis said, "an old hill fort and tribal center. Abandoned long, long ago. It goes back at least a hundred years BC. In our day, on our world, that is."

"How do you know?" I demanded.

"Research, Ed. I'm a college professor, remember?" He looked around, eyes gleaming. "But to actually be here. Wow. And this is where your mom and dad first met."

"Why did we come through here?" Josie asked.

"There must be star iron buried in the hill beneath these old walls," he said.

"Never mind that – where's Mom?" I asked.

Uncle Alf just grunted and led us through one of the gaps in the wall, onto the brow of a hillside. We were high up, overlooking a partly wooded valley, all shadows and odd shapes. There were more hills in the distance, black heaps ranged against the charcoal sky. The stars were amazing, more than I'd ever seen at home, and almost as brilliant as they'd been in that in-between place.

Uncle Alf pointed toward a dot of light in the valley below. "A fire. Urien's camp, maybe."

"Who else could it be?" I was still whispering. I couldn't help it.

"Travelers. There is a road."

"Even so, we'll need to be careful," Dennis said. "Ed, you stay here with Josie."

"If Mom could be down there, I'm going," I said.

"We all go," Uncle Alf said. "This is not a good place. Things live here. And when we get closer, I go first. Move silently. If you cannot, stay back and wait."

"So be it," Dennis said. "Josie, take this." He undid his belt and handed her his *seax*, sheath and all. It was eighteen inches long, fourteen of it blade. *Seax* just means *knife*, but this one was more like a short sword with a single edge and no guard. Dennis kept it razor sharp. "Just remember," he told Josie, "if they don't kill you outright, they'll make you a slave. They'll probably . . . assault you, too."

"You mean rape me?"

"In a word, yes. Are you prepared for that?"

I wasn't. I mean not ready to risk her. I knew *I* might die in a fight, but I planned to make so much trouble they'd rather kill me than take me prisoner. I hadn't been thinking about Josie. She wasn't supposed to be there. Now that she was, it was harder. We'd grown up together. Dennis had just about pushed us together so I'd have someone to play with. I'd been pretty much a loner before then. Josie knew all about the faires and she wasn't shy. She introduced me to everybody. She was like a little big sister. There was no way I could even think about her getting killed or raped. But, as usual, I didn't have much say about what she did.

"I'll be careful," she said. "You just worry about Alrun."

I wondered if maybe she'd let Egili chase after us on purpose.

Uncle Alf led us down the side of the hill and into the trees near the base. The moon was dipping close to the hill tops by the time we saw the fire again. We were close enough now to see it was flickering. Uncle Alf was a good hunter and moved quietly. He'd taught me, so I was pretty good at it, too. The ground was damp and spongy, which helped. When we got close enough, Uncle Alf made Dennis and Josie stay put behind some trees. He and I slunk forward about ten feet apart. He had his spear and shield ready. I had my bow braced, an arrow nocked, and my *seax* loose in its sheath. I was tense, almost shivering, ready to let fly at anything.

But there was no war party waiting for us, just a small horse, a little wagon and a single person rolled up in a blanket between the wagon and the fire. They were in a clearing beside a rutted track; what Uncle Alf called a road was hardly a wide footpath.

Uncle Alf motioned me to stay where I was, then crept out of the shadows. The horse snorted and pulled back, but it was tethered to the wagon. The blanket didn't stir. The person was either dead asleep or just plain dead. The hair rose on the back of my neck. Uncle Alf reached across the fire with the butt of his spear and prodded the blanket. Nothing happened. He prodded harder, and someone jumped from the wagon, swinging a long sword at his head.

I loosed my arrow. It tore through the edge of the attacker's sleeve and disappeared harmlessly into the darkness across the track. I swore and fumbled for another arrow.

Uncle Alf just managed to deflect the blow with the rim of his shield. He swung his spear in an upward arc, slicing at the sword with the blade-like head, but the attacker leapt back, then darted around and in, stabbing inside Uncle Alf's shield. He twisted away, trying to bring his shield around and his spear into play, but right in my line of fire. I couldn't get a clear shot. The sword jabbed into his gut. Uncle Alf let out a grunt, and the sword lifted for another blow.

I ran out, trying to aim around Uncle Alf. "Dennis!" I cried. "Hurry!"

Then Uncle Alf threw down his shield and grabbed the sword blade with his bare hand.

"Thunor's stones, woman!" he bellowed. "Stop that!"

Long blond hair, a gown: I finally realized the attacker was a woman.

Uncle Alf wrenched the sword from her grip and threw it down. I expected to see fingers go flying, but his hand was whole. The woman pulled a small *seax* from her belt, just a little utility knife, and backed against the wagon, blade out. I stepped closer, aiming at her chest, and she drew herself up, as if daring me to shoot. My heart lurched. She looked just like Gail Silverton.

Dennis came crashing into the clearing, sword drawn, shield up. He stumbled to a stop and took in the scene.

"Is everyone all right?" he asked.

The woman, girl, whatever, glared at him suspiciously. Uncle Alf was still muttering curses, holding her at bay with his spear and clutching his stomach with the other hand.

"She stabbed him," I gasped. "Right in the stomach."

"What?" Dennis cried. He hurried over to Uncle Alf, sheathing his sword. "Where? Is it deep? How much are you bleeding?"

"It's nothing!" Uncle Alf growled. "Just a weaving sword." He kicked it.

"A weaving sword?" Dennis repeated. He picked it up and looked it over. It was like Mom's, only metal, about three feet long and two or three inches wide, but without a hilt or guard; just a forged grip at one end. Luckily, the other end was rounded and the edges weren't sharp. "How did she manage that?"

"She's fast, the little hag," Uncle Alf muttered. "Watch her!"

I had looked away, and the woman was edging around the wagon. I raised my aim. She stopped and glared again. She'd lowered her knife hand, and I could see the tear in her sleeve. I felt a little queasy, glad for once that I'd missed.

"Do not worry, maid," Dennis said, in *Anglisc*. "We do not wish to harm you."

"But I will if you try to stab me again, little hag," Uncle Alf added.

"You're not helping, Ælfweard," Dennis said, in our English.

"You weren't stabbed."

"We need to question her. She may have seen something."

"And she may have friends hiding in the woods. A woman would never travel alone here. Even a warrior would hesitate."

"She's alone," Josie said, coming into the light. "I looked around."

The woman stared at Josie, wide-eyed. I think I mentioned that Josie's a little dark-skinned. She's adopted, from El Salvador. She's part Spanish, part Indian, and even a little bit African. Her hair is dark brown and so thick it's almost kinky. Lately, she'd been wearing it in skinny, snaky braids, only now all the little braids were twisted into two fat braids, one behind each ear, like Mom did. Only not. Josie stood out, no matter what world she was on. And then there was Egili, who chose that moment to push his head out from under the flap of his bag. The woman pressed back against the tree and made a warding sign. She certainly hadn't been that afraid of me.

"What is she? What is that?" she asked, in Old English. Or *Anglisc* or whatever. It wasn't exactly the same. She had an accent. Or maybe Uncle Alf did.

"What did she say?" Josie asked.

"What did she say?" the woman asked.

"She asked what you said," Dennis replied, in *Anglisc*. "She is a young woman, like yourself, but from a very distant land. And the animal is a type of stoat, a pet only, though he thinks we are his pets. We are travelers, seeking a friend."

"Speak slower, please," Josie asked, also in *Anglisc*. I whispered a quick translation.

Dennis told me to put down my bow. Uncle Alf refused to put down his spear, so Dennis told him to at least stop acting like he was about to slit the woman's throat. He kept speaking in *Anglisc*. He went to the fire, knelt, and added another couple of sticks. He offered the woman some water and food. She didn't budge.

"Tell us, at least, how you come to be here. Is it safe now to travel alone in this land?"

She didn't answer.

Dennis smiled. "Please, fair maid. We have lost a companion, abducted just this past day by a band of warriors of the *Beornice*. We are trying to rescue her. Have you seen such a war band go by? We think they would have passed this way, yet here you are, unmolested."

She laughed sharply. "I have seen such a band, led by a warrior in a bronze helm. I was not alone before they appeared, but my master has a weak heart and tepid water in his groin. He fled, he and his churl both, leaving me to defend myself with only a weaving sword."

"Not helpless then," Uncle Alf muttered.

"I see no field of slain, brave maid," Dennis said. "They went another way?"

"They would have chased my master, and slain him for all I care," the woman said, "and they would have slain me, too, for none would have touched me without I touched them first, hard enough to crack their skulls. Their thane made them stop and led them away."

"Which way?" Uncle Alf demanded.

"That way," she said, pointing westward.

"Toward Regensburg?"

"It lies that way, yes."

I butted in, sick of all the talk. "Did they have a woman with them? A captive?"

"Two women," she answered. "One was bound, her mouth covered, and rode behind the chief. She did look like you," she added to Uncle Alf, "though not so hairy."

"She is his sister, and this young man's mother," Dennis said. "The other, was she dark-haired, one of the *Wealcynn*?" *Wealcynn* meant British, Welsh, Pict, not Angle or Saxon.

"She was, yes, with painted skin, and she rode beside him, a leader."

"Morgwydd," Uncle Alf growled.

Dennis nodded and said, "Thank you, brave woman, you have helped us greatly. We must follow these people now, but I hesitate to leave you alone. Where were you bound?"

"My master was taking me to his home, in Regensburg."

"Then we will escort you there if you will allow us,"

50

Dennis said. "We will need horses to catch our prey. Perhaps we will find some there."

"If the people there are all like my master, they will offer you nags like this at twice their worth, but they will hide in fright if you frown. Just take what you need."

"We will bargain with them," Dennis said. "Dawn is near. Will you leave with us then?"

"I will, and join in your hunt," she said, sheathing her little *seax*. "Better to follow a warrior to certain death than cringe in safety with a coward like my master."

"You are brave and strong, but this is not your battle," Uncle Alf told her, "and we have women enough in tow."

Dennis gave back her weaving sword. "What is your name?" he asked.

"Milde," she replied, lifting her head. It means just what it looks like: mild.

Dennis laughed. Uncle Alf just shook his head.

Feoh

# *Chapter 6*

It took us half the morning to reach Regensburg, but it seemed longer, right from the first step. Uncle Alf had decided the wagon would slow us down and unhitched the little horse. Milde picked up her weaving sword and a small bundle that was all she owned and said "Shosefina" should ride. Josie said no, it was Milde's horse, she should ride. Milde said no, Josie was the lady and *she* should ride. And of course Josie wouldn't. Uncle Alf and Dennis threw up their hands and set off, leaving me in the middle. I thought, *great, I'll probably get my eyes scratched out trying to be a nice guy*. Egili saved me. He jumped out of Josie's arms and up onto the horse's back like he was born to it. I took the reins and started leading the horse up the road.

"Our chief has decided to ride," I said. "You will both have to walk."

Josie started laughing, and a moment later, Milde joined in. She had a great laugh, deep and rich, right from her chest. Like Mom's.

The two of them followed me, side by side. Milde was still a little stiff, treating Josie like she had two heads, but Josie started pointing at things and asking what they were. Before long, Milde was jumping in before I could answer. Which was good, because there were a lot of things I didn't know the words for. The horse's name, for one thing – Bil – but also the names of trees and flowers and other things that had never come up talking with Dennis or

Uncle Alf. Josie caught on quickly – she'd already learned a bunch from Dennis and Uncle Alf, but she also knew Spanish already and was taking French. She was just plain good with languages, and she tried so hard and laughed so easily at herself when she messed up a word that she won Milde over.

From plant life they moved to clothes. Milde was fascinated by Josie's tunic and cloak. Josie had made then herself from commercial fabric. The threads and weave were obviously tighter and more even than the hand-spun and -woven cloth of Milde's clothes, or even Josie's gown, which Mom had made from scratch. Josie let Milde try on her cloak, and before long the two of them were feeling each other's clothes, studying the stitching, comparing the patterns, the belts, the brooches, everything. They got way past pointing and naming to colors and even verbs, like braid, spin, hem. The language was coming back to me, and a lot of the words I did know, but now I couldn't get a word in edgewise.

By then, Egili was trying to get off Bil, so Josie handed him over to Milde. He charmed her in an instant. She let him wander around a little and do his thing. Then she draped him across her shoulders, tucked up under her long, golden hair, which was braided and held back by a braided cord tied around her forehead. Her neck was lightly tanned, and he snuggled right in, with his nose tucked behind her ear. Lucky ferret; I couldn't stop staring. Milde noticed and I blushed like an idiot. Milde smiled that tiny smile girls get when they know they look good. She whispered something to Josie, and they both started laughing. Egili woke up and blinked at me and hissed, which made them laugh some more. By the time we reached Regensburg, they were close to being best friends forever, and I was pretty sick of both them and Bil, who kept trying to stop and eat, or chew on my cloak. My boots were soaked, too. It was damp, that country.

We'd come out of the trees early on. The ground was rolling, covered in coarse grass and scraggly bushes. There were a lot of marshy areas in the low places, and the track wound between them and the slopes of the hills. Then it curved into a wide valley and followed a silty stream to Regensburg. I'd been expecting a little town – after all, that's what *burg* means – but what we came to wasn't even a village: just a few rooftops poking up behind a palisade wall that was maybe ten feet high, made of sharpened logs. People were outside, working in tilled fields between the palisade and the river. Some sheep were grazing in another, larger field farther off. There were scrawny cattle bunched halfway up the hillside. You could smell manure and worse a long ways away. Egili's nose was working overtime, and he kept trying to jump down from Milde's shoulder, so Josie put him into his pouch and closed it tightly.

By the time we got close enough to hail, the people had congregated in front of the open gate in the palisade and more had come out to join them, along with a handful of dogs of different sizes. I think the whole village was there, maybe twenty-five or thirty people, including a couple of babies and a handful of older kids. Only one person, a woman, had wrinkles and white hair. Most of the men looked like Uncle Alf, blond and tall, but really thin, like Milde. Most of the women were smaller and dark haired, but just as thin. They looked strong and healthy, but they were a rough bunch, more like some kind of foreign tribe than Americans. Of course, the place wasn't anything like America.

One man stood in front, leaning on a hoe. He wasn't armed – none of them were, except for the usual utility knives – but he looked like he could use the hoe for more than weeding.

"Greetings, travelers," he said. "What brings you this far from *Din Giardi*?"

"Greetings, Regenswig," Uncle Alf replied. "What brings me is what brought me before."

The man started. "Ælfweard? Ha! I should have expected you. Your old friends rode by yestereve."

"Urien?" Uncle Alf demanded.

"Yes, that one. And the *dry-wicce*." Morgwydd.

"How many with them?"

"Huni counted six." Regenswig looked at a younger man, who nodded.

"Four men and two women," Huni said. "They passed on the opposite bank of the Wyrrin. The *wicce* rode alone, a fine black horse. The other rode behind the thane."

"That was my sister, Alrun," Uncle Alf said. "Urien took her yesterday."

Huni looked shocked. "Had I known, I would not have let them pass unchallenged."

"You didn't know, and it is not your fight," Regenswig said. "We have seen nothing of Urien and his ravens since you left us, Ælfweard. Nor the witch. Others of the *Beornice*, yes, but none have threatened us. None have dared since Ida took *Din Giardi*, slew their leaders, and wed the chieftain's daughter. These have been quiet times since you left."

"I see you have prospered," Uncle Alf said, which made me wonder what the people had looked like before. "Can you spare us a small meal and a place to rest for a few hours?"

Regenswig frowned. "So you will follow them."

"We must. This is my nephew, Eadgar, Alrun's son. He will have his mother back."

Everyone stared at me. Nobody smiled. I don't think they thought much of our chances.

"You are welcome to rest here as long as you need to," Regenswig said.

"Just long enough to eat," I said, stepping forward. I wasn't going to let them write us off that quickly "A bite only, then we'll be after them. They won't escape us."

"Not so fast, Ed," Dennis murmured behind my back. "We still need horses."

"Then ask," I snapped.

"We're not rich." Dennis replied. "Let Alf warm him up first." He smiled at Regenswig, who was looking a little suspicious. We'd been talking in English.

Uncle Alf was glowering, too. "Excuse my nephew," he said. "He is rash and unfriendly."

"And hungry from the sound of it," Regenswig said. "The harvest is long way off but we can spare for a few who travel in friendship. Come and name your companions, and tell us how you happen to be leading Osweald's horse."

The villagers divided and he led us in. The palisade enclosed an area that was half, maybe three-quarters the size of a football field. A dozen buildings were scattered inside, and chickens were scattered among the buildings, scratching at the dirt. Most of the buildings weren't much bigger than my bedroom. They all had walls made of vertical wood planks, with a doorway and one or two windows, just square holes really, with heavy wooden shutters swung wide. The roofs were all thatched. There wasn't a sign of paint anywhere; everything was gray, even the thatch. Some of the buildings had garden plots beside them, fenced with woven branches, and there was one smaller hut that smelled like an outhouse. It was actually a dying shed. Poles out front were strung with lines, holding skeins of dull blue, green, and yellow yarn hung out to dry. They were the only spots of color in the place.

Regenswig took us to the one biggish building, in the center, with taller walls and a higher roof and a wider doorway. It was the chief's hall, for meetings and feasts and all that. The mead hall. It's hard to describe how important the mead hall is in Old English poems, but this one was so plain it would have made a re-enactor cry. I could tell Dennis was disappointed, but he was a good actor and recovered his smile and went on helping Uncle Alf tell Regenswig how we had come upon Milde, alone on the roadside. Egili interrupted by scratching like crazy on the inside of his pouch. The tip of his nose wormed out beneath the flap, and Regenswig stared. Josie pulled Egili out and tried to calm him. Now everyone was staring.

Dennis laughed "Forgive our smallest companion, Egili. He does not like being closed off from new sights. He comes from the land of the *Speonas*—" that's Spain "—far to the South. His mistress is Shosefina, a chief's daughter there."

Regenswig did a doubletake. "Forgive me, maiden," he said, bowing his head to her. "I had taken you for a Pictish girl or one of the dark *Wealcynn* of the West."

Josie bowed back and said something that was supposed to mean, "That's okay, everyone makes the same mistake," only she messed up the grammar big time.

"She is still learning our language," Dennis said smoothly.

Regenswig laughed. "I understood enough. You are welcome, Shosefina. Come inside, you and your slave. We have only plain fare, but you will have the best we can offer."

Josie looked puzzled as she worked out his speech. "Did he just say 'slave'?" she asked.

"He meant Milde," Uncle Alf replied.

"She's not my slave," Josie said, and then tried to say it in *Anglisc* to Regenswig.

Uncle Alf cut her off. "She's somebody's slave."

"But he abandoned her!"

"He will come back for her. And the horse and her baggage, they are still his."

"Look, Josie," Dennis said, butting in, "we're not in New York any more. Things are very different here."

"I know that!" Josie snapped. "But we are also talking about a person, not a horse."

The argument probably would have gone on a long time, except that Milde's owner arrived. One of the little girls ran in from the fields, yelling that two men were coming with a wagon. Milde swore under her breath.

"Do you think that's him?" Josie asked, then translated herself. "*Issa Þæt hine?*"

Milde nodded grimly.

Regenswig tried to make a joke about how busy the road was becoming and went back to the gate with the girl. Milde followed, with a frown that could have curdled milk.

As the men drew near, the one riding called a greeting to Regenswig. Then his companion, leading the wagon, noticed Milde.

"Look, Osweald, the slave girl!" he cried. "I told you she'd be here."

Osweald frowned. Maybe it was just because I knew he owned Milde, or maybe it was his name, or maybe it was both, but I hated him on the spot.

"Did you lose a little something on your way, Osweald?" Regenswig shouted, laughing.

"Where is the horse?" Oswald demanded, dismounting and tossing his reins to one of the boys. "Speak, girl! Where is the horse? Did you let him run off?"

"Bil was not the one who ran," Milde said loudly. "He stayed by me, shield-companion."

"Your little horse is safe inside," Regenswig said. He was trying to play peacekeeper, but he got in his digs. "We heard a mighty warband set on you. How many did you account for before you were overwhelmed and had to flee?"

"There were a dozen at least," Osweald said. "It was hard to tell in the dark. Their leader wore a golden helm, and a *wylisc* war-maid rode by his side. Her eyes glowed red with—"

"Yes, we saw them," Huni called from the edge of the crowd. "All five of them."

"Six, if you count the prisoner," Regenswig allowed. "They rode by early this morning."

"They brought her to you?" Osweald exclaimed.

"No, she was not their prisoner. She came with these people." Regenswig gestured our way and added, "You owe them some thanks for protecting your goods in your absence."

Osweald glowered at us, obviously put down, then forced a smile. "Thanks to you all," he said. "When she snuck off in the dark, I was afraid we'd lost her."

"Two ran off in that darkness," Milde said, "and they did not sneak, they fled."

"While you cowered under a horse's belly, too frightened to save yourself!" Osweald yelled. He strode over to her, fist raised. Milde didn't flinch. His blow snapped her head back and made her stumble, but she took it without a sound.

I couldn't believe it at first. Then Egili hissed and Josie cried out and ran over to Milde, and I saw the red weal burning on her cheek.

"You stinking coward!" I yelled. It would have helped if I'd remembered to say it in *Anglisc*, but my tone was pretty clear.

"What did you say, whelp?" Osweald demanded.

I couldn't remember the words. "*Stin–Stincan!*" I stammered. "*Stincan . . . yrhðu!*"

It wasn't quite right, but it must have been close enough. Osweald put his hand on his sword hilt and stalked over to me. He was taller and tried to lean over me, to make me step back. But I'd run into bullies like him at school. I stood my ground and put my hand on the hilt of my *seax*. It wasn't much of a show.

Osweald sneered at me. "Your tongue is clumsy and your sword is tiny. Would you like to borrow a real weapon, or should I spare you the shame and just kill you?"

Dennis laughed. "Very brave, Osweald. You surely have no fear of striplings and women. He called you a stinking coward. but I think he was wrong. I would call you simply brute; also girl-beater, turn-tail, and cur, weak-hearted, with water in the groin. But I am sure you have been called all these things before, so I won't."

"Stay out of this Dennis," I said. "I don't need your help."

"You're out of your league, Ed," he replied. "He's a professional."

"I don't care, I— "

Uncle Alf grabbed my shoulder. "This is not play-acting," he growled. "I say that to you also, Dennis."

"I knew that as soon as he hit Milde," Dennis said.

"And you still recite insults! Have you forgotten Alrun already?"

"I'm afraid Ed has put us beyond apologies," Dennis replied. Then he finished trashing Osweald. "I will only say that you, small thane, are not worthy to be her slave." He pointed to Milde, who was standing tall again. "She stayed and faced her attackers, with no more than a weaving sword. You fled."

"He will have to challenge you!" Uncle Alf cried.

"We'll see if he dares," Dennis replied, in *Anglisc.*

Osweald's face went red, but he wasn't the Oswald back at the renfaire. You didn't get to wear a sword in that country unless you knew how to use it. Only a warrior could afford one.

"You mumble pretty words, stranger, and bear a pretty shield," Osweald said, "but I have killed many pretty men like you."

"What stopped you from killing last night?" Dennis asked. "A bad headache?"

That brought a chuckle from some of the onlookers, but Regenswig wasn't smiling. "Urien and his *hægtesse* have barely returned," he said, "yet already they have brought fighting into my home, without lifting a sword. Ælfweard, can't you control your thane?"

"Can you control yours?" Uncle Alf replied.

Regenswig threw up his hands. "It is too late for that."

# *Chapter 7*

There was no "duel at dawn" rule with these people. They all went to the space outside the hall, where the ground was flat and packed hard. Osweald stripped off his baldric and belt, then his tunic and shirt, handing everything to his churl. Dennis stripped down, too, and gave his stuff to me, even his leather helmet. It was just going to be the sword and shield. Osweald was all muscle and bone. He made Dennis look fleshy. Dennis was a little shorter, too, and it crossed my mind that he might have a hard fight of it. But he practiced his acts every day, and I'd seen him spar. I'd even sparred with him, and he'd whipped my butt. I didn't think he'd lose, but if he did, I was ready to go after Osweald myself.

A woman came out of the hall with two cups and gave one to Osweald and the other to Dennis. Dennis took a sip and grimaced, but he smiled, thanked her, and took a second sip. Osweald tossed his back, wiped his mouth with his arm, and took up his sword and shield.

"What is your name, stranger?" he called. "I like to know who I'm about to kill."

"I am called Beorhtscyld," Dennis replied. "Your name I already know, and enough about you not to fear your boasting."

Dennis handed the cup to Josie and took his shield from Uncle Alf. It was painted bright gold, with a polished steel boss in the center and a brass strip around the rim.

Next to the boss was a snake-like brass dragon with six wings, copied from a real dark-age shield found in a grave in England. Uncle Alf always gave Dennis grief about his character name and the bright shield that went with it. Standing there on the edge of that circle of hard ground, I could see why. The people watching were dead serious. This was real. This was part of their lives. There was nothing made-up about it. Osweald's shield was a little bigger, maybe twenty inches across, but it wasn't fancy at all: half yellow and half blue, with a dark boss. Both shields looked solid, but they were still only three-quarters of an inch thick. Just disks of wood covered with a single layer of painted linen. Against swords that were thick, heavy, and double-edged. It was hard to imagine these shields would stop one for long.

"Any advice?" Dennis muttered.

"Don't let him kill you," Uncle Alf said.

"I'll keep that in mind," Dennis replied. "Wish me luck, kiddos."

"Break a leg," I said, trying to smile.

Josie tried to smile, too, but she looked even more worried than Uncle Alf. Her fingers were clenched around the mug, white. She had closed Egili back in his pouch, and a single rune twig lay in her right palm. The rune was ᚠ, *feoh*.

"Treasure," I whispered. "That's got to be good, right?"

She shook her head and put the rune away. Then she laid her hand on the hilt of her *seax* and glared at Osweald like she was willing him to drop dead on the spot. He was grinning at Dennis, mocking him.

"Come, Beorhtscyld," he drawled. "Show us how bright your blood is."

Dennis actually had the cool to steal some lines from *Beowulf*. "Well, friend Osweald, you have had your say, but it is mostly fear talking. This time you'll be worsted."

It was what he would do in one of his stage fights. I wondered how he could slip into that role so easily now, when he didn't know the moves ahead of time. When the guy with the other sword really meant it. Dennis nodded at Milde, who nodded back, all straight and proud, as if she was part of the script.

For a minute, Dennis and Osweald just stood there looking at each other. Osweald had his sword half raised. Dennis let his hang at his side, waiting.

Osweald struck first, two quick steps and a slash at Dennis's head. Dennis parried like he did know the moves: slip left, block with his shield, then twirl all the way around with a backhand sweep at Osweald's open side. He caught Osweald's sword just beyond the hilt, twisted down, and sent it flying into the dirt. It stuck near Milde's feet. Someone gasped, not her.

Dennis stepped back, letting his sword hang loose again. Osweald clenched and unclenched his empty fist. Everyone stared at Dennis, waiting for him to move in. He didn't. He tipped his head toward the fallen sword. Osweald chewed on nothing, glaring. Finally, he stalked over and bent down to grab the hilt. He did it slowly, but I could see his legs flex, the way his body never paused. I bit back a warning shout.

He came up swinging, out and low, at Dennis's crotch. Dennis blocked with both his sword and the edge of his shield. Osweald's sword bit through the brass rim, the blades rang. Osweald jerked his sword loose and followed round with a high cut. It was sword on shield, back and forth, five, six blows, thudding, quick, heavy, panting. Till Dennis somehow hooked Osweald's shield behind his own, jerked it loose, and came down hard on Osweald's wrist. Osweald lost his sword again, and I thought his hand, too. But no. No blood. Dennis had used the flat of his blade. He lifted the point now and took a single step toward Osweald, forcing him back, away from his sword and shield. They were both breathing hard, covered with sweat. Dennis waited, sword still raised, till Osweald retreated two more steps. There was muttering among the crowd. They were angry.

"End it," Uncle Alf growled. "They think you're playing

with him."

Dennis shook his head and lowered his sword. He turned to Regenswig.

"Osweald is brave in an even fight," he said. "Only speed and a better blade saved me. I would not betray your hospitality by killing a warrior you may soon need against real foes."

Uncle Alf muttered a curse, but Dennis ignored him. He started to say more. Osweald didn't let him. He stepped to his churl, snatched a hand axe from the belt he had given him, and threw it spinning at Dennis's back. There were shouts, cries.

Josie threw the cup. Left-handed but hard and sure. It shattered against the axe blade. Shards sprayed. Dennis was turning, the axe twisting, and the butt struck him hard just above the eyes. Not the edge at least. Dennis staggered. He shook his head, eyes clenched. Osweald grabbed his churl's spear and rushed toward him. Milde cried out. I took a step forward, groping for the hilt of my *seax*, but Uncle Alf grabbed me.

Dennis opened his eyes and threw himself sideways, just dodging Osweald's first thrust. He took the second on his shield, the third with his sword. Barely. He was slow, still off balance. Blood was seeping from his forehead and into his eyes. The next thrust slid past his guard, and a thin trail of blood lined his cheek. The crowd went silent. I could hear Egili scrabbling and hissing in his pouch. Osweald laughed and slashed the spear head at Dennis's neck.

Dennis ducked. He lurched forward, riding his shield along the shaft of the spear, holding it down, and fell into a deep lunge. The tip of his sword jammed into Osweald's stomach. Osweald grunted and bent over the blade. Dennis sliced sideways, spilling snakes of bowel as he freed his sword, then slashed upward, through the tip of Osweald's shoulder and into his neck. Osweald curled forward, eyes wide, head flopping sideways, and fell on his own bloody guts. Dennis settled to his knees, propped up by his shield.

We all ran to him, but he shrugged off our help and heaved himself to his feet. He took a step toward Osweald's churl.

"I have no fight with you," the churl said.

"Nor I with you," Dennis replied. "You followed your thane's orders last night. Today, he stole your weapon. Dishonored you. You deserved better."

The churl shrugged, grim. He didn't say anything else.

Dennis turned to Regenswig. "I'm sorry," he said. "You are short a warrior."

"The fool brought it on himself," Regenswig replied.

Dennis nodded, then swayed, shaking his head.

"Are you all right?" Josie asked.

"Depends on how many of you there are," Dennis said. "I'm seeing about three each. Hoh boy." And he threw up.

↑

It was a concussion, they decided, Josie and the woman who'd brought the cups. Uncle Alf stood back, trying not to show how worried he was, so I did the translating again. It was a good thing, because it forced me to focus, and I was feeling pretty queasy. Dennis's forehead was still oozing thick blood where the hand ax had hit him, and the slice on his cheek was, too. And there was the smell of puke on his breath, and Osweald's guts were beginning to stink. And I kept thinking *Dennis almost died. I insulted Osweald and Dennis almost died.*

The woman led us to the biggest hut across the packed circle from the mead hall. It was Regenswig's home, and she was his wife, Leofrith, one of the few blond women. Milde and I half carried Dennis. He was stumbling every step and had to stop once for some dry heaves. When we got him inside, Leofrith had us lay him down on a raised pallet covered with fleeces. His face looked as grey as the wool. Josie finally freed poor Egili and handed him to Milde, then she and Leofrith went to work on Dennis with some rags, staunching the blood.

A little girl had followed us in, a daughter. Leofrith

told her to fetch clean water, and the girl grabbed a wooden bucket half her height. Milde offered to do it, but Leofrith said it had to be brought by a virgin. Milde stopped. I stared at her, then blushed when she stared back. Josie made me translate and rolled her eyes when I blushed some more.

"I can get the water," she said

But Leofrith said no, Josie could help her better by staying. And then she told the girl to make sure she came to the water on her right side, dipped the bucket three times, and walked back without looking to right or left. I was glad Josie stayed then, to make sure Leofrith didn't put leeches on him or something. I started worrying again when she took five or six kinds of herbs out of small pots, along with some tiny bones and something that I swear looked like deer poop. She ground them all together with a mortar and pestle and made a paste of it with honey. And then she spit in it and whispered some words I didn't catch. Josie just leaned close and watched and listened and didn't say a thing when Leofrith smeared the stuff all over Dennis's cuts. She did suggest they boil the water when the girl came back.

"Tell them in my country we have learned that boiling strengthens the water's spirit against venom and bile," she told me.

*Whatever*, I thought, but I told Leofrith, and she nodded and did it. The hearth was in the middle of the room, and the smoke from the new fire collected in the high peak and drifted just above our heads, looking for places to seep out through the thatch. It got thick before the wood fully caught. Meanwhile, Leofrith laid a white square of linen on the floor and took some runes from a pouch hung on her belt. She whispered another charm and cast rune twigs onto the linen. With the smoke and the shafts of light from the windows and dark wood walls, the scene was like something out of a movie, but the action was also familiar, just what Mom would do.

We should have been following her already. On

horses. Only I had gotten Dennis in a fight. Osweald deserved what he got, maybe. Milde didn't belong to him anymore. But Mom was still a prisoner, getting farther away every minute that Dennis lay half conscious on that pile of sheepskins. I choked up. And there was Milde, kneeling by Dennis' side, watching me. I smiled and looked away, hoping she didn't notice how wet my eyes were.

Leofrith had picked out three of the runes, including ᛒ, *beorc*, for Beorhtscyld. Josie chose another one and offered it to her. It was ᛗ, *Dæg*, the *d* for Dennis. Leofrith took it with a nod. Between gestures and glances, they hardly needed me to translate any more. Leofrith carved the four runes onto a single slip of wood and put the slip into the boiling water, along with the rags they had used to clean Dennis's wounds. After a couple of minutes, she scooped out the slip with a wooden spoon and carried it over to Dennis. She scraped a little of the goo off his forehead, till the wound began to seep again, and she painted the thick blood into the runes with the back edge of her *seax*. Josie smeared more goo on Dennis and wrapped his forehead with a strip of boiled linen while the blood in the carved runes dried.

Finally, Leofrith made Dennis sit up and throw the slip of wood over his left shoulder into the pot of water, while she chanted, "Water to blood, wood to bone, mallow to marrow, fur to flesh, evil to breath, all venom washed away." And the little girl hurried out with the pot to empty it into the running river at the same place where she had dipped the water.

"Thank you, dear ladies. I feel better already," Dennis mumbled.

Leofrith and Josie shared a glance. They made him drink some concoction of herbs, and he fell asleep almost as soon as he lay back down. Milde set Egili beside him. The little guy sniffed at Dennis's face, then climbed up on his chest and flopped down wearily. Milde pulled up a stool, like she was planning to keep watch until Dennis was healed. She took a drop spindle and a clump of wool out of her bundle, and began to spin yarn. It was something Mom did whenever she had a spare moment.

My throat tightened. It was obvious we weren't going anywhere for a while. I sank onto a bench by the fire. I was exhausted myself. We'd been up for two days and a night without a break, except for maybe one hour before dawn, and I hadn't slept a wink then. I rubbed my face and tried not to think about Mom.

Josie put a hand on my shoulder. "He'll be fine, Ed," she said.

"Right. Nothing like a little spit and deer shit to chase the evil venoms away." It was mean, but that's how tired and bummed I was.

"If the charm is right."

"Yeah. Just like the *feoh* rune you picked. A real treasure."

She sat beside me. "Runes have more than one meaning, Ed, you know that. There's always the reflection. *Feoh* and *facen*."

She was right, of course. Mom had taught us both about reading runes. Nothing is ever what it looks like at first glance. *Feoh* and *facen*. *Treasure* and *treachery*. I rubbed my face again, wondering if Osweald's treachery was all of it. Or was Leofrith—Lovepeace—trying to poison Dennis?

# *Chapter 8*

I felt terrible the next day. I'd made the mistake of going to the mead hall to find Uncle Alf and get something to eat. The food was nothing special, just a thin stew with barley and bits of tough beef and some chopped-up greens. A lot more broth than beef. It was *briw*, something Mom had made at least twice a week before Dennis had moved in. Eating it almost gave me another lump in the throat. But what got my head was the beer. It was the only thing to drink, and it tasted terrible. I'd never liked the taste of beer the couple of times Dennis let me try a sip. This stuff was worse, and it wasn't even very alcoholic, near as I could tell. It was just vile. The next morning my head was pounding, like I was the one who'd been hit in the face with an axe.

But Dennis was fine. His stomach was fine, his vision was fine. If it hadn't been for the scabby bandages, you would have thought the duel had never happened. He said his head still hurt a little, he didn't feel a hundred percent, but he ate a full bowl of the thin *briw* and complimented Leofrith so much Uncle Alf had to tell him to tone it down before Regenswig decided to challenge him to another duel.

Leofrith just laughed, and then she and Josie made Dennis sit still while they checked his wounds. I couldn't believe it; the slice on his cheek was hardly more than a scar, and his forehead had scabbed right over. The big bruise was already yellow and fading. Mom had given me herbal teas and made salves with beeswax and oil and herbs, but she'd never done anything like this. Josie gave me a told-you-so look, and all I could do was shrug. Leofrith was pleased, too. She had her little girl boil up some more water to rinse the scabs, and then she spit on them, smeared on more of the deer-poop-and-bone-dust goo, and put on new bandages.

By the time we got outside, most of the village was working in the fields or the dye shed. Regenswig was waiting for us in the mead hall. It was time to finish up the mess with Osweald. I thought maybe Osweald's family would demand *weregild* – payment for his life – but Osweald's wife had died the past winter in childbirth. The baby hadn't lived more than a month, and she'd been the first child. The only people with a claim to Osweald's goods were his churl, Regenswig, and the man who'd won the duel, Dennis. The churl's status was more complicated, because Dennis had a right to become his thane. A churl is a freeman, but he serves a thane, who serves the chief, in this case Regenswig.

And then there was Milde, who had been hovering by Dennis's side. She was sitting across the table from him, spinning yarn on her drop spindle, with Egili curled up on her lap.

Dennis made the churl happy by telling him to serve Regenswig, and giving him all of Osweald's weapons: sword, shield, spears, the works. Except for the little hand ax that had almost killed him. He handed that to Josie.

"May you use it to save my life again and again," he said, acting all formal. She laughed, a little embarrassed, but she gave it a quick double flip, testing the balance, before sliding the haft under her belt and handing back Dennis's long *seax*. Regenswig looked a bit startled, but I guess he already thought we were all nuts.

Then Dennis told Regenswig that he made no claim to Osweald's other goods; they should be divided among the churl and the village as Regenswig and Leofrith saw fit.

Except for the horses. That did not make Regenswig happy, because horses were important, expensive, and very high status. Osweald had owned three, if you counted little Bil. Dennis had a clear right to the weapons, but this was stretching it.

"You know our quarry," Dennis said. "We can't hope to catch them on foot. We need three horses."

"Four," Josie said. She'd been listening closely and had made out the gist.

"You're staying here," Uncle Alf growled.

"Like hell I am," she replied.

He glared at her, and she glared back. "If something happens to us—," he began.

"If something happens to you, I'm trapped here. Unless Ed stays, too."

"No way I'm staying," I said.

Dennis came in on her side. "Let her come, Alf. These aren't her people. Alrun is, and I think she expected Josie to be with us."

Uncle Alf grumbled, but he never could refuse Dennis.

"So we'll need four horses," Dennis said to Regenswig, and he offered to buy one, and to pay in gold, and to return them all if we succeeded.

"That is a large *if*," Regenswig said. He glanced at Leofrith, who nodded, all stern. "But if you do succeed in ridding us of the *dry-wicce*, it will be a good thing."

He and Uncle Alf haggled over the price, but not too much. Regenswig knew we were in a hurry and didn't have any other showroom to visit. Uncle Alf and Dennis pulled lengths of gold chain out of their haversacks, chunky fat links, clinking flatly as they handed them over to Regenswig. That startled everyone. I wondered how much of the stuff they were hauling around. It made sense, though. No ATMs in the mead hall, and gold has always been hard cash.

"There is one more thing," Dennis said. Regenswig looked up from the chains in his hands, eyes narrowed. "Milde. I claim her as mine."

"What!" Josie yelped.

Dennis held up his hand. "Hear me out," he told her. She clenched her lips, seething. To Regenswig, Dennis said, "You heard how she speaks her mind. I like that. Osweald did not and fought over it. I would save you and her from further such troubles."

I think Regenswig was going to argue, but Leofrith gave him that stern look again. He laughed. "She is all yours," he said. "May she bring good service to the end of your days, and more peace than she brought to Osweald."

That ended the business meeting, with everyone more or less happy. Milde certainly was. Josie wasn't.

"She's not a horse or a sword," she muttered. I kept my mouth shut.

We went out and got the horses saddled up and led them to the gate. Regenswig had thrown in a saddle and saddlebags for the one we'd bought. That was Dennis's. Uncle Alf got the biggest, Osweald's. I got the one the churl had been riding, and Josie got Bil. Mine was mostly brown, with one white hoof, and not as big as you might think. Nothing like the tall, hefty horse Gail Silverton rode in the jousts – none of them were close to that big. But it was still a horse, and I couldn't help thinking she'd be impressed to see me, armed and on horseback, riding into a real battle.

Before I could even figure out how to mount up, Milde appeared beside Dennis, carrying her bundle and her weaving sword.

Dennis smiled. He took her by the shoulders and turned her, so they were facing Regenswig and Leofrith and the few others who had come to see us off.

"Hear me, all of you," he said, shifting into his royal speech act. "This is Milde, a strong and brave woman. She has the heart of a warrior and the free spirit of an eagle. I yield up my claim on her. She is a free woman now."

"All right!" Josie cheered. Milde looked clobbered. Everyone else looked confused.

"Not now, Dennis," Uncle Alf moaned.

"What?" Dennis said. "What's wrong with it?"

"I have no more horses to sell you," Regenswig said. "She will have to walk."

"Walk?" Dennis said. "She can't – I didn't mean – I meant she was free to stay here. To start a new life. With ... um ..."

It was funny to see Dennis, the great actor, struggling for words. Not to Milde, though.

"I will not stay," she said, glowering as deeply as Uncle Alf.

Dennis started stammering again. Amazingly, Uncle Alf came in on Milde's side.

"These aren't her people," he said, echoing Dennis's own words about Josie. "She is *Seaxisc*; they are *Anglecynn*. She has no family, no house. She would have to marry quickly, or else put herself under Regenswig's protection."

"You mean become his slave, don't you?" Josie said.

"Yes, that's what he means," Dennis replied. He rubbed his face, then groaned when he hit the bruise. "It must be this knock on the head. I can't believe I didn't think of that. I don't suppose she'd want to marry Huni or ..."

One look at Milde's scowl shut him up again. She was no dummy; she knew what we were talking about.

In the end, she came with us. She and Josie shared the biggest horse. Uncle Alf took mine, and I wound up straddling little Bil, with my knees sticking out. Even so, being up there felt higher than I'd expected. I clenched my legs on the saddle and tried to look like I knew what I was doing. I sure didn't feel like it. I was really glad Gail Silverton couldn't see me then.

↑

We forded the river a little way upstream from Regensburg, and I almost fell out of the saddle trying to steer Bil around the rocks. He kept tugging against the reins and skittering sideways. Milde told me to let him pick his own path and spoke to him quietly. He calmed right down and followed her and Josie without any trouble.

Uncle Alf set a fast pace then, scanning the ground for

tracks. He was a good tracker, but even I could see the hoof prints in the soft ground. It was just a narrow path that followed the driest, smoothest route beside the river, curving out and back around cuts, seeps, and fallen trees. The valley wasn't heavily wooded, just an occasional clump stretching down from the forests on the hillsides, usually marking a small brook that trickled into the river. There were plenty of them. Some the horses could step over, others not. Bil's belly got soaked, and so did my legs. Everyone was pretty spattered by the time we stopped in mid afternoon to eat something from the haversacks and give the horses a chance to chomp some grass.

Dennis asked Uncle Alf if we were gaining on Morgwydd's band. Uncle Alf shook his head and said, "I fear not. We must ride faster. Even then it will take two or three days at least."

"At least they won't be expecting us," I said.

"Maybe not so soon," Uncle Alf replied, "but they will be watching. Urien is a war chief. He is not stupid. We will have to very careful." He glared at Josie and Milde, down by the river. They were rinsing their faces and talking, all gestures and big expressions. "We will have to leave them behind at some point. They will only be in the way in the fight. Urien will not hesitate to use them against us."

"We'll cross that bridge when we come to it," Dennis said.

I'd thought we'd be riding into the night, but we only made a few more hours. Dennis was swaying in his saddle, looking gray again. When Milde said something about it, Dennis tried to act like he was fine, but we could all see he was lying. Uncle Alf reined up like we'd come to a cliff. He glanced at the tops of the hills. The land had been rising and closing in as the stream narrowed. The rounded top of the nearest hill was bare and jagged, as if an old wall was slowly crumbling into ruin there. Uncle Alf stared at it a long time. Then he took another long look at Dennis and said we'd better stop. He looked even grimmer than usual

I was just as glad; my butt was aching. We dismounted

and staggered around making camp. Josie forced Dennis to sit down and drink some water mixed with a little mead Leofrith had given her. Milde started making a fire. Uncle Alf and I hobbled the horses and took off their saddles, and then he told me to go shoot some fresh meat for supper.

"I'll go upstream," he said. "You go down. Stay off the hillside."

I asked why, and he repeated what he'd said at *Ad Gefrin*: "It is not a good place. Things live there." And off he went, bow in hand, silent as a cat.

Uncle Alf had taught me to hunt as soon as I was big enough to handle a bow. He'd made a small one just my size. This was before Dennis and his car and salary. We ate a lot of game. We'd walk all the way out of town and across the fields into the woods, hiking the steep hillsides until we were in the thick of the upstate New York forest. Uncle Alf shot all the game to begin with, but he taught me how to track, how to wait quietly by an animal run, how to gut and skin deer and hares and turkeys and Canada geese. And ravens and swans, for the feathers. We never ate the ravens, but swan was pretty good. Of course, the swans weren't actually wild; he shot them by the pond in the park. He shot a coyote once, too, but they were hard to track. Too tricky. He didn't bother with squirrels, but he had me shoot at them, and was proud as a park swan when I finally hit one. We stewed it for dinner that night. It wasn't much, but it sure tasted good.

After that, I started getting more game. My first deer was a big deal, that's for sure. But I had the same trouble hunting that I had at competitions. Sometimes I couldn't concentrate. I couldn't see just the target, that spot above the heart. Once Uncle Alf didn't bring his own bow. He said we'd eat what I shot or nothing at all. That was a hungry two days.

The same thing happened on that hillside. I missed a hare. I glimpsed a small deer, but didn't even get a shot off before it bolted. I accidentally flushed a huge, dark grouse and almost jumped out of my skin. That arrow went way wide. I managed to find it, but nothing to eat. I decided to make one last slant across the hillside, and maybe went higher than I should have. I stumbled into a sump, a hollow under the trees where a small spring turned the ground to muck. A thick stand of pale green ferns rimmed the place, and bright little dragonflies darted in and out, snatching at midges. It was beautiful, and I stopped for a minute to rest from the climb. I glanced down. There in the mud was a long, broad footprint. I thought for a moment it was a boot print; that a person had been there. When I looked more closely, I realized it was too big. And it had toes, three of them, with claws. My next thought was bear, but that was stupid. Bears have four toes. And this track just wasn't shaped right. It was too long, particularly the claws.

A shiver ran down my spine. Suddenly, I was sure I was being watched. Then I laughed at myself. Something this big I would have heard. Besides, the track wasn't that fresh. Still, I decided I'd hunted long enough and headed back down the hillside a lot faster than I'd come up.

I stumbled back down to the river in twilight, to be greeted by the wonderful scent of roasting meat. Uncle Alf had bagged a fat hare and a grouse. Even Egili had caught a good-sized rat, which he'd already half devoured. Uncle Alf didn't say anything when I showed up empty-handed. He didn't have to. His frown said it all.

I had a hard time sleeping that night, what with the saddle sores and the chill and damp by the river, the light from the half moon, and all those stars. And the noises. There are always noises when you're camping in the woods, but I kept listening for something bigger. Something with three long claws on each foot. Whatever it was, it didn't show up.

The next morning, Dennis felt fine again. He joked about brewing a hot cup of coffee. I could have used one myself. Josie gave him some herb tea to drink with his breakfast – nothing for me – then unwrapped his bandages, spit on the wound, and added more goo.

"Josie! Yuck!" I said. "Do you have to spit on it?"

"When in Rome, Ed," Dennis said. "Besides, it's working, isn't it?"

There was nothing I could say to that. The cut on his cheek didn't even need a bandage any more. Josie stuck her tongue out at me, and Milde laughed. I went down to the water to rinse my hands and hide the blush on my face. Milde still reminded me too much of Gail Silverton.

Dennis came down to join me. "Sorry to embarrass you, Ed. She is an awfully attractive young woman."

"Yeah, I guess so," I replied. "Not really my type though, you know?"

He grinned. "There are types? I don't recall being all that particular at your age."

"Dennis, please," I moaned.

"Sorry. Just trying to lighten the air." He shook off his hands and started to go.

I stopped him. "Dennis. I'm sorry about Osweald. The duel, I mean. You almost got killed because of my big mouth."

He smiled again. "That's okay, Ed. If you hadn't spoken up, I would have stayed silent, and then I would have hated myself for the rest of my life."

"Which almost wasn't much longer."

"It's okay," he repeated. He started to go, and I stopped him again.

"Dennis. What's it like to kill someone?" It was hard to ask, but I hadn't been able to forget the look on Osweald's face when his guts had spilled out.

Dennis looked like he was going to make one of his quick, cute answers, or maybe quote some poem, but he just shook his head and said, "I'm still trying to figure that out, Ed. I hadn't planned on killing him. Go ask Alf. He's had to do it a lot more than me."

The thought had never occurred to me. I followed Dennis back to the campsite and looked at Uncle Alf. He was rolling up his cloak to tie behind his saddle. He had his spear and shield close at hand, and the *seax* on his belt was loose in its scabbard. He moved smoothly, quickly but not rushed, like he was making a bow. No smile, as usual. But I realized he wasn't actually frowning. He was just busy. Focused. Not mad at any particular thing.

Then he looked over at me, and a small frown creased his brows.

"Are you all right?" he asked.

I thought about him killing someone, but I couldn't ask. I just nodded.

"Good," he said, and his face relaxed a little. "Come, help me saddle the horses."

He took the lead again when we left, and set a harder pace. The first few miles were agony, but then my butt went numb and I could bear it. I really needed some calluses on the inside of my thighs, though. By afternoon, it was all I could think about. I wasn't the only one, either. Josie and Dennis were both walking softly when we stopped briefly for a quick bite. Dennis couldn't even joke about it. He begged Josie to rub some of the deer-poop goo on his chafed spots, but she said it would only work on his head. Uncle Alf and Milde seemed immune, and I was beginning to resent it.

We left the riverbank about then. The stream had dwindled to a brook and was about to disappear into a narrow, heavily wooded ravine when the path veered to the left. We wound up a rocky incline toward a dip between two of the tall, round-topped hills. There were more hills west of the pass, taller, bald-headed. Gray clouds were moving toward us above them, swallowing big chunks of blue sky, chilling the already cool sunlight.

The way steepened as it neared the crest of the pass. The trees closed in on the left, forcing the path toward a rocky outcrop. We swung around a grassy knob, then through a short lane in the trees, then out into the full stare of the lowering sun. I had to squint to make out Uncle Alf's silhouette ahead me. He was bent to the side, studying the tracks again. A horse whinnied. Bil cocked his ears and whinnied back.

Uncle Alf jerked upright and reined in, staring around. I wondered what had startled him, then realized the whinny hadn't come from any of our horses. By then I was almost on top of him. Bil stopped on his own, and the others almost plowed into us, milling, heads turned toward the woods.

"Go back!" Uncle Alf growled.

"What is it?" Dennis asked.

"*Træppe!*" Milde cried. She turned their horse sharply, pointing. Josie almost slipped off.

Morgwydd stood on the next outcrop, Urien beside her. His men appeared from the trees behind us, shields raised, spears leveled. There was nothing we could do, because Urien was holding Mom, with his knife pressed to her throat.

# *Chapter 9*

Urien was holding Mom by the hair, pulling her head back. The point of his knife made a dent in her skin. I froze, certain he'd already started to cut. But Mom was watching us, eyes clear, no sign of pain. No blood.

Morgwydd stood beside her, gripping her left arm. Morgwydd's hand was dark against Mom's pale skin. It was tattooed, or maybe painted: dark blue swirls that wound between her clenched fingers and spiraled up her arm. More blue swirls patterned her cheeks. Her hair was dark and thick and half covered her face. She was smiling. Mom's mouth was gagged with a coarse cloth bound tightly from nose to chin. I wondered if Morgwydd knew Mom didn't speak.

Mom's hands were tied together at her waist and hooked under her belt. There was no way she could gesture. She just kept watching, glancing from Uncle Alf to me, as if wondering what we would do. I wanted to do something, but what? What, with Urien's knife already half through her skin?

Morgwydd laughed. "Well met, Ælfweard. I was beginning to worry you had lost our trail, a great hunter no more, turned foolish in the spirit world. But no, you still have skill, if not wit." Her *Anglisc* had a thick, lilting accent that rolled past half the consonants. She laughed again. "Loving brother, your sister was not worried. I should have paid her mood more heed."

81

"What do you want, *dry-wicce*?" Uncle Alf growled.

"You, bow-maker. You, sister's strong arm and pet. You, both." Her mouth turned from smile to scowl. She shook Mom's arm, and a spot of blood appeared at the tip of Urien's blade. Mom just took it. I wanted to scream. I couldn't think of a single way I could help her.

"Seven years!" Morgwydd almost sang it. "Seven years I waited for you two, while the *nicor* bred, burrowed, and waxed, and your people spread farther and farther, a pox fouling the face of our land. You didn't take the bait. You wouldn't come. I had to come for you. This bait—" She shook Mom's arm again and I almost drew my *seax*, but Urien saw. His knife arm tightened. His glare dared me. "—this bait worked. Dismount. Now! Off! Come to me!"

Urien barked an order in his own tongue, and his men stepped closer.

Uncle Alf stared at Mom. She flicked her bound hands slightly. *Come.* He slipped off his horse, and handed the reins to Josie.

"Alf?" Dennis muttered. "Are you sure?"

Uncle Alf gave me a quick look and nodded. I couldn't tell what he was thinking, what he wanted me to do. Then he turned away and started walking toward the outcrop. Urien gave another order, and his men circled around us. Uncle Alf seemed to ignore them, until the first came within reach. Uncle Alf grabbed the man's spear, yanked him forward, and had his *seax* out against the man's throat in an instant.

"If you harm my companions, this slave will be the first to die," he called.

"She will be next!" Urien yanked Mom's head back.

"Then all will die," Uncle Alf bellowed, "and Woden's black birds will share a glorious feast on your guts, Urien. If you want me, my companions must live!"

Morgwydd laughed again. "Someone has taught you to rhyme, bow-maker! 'Glorious feast?' What next? Will you read your sister's secret runes and sing in a girl's voice?"

"I will slit this throat and then yours, *dry-wicce*." Uncle

Alf lifted the warrior right off his feet. "Answer!"

Morgwydd's smile became a snarl. "I will spare your pretty friends, bow-man."

Urien started. He spoke to her quickly, arguing.

Morgwydd looked right at me, eyes narrowed. I glared back, hoping she'd order me to come, too. So I could get close enough to do something. I didn't know what, but I couldn't just sit there. I willed her to take me.

But she shook her head and answered in *Anglisc*, so we would understand. "I said all. Even her man-child may go. Hear that, bowyer-brother? I keep my word." She smiled again. "And you will serve both needs well enough."

She began to chant then, in her own language, a nasal, trilling sound. The words echoed from the peaks on either side of the pass. My ears rang. Egili burst from his pouch, hissing, fangs bared. He scrambled past Milde to the top of the saddle bow and tried to leap toward Morgwydd. Milde caught him just in time. Her horse started, ears back, and the others began to mill and shift. Uncle Alf's horse reared, dragging Josie off her feet. Dennis and I both tried to reach her, grabbing for the reins, the horse's bridle. She scrambled up between our horses and we almost knocked her over again. Milde struggled with Egili, squirming in her arms. She spoke to her horse, holding it calm with words and knees. And Morgwydd kept keening.

The wind picked up, blowing hard from the West. Urien never shifted, but he was angry. Frustrated, maybe. He kept glaring at me. Mom stood like a stone, eyes closed, bearing the point of his knife. Uncle Alf threw down his captive, who scrambled to his companions on hands and knees. They pulled him up and edged away from us. And from Morgwydd. Her face was twisted with effort. Her eyes burned. Still singing, she raised her free hand and pulled the brooch from her left shoulder. The dark cloth sagged, baring a small breast criss-crossed with fine white lines. She scraped the point of the brooch pin across her skin, adding a red weal to the pattern of scars. Bil snorted and tried to turn away. I jerked at his reins, twisting in the saddle. I couldn't take my eyes off Morgwydd. Her voice went up an octave, then broke into a harsh chord, as if she had two throats singing in different keys. The wind increased, singing through the coarse grass and trees. There was a tearing sound behind us. Cold struck my back. I glanced around to see a dark slit widening in the air between us and the trees. Stars showed in the gap.

I spun back, almost falling. "No!" I cried. "We're not leaving you!"

Mom's eyes opened. Her fingers flicked. *Go.*

I screamed at her. "No, damn it! No!" I tried to ride toward her, but Dennis and Milde were both in the way, trying to help Josie, still on the ground, jerked right and left by Uncle Alf's shying horse. Bil kept trying to turn, and I didn't know how to control him. I shouted at Dennis to get out of my way, shouted at Uncle Alf, at Mom. I cursed Urien and Morgwydd.

She probably didn't even hear me. Her singing almost drowned out the wind. It had gone past singing to a wild, wordless cry. She scraped the brooch pin across her breast again, harder, drawing blood. The wind gusted. Dust and leaves flew in our faces. The horses fought to get away from it, and from that horrible song. Morgwydd lifted her arm then and drove the point of the brooch into Mom's shoulder. Mom jerked and Urien's knife went deeper. I screamed.

Blood welled down Mom's arm. Morgwydd dropped the brooch and scrubbed her hand through the blood, across her own bloody breast, across her mouth.

The noise stopped, all of it: singing, screaming, breath. Then a fresh blast of wind scoured the hilltop. The horses turned and fled through the gap, into the cold place between.

The wind eased the slightest bit and I managed to rein in Bil. He stood quivering beneath me, blowing again and again. Dennis was beside me, still struggling to calm his own horse. Milde was behind me. Behind her, the slit was still open, a gash of blue rimmed by black. I tried to turn

Bil toward it, but he shook his head and planted his feet and wouldn't budge. I cursed him and kicked my boots free of the straps, tumbling to my knees. I heaved to my feet and struggled against the wind toward the gap. Dennis and Milde were shouting, but I couldn't make out the words. Then a shadow blocked the gap, a horse, bolting through. It was Uncle Alf's horse, dragging Josie at the end of its reins. She lost her grip and fell, half through the gap. It started to shrink.

Josie screamed, and I threw myself against the wind, grasping for her hands. She was trying to get on her feet, but the gusts kept knocking her flat. I fell to my knees again and lurched forward, reaching as far as I could. Our arms touched. I got hold of one elbow. I rolled back, pulling with all my weight, and she slid forward on top of me as the wind rolled us over and over until we jarred to a stop against Bil's legs. Josie hugged me, fighting back sobs. I hugged her back, but all I could think of was Mom. I tried to untangle myself, to crawl back toward the slit. Too late. It pinched shut while I lay there, trapped between Josie and Bil.

Now there was only starlight. I could barely make out Milde, off her horse, holding it by the reins while she spoke to Dennis's mare, calming it. Egili perched on her shoulder, a pale blur with gleaming eyes. Josie and I helped each other up.

She wiped her eyes, gave my hand one last squeeze, and said, "The arrow, Ed. Use the arrow. Get us out of here."

I could have kicked myself. I'd never even thought of it. Idiot. I drew it out of the quiver and gripped it tightly, then swung it into the wind, toward the spot where the slit had been, where a familiar star now burned. My throat was dry, raw from cursing. I swallowed and started to sing. At the very first word, the wind gusted hard enough to knock me back against Bil.

"No, Ed!" Dennis cried.

"What do you mean?" I yelled. "Mom is back there!"

"So is Alf, but we're not ready!"

"Urien cut her . . . her thr—" I couldn't say it. "We've got to get back! We have to! Josie has the salve! And Leofrith's charm. We can sing for her!"

Josie grabbed my hand, pulling it down, with the arrow. "No, Ed. She's all right. I saw her just before the horse dragged me through. She was hardly bleeding. Alf was with her. Urien had let her go. She's all right." She pressed her other hand to my cheek, making me look at her, not the star.

"You're sure?" I asked. She nodded. I managed to take a breath, and it numbed my chest. I was suddenly aware of the cold and the ice-bright stars. "Okay, what now? We can't stay here."

"Home," Dennis said, pointing at the stars ahead of us. He and Milde had come close, leading their horses. We huddled together, shouting against the wind, hunched against the cold. "We can rest there and plan, then come back when they aren't expecting us."

There was a star in the center of the cluster he was pointing at, a star that felt familiar. It seemed closer than it should have, but the one behind us seemed farther away now, as if the wind were pushing us across the space between. *Or maybe the star is drawing us back*, I thought. Morgwydd wouldn't try to send us home. She wouldn't care where we ended up. She would have stranded us here, in the cold between. That I was sure of.

I held up the arrow and began walking sunwise circles, singing. The wind whipped the words from my lips, but when I passed near Josie, I could hear her singing with me. I moved as quickly as I could. There wasn't the same pressure now, that thickness against my legs, and when I turned moonwise and lowered the arrow to point at the star, the wind fairly blew me across the darkness. Dennis grabbed my belt and slowed me down. I didn't dare glance back to make sure the others were behind him. I was afraid to look away from the familiar star. There were too many others around it. The cold was making my eyes tear, and the stars blurred and swelled, trying to run together. I kept blinking, kept singing, kept walking, dragging Dennis behind me. The others, too, I hoped. Then I saw an edge opening in front of the star. The darkness pushed back, stronger than the wind, but I forced the point of the arrow against it and kept walking. I could see blue sky, a yellow sun, grass. The grandstand at the fairground.

Then I was through, and Dennis was pushing me forward. Bil whinnied, and I knew the others had made it through with me. I stopped singing and stumbled forward a few more steps. The air rumbled behind me as the slit closed. I drew in a lungful of air. Smelled grass, horses. And exhaust fumes. Diesel and gasoline. I could hear engines running. A loudspeaker, booming with static in the distance. A jumbo jet, high overhead. I looked up and saw the contrail, streaking a hazy sky.

"Frige's heart!" Milde cried. "What place is this?"

She sounded terrified, and looked it, so much that it frightened me. She had stood up to Osweald, faced Morgwydd and Urien without a tremor, kept her cool when the sky split, and kept the horses under control in the cold other place between worlds. But this world terrified her. The horses sensed her panic and begin to fret. Egili hissed and clung to her shoulder, cowering.

Josie was right there. She took Milde's arm and held it, telling her not to be afraid, that we knew this world, that it was safe. Milde didn't believe her; I could see it in her face. She stared around, wide-eyed, clinging to the horses's reins. Dennis went over and put his arm around her shoulder, holding both her and Egili. There's was no room for me. All I could do was smile and nod at what Josie was saying. Milde started to calm down. She took a deep breath, nodding back, trying to smile at Josie and Dennis.

Then the cop showed up. I think it would have been okay if he'd just walked up, but he came tearing toward us on a four-wheeler. There were RVs parked all around the field – I hadn't noticed till then – and horse trailers and huge pick-ups. The cop wove through them and sped across the field, throwing up dust and exhaust. He was wearing a shiny black helmet with a tinted visor, like he was part of the machine. Milde swore again. Egili scurried down her dress and into his pouch. The horses snorted, and the big one tried to rear.

"Milde!" Josie said, punching her arm. "The horses! They need you!"

Milde gave Dennis a quick look. He nodded, handed her the reins of his mare, and turned to face the on-coming cop. Milde set her jaw and started to calm the horses.

The cop braked not five feet away, leaned back in his seat, and tipped the visor up. It was Officer Quincy, the same cop we'd spoken to at the renfaire just a couple of days ago, but he acted like he'd never seen us before.

"What the hell was that noise?" he demanded. "One of you shoot off a cherry bomb or something?" He sure didn't talk like the cop at the renfaire.

"Not us, officer," Dennis said, matching the cop's accent like he was born to it. "I'd like to catch whoever did it myself. You can see how it spooked the horses."

Cop Quincy crossed his arms and watched Milde and Josie for a moment as they got the horses under control. "Good thing you brought the girls along," he said. "What is it with chicks and horses, huh? So, who the hell are you, anyway? What's with the swords and stuff?"

"Yeah, a bit strange here, I guess," Dennis said. "We're one of the featured groups. We do a specialty riding show, historical thing, like they did it back in the days of King Arthur."

"King Arthur?" Quincy frowned. "You mean like a, whaddya call it, a joust? Where's your armor?"

"Not that version of Arthur," Dennis said. "The real Arthur, back in 450 AD."

Quincy nodded, pretending he knew what Dennis was talking about. "So the pretty blond there must be Guinevere, huh? And you're Arthur, I bet." He winked.

"No, Arthur couldn't make it," Dennis said. "I'm Lancelot."

I wanted to gag. Quincy just laughed.

Josie went over to him. "Excuse me, officer. Can I borrow your cell phone?"

He immediately looked suspicious. "My what?"

"Your cell phone, your . . . ?" Josie stammered.

"Your mobile," Dennis said. "You know, your portable, your hand-held."

"You mean my netphone?" Quincy laughed again." Is that what you call 'em in 450 AD, Lance? Hand jobbies?"

"If I could, please; I need to call my parents," Josie said. "I left mine back in the car, and I just remembered I was supposed to call them as soon as we arrived." She put on her worried innocent puppy face. "They only let me come all this way because I promised to check in all the time." She shrugged. "You know, parents."

"They're a little bit, um, overprotective, to put it nicely," Dennis said.

Quincy fell for it. "Hey, you can't be too careful in this day and age. Here." He handed Josie the phone. It looked ancient, like a two-way radio.

She stepped off to the side, dialing, waited, and then brightened. "Dad! It's me. We're—" She stopped, mouth wide, listening. "Josie. Who else? Look—" She listened again. "Wait, isn't this Jonathan Mayer? . . . But I'm . . . I . . . No, I'm sorry. I must have dialed wrong."

She stared at the phone. She looked like she was about to throw up, but she swallowed and straightened and handed the phone back to Quincy.

"Some kind of bad connection," she mumbled. "I'll have to try later. Thanks."

"No problem," Quincy said. "Now you better get your butts in the saddle. The parade's about to start, and I'd say you're about to be in big trouble. Here comes the Marshall."

A woman was riding toward us on a big gray horse. She was decked out in western style, complete with a big Stetson, cowboy boots, and bright red shirt with swirls of sequins and two rows of white buttons down the front.

"Quincy!" she shouted. The cop waved. She reined in and glared at us. "What's the trouble here? The parade starts in five minutes!"

It was Gail Silverton.

# *Chapter 11*

Talking with Quincy had confused me. Josie's phone call had worried me. Seeing Gail Silverton done up like a country-western star totally threw me. With lipstick and eyeliner, even. She'd never worn makeup at a renfaire, not even at school. But it was still Gail, on the same big horse she used for jousting. She rode it like she was wearing armor, ready to attack. Dennis fed her the line about an Arthurian horse show and all she did was frown.

"Nobody told me about this," she snapped.

"I think it was a last-minute thing," Dennis drawled. "We only got the call last week. Fellow name of, uh, Oswald? Talked like he was running things."

Her scowl deepened. "He would," she muttered. "Is this all of you?"

Quincy laughed. "Arthur couldn't make it, Miss."

"I can see that," she snapped, staring at Dennis's bandaged forehead and dirty face. She ran her eyes over the rest of us, pausing a moment on Milde. When she got to me she said, "I know you from school; the junior with the funny name. Egbert or something, right? I didn't know you rode."

I shrugged and said, "It's a new thing for me, but, yeah, I'm liking it."

She smiled for the first time, but it wasn't pretty. "You might like it more on a real horse." Her eyes went back to

Milde. "I know you from somewhere, too, don't I?" she asked.

Milde's look was like a mirror: puzzled, but the same face. A bit leaner, is all; smudged with dirt instead of makeup. She glanced at Josie and Dennis, obviously wondering what we were talking about.

"I don't think so," Josie said. "She's just visiting for the summer. She's my cousin from Germany."

I couldn't believe she'd said it. She looked as much like Milde as she did like Gail Silverton.

"Let me guess," Gail said. "You're adopted."

Josie looked ready to kill. "Oh, no," she said, "she is."

Dennis coughed to cover a laugh. I almost felt bad seeing Gail put on like that, but I had to admit she deserved it.

She flushed. "Well, get your cousin on her pony and get over to the grandstand. The parade starts in five minutes."

Egili picked that moment to poke his head out of his pouch. He peered up at Gail Silverton, looming over us all on her high horse, and hissed. The horse snorted and stamped one of his huge front hooves.

She patted its neck, staring at Egili as if he was just the sort of thing she'd expect from the likes of us. "If you'd had the courtesy to get here on time we might have been able to give them a brushing at least. As it is . . .? I guess, you'll just have to go for the authentic medieval look. Quincy, squeeze them in behind the rodeo clowns. And make sure they keep that rat out of sight. Pets aren't allowed."

She wheeled her horse and galloped off.

Officer Quincy watched her go the same way he'd eyed Milde. He shook his head at us. "Oh, you got her angry, all right. Better scurry on over. Her daddy runs this thing, you know."

He started his engine, which startled the horses, but Milde was back in control of herself and they didn't spook. Quincy waited, revving the throttle off and on, just to keep them nervous. Dennis finally had to tell him to drive on ahead so we could get mounted. "They may not look like much," Dennis said, "but medieval fighting horses are trained to kick."

"Whatever you say, Lance," Quincy replied. He vroomed off toward the grandstand.

"Are you all right, Josie?" Dennis asked.

She nodded. "Fine."

"Wrong number?"

She shook her head. "It's okay. Let's get this over with."

"If you say so," Dennis said. "We can rest and regroup later."

He took a moment to explain as much as he could to Milde, then we all mounted and started plodding toward the grandstand.

I felt stupid in front of the crowd. We had clowns in front of us, complete with a dressed-up pig in a baby carriage, and there was a row of baby oxen behind us, all led by gawky kids in a mishmash of jeans, cowboy shirts, and frilly dresses. Tractor engines growled and snorted at the rear, behind teams of full-grown oxen. Gail was at the very front of the parade, leading a whole army of over-dressed people on big, fancy horses with flashing saddles. Marching music blared from the loud speakers, cut through by the sharp voice of the announcer. The crowd was cheering and laughing and making catcalls and raspberries at the clowns. And at us. Milde was in the lead, on Uncle Alf's horse. She was the only one of us who could keep him from rearing. All I could see of Egili was the very tip of his nose, sticking out from under the flap of his pouch, twitching at every scent. Dennis and Josie came next, and it was all they could do to handle their own horses. Josie kept fighting back tears, and I was worried she might lose it completely. I was right behind her, the guy on the runt, knees and legs sticking out like oars. Poor Bil laid his ears back and plodded ahead, looking disgusted. We were a pretty ratty sight.

The parade seemed to go on forever. Each group of

riders stopped in front of the judging stand and made their horses rear and bow and ride around each other, while all the rest of us waited in the noise and the flies, and the big-wheel tractors revved their engines. The clowns put on a stupid skit with the pig in the carriage. Finally it was our turn, and Dennis called to Milde to just lead us in a circle once or twice. Gail Silverton was parked there on her horse, looking down on us like some kind of cowgirl goddess. It was stupid, I know, but I didn't want to plod around in a circle in front of her like a kid on a pony ride. I'd figured out this wasn't really our world, and this Gail wasn't really the Gail I knew, but it didn't matter. I still wanted to impress her. And there was only one way I could think of to do it. I gave Bil a kick in the ribs, steered him around Josie, Dennis, and Milde, and took the lead, pulling out the rune arrow as I went.

Then I started to sing.

Josie joined in on the second line, and Dennis followed her lead. He even drew his sword and held it up like my arrow. Then Milde pulled out her weaving sword and Josie lifted her ax. People cheered and started clapping in the slow rhythm of the song. I sped up and tightened the circle, and the clapping got louder. I managed to turn Bil back moonwise with only one hand on the reins. I felt him slow as the air thickened around us, and urged him forward through the final circle. Then I was looking right at Gail Silverton. I lowered the arrow and the star-iron head began to glow. The air wavered. Her image rippled like water. The gate split open and I led us off the parade ground, onto the path between worlds.

Bil pricked his ears, not at all afraid this time. Maybe he wanted out of that fair as badly as I did, badly enough to prefer the cold, dark path to the hard-packed racetrack. Milde's stallion snorted, but she calmed him with a stern word. The others followed without a pause. The gate boomed shut behind us, cutting off the grating noise from the fairground. I kept singing, and Josie sang with me. Her voice made mine stronger; that's what it felt like at least. I also knew what to expect now, not only the gate and the path, but where we were going. I knew how to make the gatekey work.

I thought, if Morgwydd knew I could do this, she never would have let me go. And it felt good. I could do something that helped. I just had to see the right star, only the right star. Close enough wouldn't do. I had to ignore the thick pressure washing against Bil's broad chest and flowing past my legs, the cold biting my face. And so I did. I thought about where I really wanted to go. I thought about Mom – my real mom, not an almost Mom like the almost Gail, not a Mom who looked like her and maybe shared some of her past, but none of the important parts, the important people, my father and me, Uncle Alf and Dennis and Josie. I pictured what mattered, what made my life what it was. I looked for the star that felt like them.

I saw it then, the small, yellow star, almost by itself. I knew it for certain. I pointed the arrow tip at the star, right at its heart. The pressure eased at once, almost became a pull, magnetic. Bil quickened his pace, as if he recognized his home. The arrowhead drew us toward it, touched the corona, glowed brightly. A dozen bright green spots flashed in response. There was the slit, widening quickly with hardly a sound, then a glimpse of dim light and stone.

Milde's stallion surged forward, shoving Bil aside. Then we were all churning through, a press of horses and humans and one frantic ferret, into warm, musty air and silence.

But it wasn't the hilltop where we'd first come out, or even the high pass where we'd been ambushed. We weren't even outside. We were surrounded by stone walls, beneath an arched ceiling that looked like it was covered with faded paint. Slender columns that flared at the top and bottom were arranged in a half circle in front of us, as though someone had planted a ring of stone saplings inside a cave. Light flowed in through a round hole in the center of the ceiling, directly above a small cart carved out of a block of stone. The horses shifted nervously, their hooves clopping on the stone floor. The room wasn't all that large; we crowded the end.

"Frige's heart," Milde muttered. "Where have you taken us now?"

I had no idea. It had never occurred to me that the gate could open indoors. Some of my newfound confidence faded.

"It is a temple of some kind," Dennis said, turning his horse to look around.

"There is a door," Milde said, pointing behind us to an open rectangle flanked by two more of the flared columns. The stallion pulled at the reins, and she let him head for the daylight bleeding in through the doorway.

"Wait!" Josie called. Milde ignored her. Josie reached over and grabbed my arm. "Ed, wait!" she repeated, pointing at the stone cart. "Dennis, you too. Look."

Resting atop the low sides of the cart was a broad, shallow bowl with leaves and vines cast into its surface. It was a deep shade of copper-brown, probably old bronze. A few real leaves, dried with age, lay inside, half hiding a split ring in the very center of the bowl. It was a torque of twisted iron, with two half-human faces staring at each other across the narrow slit. Its surface rippled, almost glowing. Sky iron.

"Look, Ed," Josie repeated, shaking my arm. "Don't you recognize it?"

I didn't recognize it. It didn't even feel familiar.

She shook my arm again. "Morgwydd's brooch! How could you not notice?"

What I'd noticed about Morgwydd were the tattoos on her arms, the scars on her breast, and mostly the madness in her face. Her clothes? Her jewelry? I jerked my arm free. Bil shook his head irritably. "There was this knife at Mom's throat. Or didn't you notice that?"

"Of course I did!" she snapped. "But I also—" She stopped herself, took a breath. "I'm sorry, Ed. Alrun's your mother. How could you think of anything else?"

"Forget it," I said.

"I should have realized, particularly after—"

"Forget it! All right? It's okay." I stared at the torque in the bowl, but I didn't really see it. I just didn't want to look at anybody right then. The mention of Mom and Morgwydd had brought everything back to me. We'd walked right into Morgwydd's trap. Maybe if I'd been paying better attention I would have seen something to tip us off, spotted one of Urien's men in the woods or something. And why didn't I have my bow ready? I could have taken out Urien with one shot, and Morgwydd with the next. Even so, even without the bow, there must have been something I could have done to change what happened. To rescue Mom. To keep Uncle Alf out of their hands at least. All sorts of wild scenes began to run through my mind.

Dennis brought me back to reality. "What about Morgwydd's brooch?" he asked Josie. "I didn't notice it, either. Me of all people, huh?"

"Her brooch was smaller," Josie said, "but it had the twist and the same two faces, and it was the same shade of gray."

Dennis thought for a moment. Then he asked me to hold the tip of the arrowhead close to the torque in the bowl. When I did, the arrowhead shone with the same light. It wasn't just the reflection of sunlight from the hole in the roof; they were both glowing. The wrought patterns were moving, faintly, but it was there. And I could feel it – the glow, the energy, whatever – I could feel it flowing up the arrow shaft. That feel I recognized: It had filled my hand each time I sang the song and opened a gate between the worlds.

"Well, there's the reason we wound up here, I'd guess," Dennis said. "This sky iron must come from a piece of the same meteorite."

*Part of the reason*, I thought. *But if Morgwydd has the brooch I was looking for, why didn't we end up there?* There was still so much I didn't know about how the gatekey worked.

97

Dennis was all for taking the torque, but Josie wouldn't let him. "This is obviously a temple to one of Morgwydd's gods."

"A goddess," Dennis said, pointing out some Latin inscribed around the sides of the cart. "Her name is Brigantia."

"Whatever, she's not our goddess. Her torque won't be any help to us," Josie insisted. She was so serious it surprised me. Her parents were Jewish. What did she care about a heathen goddess? What did I care, for that matter? Sure, Uncle Alf swore by Woden and Thunor, while Mom . . . Well, I'd never heard her swear, but she cast runes that stood for heathen gods. And there was the arrowhead, dedicated to Tiw.

To tell the truth, I didn't know what to think. I had grown up surrounded by Christians. I'd learned about Jews from Josie and about Muslims in Civics at school. But here was Dennis, who pretended to believe whatever he needed to for the part he was playing at any one time, who explained the gatekey with dopplegängers and molecular attraction – *he* wanted to steal from the altar. I wasn't sure I believed in any god, but if it would weaken Morgwydd's goddess, I was all for taking the torque out of the bowl, melting it down, and scattering the drops in the nearest ocean.

I couldn't get it out though; it was welded to the bottom of the bowl. We had to leave it there, glowing, doing whatever it did. Or didn't. I wished I knew.

# Chapter 12

Outside, the sky was as gray and water-stained as the ceiling of the temple. We led the horses down three broad steps to a lawn of thick grass gone wild in some kind of shrine village. We were surrounded by stone temples with grooved columns and carvings around the eaves, even a round one, like a stone bandstand. And statues, some fallen. The faces and doorways were all staring down on the patch of wild grass that had dared to engulf their bottom steps. They were built like Greek and Roman temples, but none of them were very big, not like in pictures of the Acropolis or the Roman Forum. The one we'd been in wasn't much bigger than the hall in Regensburg, and it wasn't even the smallest. But they really made me worry. I couldn't believe I'd brought us to the wrong world. It had felt so right. It still did. Even the horses seemed to think so. They had joined the stallion and were calmly chomping away at the thick grass. But where did all these temples fit in?

Milde was waiting for us in the center of the meadow, standing by a curved stone bench. She had her weaving sword in her right hand, and Uncle Alf's spear was leaning against the bench. She asked what had kept us so long, and Dennis explained about the bowl and the torque. She glared at the temple as though it was personally responsible for all our troubles.

"Dennis?" Josie asked. "Do you have any idea where we

are?"

He shook his head. "Milde? Have you ever seen or heard of such a place?"

"*Enta geweorc,*" she replied. The work of giants. She peered into the shadows inside the temples, gripping her weaving sword as if she might need it at any moment. Egili perched on her shoulder, nose twitching. But the place was obviously abandoned. The wall that surrounded it had gaps along the top, and some of the buildings were sagging, with stones jutting at the corners, sections of column out of line.

"*Wrætlic is þes wealstan, Wyrd gebræcon,*" Dennis recited. "Wondrous is this stonework; Fate broke it, the wards of the city have crumbled and the work of giants is rotting away, tumbled roofs, towers in ruins, they were bright city buildings, a wealth of lofty gables, many a mead-hall filled with human revelry – until mighty Fate changed that." He bowed at us, smiling. No one applauded. "Philistines!" he cried. "Do you know how many times I have recited that without truly appreciating its force?"

"Yes, you're brilliant, Dennis," Josie said, "but where are we?"

"In a Roman town deserted when the legions were pulled back to defend the core of the falling empire," he said.

"You mean we're on the right world at least?" I asked.

"I never doubted it, Ed," he said, and my heart lifted a little. "The Britons occupied some of these towns at first – they were very Romanized by then – but the Anglo-Saxons avoided them, at least for a while. Superstitious. These were the cities of giants, as Milde said."

"All right," Josie replied. "Do you know which one?"

"Not really."

Dennis turned slowly, studying the faces of all the little temples. He pointed at one and read the Latin carved over the doorway. "Apollo-Maponus, a Romano-Celtic god. I don't know a lot about him, I'm afraid – the Romans aren't really my period of specialization – but I remember there were several hybrid gods worshipped by the legionnaires recruited from the local tribes, particularly in the North. That's a good sign."

"Why?" Josie asked.

"It could mean we're in one of the fortified towns along Hadrian's Wall. That would put us only two or three days' ride from Regensburg."

My heart sank again. Two days lost, maybe three. Plus two more just to reach the spot where we were ambushed. And who knew how much farther we'd have to go beyond that. Assuming I could follow the trail. I wasn't half the tracker Uncle Alf was.

"I'm sorry," I muttered. "I thought we'd come out back at the hill fort."

"Me, too," Dennis said. "For some reason, this torque exerted a stronger attraction."

I was pretty sure he was right, but I knew there had to be more to it than that. Something I did that changed the aim. I mean, if this torque was just like Morgwydd's, why didn't I take us right back to the ambush? If I could figure out that, maybe I could also figure out how to use the sky road as a shortcut to Mom and Uncle Alf.

Dennis patted my shoulder, then went over to the bench and sat down with a big sigh. "Let's take a break. The horses need it and so do I."

A break. The minute he said it, I realized how tired I was. We had ridden hard for hours, survived an ambush, gone to the wrong world, marched in a frigging parade, and traveled the freezing world path twice, and it was barely past mid afternoon.

My legs began to shake. I had to put my arm across Bil's shoulder to keep from dropping on the spot. Bil lifted his nose from the grass and glanced back at me, one ear askew, like he would be happy to have my weight off for a while longer. Milde was frowning at me, too, like she was worried. Josie had flopped on her back in the grass with a big sigh, one arm across her eyes. I would have loved to do the same, but not with Milde watching me like that. I gave

Bil's shoulder a quick rub and carefully made my way over to the bench. I sagged down on it, then wished I had flopped with Josie after all. My butt ached. So I stood back up and stretched and walked around a little and drank some water.

"Feeling better?" Dennis asked. He looked raring to go.

I shrugged. "Okay, I guess. A lot's happened today."

He nodded and patted my shoulder again. "Don't worry, Ed. We'll get them back, safe and sound; trust your mother on that. She wouldn't have gone with Urien so readily if she hadn't seen something in the runes to make her think she should. I'm certain she saw victory for us. I'm even more sure she wouldn't have come at all if she'd seen the slightest hint of danger to you."

I shrugged again. I could only hope he was right.

Milde hadn't sat down. She kept scanning the doors of the temples, sword ready. The way her jaw was set made me think she didn't approve of these foreign gods. I thought, *Maybe she can feel they don't approve of her.*

"Evil things live here," she said, like she had read my mind. "We should be far away before nightfall."

None of us were going to argue about leaving. We collected the horses and rode down the overgrown lane between the temples to the nearest gate. The huge doors were ajar, the corners sagging into the dirt on failed hinges. We rode out two abreast onto a wide, stone-paved roadway between two walls. A gatehouse with two tile-roofed towers and a crenelated walkway faced us across the roadway. Its gate was still solid, and shut tight. The long stone capstone over the gate had been carved with the name of the fort: *Corstopitum.*

"*Hwæt!* We know now where we are!" Dennis exclaimed theatrically. "This place is Corbridge, near the east end of Hadrian's Wall. The north-south Roman road goes right through it."

"North is there," Milde said, pointing back toward the gate to the temples.

"Then we shall go this way," Dennis said, pointing east.

102

"We can turn northward when we reach the end of the walls."

"Why don't we just go back through?" I demanded.

"Milde has called that place evil," he said. "I see no reason to argue."

"Coward," I muttered.

"Choose your battles wisely when you can, Ed." he replied. "Why should I risk the wrath not only of strange gods but also of Milde? These walls will end soon. Onward!"

*We should be riding straight north*, I thought. *Uncle Alf would never have let himself get sidetracked.* But Dennis was our leader now, so I plodded behind on little Bil.

Dennis was right this time at least: we could see the end of the walls in a couple of minutes, and reached it soon enough. The land opened up to the north. There were fields, clumps of stone buildings – mostly ruined – patches of trees, and the gray outline of hills. Low, rounded mountains rose beyond them, dark in the distance under spreading clouds. My stomach knotted when I saw how far we actually had to go. I scanned the peaks, looking for the two hills where we had been ambushed. I was sure I'd be able to recognize them, but the distance was too great.

The others weren't even looking that way. Straight ahead of us, maybe a mile away on a dirt track that veered off from the stone road, was a large, walled village. A town, really. Smoke rose from dozens of points behind the palisade, and I could make out people by a large gate. We reined in.

"So. The locals have not completely avoided the old fort," Dennis said.

"But who lives there," Josie asked, "*Angelcynn* or *Wealcynn*?"

"It would be *Angelcynn* by now," Dennis said. He looked up. "It gets late."

"Wait a minute," I said. "We're not planning to go there, are we? How are they going to take to strangers? We don't have Uncle Alf to speak for us now. And Milde is not an Angle."

"Good point. I supposed we could go back through to the western end."

Josie sighed and Milde didn't look too happy, but they agreed it might be the best way. No one seemed to have spotted us yet, so we could just slip back between the walls. But before we'd made up our minds, we got caught.

The east wall of the fort stretched southward for a couple of hundred yards, broken in one place by a fallen heap of stone that had been another gate. Beyond it, a winding line of trees marked the bank of a wide river. Suddenly, a great bawling herd of cattle appeared from behind the wall. Two men walked ahead of them, leading a packhorse, two others rode alongside, and several more walked in the cloud of dust behind, driving the herd forward with hoots and cries and long switches. They were moving along a dirt road that angled from the river toward the town. One of the escorts spotted us and waved. With a long spear.

"What now?" Josie asked. "It will look very bad if we turn and flee."

"We put on a bold front," Dennis said. "That was a friendly enough wave."

"They think we're from the town," I said. "One word and they'll know better."

"True enough," Dennis agreed, "but they will always welcome a *scop*. I will adopt Beorhtscyld's alter-persona and sing for them, recite poems, tell riddles. You have a good voice; you can be my young apprentice. Josie is even better voiced, and she can juggle. She will be your fiancé from Spain. And Milde—"

"I cannot be a *scop!*" Milde cried. "I have no gift for poetry or stories!"

"Than you can be my goodwife," Dennis said.

I thought, *Figures he'd stick me with Josie and claim Milde for himself.* "You're hardly dressed like a wandering minstrel," I pointed out. "You're the one who told me only professional warriors owned swords."

Dennis shrugged it off. "Even a *scop* has to know how to defend himself. But if you're too shy to sing in public, you can carry the sword and be my bodyguard."

"Would a *scop* even have a wife?" Josie asked Milde.

Milde blushed. "Yes. And big families, sometimes."

"There you are," Dennis said, "we have our parts to play. Now for a full meal, a poem, and a good night's sleep in a bed. A straw pallet would be a godly gift."

Milde blushed even deeper, but Dennis didn't notice. He was staring ahead with a look I recognized, already rehearsing the riddles and poems he'd recite. I hoped Milde wasn't taking a big liking to him. He was Uncle Alf's partner, and unlike Uncle Alf, he wasn't even bi.

We hurried the horses to the intersection, then waited until the men in the lead reached us. One of them was carrying a spear and a shield. The other was older and carried no more than a small *seax* on his belt and a fur bag over his shoulder.

"Greetings, friends," Dennis called. "Have you come far?"

"Not so far as you from the look and sound of it, but far enough for sore feet," the unarmed man replied. "Had we been going straight up, we near could have reached the groves of the moon! Yes, these cattle are better traveled than most, but miles don't make a beast wise. Men the miles make stupid. Plod, plod, plod, the step-drum beats from road to foot to heart to head, thoughts turn to dust, always a coarse meal, a *briw* too thin to feed thoughts. A meal of dust and flies adds little weight to body or words. Your answer, then: two feet-full of days from Deira to the Wear, a handful more from Wear to Tyne, and a handful in front of us still to Din Giarde. By then both cattle and men will all be mad as me."

The man did look a little crazy. His companion with the spear was dressed in coarse brown clothes, but his hair and beard were trimmed, and his plain face seemed normal enough, just maybe a bit wary. The self-proclaimed madman wore finer cloth, but his hair was shaggy, his beard was tangled, and his right eye was covered by a dark leather patch painted with a gold spiral that made it seem like he was staring at you. It was almost impossible not to stare back. The eye-patch half-covered a puckered scar that slanted through his eyebrow, under the patch and back out, curving along his cheek to the crooked bridge of a large, ruddy nose. His face was tanned, gaunt, and streaked by dust and the white scar. His left eye *was* staring, bright blue, flicking from face to face as though he'd never seen anything like us. And he never stopped grinning. His teeth were straight and white, the only tidy things about him.

"We are bound for Coria this evening," he said. "Will you walk with us?" Which was crazy enough, since we'd been trudging along ahead of the cattle all the time he was spouting.

"It would be a pleasure," Dennis replied. "We have traveled a long, roundabout way ourselves, with more than one wrong turning. Not till we reached the stronghold behind us and saw its name carved over the gate did we know for sure we were on the right road."

The madman's bright eye stopped wide on Dennis. "You can read the language of the giants?" he exclaimed, and the man with the spear frowned. "How can that be? There is more to you than meets the eye, and what the eye meets is very odd already."

Dennis cleared his throat, then shrugged. "It is rare, I know," he said, "but my mother was a Frank, and I lived a while in her country. Her father knew the *Romanisc* words and it amused him to teach me, his only grandson."

"You have indeed come far, whether it took one journey or many," the madman said. His one bright eye lingered on the bandage on Dennis's head, then on Josie, then stopped on Milde. She must have looked the oddest of us all, riding the biggest horse with the best saddle, with Uncle Alf's shield hung on one side and his spear on the other. And Egili, still perched on her shoulder and peering back at the madman with his own eyes bright. "I imagine you all have such a tale to tell, your furred companion most of all. What do you call him, a stoat-elf? Can he talk?" He laughed, a rowdy bray of a sound. "But that can wait till evening in the hall. What say you, Cenryth? Let's not spear these strangers; we'll let Coria's famous mead bring them low." He laughed again, and Cenryth, the spear-bearer, finally relaxed.

"Beware everything Rædwod tells you," he warned. "Coria's mead is famous for being vile. Only the *Beornician* beer is worse!" He shook his head.

I could vouch for that after our night in Regensburg. Cenryth at least seemed sane, but Rædwod only got crazier. When Dennis introduced us and said he was a traveling *scop*, Rædwod almost danced in the road.

"What an evening we shall have!" he cried. "Story upon story upon poem! Tell me, then, where do you come from and where are you bound and what brought you along the giant's stone road through the cold, damp, gloom-ridden home of *Wealcynn, dry-cræft, ond wyrmum*?"

Strangers, druid magic, and dragons: It was too perfect a way to describe what we'd been through. We hadn't seen any dragons yet, but maybe the tractors would count as *wyrmum* to Rædwod. Maybe the eye under the patch gave him second sight. More likely it was just how these people thought of the Britons, as a bunch of druids and vipers. But who knew what could happen on this crazy world? Maybe Josie really could read the future in the runes. Maybe Rædwod really could see our past. Maybe Egili really would start speaking. What did I know?

Rædwod handed me the lead rope of the packhorse, called me a stout lad, and walked alongside Dennis's horse. Milde and Josie followed, and I fell in with Cenryth. He was the silent type, which was good because I was in no mood to talk. I was tired, strung out, hyper, and really pissed at Dennis for pretending to be a *scop*. This Rædwod was going to make us all perform in front of the whole town that night, I could foretell that much of the future. I glanced at Milde. She looked cool as a cucumber, but she was playing the goodwife. She could just sit in a corner spinning yarn and looking beautiful while the rest us fell on our faces. Oh, Dennis and Josie could probably pull it off, but I knew I was going to look like an idiot.

Coria was built like Regensburg, but on a larger scale. There was a mound and ditch in front of the wall, which was taller and built from tightly fitted hewn planks instead of raw logs. The crowd of gawkers was much bigger and more varied: more children, more light-haired women, even a few more old folks. I guess because it was the end of the day, most of the townsfolk were coming in from the fields. We were met at the gate by three official guards, complete with shields, spears, and swords. They sent Cenryth and the cattle around to a corral, but one of them recognized Rædwod, who then proclaimed in a loud voice that Dennis was a *scop* and would perform that night. "Come one, come all" – he was worse than a carnival barker. They ushered us right in. I almost turned around to follow Cenryth, but Josie flashed me a smile and a shrug, like, "Oh, well, here we go." So I went.

Inside the wall, Coria looked even bigger. Not only were there many more houses, but many were bigger than the ones in Regensburg. There were actual lanes between the little garden plots that fronted each house. It smelled the same, maybe worse; there was more than one dye-shed reeking among the latrines. One of the guards had come with us to lead the way, and a bunch of little kids tagged along behind. People stood in doorways to watch us pass. Rædwod called out hellos, waving to the adults and bowing to the children. Then he reached into a long pouch hanging from his belt and pulled out two bone whistles. He stuck a mouthpiece into each of his nostrils and played a crazy duet through his nose. Then he played a round, a different part from each nostril, with just enough sour notes to make it twice as funny. Everyone roared, grownups and kids alike. He capered around the children, playing and dancing. And when he took his bow, he lifted his eye-patch. I thought, *gross, that's sick*, but it turned out he had a second patch under the first one, with a winking eye drawn on it. The kids absolutely shrieked, so he did it again, concert and all, dancing up the lane like a mad pied piper.

That was how we arrived at the mead hall, where the chief and his wife were waiting on the long, front stoop, flanked by another pair of official guards.

The kids hung back and Rædwod ended his tune with a flourish right in front of the chief.

"Greetings, Grimmære, son of Grimwine, and fair Hwite, Hudde's daughter," he exclaimed. "You have not aged a day since we last met. A year, maybe, but never a day."

"It has been five years, and you have only grown more mad," Grimmære replied.

"Yes but no! I am still no madder than suits the way of the world."

"Your words remain half wise," Hwite said. "Have you come to sing for us, Rædwod, or is cattle-driving now your craft?"

"Even better, I am a *scop*-driver!" And he called Dennis forward to introduce him.

Dennis played his part more humbly than I'd expected, saying he was just a simple man who knew a few poems and riddles. I think maybe he had already realized what Rædwod was. Grimmære greeted him warmly anyway and insisted he would hear Dennis perform that very night, and also hear the story of our journey. He glanced at Milde, Egili, and Josie as he said it, reminding me just how odd we must look. But Grimmære turned his attention back to Rædwod.

"We hope you can calm your wild thoughts long enough to tell us the news from Deira and the Saxon lands," he said.

"My memory has its sharp moments, particularly

when it is whetted," Rædwod replied, bowing again. It was a terrible pun, but Grimmære laughed.

"Good. See to your horses and come back when you are ready to eat and drink."

"And play, we hope," Hwite added. "You have a *gliw-beam* on your back, I see."

Rædwod patted the fur bag slung over his shoulder. "I would be more than mad to lose this, fair Hwite."

*Oh, crap, we're screwed!* I thought. *He's a gleeman!*

# *Chapter 13*

Dennis was staring at Rædwod's fur bag, struggling to keep the smile on his face. I had no sympathy for him.

"I will tend to your horse, uncle," I said. "You stay here and tell our good hosts the tale of our journey." I was thinking he'd probably dig us deeper into the hole he'd created, and I didn't want to be sitting there squirming while he did it.

Josie came with me, leading her horse and the stallion. Milde would have come, but she was supposed to be Dennis's wife. Her, I felt sorry for. Grimmære had said "Saxon lands" like things weren't too friendly between them. Milde's accent would give her away immediately. Maybe Dennis could say she was some relative of his Frankish mother. But how he'd explain her shield and spear I had no idea. Sure, there were stories about shield-maidens, but not as the wives of wandering minstrels.

"You realize what happened back there, right?" I asked Josie. "About the *gliwbeam*? It's a harp. Rædwod really is a *scop*."

"I thought it was something like that," she replied. "Don't get too bent out of shape over it, Ed. Dennis is great at improv."

"Yeah, and I'm supposed to be his apprentice. I can't recite in front of all those people! I don't remember any of those long Old English poems!"

"Just tell a riddle. Come on, Ed, it's only a big deal if you make it one."

"Says the queen of the mud beggars," I muttered.

She frowned. "Not much call for that here; it's too much like reality. But you're right, I like performing. Look, I'll cover for you. I'll say you have a sore throat. Or we can pretend to be making out in the corner. I'm your hot Spanish fiancée, right?"

"Josie, you're not helping!"

Bil tipped his ears back and gave me his disgusted look. Josie just grinned.

By the time we'd taken care of the horses and made our way back to the hall, Dennis and Rædwod were settled comfortably on benches near a raised fire pit in the middle of the long room. Grimmære and Hwite were with them, and a few other people were already seated nearby, obviously listening in. Milde had found a stool in the light near the doorway and was quietly spinning yarn.

Grimmære's mead hall was the real thing, much bigger than the one at Regenswig, with high walls, massive beams, and a tall, peaked roof. A single torch burned on each of the four walls, barely lighting the space. There was a raised platform at the left end of the hall, holding two carved, backless chairs – thrones, sort of. The fire pit fronted the doorway, so the tables there were the warmest and the brightest. Three women were cooking something in big pots over the fire. It smelled delicious, and my stomach growled. Rædwod laughed.

"Welcome again, young Eadgar," Hwite said "Beorhtscyld has told us the sad tale of your mother and father."

"I told them how your father was killed and your mother, my sister, carried away to slavery," Dennis said quickly. "How we have tracked her westward and northward as she was traded, not once, but three times, the last to a man of the *Beornice*."

"You are brave to think you can find and free them from their captors," Hwite said. "The *Beornice* are not so tame as the *Bretwealas* in your Southland."

"A fool's quest, I call it," Grimmære said. "It will make a fine poem, but there will be no one to sing it. You will all be dead."

"Our good hosts have tried to convince me to return home and turn our thoughts to grief," Dennis remarked, as if it wasn't obvious.

"Grief is good," Hwite said. "Sing that song to mourn them, as you should. He is dead, and she is dead to all but memory."

"Then sing vengeance as you seek it, and die in honor," Milde said quietly, eyes still on her twirling spindle.

Grimmære sighed. He was older than Regenswig, with a lined face and a long, graying mustache, and his age showed now in his eyes. "Honor in battle, yes, but you four are no army. It will be slaughter and slavery before you even find her."

What he was saying made sense, but I didn't want to hear it. "We will find them," I said. "We will find them and free them."

"Them?" Rædwod asked. His eye was fixed on me. Even the swirl on his eye patch seemed to be staring.

"Her ... My mother and her captors," I stammered. "We will find them and free her."

"And free the *Beornice* of their hold on life," Dennis put in. "It is Wyrd's will."

"Wyrd's will, of course," Rædwod echoed, nodding, "but she is a fickle bitch. Her will turns with the seasons; no, with the change of the moon – no, a change in the breeze! Oh, what a woman is Wyrd! And aren't they all?" He flipped up his patch, showing the wink to Josie. "Aren't you, Shosefina of the *Speonas*? Aren't you, sweet-tempered Milde? And you ... ? No, Hwite, you I would never call fickle. Grimmære would slay me with one fearsome frown."

"I can see we'll get no more serious talk out of you tonight," Grimmære said. "We shall eat and let you entertain us with more cheerful words."

"We have never had two *scopen* in our hall at the same time," Hwite said. "This will be an evening to remember."

I already wanted to forget it.

Grimmære and Hwite moved to the dais, and we were seated at the table just below them. More torches were lit, which brightened the place a bit. There were hangings on the wall, scenes of hunting or battle. There were carvings on the front edge of the dais, too, vines and snake-like animals tied in knotwork. The hall had a feeling of grandness to it, in a rough-hewn way, like the townsfolk. Their cloth was woven in bold checks and plaids, their brooches and buckles flashed with designs, and many of the women wore big colored-glass beads. Hwite and Grimmære both wore jeweled brooches and tooled leather belts, and the hilts on their *seaxes* were gold, inlaid with patterns of red stone or glass. But the meal was plain, another thin *briw* with a little meat and this time some beans mixed in with the barley and greens. And the beer was just as bad as Cenryth had warned. There was thin buttermilk, which didn't taste all that great either, but I figured at least it wouldn't give me a hangover. There was no sign of mead. Grimmære wore jewels but he skimped on dinner.

More people had come in while we were talking, and more arrived while we were eating. The children came to stare at us, and mothers brought the youngest to meet Egili. He reveled in the attention, but Milde did not. She let Josie play the host at our table, ignoring the kids, and avoiding the babies as though they were catching. She seemed relieved when Grimmære finished his bowl of *briw* and stood to address his people. The place was packed and noisy, but everyone stilled quickly. Grimmære said a few words about the work planned for the next day, like the morning announcements from the principal at school. Then he introduced Beorhtscyld, which brought on clapping and cheers. Dennis stood and waited quietly, looking across the gathering, meeting as many eyes as he could. He could have been back at the Scarborough Faire. The people fell silent. But instead of starting a poem, he introduced Rædwod.

The crowd went wild. Dennis didn't even get to finish the little speech he'd started. He tried to be heard over the noise but finally gave up. The look on his face was priceless: He was some pissed.

Rædwod didn't play the noble bard role at all. He was more like a rock star, leaping right up onto the dais, arms high, nodding his head, and spouting a stream of nonsense at the children, who had all rushed up to the front. He started a little song that I swear was the original "Old MacDonald," and the kids all sang along, mooing, baaing, and clucking. Then he sang another one about a witch, a bad child, and a *puca* – a kind of goblin. It was really gory. The kids loved it of course, and half the parents joined in on the final verse, about cooking the *briw* the *puca* made from the bits and pieces of the bad child that the witch wouldn't eat.

Then he told a couple of silly poems and a riddle: I am gold on the outside, round on the inside, never breathing, never eating, I live till the day I am born. It wasn't one I'd ever heard before, but it was easy for the kids: a dragon's egg. Then he put on a serious face and stood like Dennis had, looking around haughtily. Everyone laughed, but they quickly went still.

"I have a riddle now for our gracious hosts," he said, "if I can force it through my tired, dusty throat."

This one I knew. It starts *Ic eom weorð werum:* "I am man's ransom, found everywhere; brought from forests, cliff-sides, hill slopes, valleys, and downs. By day, wings bear me in the buzzing air, lay me under a sheltering roof, a sweet craft. Soon a man bears me to a tub . . ."

The ending is harsh: "Bathed, I am binder and scourge of men; I bring down the young, ravage the old, sap strength. He who wrestles with me soon feels my fierce attack. I roll fools flat on the ground. Robbed of strength, reckless of speech, men lose power over hands, feet, and mind. Who am I who bind the men of this Middle Earth, blinding with rage and such savage blows that dazed fools know my dark power even by daylight?"

Everyone was silent, thinking. Someone called out, "A sword!" But Rædwod said no. Others tried: "A warrior?" and "Venom!" A child cried, "Mother's cooking!" and everyone laughed, but they were all wrong. I looked at Dennis; I knew he knew answer. But he shook his head slightly. He wasn't going to upstage Rædwod. People kept shouting out guesses, until finally they were drowned out by cries of "Tell us!" and "What is the answer?"

"Why it is clear as the phlegm in my throat," Rædwod exclaimed. "Mead! Brought by bees, hidden in the hive, bathed by the brewer, downed and suffered by the fool, and still treasured by every mad man on this earth. Particularly this one."

"Then you shall have it," Hwite said.

"Wait!" Grimmære called. "Has he earned it? Has he earned his cup of mead?"

The children all cried yes, and the parents laughed and agreed. Rædwod accepted the cup from Hwite with a bow and a smile and three poetic lines of thanks, to her and Grimmære and the audience. For a moment he wasn't mad at all. He sipped the mead, gave a big sigh, rubbed his throat while contemplating the far corner of the roof, nodded, and downed the rest in a gulp.

"I believe my voice will last a little longer," he announced. The crowd cheered, but he raised his hands for silence. "First we must welcome Beorhtscyld, warrior *scop* from across the earths. Let us hear my new-made friend."

"Time to earn your mead, Dennis," Josie whispered, flashing him a thumbs-up.

He grinned back and stepped onto the dais. No more poses for Dennis, not right away at least. Rædwod stepped back and sat on a stool by the wall, letting him have the stage.

"A wise man knows not to challenge a master at his craft," Dennis said, "but you have invited me, Rædwod, and I will offer up what meager fare I can. First, a riddle for a riddle: What am I, who protects my hearth, my horde, my home, wrapped with strands and filled with excellent treasure. Often by day I shoot out the spear-terror. My success waxes the more I am filled. My master sees how the darts fly from my innards. Sometimes I swallow the swart, dark weapons, the poisoned arrows. My entrails are good then, precious to warriors, this horde that I hold. Many remember what comes through my mouth, both the dark and the light."

"A beehive!" a little girl cried, and the all the other kids joined in. "A beehive, a beehive!" The parents laughed and cheered them on.

Dennis looked startled. He started to say something but changed his mind. "What a smart child!" he cried. "All of you! The smartest children on this earth live in Coria!"

"That's not right, is it?" Josie whispered.

"Nope. He always said it was a ballista," I replied. "But like you said, he's good at improv." Dennis glanced our way and I couldn't resist giving him a thumbs-down.

Dennis raised an eyebrow at me, a dangerous look from him. He motioned for silence and said, all apologies, "Good people, you are too smart for me. A riddle that easy would never earn a cup of mead. It hardly merits a sip of your beer. Even my apprentice could do better." He grinned at me. "Eadgar, come up! Show these Corians your bright mind at work."

I wanted to crawl under the table. Every eye in the place was on me, especially Rædwod's creepy, lop-sided stare. Then Milde gave me a push on the shoulder.

"Go on, Eadgar. You cannot disappoint them."

I would happily have disappointed every one of them. But not her. I swallowed hard and clambered onto the dais.

"They're all yours," Dennis murmured, and he stepped to the side with Rædwod.

I made the mistake of looking out over the hall. There they all were: the kids, the grownups. Milde. Josie. Even Egili, wriggling in Milde's arms like he wanted to join me. I blanked. There wasn't a riddle, a poem, a single word in

117

my head, It was worse than having Gail Silverton watch me screw up the archery tournament. That bad memory at least gave me the idea for a riddle. I opened my mouth and croaked. The children laughed, but I managed to make a joke out of it. I coughed and made faces like I was choking, which turned the laughter in my favor at least. Finally, I cleared my throat for real and recited as smoothly as I could.

"*Agob* is my name twisted about. I am a creature shaped for battle. When I bend and—"

A dozen voices, young and old, cried, "*Boga! Boga!*" A bow! A bow!

I wasn't surprised; the minute I said *agob* I realized it was a stupid way to start a riddle. Say the word backwards? What idiot thought that was clever? I shrugged at Dennis. He shrugged back. Rædwod actually looked kind of disappointed. But Josie jumped in.

"I will earn your mead for you, Eadgar!" she yelled, leaping onto the dais with her gown flapping. "You can decide whether to share it with Beorhtscyld."

The crowd was struck dumb. I don't think it was because Josie's a girl. The women there in the hall hadn't been shy or quiet. They'd laughed as loud as the children and yelled out answers, and I'd heard at least two young mothers singing lullabies to their babies during dinner. But you have to picture Josie in that crowd. Sure, there were plenty of dark-haired woman and children, but they didn't have Josie's Hispanic face, her native eyes, her corn-row braids. And she was better dressed than any of them but Hwite. Add to that her odd American-*Anglisc* accent – I mean, she'd only been speaking the language for real for two-and-a-half days. But she'd had a willing coach in Milde, and Josie has never been shy a day in her life. She didn't care what she sounded like. She knew some riddles, and that was all she needed to perform. I just got out of her way, all the way back to my seat.

Hwite started clapping first. The little girls decided that gave them permission and started cheering and calling her name. And then everyone else was cheering. Josie bowed in a very ladylike way, did a great imitation of Dennis waiting for them to be quiet, which only made them laugh harder. Then she pushed back her sleeves and started in. She mimed every line.

"I am a wonderful help to women, the hope of something to come. I hurt no one except he who slays me. Rooted I stand, on a high bed. I am shaggy below. Sometimes a beautiful farmer's daughter – an eager, proud woman – grabs my body, pulls my red skin, holds me hard, and claims my head. The curly-haired woman who takes me fast will feel our meeting. Her eye will be wet. Oh, yes."

Everyone knew the answer, but no one bothered to say it. They didn't care. Every gesture, every look had been perfect. And the "Oh, yes" at the end was new, Josie's own personal touch. Anyone who hadn't started laughing by then lost it. Rædwod was stamping and slapping his knee. He started chanting, "Mead, mead, mead!" and soon the rafters were ringing. Hwite poured it, and Grimmære rose to deliver it himself.

"Wait!" Dennis cried. "She hasn't told us the right answer!" He was grinning ear to ear, as if he'd told the riddle himself.

Someone started to say it, but Josie held up her hand and cut him off. She winked at me. "It was Eadgar who taught me this riddle. He can tell us which answer he prefers. Or not."

I almost threw my cup at her. Milde pushed me to my feet and I mumbled, "Onion."

Josie clapped her hands to her cheeks, faking surprise. "No! That's what it's called?"

Rædwod almost choked. Everyone roared, even the littlest kids. I guess living in one-room houses made them grow up fast. I blushed and sat back down, burying my face in my buttermilk. Milde patted my knee, chuckling. That made me blush even more. Idiot.

Grimmære handed the cup of mead to Josie and said,

"You might want to share this with your young man, if you expect any tears tonight."

It was Rædwod who saved me. He took center stage and told another one of the R-rated riddles, then sang a song about a wedding between a young man and a *scucca*, a shape-shifter. The groom had to consummate things with every new shape his bride came up with.

Rædwod turned the dais over to Dennis then, and Dennis finally earned his mead by reciting a poem that I'd only heard him do once before. It was one he'd written himself, a serious poem about two lovers who become betrothed on the day of a battle when the young man is killed. The woman spends the rest of the poem seeking vengeance, and dies alone. Dennis always said the poem sounded too modern, too Hollywood, but the Coria people loved it. Milde was weeping beside me by the time he was done. Egili woke up and nuzzled worriedly at her face till she hugged him. Then Josie reached across me and took her hand. I wished I'd thought of that, but it was still pretty nice to be pressed between them.

Dennis recited another poem, then Rædwod recited two. I was beginning to think the party would go on forever. I could hardly keep my head up. Josie had given me her mead after only one sip, and one sip was really all I needed. It was sour stuff, not a hint of honey left in it. Milde didn't like it either, but we didn't want to insult Grimmære and Hwite so we kept passing it around, taking smaller and smaller sips and sagging more and more onto the table.

Then someone called for *Beowulf*. It was Dennis's turn again, and I thought, *great, we'll be here all night*. But Dennis surprised me and said no, it had been too long and hard a day.

"We have come from hostile lands to this kind place, as though from one world to the next . . ." He actually said it, the truth and then some. " . . .from *Hel's* kingdom to a welcoming hall in *Middengeard*. I lack the energy and the wit to do right by such a song as *Beowulf*. With the chief's leave, I will yield the hall to the true *scop* among us." Dennis bowed to Grimmære and Hwite, then to Rædwod, then to the people, and came to sit with us, taking the half-drained cup of mead from Milde with a tired smile. He got a big round of applause.

And then the call went up for Rædwod and *Beowulf.* Rædwod was as serious as I'd ever seen him. He sat on a small stool near the front of the dais, opened his fur bag, and took out his harp. It was more like a lyre really, a beautiful thing of bright wood, with silver fittings where the two arms came up to meet the crossbar. The bridge was carved bone or ivory. He set the base on his thigh, holding it upright by his cheek. It only had six strings, but they sounded sweet when he plucked them to check the tuning. He spoke as he tightened the pegs.

"I have less wit than Beorhtscyld, and only a little more energy. To sing the whole of *Beowulf* would take us through the night. When I was younger I could do such things, and happily spend the next day walking in company with a herd of farting cattle. Those days are passed. So I will tell you only one part of the tale and leave the rest for my return."

"The *wyrm!*" a little boy cried. "Tell of the dragon!"

"No, tell of Grendel!" another boy cried, and then a girl shouted to hear about the *nicor*, Grendel's mother. Other kids joined in on one side or the other, and a lot of the adults, too.

"What is a *nicor?*" Josie whispered.

"A water-beast," Milde replied. "A fearsome thing."

Josie looked really puzzled. "What's up?" I asked.

"I could swear Morgwydd used that word," she said.

"What? When?"

But then Rædwod laughed and stroked a strong chord on the harp. Everyone went quiet. "I will tell of the *wyrm,*" he said. "It is a fitting part to end an evening – Beowulf's final battle, death in victory – for it is also the tale of Wiglaf, a young man of courage and honor, like the young man who spoke first." He looked intently at the boy, who was sitting on the floor right in front of the dais. "When you face such a foe, may you meet it with the same bitter-sweet honor."

Then he began to recite, from the verse where Beowulf becomes king of his people and rules in peace for fifty years, until a slave finds the dragon's horde in a barrow and steals a single piece. Then the *wyrm* wakes up and wastes the countryside, and it's up to Beowulf, now an old man, to take him on. Beowulf rides out to challenge the dragon with twelve warriors, but he tells them all to stay back in the woods; he has to battle the dragon alone, like he did Grendel and the *nicor*. He has a famous sword and an iron shield made just for this battle, and he advances into the dragon's lair knowing this will probably be his last fight.

But before that happens, Beowulf tells his men some of his history. About his foster father, and how the oldest son is accidentally killed by the youngest. How the father is destroyed by that loss. There's a lament built into the bigger poem, and Rædwod sang that part as a song.

I had been nodding off, just too tired to listen. When Rædwod started to sing, I snapped awake. Josie did, too. Dennis, Milde, we all did. We knew the tune. It was the lullaby, the song of the gatekey. My song. Only not all the notes were the same, and the phrasing was a little different. Rædwod was singing it right – not the way I'd remembered it, but the way it was supposed to be. I recognized the rightness of the tune, and I recognized his voice. Thirteen years later, I still recognized his singing voice. Rædwod was my father.

Eoh

# Chapter 14

Josie knew something was up. She leaned close and whispered, "What's wrong?"

I just shook my head. I couldn't speak, my mind was frozen. I'd thought I was already numb after that long day, but this stunned me. I stared at Rædwod as he finished the song, trying to see some resemblance to my vague memories. I tried to shave off the beard and trim the wild hair, smooth out the lines. Heal the scar away. Replace his missing eye. I still couldn't see it. And when he was reciting again, I couldn't hear it. I began to think I must have nodded off and dreamed him singing. By the end of the battle, as the *wyrm* and Beowulf both died, I was sure of it.

But then Rædwod sang again, "chanting in dirges," like the poem says Beowulf's men did at his funeral. And he was my father, singing my song.

"He's singing it wrong," Josie whispered, "but it's beautiful." There were tears in her eyes. In mine, too, I guess.

"He's singing it right," I mumbled.

I waited until the fire had been banked and everyone had left. Hwite and her daughters brought in furs and blankets for Rædwod and me. Then she and Grimmære led Dennis and Milde off to some private place more proper for a married couple, and Josie went to sleep with Hwite's daughters, because Josie and I were supposed to be only betrothed. She pretended she wanted to stay, but I was too distracted for joking.

124

"Well, young Eadgar," Rædwod said, when we were finally alone in the long, dark hall, "it has been a long day, and it bodes to be a hard night." He stomped his foot on the wooden floor of the dais, where they had laid our bedding. "It's time we tried to use this properly. Unless you have something more to tell me of your adventures."

He was staring at me, studying my face. He suspected something, I could tell, so I spoke English. "You're Edwin Lewis, aren't you. From a different time."

He answered in English. "A different Earth." His voice was hoarse. "Oh, my. Edwin Lewis. Yes. To hear that name. To hear this tongue! Shhh!" He slipped back into *Anglisc*, and whispered, "Speak it softly here."

"I think you're my father," I said.

He nodded. "Well you might think. Very well." He hugged himself, like he could barely hold himself together. "Sit. Tell me. Let's make sure."

I didn't know where to start. The renfaire? The arrow? Morgwydd and Mom? Or at the very beginning, when I first realized he was gone? I tried them all at once, jumping around, a sentence here and there. I wasn't making much sense, and he stopped me.

"Your mother . . . Alrun, right?" I nodded. "Oh, gods. Oh good gods! Tell me, what is she like? What does she do? I might know her, indeed."

So I told him about Mom: the weaving, the runes, how she never spoke after he disappeared. How she must have slipped me the arrowhead, knowing that Urien would be coming to get her. Rædwod – I still couldn't think of him as *Dad* – he asked questions, sometimes in English, sometimes in *Anglisc* when he couldn't remember the English words. He'd whack himself on the mouth or shake his head until the right word popped out and then go on in whatever language that was. He was crazy, but less and less the more we talked. Finally, I had to ask him the one question that had been stuck in my mind since I'd first met him.

"What happened to your eye?"

He withdrew a little, was more Rædwod again, hiding behind the mad grin. "Pretty, isn't it?" He flipped up his patch to show the wink. "Gentle Morgwydd decided she needed it, so she cut it out with a little silver knife while Urien's sons held me down. She slipped." He ran his finger along the scar. "She told me I shouldn't have moved my head."

"Good God! She needed it? Why?"

"She wanted to spy on your mother. She thought it would help."

"That's crazy!"

"Oh, no. No, it makes perfect sense. Who would want to see Alrun more than I?" He tapped the side of his head. "Who would always see her in the mind's eye? It's the Law of Similarities: water to blood, heart to mind, mind to eye. All the gods understand that formula."

"Jesus," I muttered.

"Except him. There is no Jesus here. Not on this world, not even a rumor. But gods, yes – more gods than you can shake a stick of yew at." He grinned again and patted my arm. "Don't worry, you get used to it after nine years. It gives you a lot more curses to swear with."

"Thirteen years," I said. "You've been gone thirteen. Almost fourteen."

"Thirteen? I knew it would be longer, but . . ." Thunor's stones, that makes you . . ." He peered at me, tipping his head like a bird. "Seventeen? I thought you looked too old."

"Did you recognize me?" I asked. The thought made me feel kind of glad.

He shook his head. "I knew there was something familiar. The whole lot of you: so strange. And bearing a ferret? Ha! Not from this world, not in ten score years! But where, then? Which Earth? And what of Milde, armed and angry and so much of this world. I admit, I was distracted by your Milde. She reminded me so of your mother."

"What?" That thought had never occurred to me.

He held up his hands. "Your mother when I first met

her, lo, those many years ago. Sixteen – no, what? Twenty? I'm lost. When are we? Never mind, before you were born. Come, come! You have to admit there's a similarity: height, complexion, mettle. Not many women would carry a spear and shield or ride such a spirited stallion."

"Mom never did that! Did she?" I couldn't imagine it.

"Maybe not," he said, "but she wouldn't hesitate if the chance came up. She took a knife to my throat once, you know. Oh gods, I've missed her! Quick, quick! Finish your story. Who are Dennis and Shosefina? A Spanish princess? Pu-lease! I knew right away they weren't from this world. But which, but which? You could have come from home, or any other Earth out there." He held a finger across his lips and whispered. "*Shhh.* I wasn't going to speak up until I was sure. I'm still not a hundred percent. Tell me everything."

So I told him about what it was like living with Mom, who didn't speak, and Uncle Alf, who didn't speak much. Then about Dennis: how Uncle Alf had heard him reciting poetry in Old English on the common at the college and had corrected his pronunciation. Before you knew it, Dennis was coming over almost every day to practice and eat Mom's *briw,* and then he moved in and life got a lot easier.

Rædwod's face fell. I mean, he just deflated. All the spirit, all the energy went right out of him. He was just a beat-up, dirty old guy with one eye. It flashed on me why.

"Not with Mom!" I said. "He moved in with Uncle Alf."

Rædwod's eye went wide. His opened his mouth, closed it, sat up straighter. "Alf?" he said finally. "He moved in with Ælfweard?"

"Yeah, with Uncle Alf," I said. "You got a problem with that?" I had gotten a few fag comments from some of my classmates. After a fight and a trip to the office, I'd learned to ignore them. Now my fists had clenched again, but Rædwod held up both hands and shook his head.

"Nooo! No problem at all," he said. "I just never expect-ed— He was betrothed once, you know?" He laughed. "Alf!

There is so much behind that frown! Does he still frown all the time? Or did Dennis change that, too?"

"A little," I said, relaxing. "He still doesn't smile much at me."

"Don't take it personally, Son," Rædwod said. "That's just Ælfweard being himself."

"Son?" I echoed. "You're sure?"

"Oh, I so want you to be!" He squeezed his hands against the side of his head, as though it might explode, and let out a huge groan. Tears ran from under his patch. "Gods! You are either my very own son, or you come from a world so close to mine it doesn't matter."

He reached out, grabbed my shoulders, and pulled me to him. It was awkward as hell on the bench, and I didn't know how to react anyway. This was my father? Really? It seemed impossible. My dad was dead. That's what one half of me thought, but the other half wasn't thinking, it was feeling. And that part of me felt like eight things at once, and wasn't sure what eight they were. I was crying, too, a little. And I also wanted to shout *yes!* as loud as I could. But I couldn't. There was a lump in my throat so big it would have choked even Bil. And I wanted so much for Mom to be in on that hug. I hugged him for that, for being there with me, who he hardly knew, when he couldn't be with Mom.

It was a while before he could speak again, but then he started asking more questions and I had some of my own. How he'd escaped, for one, and he told me, acting out half the scenes, words pouring out in his crazy mix of English and *Anglisc*. After Morgwydd cut his eye out, she and Urien kept him as bait to lure Mom and Uncle Alf back. They locked him in a shed, half conscious, but he woke up after dark and managed to claw a hole through the thatch of the roof and escape into the woods. They came after him and almost caught him, but they stirred up some wild beast – *an aglæca*, a monster – that attacked them and gave him a chance to slip away. Then a storm blew up, a big thunderstorm that raged all night. He kept moving and found a tiny cave to hide in the next day, and then worked his way south, moving by night, living on berries and water mostly, until he reached Coria. He pulled a Dennis, pretending to be a *scop* from the South, an escaped slave. They nursed him back to health, but he didn't stay.

"Urien's men began to harry the region," he said. "They raped and razed two outlying farms and then a village just to the north. I could feel Morgwydd searching for me, a weight on the back of my head. A glimpse of her shadow from the corner of this eye." He pointed to his patch. "I fled southward. I changed my name, grew the beard, stayed far, far away. For two years. It seemed long enough, unbearably long! Oh, I was young and foolish then, eh? So much still to learn. But your mother – gods, how I missed your mother! And you." He touched my cheek. His hand was trembling. I tried not to flinch. "Already the memory of your face was getting harder and harder to see. With either eye. I was afraid I'd lose even that of you. So I came back to Coria, and they welcomed me. But I nearly betrayed them. I saw *her* shadow but tried to ignore it. Then Urien's ravens came again, raiding as close as the Wall. I couldn't ignore that. I couldn't endanger these good people. I fled again. Seven long years."

"What made you decide to come back now?" I asked.

"A dream," he said. "A dream of your mother's hands casting runes on her white cloth."

"Which ones?"

"Tiw. Wyn. Ear. Oeþel."

A chill went down my back. The arrow, the gatekey, and me. But the fourth? "Oeþel?" I asked.

"*Homeland*," he said. "Oh, yes, I've dreamed of it often enough, but never in runes. That's your mother's talent. She was calling me northward, back to her."

I was thinking that was a big decision to make just because of a dream, and Rædwod must have seen it in my face. He smiled and waggled his head.

"You're thinking I'm even madder than I look. Well may I be, but this is not the world you grew up in, Son. You

129

didn't travel in time, you crossed the cold marches to a new land entirely. The rules here are different, even time moves differently. I've seen people healed and made sick by runes, ritual, and song. I've watched more than one *burgrune* predict the future and then watched it come true. I've seen a ten-foot-tall shadow attack Urien's searching men, and heard a god's voice in a thunderstorm. I've enchanted a roomful of angry men with my harp and stopped a war. I know when a dream is more than a dream."

He had begun to sing when he spoke of ritual and song, and when he finished, I realized I had seen everything he described: the shadow and the storm, and I could have picked the angry men out of a crowd of strangers. I believed him.

We talked a little more, but finally we both agreed we'd better get some sleep. I wasn't sure I could, my head was spinning so much. But the day had been too long. He'd hardly started snoring when I went out like a light.

I might have dreamed – I sure wouldn't have been surprised if I had – but I don't remember anything between his first snore and the weight of a hand on my shoulder. It was Dennis, whispering my name. The last thing I wanted was to wake up, and I tried to roll over and ignore him, but he kept shaking my shoulder, until I had to open my eyes.

He looked terrible. His face was a pasty blur in the thin dawn light leaking through the doorway. He eyes were dark spectacles.

"What?" I mumbled, struggling to sit up.

"Where's Josie?" he rasped.

I fell back onto the fur and fleece bedding. "I don't know. Ask Milde."

He sank down beside me. "She's gone, too. I need Josie. The salve. My head is splitting."

"It's your own fault. You drank too much of that awful mead."

"No, it's right here." He touched the bandage across his

forehead. "Like a knife. I need salve. And the chant. Le-ofrith said three days."

Just a few hours earlier, I would have scoffed at him, but not after hearing Rædwod's story. My father's story. I was still having trouble matching the two in my mind. I glanced over at him, sound asleep on his pile of bedding. His hair and beard were a dark tangle around his face, the eye patch a blotch across the pale scar. He was still Rædwod, but he wasn't just a crazy old stranger any more. I felt a lump stick in my throat.

I didn't wake him. I didn't tell Dennis anything yet, either. He was in no condition. I made him lie down in my bedding and went to find Josie.

Most of Coria was already awake. Smoke drifted from the holes in the peaks of the houses. Shutters had been thrown back, and I could hear low voices, the sound of crockery, farts, and yawns. Luckily, I bumped into one of Hwite's daughters, and she sent me a couple of buildings down to a workshop, a low weaving room set a foot or two into the ground. The door was open to catch the early light, and a tallow lamp hung from one of the beams. A single vertical loom stood against the wall opposite the door. Milde was helping one of the townswomen, using her weaving sword to lift a pattern from the vertical warp threads so the weaver woman could pass the weft through. Josie stood to the side, paying close attention. The low dawn light made their faces glow, as though they didn't have a care in the world but weaving. I stood a moment watching, wishing it were true. Milde passed the shuttle back – just a simple polished stick wrapped with yarn – and beat the threads upward with sharp, two-handed blows of the weaving sword. She withdrew the sword, dropped the heddle rod to reverse the warp, and paused while the other woman used a slender stick to pick out a new pattern of warp threads. Then Milde slipped the sword back in, twisted it to widen the gap, slid the shuttle through, beat upward, lifted the heddle, paused for the other woman to pick up a new pattern, slipped in the sword, slid the shuttle, beat upward. It was fine work, hard work. Her muscles showed it. I had watched Mom weave on a loom like this but had never given it a second thought. I studied Milde's face. No way did she look like Mom, but working there at the loom, she could have been a cousin.

Then Josie noticed me, and I told her about Dennis.

"We must go at once," Milde said. "He will need all his health to face Urien."

Well, that spoiled the mood. We trooped back to the hall, where Dennis was moaning theatrically. A couple of women were tending the fire, getting ready to cook. They looked up when we came in and shook their heads.

"*Scops!*" one of them muttered.

Milde shot her a frown and strode by like a queen, but Josie just laughed.

"That's right," Dennis moaned. "Make fun of a dying man."

"Don't speak of such things," Milde snapped. "Wyrd listens everywhere."

"Don't worry," Josie said, "he's enjoying himself too much to die."

"'Enjoying' hardly describes the depth of my pleasure," Dennis muttered. "Healer, work your magic, I beg you."

"Give me a smile and I will," Josie replied.

Dennis bared his teeth at her. She laughed again and asked Milde to fetch some boiled water. She unwrapped the bandage and went through the whole ritual, complete with spit. Despite what I'd heard from Rædwod, I still couldn't believe spitting made a difference. But Dennis felt better immediately, so what did I know? Milde was back by then with a small pot of hot water, and Josie made the last of the herbs into tea for Dennis. Milde had brought some food, too – stale ends of bread dipped in leftover broth and spread with lard. They were all sitting and eating when I dropped the bombshell about Rædwod.

They stared at him, curled up now with his back to us and his robe pulled over his face.

"*Feoh*," Josie whispered. "Not *facen, fæder!*" Not treasure, father.

"You're joking, right?" Dennis said.

I said no.

"Ed, this is wonderful!" Josie exclaimed. "How did you know?"

I explained about the song and the sound of his voice, and then everything he'd told me. Milde looked a little poleaxed at first but shrugged it off. After all, she'd already been on the star road between the worlds and seen her face on Gail Silverton. Dennis had a lot of questions, most of which I couldn't answer.

"Well, this certainly adds a wrinkle," Dennis said.

"No worse than any we've tripped over so far," Josie said. She gave me a quick hug. "Oh, Ed, I'm so happy for you. Alrun and Uncle Alf are going to be so glad to see him."

"Yeah, there is that," I allowed. "What do we do, Dennis?"

"About what?" he asked.

"About Mom and Uncle Alf. We can't sit around here like this, we've got to get moving. We've got to get all the way back to Regensburg, then try to pick up their trail after all that rain, so we can find our way across the hills to wherever they were going. And now everything is more complicated. I mean, he'll slow us down, he doesn't have a horse. Or weapons. Do you have more gold to buy them? Even if you did, we don't have the time to mess around bargaining with Grimmære."

"What are you saying Ed?" Josie demanded. "That we should leave him behind? Your father?"

"No, I'm just saying we should have left already. Every minute counts!"

Rædwod coughed and rolled over, throwing off his cloak. "Haste and worry, haste and waste," he said. "We have time, Son. We have till the solstice. And I know the way." He pointed to his patch. "I could find Alrun in the dark with just this eye."

# *Chapter 15*

Dennis and Josie took Rædwod at his word. Milde and I both complained, but we were out-voted by one extra eye. So we stayed in Coria that day trying to get a horse for Rædwod. He insisted we keep using his mad-*scop* name; he said Morgwydd had ways to hear his real one. That was okay by me. I still had a hard time believing my dad would say things like that.

No luck with the horse, though. Dennis had some gold left, but Grimmære was bent way out of shape. He accused us of using enchantment to lure Rædwod to certain death. We couldn't tell him I was Rædwod's son, not after the elaborate fable Dennis had made up the day before. Besides, the truth was even more unbelievable. All Rædwod could do was pretend that he'd had a dream telling him to join us, that he should be the one to sing our story. It didn't work. Hwite was just as upset as Grimmære and wouldn't take our side. Even Cenryth tried to talk Rædwod out of it.

"For once ignore your own mad counsel!" he cried. "If it's death you wish, I'll be happy to kill you myself at the end of our journey. Just don't make me travel all the way to Din Giardi with no one to talk to but cattle, churls, and slaves."

"Two more days and you'd have been as mad as me, good friend," Rædwod replied. "I'm doing you a favor."

So, early next morning, we rode northwest, up the

Roman road called Dere Street. Milde and Josie rode together on the big stallion, Dennis and Rædwod took the mares, and I was back on little Bil.

Rædwod said that Morgwydd and Urien were using one of the old hill forts for their base. The way he told it, we could have driven there in a couple of hours. On our Earth, that is, in a car. On this Earth it would take a few days' ride. The Roman road was a war zone. No one could travel on it beyond Hadrian's Wall without risking an ambush. We'd have to take to the woods.

Between Coria and the Wall, the road was rough and rutted but still mostly cobbled. It passed by weathered ruins: roofless stone houses more than half covered by lichen, with empty windows and the stains of old fires. The *Angelcynn* had done this, driving out the *Beornice*. But soon enough, we passed by the first of four burned-out *Angelisc* farms, marked by the small rotting circles of their pal- isades. Then we reached the Wall, and Professor Dennis had to waste time telling us all about it. It was still tall and imposing, though the fort and gate were a jumble of fallen stones. A few miles past that, we came to the village Ræd- wod had mentioned, a grown-over tangle of weeds and burned timbers. The palisade had been completely razed, and the hall in the center was just a low mound of brush.

"They killed everyone," Rædwod said, "took no prison- ers, not even slaves: men, women, children, all were cut down."

"Why so brutal?" Josie asked.

"Why, 'twas a message from gentle Morgwydd: her warning to bold Grimmære to keep his people south of the Wall." Rædwod looked away. "Or maybe our dear little girl just threw a tantrum because I'd escaped her. Morg- wydd rides with a war chief, but she doesn't think like one. And her slaughter flew back in her painted face. The *Angel- cynn* responded in kind, raiding farther and farther into the hills. Now we have stalemate, but this is a war of attri- tion, and the invaders are winning."

Invaders. I hadn't thought of it that way before. Morgwydd and Urien were fighting to save their land. The *Anglecynn* were fighting to take it.

"And even King Arthur failed," Dennis remarked.

"Arthur?" Rædwod laughed. "The man of myth! There was no King Arthur here."

"He really didn't exist?" Josie asked.

"Did I say that?" Rædwod exclaimed. "Did I say 'not exist'? There was not *a* King Arthur, there were dozens of him, from the pointy toe of Cornwall to the lumpy knob of Arthur's Seat at *Din Eidyn*! Vortigern and Artorius were Arthur. Cuneglasus was Arthur. Mynyddog will be Arthur, and Cadwallon, too, if a wayward falling star doesn't keep them from being born. Right now, right here, Urien is trying very hard to be Arthur, and Morgwydd is his cross-dressing, black-minded Merlin."

Okay, that explained a lot about Morgwydd and Urien and what they were doing, but not everything.

"What does Morgwydd have against us?" I asked. "It's not just that we're *Angelcynn*. I mean, she was ready to let Urien kill us. What does she want with Mom and Uncle Alf?"

"She needs a bow for some reason," Rædwod said. "That's the only thing we could think of. She needs The Right Bow. Your mother was bait to catch Alf, and he to hold her, for the witch needs Alrun, too. Only your mother can cast the runes for the bow, and the she-devil knows it. But it's more than just that. Why does she need this bow? Who does she need to kill whom Urien can't take by sword and spear? An army? A single bow can't destroy an entire army, no matter how strong a magic she lays on it. And this is no single army she fights, or a single tribe; it's a migration, an entire population of invaders sailing with gods who honor war and valor more than love and life. Morgwydd believes that Alrun and Alf will do as she bids merely to save each other. She who would die for her country cannot understand that they will do the same. Oh, gentle Morgwydd is mad, indeed, but still not half so blind as me. She can see the rising tide, the coming flood, the land-drinking wave, yet she thinks she can stop it." Ræd-wod gripped his head between his hands. "Woden's left eye! Why? How? Mad as I am, I cannot understand her."

I didn't either, and I didn't care.

"We don't have to understand," I said. "We just have to get Mom and Alf out of her hands. Come on, we're wasting time."

Rædwod let go of his head and took a breath. "Wise words, yes, but we have a week still till the solstice. Morg-wydd's strength ebbs and flows with the sun and moon. Midsummer is her peak, and the moon will be full then, too, or so said the wise old *burgrune* safe back south in Gipeswic. Now that Morgwydd has Alrun and Alf, she will wait for the skies to turn."

"Damn witch," I muttered. "Damn her and all this crazy *Wealisc* magic."

Rædwod shook his head. "Don't say that, Son, for you damn yourself. You wouldn't be born without it. It was magic that brought me to your mother." He dropped his voice and spoke English. "And she almost killed me right off; would have slit my throat as quick as last night's dinner if I hadn't convinced her I wasn't one of Urien's ravens." He steered his mare close and leaned over to whisper in my ear. "We're Welsh, too, you and I. Lewis, we are. Your grandfather was born in Llanidloes in the heart of Wales. If he'd been born in this here and now, we'd be outlaws in the hills, or dead by Saxon hands. Think about that when-ever you moon over sweet Milde. If she but knew . . ." He drew his finger across his throat.

I glanced at her, but she was feeding Egili some scraps of beef jerky.

"There are no winners here, Son," Rædwod said, "only villains and victims, on both sides. Ha! Just like any war."

He led us around the ruins and off the road, cutting across the overgrown fields toward the trees. From that point on, we would travel out of sight.

↑

We could have walked it faster, I think. Rædwod's mare hated being so closed in and made a break for every clearing. The stallion hated not being in the lead and kept nipping at the mare's flanks. Dennis's mare had a habit of squeezing between two trunks that were too close together to fit Dennis. Good old Bil just followed the leader, stepping carefully along the easiest path. I almost forgave him for being so dumpy.

We were all bushed by the time Rædwod called a halt beside a rushing brook. It was a beautiful spot, just above a steep tumble of rocks. The water rolled and bounced through a half-dozen channels into a deep pool.

"We'll ford here and then camp, " he said. "I'm foundering and fain must feed. We must feel fresh to fell our foes."

"Fresh!" Josie exclaimed, easing herself off the stallion. "My butt aches all the way to my armpits, I stink worse than this horse, and I itch like I've caught all its fleas!"

"What did you say?" Milde asked, dismounting easily beside her.

Josie laughed and shook her head. "I'm sorry, friend, I can't translate half those words."

"She aches, stinks, and has fleas," I said in *Anglisc*. "Nothing unusual."

Josie punched my thigh. I yelped and Bil snorted. I think he was laughing at me.

Milde did laugh. "After we set up camp, you and I can bathe here," she told Josie.

"Not alone," Dennis said. "We're in Morgwydd's territory now."

"We have Egili to be our watch dog," Milde said. As if on cue, he poked his head out of his pouch, testing the air.

"Not good enough," Dennis said. "He may have the heart of a wild boar, but he lacks the weight to go with it. He can't even bark. First, we'll find a camp site not too far away. Then I'll keep watch while Ed and Rædwod hunt for some dinner."

"How well will you watch?" Milde asked.

"Nothing will distract me from your safety," Dennis replied smoothly, with a little bow.

I bit my tongue. If Dennis wanted to come out to Milde he would. I looked at Josie and rolled my eyes, but she totally misunderstood.

"Sorry, Ed," she said in English. "You'll just have to keep imagining."

"What?" Milde asked.

I wasn't about to translate it.

We led the horses across the stream and found a place to camp back in the trees, near a windfall that made a clearing just big enough to grow a thin covering of grass for the horses. Josie and Milde went off as soon as they had unsaddled the stallion and let Egili stretch his legs. Dennis went after them, carrying his shield. Rædwod chuckled and started hobbling the horses.

"Do you think they'll be safe?" I asked.

"As safe as anyone can be north of the Wall," he said. "Go find our dinner and I'll tend the horses. A one-eyed *scop* makes a miserable hunter. A harp makes a poor bow."

True enough, I thought. I could only hope I'd live up to his expectations. I braced my bowstring and set off into the woods, moving slowly and quietly, looking for tracks. There were plenty of them, also scat – deer, hare, squirrel, grouse – but I didn't see a single living thing besides myself and a couple of tiny bold birds. I made a big loop and wound up beside the brook. There were some fresh deer track in the mud, and I followed them on a zig-zag path to the tumbling channels above the deep pool. I couldn't resist looking down. There was nobody there, just a couple of big geese out on the water. And no sign of Dennis.

I wondered if they could have finished washing up already. Maybe the water was too cold. If so, they were back at the camp, wondering what happened to dinner. I watched the geese and thought, *Dinner.*

I slipped back into the woods and crept downhill, bow ready. When I was below the pool, I snuck closer, keeping the light of the sun behind me. The water flashed and rippled, but I couldn't see the geese. The brook cascaded into the pool, covering any sound except the slight rustle of a breeze in the trees and the occasional trill of a bird. It was like soft music. I shifted a few steps closer, and there were the geese, gliding into sight. Only they weren't geese, they were swans, one white and one dark. They were beautiful, regal, graceful, all those words that go with swans. I knew the other words, too: strong, quick, touchy, and downright vicious if you threatened them. But they tasted good. They glided out of sight, and I followed them behind the trees, bow at half draw, looking for a clear shot.

"Bad idea, Son."

It was Rædwod, right beside me, leaning against a broad oak tree, facing away from the pool, stroking a tune from his harp. I almost tripped over him.

"Jesus! What are you doing here!"

"*Shh*," he whispered. "You'll startle them."

"Not like you startled me!" I muttered. I couldn't help whispering, too. There was something about his music that made you want to leave it alone.

He grinned. "So sorry, my good hunter. You're so quiet, so feline and feral, you were on me before I could warn you."

"What are you doing here anyway? Where's Dennis?"

"Lurking higher up, as promised. And keeping his eyes averted, also as promised. A man of his word is our Beorhtscyld. As for me . . ." He stroked a few sweet chords on his harp. ". . . I am simply doing what I can to help."

"By making noise? Besides, Milde and Josie have left. There's just a couple of swans on the pool. Dinner, if I'm lucky."

I glanced at the pool, and there were Josie and Milde, chest deep in the water.

I must have looked really stupid, because Rædwod stifled a laugh. "No-no-no-no-no, don't look," he told me. "It is boorish, oafish, crude, and unkind. Not to mention uncool."

"But how—?" Josie and Milde were right in the sun,

plain as day. I couldn't understand how I'd missed seeing them.

"*Shh*. If you can see them, they can see you."

I was barely shadowed by the overhanging branches, with just one low bush between me and the water. But they were facing mostly away from me. Milde was washing Josie's hair, and the water flashed and sparkled as she tipped Josie back and scrubbed her fingers through the thick, dark mass. Milde's hair was unbraided, too, and hung down into the water in a wet, pale fall. Her skin was as white as the linen shawl Mom used to cast her runes. Beside her, Josie was . . . hard to describe. Half standing, half floating on the water, arms out. Her breasts just broke the surface.

Rædwod grabbed my shoulder and pulled me toward him. The sudden gap in music was like a shout. Milde started to turn just as the broad tree trunk came between us.

"*Shhhhhhhhh*," Rædwod breathed. "Gawk not, young geek. They are your friends; do not betray their trust. Someday maybe they'll invite you to join them. Until then, you are blind on that side."

He turned me away from the pool and began to play again. The soft music blended back into the sounds of water, breeze, and bird calls. It slowed my heartbeat, which was pounding pretty frigging hard, I have to admit.

Quietly, Rædwod began to sing. "*Hrægl min swigað, þonne ic hrusan trede.*"

*My gown is silent as I thread the seas, haunt old buildings or tread the land. Sometimes my song-coat and the supple wind float me high over the halls of men; the power of clouds ferries me windward over cities. Then my bright silks start to sing, whistle, roar, resound, and ring, while I sail on, untouched by earth and sea, a spirit, ghost, and guest on wing.*

"*The Swan*," I breathed. "Yeah, that beautiful."

"She is indeed. A rare beauty. And Milde, too."

"Well of course," I said. "That's who I meant. I mean,

sure, Josie is . . . Sure, she's pretty enough—"

Suddenly I was embarrassed. I mean, here was my father, and we were talking about Josie, my almost sister. "I meant Milde," I repeated, feeling lame.

"Either one, beautiful is the right word," he said. "Choose words carefully, Son; they have power, as much as music." He played a few bars without speaking. "Do you have a girlfriend back home?" he asked.

"Don't I wish," I said.

"An interest, then?"

I shrugged. "Yeah."

"Any interest back?"

I thought about that glimpse of Milde's back and wondered if Gail would look like that. Probably not so thin, more tanned, but still . . .

I sighed. "Not really. She's older and, I don't know, more mature. More sure of herself. More exciting. I guess I must seem pretty plain to her. She's a lot like Milde, actually, looks and everything. I mean, not that I've seen . . . everything. Much of anything. I mean she has the same guts. Spirit. Like that."

Rædwod chuckled. "Oh, my, that is saying something indeed. A veritable Valkyrie. How do you plan on catching her interest? Please do tell me you at least plan to try."

I remembered the archery competition. "Yeah, I've tried. It didn't go so well."

"Ha! No more than a setback. Keep trying, Son. If she is truly worth it, keep trying."

"Yeah," I said. "That's all you can do, right? Keep trying?"

"In love as in life, and both drive us mad," Rædwod replied. "Why don't you head back to camp and make a fire. Our swan maids will need one to dry their feathers. I'll stay and keep watch till they leave." He strummed a few more notes. "It helps the music when I'm closer."

I suddenly realized what he thought he was doing. "No way. You don't really think—?" I turned to look at the pool and didn't see Milde, Josie, or even swans. Then movement caught my eye, and there they were, walking out of the water off to the left.

"Tut-tut!" Rædwod dug his elbow into my side without missing a note in his song. "Now that you know they're there, you can see them. Go. Go on. Go-go-go. They'll be safe without Little Brother watching their every last move."

He was teasing but I still blushed. I started walking directly away from the pool.

"Start dinner, too," he whispered. "I'm starved."

I glanced back, wondering if he'd noticed that I wasn't carrying any game, and for a moment, I couldn't even see him. Or hear the music. There was only the cascade and the breeze and the trill of a bird. Then he smiled and waggled his head, and there he was, leaning against the oak tree, playing his harp.

# *Chapter 16*

I just had time to get a small fire started before Milde and Josie showed up. They hung their wet cloaks over some branches, then huddled by the fire, holding their gowns near the flames. They were wearing their undertunics – calf length, with long sleeves – but I couldn't stop remembering the glimpse of them in the water. I went to check on the horses. By the time I'd finished, Dennis and Rædwod were back, and Rædwod was plucking one of the big, dark grouse that had startled me after we'd left Regensburg.

"I thought you said you couldn't hunt," I grumbled.

"And so I can't," he replied. "Noble Egili brought down this regal fowl, in exchange for the best bits."

The little ferret was crouched beside him, chowing down on the bird's guts.

"That thing is huge," I said. "How did he manage it?"

"With a blazing sprint and a lunge for the jugular!" Rædwod exclaimed. "Our little friend has an arrow's speed, a lion's jaws, and a boar's heart. This horse grouse will feed our small army well. With the goosefoot greens Milde collected and the bread from Coria, we shall have a chieftain's feast. What else is in those haversacks, eh? A sweet, perhaps, to cap our meal?"

Dennis and I dug out what we had left from home: a few more strips of jerky, a bit of hard cheddar, dried apple slices, and the crumbling remains of some oatcakes.

Rædwod waved it off. "Filler for dire straits; save it. We'll hunt and forage as we go."

*Easy for you to say*, I thought. But at least no one had mentioned my own empty luck. "I don't see why Grimmære couldn't have spared us a little more than these tiny rolls," I complained.

"Ingrate, these tiny rolls are a treasure!" Rædwod replied. "It's the fasting season. The year's crop is a long way from the table. They're down to the last of the grain and ham and lard, the cattle are lean and the milk thin. They've culled the hens who've stopped laying, and the rest cower in the coop, afraid to follow in that fowl fate. The feast Grimmære and Hwite put on for us was an expense they could hardly afford. We were lucky to get even these. Apologize!"

He held up two of the loaves; back to back they were no bigger than a softball. He waggled one and spoke in a deep voice, "Yes, apologize slave, or I shall have your bowels for breakfast." Then the other, in a squeak, "Oh, no, brave Grimmære, you brute! The lad is unschooled in manners but he means well enough. Leave him bowels, else how could he speak. Just take off his *beallucas*."

Dennis chuckled. Milde, who was braiding Josie's hair, whispered in her ear, and they both laughed. *Beallucas* means balls.

"Ha ha, very funny," I muttered.

"Ah, but you shall have the last laugh, my son . . . ," Rædwod handed me one of the tiny loaves. ". . . for you shall have the first bite."

We roasted the bird over the fire, then ate it with our fingers, wiping our hands on the coarse bread before gnawing that down with the greens. It wasn't enough, but it tasted good.

"Thank you, Egili," Milde said, picking him up and giving him a hug. "You are a brave hunter. He could have protected us without you, Beorhtscyld."

"He certainly would have tried," Dennis replied. He

had used Josie's ax to cut some saplings for a clothes-drying rack, and was honing its blade on a small stone.

"Also he wouldn't have been tempted to watch us instead of the woods," Milde added.

"You offend me, Milde," Dennis replied. "Did I not promise that nothing would distract me? I assure you, I didn't glance your way more than once, and saw nothing more than the flash of reflections on the water."

"What is worse, Shosefina?" Milde asked, frowning. "That he broke his promise and looked, or that he bothered to look only once?"

Josie was braiding Milde's hair now. "It's hard to know with Dennis, but we may have been insulted."

Dennis laughed. "You are a tough one to please, Milde. I'll say only that you couldn't be any more beautiful in the water than you are on land."

I remembered the riddle of the swan and said the first line. Milde looked over at me, half smiling, and my mouth almost went dry.

"Go on, Ed" Josie urged, so I swallowed and managed to get it all out.

"Well done!" Dennis cried, and Rædwod gave me a wink with his good eye.

Milde raised her eyebrows. "I think more than one man looked."

I blushed and shook my head, totally dried up.

Then Josie began to recite. "*Bliðe seo bryd hwa me hæfþ* . . . Joyful the wife who has me; Wyrd smiles on that chosen one. The longer and stronger I grow the more true I prove to her, the bearer of life's sweetness, maker of children and joy. Joy night and day, through week, month, and year. In field, hearth, and bed, I shine brighter than gold, stand stouter than ash and stronger than steel, a chieftain's gift bestowed by a good man to a good willing wife. Oh, what joy I bring."

We were all silent for a minute when she finished.

"I haven't heard that one before," Dennis said.

"Nor I," Rædwod agreed. "Nor you, Milde? Ah, I see

not."

Milde shook her head. Her face was sad.

"Is it any good?" Josie asked.

"Good? It is excellent!" Rædwod replied. "Did you craft this gem, Shosefina?"

She smiled ear to ear. "I did. What do you think it's about? Any guesses, Ed?"

Nothing I wanted to say out loud. My cheeks were burning again.

"A long night with a good man?" Rædwod offered.

Josie groaned.

"A good night with a long man," Dennis said.

"Dennis, I'm being serious here!"

"For once," he allowed.

"A faithful lover?" Rædwod guessed.

"Warmer, sort of," Josie replied. "How about it, Ed? Gotten any clues?"

I had been thinking more like Dennis. I shrugged, trying to think like a girl. "I don't know. Eternal love?"

"Faithful, eternal; lover, love – you're splitting hairs," Dennis remarked.

"But such lovely hairs," Rædwod said. "Braid them with yours, and the pattern is plain: a true and truly talented lover. How else could love stay eternal?"

"A long life with husband and child," Milde said. She was blinking hard against tears. Egili climbed from the cradle of her arms and nuzzled at her cheek. She hugged him tightly.

Josie's face fell, and she put her hand on Milde's back. "Yes," she said quietly, "that's the best answer."

I don't think it was the right answer, but Josie did right to say it was. I grabbed a stick and poked at the fire. Josie went back to braiding Milde's hair. Dennis focused on honing the ax. Then Rædwod took out his harp and began to play a slow, gentle tune. His own cheeks were wet. I wondered if he was thinking about Mom. I wondered what she and Uncle Alf were doing then, if they'd had a meal at

all, or a fire nearby to warm them. Were they even together? Or tied up in separate cells in some stone hut. Were
they even alive? I stared into the flames, wishing they were
with us. Or could at least hear the music. I wished I could
do something like that; play the harp, sing, just something
to fill an awkward silence and maybe ease a person's heart.

↑

The next day, the clouds were back. Josie and Milde
started out damp, and the rest of us were sodden soon
enough. Rædwod led us deeper into the hills, keeping to
woods whenever we could. It was maddeningly slow. The
valley floors were mostly clear meadows, and we went out
of our way to cross them quickly. Even the hillsides had
openings to avoid. We bypassed two or three walled farm-
steads that had been built on terraces cut into the turf and
stone. They were ruins now, destroyed in the first invasion
of the *Angelcynn*. We passed below a ruined hill fort, too,
but we didn't see a single sign of a living person.

When I mentioned it, Rædwod grinned. "Ah, but that's
the point, isn't it? Urien's ravens are watching the road and
anything that's half a path. You can be sure there's more
than one keen-eyed spy sited on all the highest hills. Be
thankful Morgwydd can't fly."

"How can we be sure they won't see us?" I asked.

He leaned close and whispered, "I can't, but don't let
them know that."

"It's not funny," I said. "If they spot us, we're as good as
dead."

"Maybe, maybe not. All the more reason to keep them
in the dark until we're at the very gates of their citadel."

"Then what?"

He winked his eye-patch at me "We run like hell.
Hopefully, we'll have your mother and Alf out of there
first."

"And how's that going to work?"

"That depends." He held up his hand and began ticking
off the points. "Are they together or kept apart, what sort

of prison has Urien contrived, how many men has he set to keep watch, do they have dogs, do they have bows, do they rings on their fingers and bells on their toes, ho-ho? We won't know till we take a look."

"And how's *that* going to work?" I demanded.

"Very quietly, Son. Vewy, vewy qwietwy. Heh-heh-heh-heh."

We stopped early again that afternoon. While everyone else set up camp, I gritted my teeth and went off to hunt up some dinner. I almost lost an arrow instead, and wasted ten minutes hunting for it. I wanted a full quiver when we finally reached Morgwydd's hill. I found the arrow undamaged, but the hare I'd been aiming at was gone. Then I caught a glimpse of something larger – a deer, I was sure of it. I started to creep closer, arrow half drawn, before I realized they were horses. Just to prove the point, one of them whinnied softly. It was Bil, saying hello.

I muttered and turned away and there was Milde, with Egili in her arms. We both nearly jumped out of our shirts. Egili hissed at me.

She stroked his head. "Eadgar, you're so quiet! What did you catch?"

"Nothing yet," I admitted. "I was tracking a . . . a deer, but I've lost the trail."

"A deer would be nice," she said. "I've seen only hares. Look, there's one now!"

I swear it was the same little bastard I missed before, come back to tease me. But this time, it came out into the clear and began nibbling on a spray of ferns.

Egili tried to squirm loose. Milde nudged me. "Shoot it quickly!" she whispered.

"*Shh!*" I hissed. I raised the bow slowly, aimed very carefully, trying not to think of Milde two inches away from me, face flushed, lips a little open as she stared intently at the hare, waiting for my arrow to take it. Then I saw Gail Silverton, imagined her wearing that same look. I loosed the arrow just as the hare took two quick hops toward a fresh spray of ferns. The arrow missed. The hare bolted into a thicket.

I bit back another curse. If I'd just aimed and loosed, I would have had him. Idiot.

"He hasn't gone far," Milde whispered. "Brave little Egili will find him."

"In that thicket?" I replied. "How is—?"

She touched her fingertips to my mouth to silence me. It worked. I couldn't even breathe for a minute. Milde stooped, loosened her grip, and Egili shot out of her hands. He bounded into the brush without rustling a single leaf. Everything was still just long enough for me to begin to worry we'd lost him. Then the hare burst from the side of the thicket and loped away, with Egili right behind him.

"Run, brave one!" Milde cried. "Take the foe!"

Ferret's don't run, they undulate. A long, thin body on short, bounding legs, Egili gave the hare a race for its life. And the hare made a fatal mistake: It went to ground in a hole at the base of a dead tree. Egili slipped in after it without a pause. I ran to the hole and dropped to my knees, listening. Milde joined me in an instant, bending so close her hair brushed my cheek. There were sounds of a scuffle, a hiss, a squeak, then a shriek that stiffened the hairs on the back of my neck.

Milde grabbed my arm. "What was that?" she whispered.

"The hare, I'm guessing," I replied.

She bent closer to the hole and called Egili quietly. There was no response. The hole stayed quiet, not even the sound of chewing. So she started to sing, a song I hadn't heard before. The tune was like a lullaby, but the words sure weren't. "*Ne wearð wæl mare æfre gieta folces gefylled beforan þissum sweordes ecgum...*" Never before this were more men slain by the sword's edge ... Milde's voice wasn't as pure as Mom's or as sweet as Josie's, but it was strong and clear, and it worked. Egili poked his head out and peered up at her.

Milde scratched under his chin. "Thank you, little boar," she said. Then she bent low and kissed the top of his head. "Now fetch out the hare so all can eat."

And he did.

I did manage to shoot a horse grouse the next night, and Milde found some wild garlic and water cress, but I was too distracted to enjoy it. I was too worried about Mom and Uncle Alf, and also worried about whether Ræd-wod actually knew where we were going. It didn't help when Dennis decided that we should spend half a day practicing with our weapons.

"You're kidding, right?" I said.

"We need it," he replied. "We have the time and—"

"What time?" I exclaimed. "We don't know what day it is. Only that it's almost the solstice, and maybe – maybe! – Morgwydd is going to wait that long before she kills Mom and Uncle Alf."

Dennis gritted his teeth. "I'm as worried about them as you are, Ed, but I believe Rædwod's right."

"Sure, why not? Anything makes sense on this crazy world. So what if we don't know what day it is. So what if he's just one day late on the solstice and we are totally screwed."

"Right or wrong, we have to be ready to fight. I am. You might be, but I know you haven't handled a blade in over a year. As for Josie and Milde, I'm not going to drag them into battle completely untrained. Now you get off your high horse and get ready to defend yourself." And he made me put down the bow and take him on with just my *seax* and my little utility knife.

He sliced me up like a salami, or would have in a real fight. And just when I thought I was starting to get the hang of it back, using the *seax* to parry and thrust and the small knife to jab and slice, he told me to pick up my bow. Then he came rushing at me like a mad man. I had to drop the bow and draw the blades before he reached me. He knocked me down with his shield three times, then whacked me with the flat of his sword the next three. Finally, I got so fed up I just screwed the blades, pulled out an arrow and speared it at him. He caught it on the shield, but that gave me time to draw my *seax* and sneak under his guard, whacking him hard on the thigh. He gave out a satisfying yelp.

Rædwod roared with laughter. "A hair to the left, Son, and you'd have shortened his onion for sure!"

"A touch, I do confess it!" Dennis squeaked. "My nightlife is ruined." Then he got serious again. "A leg wound won't stop a trained warrior from getting in one last blow with the sword. You have to follow up immediately. Go for the throat." He showed me how, several times. I was royally bruised before he'd finished with me and sweaty enough to drown an army of fleas.

He didn't go as hard on Milde or Josie. "You know what will happen if they catch you," he said, "so be prepared to run the minute things start to look bad."

"It will not go badly," Milde said.

"Your confidence warms my heart," he replied, bowing, "but Wyrd is a fickle hag and will grant victory to whomever she favors that day. You must know how to protect yourselves long enough to flee."

"And how to die bravely if we can't," Milde said.

Dennis sighed, then went to work with Josie. Her ax was made for throwing. What with all the juggling she'd done, she nailed that part in ten minutes, and he moved on to hand-to-hand combat. Not just hacking, but how to thrust with the ax's sweeping upper point, how to slice with the edge and use the lower point like a hook, to catch a shield or a sword and make an opening for the knife in her other hand. He whacked her a few times, but not like he'd whacked me.

Dennis offered his long *seax* to Milde, but she wouldn't give up her weaving sword. This is longer," she said, "and it was made for my hand."

Dennis hesitated only a moment. "I saw how well you used it against Ælfweard. But remember, bold Milde, you surprised him. You will have that advantage only once. After you best the first man, the second will be more wary."

She smiled coldly and held up her other hand. Her

small knife was tucked in her sleeve.

He smiled back. "Good. Now to teach you some tricks."

She was light on her feet, strong in the arms, and a quick study. Dennis showed her how and where to strike with the edge to break an arm or a jaw, and where to slash or stab with the little knife. Even down on the ground, under a man. More important, he showed her how to think ahead three or four strokes at a time. Swordplay is chess in motion, he always said. Milde had never heard of chess, but she got the idea right off. And she didn't pull her punches. Practice ended when she whacked him in the ribs so hard she knocked the wind out of him.

When he bent double, gasping, she dropped her weapons and helped him sit down, apologizing again and again. Josie rushed over, made Dennis lie on his back, pressed both legs in on his stomach. When she let up, he was able to draw in a breath. Meanwhile, Milde slipped off his shield and leather cap and began rubbing his forehead, still apologizing.

Rædwod nudged me in the ribs. "If I didn't know brave Beorhtscyld was gay, I'd swear he did that on purpose."

I shook my head. "He'd never fake losing." And I thought, I wouldn't either. I would have loved the stroking, sure, but I wanted to earn it. If I'd been sparring with Milde, I'd have done everything I could to whack her, not to get whacked.

That night, after my watch, I lay down feeling too bruised and bitten to ever fall asleep. The next thing I knew, Josie was shaking me awake. She was leaning over me, face shadowed from the moonlight. She bent close, and for some reason I thought she was going to kiss me. But she just wanted to whisper in my ear.

"Come on, Ed, wake up! There's something moving out there. It's getting closer."

That woke me for sure. "Where!" I whispered, sitting up. Then I heard it: a rustle in the leaves, a branch snapping. I could smell it, too, a musty odor, mingled with a faint musk, a damp animal smell. I grabbed my bow and slipped it out of its leather case as I stood, then braced the string, peering into the broken moonlight beneath the trees. The fire had gone out. The shadows were deep as a cave. I pulled two arrows from my quiver, set one, and held the other in my left hand, alongside the grip, ready for a quick second shot. If I had the chance for even one.

Dennis was up already, holding Uncle Alf's spear. Milde was beside him with her weaving sword. Egili was inside his bag, scratching at the flap. I could hear the horses shuffling and snorting, pulling at their tethers.

"Where's Rædwod?" I whispered.

"With the horses," Josie breathed. She drew her ax, and we tip-toed over to Dennis.

"Any idea what is it?" Dennis asked.

"Not a deer," I said. "Wrong smell. A boar maybe. Or a bear." Even as I named them, I knew I was wrong. That moldy musk was too odd, the creature's movements too careful. Whatever was out there was circling our campsite, checking us out.

"*An nihtgenga,*" Milde murmured, "*an scucca.*" A night creature, and not a good one. She gripped her weaving sword in both hands and began whispering a spell. "*Ic me on þisse gyrde beluce and on Frigges helde bebeode, wið þane sara stice, wið þane sara slege, wið þane grymma gryre...*" I gird this staff and call on Frig's protection, against grievous cuts, against grievous blows, against dire horror...

We turned slowly in the dark, following the thing's progress, the rustling whisper of a body pressing through underbrush. Not a small body, either. Then it stopped, and even the horses went silent.

"Spread out," Dennis breathed, and I took a few steps to the side. Josie and Milde slipped closer together. I kept watching the place where the creature had last moved. I could sense a shadow there, a block of darkness that wasn't the right shape for a tree.

"Milde, light a torch," Dennis whispered.

"No!" A burst of breath.

We all spun toward the sound. I pulled to full draw,

almost loosed the shot.

It was Rædwod. "You'll only enrage the thing," he whispered. He came toward us, pulling his harp from its bag.

"Do you know what it is?" Dennis asked.

"Oh, yes, I would know that smell in the frigid halls of Hel," Rædwod replied. "I've seen it once before, when I fled Morgwydd's camp."

"A *nicor*?" Josie asked.

"No, a land beast, a *ðyrs*, troll-like; tall, strong, and vicious. Urien's men were on the hunt, about to run me to ground. It attacked them, dear beast, killed two at least, easily, and drove the other ravens back up the hill. I ran the other way, singing thanks in my heart. I should have stayed to give them in person, perhaps, but the enemy of my enemy was still no friend. Fear was, and is."

He started to play his harp very softly. At once, the creature responded, a low, growling moan. Milde started her spell again.

"Louder," Rædwod said, and he joined her, fitting his tune to the rhythm of the words. Josie added her voice, humming, then Dennis. I watched the darkness, bow ready. The creature moaned again. Then it came toward us.

# Chapter 17

I raised my bow, but Rædwod stopped me again.

"No-no-no! Sharp things make it angry, and angry does as angry is."

He played his harp louder, strumming chords. He sang the melody without words, just notes. It was a simple tune, but the background was shifting and rich, accented with bell-like notes plucked with his left hand at the same time his right strummed the chords. I began to feel a little loopy. Overfed, like I'd had too much of Regenswig's bad beer. And I wasn't the only one. Bil snorted and shook his head. Egili gave a little cough and stopped trying to get out.

The creature hesitated. It grunted and punched the tree next to it. The branches shook and rattled. Rædwod played faster. He raised his voice an octave at least, to a falsetto that was sickly sweet, almost inhuman. The horses all began to mill and blow, and Milde hurried to hush them. The creature let out a final groan and turned away. As it shambled off through the trees, I caught a glimpse of it in a shaft of moonlight. It was twice my height, maybe more if it straightened, with a rounded block of a head and long limbs on a squat body. It disappeared into the shadows, and the sound of its footfalls grew fainter and fainter. Rædwod didn't stop playing until they faded completely and the horses stilled.

"Thank you, lord of *scops*," Dennis said. "I'm glad we

didn't have to fight that thing."

"It would have been a short fight," Rædwod said. "Spears and swords glance of its hide like advice off a young man's head. You'd do better to slink into the bushes and hope it only wanted the horses."

"Do you think it'll come back now that the music has stopped?" I asked.

"Only Wyrd knows," he replied. "If it does, wake me first."

"It's your watch, anyway," Dennis said.

"I'll take his watch. I'm wide awake now," I said. My stomach was still twisting.

Dennis started to argue that I'd been on watch already, but Rædwod cut him off. "I accept! To your own blanket, Beorhtscyld. We ancients will get a little rest for once."

↑

As soon as the sky was light enough, I went out to check for tracks. I found the tree where the thing had been standing, marked by torn bark and a deep dent in the trunk. Farther out I found a footprint in a hollow: long, broad, three toes, with the faint indentation of a claw on the middle one. It was the same type of print I'd seen on the hill above our first campsite when we left Regensburg. Only it was a lot bigger.

As soon as Dennis woke up, he got us moving. We had cold leftovers for breakfast, saddled the horses, and set out within a half hour. A few miles on, as we were skirting a marshy patch, I looked down and saw more of the footprints. Dennis suggested we swing wide, so we didn't stumble on it sleeping somewhere along the way. Rædwod said the thing would find us on its own if it wanted to, but he led us up and around. We skirted the bare top of the hill and started down the opposite side. The trees were smaller here, and the woods had a young feel to them, with more underbrush and bare spots where ledge stuck out. Milde stopped her horse at the edge of a gap and pointed to the northeast.

"Smoke," she said. "A hearth fire on that peak."

"Your eyes are sharp, Milde," Rædwod said, squinting toward the thin line of smoke, barely visible against the low, gray clouds. "See the level top on that hill? There stands the wall around Urien's camp. It was a village once, but he moved his people to the North, beyond easy reach of Ida and Grimmære. He keeps a small flock of his ravens here to man watch-posts along the road. And I think to keep Morgwydd away from his people."

"If we can see them, they can see us," Dennis said. "No fire tonight."

"That means no dinner," Josie said.

"And no whining above a whisper," he added.

Josie stuck her tongue out at him, but Milde took his side.

"Beorhtscyld is right!" she whispered fiercely. "They are not blind or deaf. They are smart and cruel, all of them. Be quiet, if you want any hope of killing them." She looked as grim as she had when she faced down Osweald.

We moved slowly and carefully from then on and made camp in a hollow on a southeast slope. One last, broad hill shielded us from the eyes in Urien's fort. We unsaddled and tethered the horses without a word. Milde rubbed each one down with a coarse wool rag, calming them to near silence. We nibbled on the bit of food left in the haversacks, but no one except Egili seemed hungry. I sure wasn't. Afterward, Milde got out her spindle and wool and began to spin. Josie had picked up a few round stones at each place we camped. Now she kept five of them in the air, juggling. Dennis looked to the weapons, his and ours, honing each edge, wiping each blade. I braced my bow and checked the string for chaffed spots, rubbing it gently with a bit of beeswax. Then I checked my arrows. Their edges were still keen, the fletching straight and tight. I had lost two, but that still left me with twenty-two. And the rune arrow.

Rædwod sat by me, cradling his harp in his lap. He nodded at the rune arrow, and I handed it to him. He studied the arrowhead closely, then pricked the heel of his left palm, drawing blood. Mumbling some quiet words, he dabbed a few drops with a finger tip and rubbed blood into both runes. I stared, amazed. Then he dabbed more blood and drew a line across each of his cheeks. And I recognized what he was mumbling; it was the charm to open Tiw's gate. A chill slithered down my spine and into my gut. Rædwod wiped the point clean on his tunic, and handed the arrow back with a nod, like he was returning a pen he'd borrowed.

*Oh, Dad,* I thought, *you have been here way too long. You really are Rædwod.*

He pressed hard on his palm until the bleeding stopped, then began to play his harp. Very softly, but everyone paused what they were doing. Egili popped his face out of his bag. Even the horses looked up. Dennis started to shush him, but listened a moment and relented. Everything went very quiet, like it had by the pool when Milde and Josie were bathing. I glanced at them, but they didn't seem to recognize the melody or the effect. Milde smiled and went back to spinning. Josie put her stones back in her pouch and sat beside her. I slid the rune arrow into my quiver, and now I was thinking maybe having Dad be all Rædwod wasn't such a bad thing if it could make us invisible.

I spent most of the night trying not to think about what we might run into the next day. I almost would have welcomed another visit from the *ðyrs* to give me something else to worry about. But I did get a little sleep, so I wasn't a complete zombie the next morning.

Dennis woke us up before dawn. We saddled the horses as quietly as possible in the dim light and set off as soon as we could see enough to pick out a path. There was a stream in the valley below us, but it was too open there. We kept to the slope, where the going was rough but the cover was better. Rædwod led us around the curve until we were on the back side of Urien's hill, opposite from the Roman road and the track that led up to the fort. We went down through the valley, too close to the hillside now to see the fort on its top, or to be seen. A hundred yards uphill we came to another stream, a brook really, rolling and tumbling through the trees. We left the horses there with Milde and Josie – Dennis's orders – to watch the horses and be ready for a quick getaway in case the three of us were spotted. This was not an attack, it was a reconnaissance, to feel out the defenses and see if we could spot where they were keeping Mom and Uncle Alf. Milde and Josie hid near the horses, weapons ready. Dennis, Rædwod, and I started to climb.

It wasn't the highest peak in the range, it was just the steepest, and this was the worst side. But that was the plan: to sneak up from the least likely direction. We climbed carefully, scrambling where we had to, trying hard not to make noise or get too winded. I had my bow in my left hand, string braced. My quiver hung next to my right hand on a baldric. Still, if we'd been ambushed on that steep hillside, it would have been all over.

When the slope finally eased off, we stopped for a minute to rest. I nocked an arrow and held a second in my left hand. Rædwod took out his harp. Dennis settled his shield and drew his sword, then looked us over. He shrugged, grinned, and led the way to the edge of the trees.

The cover ended a lot sooner than we'd hoped. From the look of it, Urien's men had cut it back not too long ago. We had a good fifty yards of stumps to weave through to reach the base of the wall. The hilltop was a broad, uneven oval, sloping gently upward from where we were. The wall itself wasn't tall, maybe eight feet high, made of packed earth. There was a shallow ditch all the way around it, sort of a dry moat, with a steep, grassy slope about five feet high to the base of the wall. The top edge of the wall was very ragged. Piles of dirt and a few dirty balks of wood littered the base. It must have been a couple of feet higher once. More important, the wall top were empty. No one was keeping watch. Dennis led the way into the open.

We hurried through the stumps, then down across the ditch and up the steep pitch to tuck against the base of the wall. Dennis had picked a low spot, where a mound of fallen wall right at the base gave us a little boost to a narrow gap just about head high. Dennis crept up the mound to one side of the gap and peeked in. I leaned my bow against the wall and shinnied up the other side.

There was a wooden walkway inside just below the gap. What caught my eye was a small fire, with a pot hanging on a tripod. No other sign of life. The fort was maybe three hundred feet across, smaller than it looked from the outside, and the fire was burning about in the middle, in front of a low building, its doorway facing us. There were other buildings around it, all low and round with thatched roofs. A lean-to stood against the far wall, near a gate. The walkway went right over the gate, where the wall was higher. I could see part of a corral and a couple of horses next to the lean-to. If I craned my neck, I could see the backs of more buildings on our side. Then a warrior came out of the building by the fire, checked the pot, and started walking across the compound. Dennis and I ducked back, and I almost slipped off the mound. He grabbed my arm to steady me, and we perched there for a couple of minutes, stiff and silent.

Dennis risked another look and pointed to the side. When I got my head at the right angle, I could see another lean-to beyond the two huts closest to us. It was just some poles and a flimsy roof stuck against one of the larger huts. Uncle Alf was under it, bent over a crude bench. Working on a bow. As we watched, he turned and hobbled toward the back of the lean-to.

Hobbled. Both of his knees were wrapped in crusted bandages. He'd been lamed.

Dennis went white with fury. He looked like he was going to leap over the wall and take on everyone inside. And right then, I was ready to go with him. I gripped his arm, nodding. For some reason, that cooled him off. He shook his head, and pulled me down from our perch.

Rædwod looked at both our faces and cocked his head, shrugging a question. Dennis put his mouth close to Rædwod's ear and whispered what we'd seen, and Rædwod stopped stroking his harp. Only in the silence did I realize he'd been playing at all. He looked stricken, more sad than angry. He sighed and whispered, "Any plan?"

Dennis shook his head. "We need a better angle."

"Risky-risky."

"Just keep playing."

"Just keep praying they do not look too closely. This is but a distraction."

Still, he didn't hesitate when Dennis led the way around the curve of the wall. Twenty or thirty paces on, we came to a tiny, stone-lined channel. It ran from a culvert under the wall, crossed the ditch, passed through another culvert, and emptied into a small brook that trickled down the slope and into the trees. The stonework around the culvert had settled, and the earthen wall above it had sagged, showing some of the timber in its core. Three or four culvert stones had fallen out, making the wall slump in another gap. Dennis and I were just about to crawl up for a look when one of Urien's warriors walked into view around the outside of the wall, looking out at the tree line.

We sank back against the slope of the ditch. Rædwod played more softly, lowered the pitch, slowed his tempo. I think I stopped breathing. The sentry kept looking out. He was on the other side of the ditch, not in any hurry, maybe enjoying the view. Carrying a spear and dark shield, big dagger at his belt, leather helmet, leather armor. Getting closer. Very slowly, I slid my hand over the grass and picked up my bow. Then an arrow. Dennis noticed. Rædwod was between us, but Dennis reached behind him, to stop me. He bumped Rædwod's shoulder, just barely, just a brush. Just enough. Rædwod missed a note.

The harp whined. The warrior heard it and turned.

I was standing and drawing even as his eyes went wide. His mouth opened to shout and I loosed the arrow, knowing it was too late.

At that instant, a stone struck the back of his head with a hollow thump. My arrow stuck deep in his shield. The warrior choked on the shout, stumbled, dropped his spear. He lifted his head and tried to shout again, but a second stone hit him, and before he could even start to fall, Milde came racing up the slope, swinging her weaving sword two-handed. It struck his neck with a sharp *chunk!* Weaving swords aren't sharp, but he toppled across his shield, neck broken, head crooked at a right angle. His eyes were empty, but his legs kept kicking at the ground. Milde drew her little knife and plunged it into his back. It wasn't long enough. He kept twitching, making small noises as his heels hit the turf. Finally, Dennis ran over and rammed his long *seax* in beside Milde's knife. The sounds stopped. All but the soft tune from Rædwod's harp.

Dennis pulled out his *seax*, wiped it carefully on the man's tunic, then did the same with Milde's. He handed it to her with a nod and a whispered, "Thank you." She smiled very slightly and slipped it into her sleeve.

By then Josie was there. "Next time *you* can stay with the horses," she muttered. She looked at the dead man. He was face down at least, not like Osweald. And not as bloody. She swallowed hard and started looking for her stones. I spotted one of them under the man's leg, but I didn't tell her. I gritted my teeth and got it for her. Her hand was shaking when I gave it to her. So was mine, and it kept shaking as I pried my arrow from the dead man's shield. We found Josie's other stone in the ditch, then huddled against the wall. There was no question of sending Milde and Josie back down the hill. They kept watch and Rædwod kept playing while Dennis climbed up for a look. I leaned my bow against the wall and climbed up on the other side of the gap.

The stone channel led in from the culvert to a low stone block at the center of the fort. Water bubbled from a hole in the top of the block, where another warrior was filling a bucket. Uncle Alf's lean-to was right across from us. He was back at work with a scraper, which meant he was close to finishing the bow. We could also see three other warriors by the far gate, plus two goats in a pen near the horses, the usual chickens here and there, and a small pig rooting around outside one of the buildings. No dogs at least, but there was no way to tell how many other men were inside. And there was no sign at all of Urien or Morgwydd. Or my mother.

The warrior by the fountain straightened and carried the bucket a few paces to a wide, shallow basin standing on a metal tripod. The basin was polished bronze, with a pattern cast into its surface, a twisted maze of vines and leaves. Just like the one on the altar in Corspotitum. I couldn't see if the bottom of the basin had a sky-iron torque welded to the bronze.

It turned out it didn't need one. Morgwydd came out of the hut nearest to Uncle Alf's lean-to and crossed the open yard to the basin. She was wearing the matching brooch. The warrior stepped back quickly as she neared. She looked into the basin and brushed her hand across the surface of the water, as though smoothing a sheet. Then she unpinned the brooch, letting her dress fall off her shoulder. I shuddered as she scraped the scars on her breast with the point of the pin, drawing blood. A few drops fell into the basin. She watched for a moment, then lay the brooch on the surface of the stained water. It sank without a ripple.

Now she began to sing, and I shuddered again at the first note. If I'd had my bow I would have tried to kill her then and there. I covered my ears and tried to ignore the clashing notes. The first few lines were bad enough, but her voice changed, as it had on the hillside, as though two voices were singing through her mouth. The warrior took another step back. Uncle Alf looked up, glaring. I could see him muttering, maybe a charm to counter the magic, but probably just a curse. Urien appeared in the doorway to the hut, scowling.

Morgwydd turned toward the little pig. It looked up at her and shook its head, backing away just like the warrior had. She sang to the little pig in her two voices, and it jerked like the notes had reached out and grabbed it. It began to walk toward her, slowly at first, then more quickly, finally trotting the last few yards. Morgwydd stooped, and the little pig leaped into her arms. And all the time, it whimpered, trying to turn its head away, turn its feet, to flee. Morgwydd lifted it in the crook of her left arm, reached to her belt, and drew out a slender, silver knife. Still singing, she held the piglet's head over the basin and smoothly slit its throat. Blood spurted into the bowl. The piglet squealed once. Then Morgwydd threw it aside, to totter and flop in the dirt as the rest of its blood poured out.

Finally Morgwydd stopped singing. She peered into the bowl, frowning at whatever she saw. She called to Urien in her lilting, thick-tongued language. Urien stepped back into the darkness of the hut, and reappeared a moment later, dragging Mom with him.

# *Chapter 18*

My heart raced when I saw her. She was still alive! I'd been acting like she was, but I'd never been sure. Morgwydd had promised, but Morgwydd was crazy and cruel. Now, here she was, Mom, alive. But she looked terrible. When Urien dragged her out of the dark hut, I could see scabs on her neck and arm, surrounded by yellowed bruises. Her cheek was bruised, too, and she was dirty. Her hair was matted, her clothes smudged and rumpled. She hated being dirty, hated when her hair came undone. There was hate in her eyes as she looked at Morgwydd.

Still, she was alive, with only Urien and a few of his men in sight.

Dennis gripped my arm. This time I was the one starting to climb over the wall. I hadn't even realized it. I glanced down at my bow, leaning against the wall at my feet. I felt useless without it. Josie caught my eye and mouthed *what?* I mouthed *Mom, she's okay,* and Josie pumped her fist.

When I looked back through the wall, Mom was standing next to Morgwydd, by the basin. Urien was holding her tightly. I could see his fingers digging into her arms right where she was cut and bruised. Mom glared at Morgwydd, as if daring her to use the knife. Morgwydd didn't even seem to notice. She began to sing again, a different song, low and monotonous, almost tuneless. She reached up and took Mom by the chin, forcing her head to the side. Her voice rose and the chant rang against the wall. She lifted the dark knife and slowly moved the point toward Mom's eye.

Rædwod stopped playing. "What is she doing?" he hissed.

I couldn't look away.

"Morgwydd!" Uncle Alf roared. He held the unfinished bow over his head, hands clenched near the tips. "I will break this!" he cried. He stepped into the sunlight and began to bend the stave.

Morgwydd kept singing, but the knife paused. She let the tip droop. Shrieking the final words, she pricked Mom's cheek just below the eye. Mom let out one sharp cry.

Blood leaked from the wound and ran down Mom's cheek into Morgwydd's hand. I saw it, but it hardly registered. Mom had cried out. She had spoken, not words but . . . Her voice. I hadn't heard it for thirteen years, but I knew it, like I had my dad's when he sang the lullaby tune.

Rædwod whispered her name, *"Alrun."* And I could hear my dad again.

Then Josie said, "What's happening? Is it—? Milde," she hissed, "watch out! Ed, catch him!"

Egili scrambled up my back, across my shoulder, and over the wall. I tried to grab him, but it was too late. He was loose in the fort, and he was furious: hissing, fangs bared, bounding across the packed earth with his little ears laid flat and his short tail straight out behind him.

Morgwydd had turned back to the basin. Her hand was wet with Mom's blood. She was chanting, staring into the water, tilting her hand to let the blood run in. Mom saw Egili, looked past him and saw me.

"No, Eadgar!" she cried, in English. "Not yet!"

I froze. I couldn't believe I'd heard her speak. But around me all hell broke loose. Urien bellowed a curse. The warrior by the spring threw down his bucket and drew his sword. Morgwydd looked up from the basin, startled, silent. She saw me and her face clenched with rage. She pointed her bloody knife, screamed a command. Then she began to sing again.

But Mom kicked her and cut off the song. Morgwydd screamed again. Urien jerked Mom off her feet, slapped her across the face, threw her to the ground. I started over the wall, but Dennis yanked me back, and I stumbled down the rubble, falling into Josie.

"Run!" Dennis cried, drawing his sword.

I tore free of Josie and grabbed my bow. "We can't leave her there!"

"You heard her, Ed," Dennis cried back. "She said not yet!"

I nocked an arrow. "She couldn't have! She can't talk! I'm not going!" I was being an idiot, but I couldn't think straight. I wasn't thinking at all. I tried to climb the rubble again, to shoot over the wall. But I couldn't do it with the drawn bow. Cursing, I stumbled back down, ready to run around and storm the front gate.

Urien's men had already thought of that. Three of them came tearing around the curve of the wall. I almost shouted with joy. Here was someone to shoot at. Without a thought, I drew and shot at the first warrior.

The arrow went true and took him in the face. I did shout then, and Milde joined me, a howl, a wild battle cry to Thunor. She waved her sword over her head. I drew another arrow.

"Ed, they're at the wall!" Dennis yelled. "Let's go!"

"Shoot!" Milde cried. "Shoot them all!"

For an instant, I froze again, realizing what she had just said. What I had just done. This was real. It was kill or be killed. Right now.

I loosed the arrow but it went wide. " Ræd—Dad! Play something!" I cried. "Like you did for the *ðyrs*! Confuse them!"

Instead, Mom began to sing the lullaby, the song of the key and the world path. In a moment, Dad joined her, with voice and harp. Then Josie.

"No!" I screamed. I notched a third arrow and drew

back, concentrating, letting the two warriors come on, trying to see a target behind the shields, a leg, a side, something. Trying to see only the target. I drew farther. I drew too far.

My bow snapped. More like exploded. Splinters flew into my face and a jagged end tore across my brow. Blood ran into my eyes. I stumbled backward and sprawled among the fallen stones in the ditch.

"Eadgar!" Milde came to me.

I was still holding the middle of my shattered bow. I threw it away and tried to wipe the blood from my eyes. Milde grabbed my other hand and heaved me to my feet. The bowstring, one tip still attached, had wrapped itself around my throat and was caught in the fletchings of my arrows. Milde tried to untangle it.

"Forget that, Milde!" Dennis yelled. "Get him out of here!" He was facing the oncoming warriors, I shoved her away and fumbled with my *seax*. "I'm okay! Go with the others!"

She ran to stand by Dennis instead.

Dad stopped singing just long enough to shout, "The key, Son! The key!"

I fumbled with the string, but blood kept getting into my eyes. I couldn't wipe it away fast enough. And nobody was stopping to let me. The third warrior was carrying a spear, and he threw it. Dennis and Milde jumped apart and it sailed between them, to stick in the ground barely a foot shy of Josie. Still singing, she came to me, freed the rune arrow, and forced it into my hand. The arrowhead began to glow. Dennis lunged against the first warrior, catching him by surprise. The blow tore the man's shield free, and Milde swung her weaving sword against his ribs. Dennis cut the man's chest half open and turned to face the next one, side by side with Milde. The warrior, the spear thrower, had drawn his sword but he hesitated. Green light rippled along the pattern in the arrowhead. Josie took my wrist and raised my hand. All the time she was singing, Dad with her. Then Urien appeared at the top

169

of the wall, two more warriors beside him. Josie let go of me and threw a rock at him. He ducked just in time.

Josie slapped my face. "Sing, Ed! Dammit, sing!"

I sang. There was nothing else I could do. Two more warriors came around the curve in the wall, and Urien jumped down. Blood kept running into my eyes. Dennis and Milde backed up beside me, and Josie drew her hand ax, held it ready, singing again.

I sang, and as soon as the first word came out, the arrowhead flared. The shock of it ran down my arm. The gate opened right beside me, with a boom that deafened my right ear and made the warriors jump back. All but Urien. He came toward us, shield held high against the glare of the arrowhead, sword ready.

Dennis stepped forward to meet him. "Go on! Get through the slit!"

But Milde grabbed him and hauled him backward. Josie pushed me through ahead of them. Dad came last, striking a sharp chord that shut the gate behind us.

We were standing in silence. There was no wind this time, only bitter cold and the hard light of the million stars above and below and all around us.

I wiped my eyes again. "She spoke to me," I mumbled. "Mom did. She sang."

"She did, Son," Dad replied. "By all the gods, she did. As beautiful as my memory."

"She can't sing!" I cried. "Dennis, how can she sing now?"

"Later, Ed. We can't stay here," Dennis said.

"But—"

"No buts. Pull yourself together. They may come through after us."

"It will take Morgwydd a minute or five," Dad said. "Time to look to Ed's wound."

Josie had already untangled me from the bowstring and was trying to staunch the bleeding with the sleeve of her shirt. Milde took out her knife and cut a strip from the hem of her dress. She also pulled a wad of wool from her bag, and Josie started tying up my wound.

"Just don't spit in it," I muttered.

"Kiss it, make it better," she chanted, standing on tiptoe to do it, then wiping the blood from her lips. "Ew, salty."

I laughed. Really. That's how fried I was. Blood doesn't bother me, but too much had happened too quickly. And I had killed someone. And Mom . . . I suddenly felt dizzy. I took a deep breath and held myself together, and as soon as Josie had tied the knot in the cloth, I lifted the arrow and started singing.

"Wait a minute," Dennis said. "Where are you planning to go?"

"Back," I said. "We can't leave them there."

"Urien's ready for us," Dennis said. "We can't go straight back."

"It's the last thing they'd expect." I started singing again.

"Wait!" Dennis insisted. "Alrun said wait. We could go back home—"

"No!" I snapped, and Josie echoed me.

"We have time," he argued, "a couple of days at leas—"

"No! There's too much at stake! What if the van breaks down? Or we have an accident?"

"Or we reach the wrong world?" Josie added.

"But—"

"*Na!*" Milde yelled. No, loud and clear. We all looked at her. "We are lost in these marches. We can go only forward now."

"The lady has a point," Rædwod said.

Dennis shook his head, angry, but we had him outnumbered.

"Can you do it, Ed?" Josie asked. "We could wind up back in Coria."

"I'm getting the hang of this. Now, all of you, sing or shut up!"

Dad began to pluck the tune. "Flatten the third and fourth notes, Son. You're too sharp." He led me through the parts I had gotten wrong, fixing my broken memory. "Right here it goes up a fifth in a triplet." I'd never studied music but I could hear what he meant. We sang it together, and that's when I really stopped thinking of him as a stranger. He was still Rædwod, but he was also truly my father. Dad.

"Don't forget to turn," Josie said, but Dad shook his head.

"There's no need if the melody's right."

"But Alf said—"

"Alf was terrified of Alrun's magic," Dad said. "All the turning and twining was just to keep him too busy to fret. It's all in the song."

"Alf can't carry a tune in a bucket," Dennis muttered. Then he shouted, "Damn her!" He blinked back tears and began to sing.

"No, Dennis, no. *Shhhh.* Don't help," Dad said. He stopped playing his harp. "You, neither, Josie. *Shh-shh-shhhh.*" He covered her mouth with a hand. "Save your love and your anger for later. Eadgar has the tune now. The spell is his."

So I sang it alone, and the glowing arrowhead brightened. I walked toward the star, lowered the point. And it was easy; no back pressure, no wind, nothing to block me. Dad was right – I owned that spell.

Dad caught my shoulder just as I started to push through. "Heed your mother, Son," He said quietly. "If she told you 'not yet,' you can be sure she had a good reason. Don't go straight back. Roundabout is best. Sneaky wins the race. Seek nearby for another piece of sky iron. Even a tiny one will do. Take us somewhere out of sight, out of mind."

I could already glimpse a small, bright ring that I knew was Morgwydd's brooch. I squinted into the glare and saw other points of light, some larger, some even smaller, all pulsing with the same green glow of the arrowhead. I pointed the tip toward a dot a bit to the left of Morgwydd and pushed gently. The gate eased open. I saw a broken earth wall, collapsed huts, a view over hilltops under a gray sky. It was another hill fort, this one long abandoned. I pushed through, singing till everyone was with me. When I stopped, the gate snapped shut with a roll of thunder.

"Well, if they heard that, they know we're back," Dennis said.

Dad patted my shoulder. "It always does that, Ed, even for your mother, and she could sing an egg out of a gander and make him enjoy it."

I stared at the arrowhead. "What about that, Dennis? She sang. She spoke." I looked him right in the eyes. "How come she can do it now?"

Dennis glanced down, then faced me. "She always could, Ed. She chose not to."

"She what?"

"She was afraid to, for the same reason we haven't been using your father's name. She was afraid Morgwydd could hear her." Dennis shrugged. "It sounds ridiculous, I know, but—"

"But Morgwydd has long ears," Dad said. "She knew your mother and I were planning to open the gate and come back that first time, that failure, that ruin. She was ready for us. As if she had heard us making our plans."

Dennis nodded. "That's what Alrun thought, too. Alf told me, and he believed her."

"He never told *me* that," I said, "and neither did you."

"We would have," Dennis replied.

"Yeah, I know – when I was older. Thanks, Dennis. All this time, I could have—"

"What?" Dennis demanded. "Talked with her? Sung with her? Could you have kept it a secret when you were six or thirteen or even last month? Would you have let her stay silent during all of those inane arguments you had with Alf?"

"Beorhtscyld," Dad said, raising a hand.

"You weren't there, Rædwod," Dennis said. "I wish to God you had been, but you weren't. You didn't have to live through the onslaught of puberty in this boy."

"This young man, you mean," Dad said. "He's not a boy any more. I missed that part."

"Thunor's stones," Dennis moaned, "don't you start pouting, too! Look, I'm sorry. You've both missed out on so much, and I will make it all up to you as best I can as soon as we are safe back home. Can we save this argument till then, please?"

Dad threw back his head and laughed. "Thunor's stones, yes! And Frige's sweet lips! How can we argue at all when we are still alive and have loved ones to rescue? Beorhtscyld – and Dennis, too – you both have the patience of saints, not that there are any to compare you to on this world." He turned to me. "Son, Ed, let it go. What's done is past. Put your mind back to saving your mother and uncle."

*It never left there,* I thought, but I didn't trust myself to say anything without turning it into another argument. I just nodded and looked away, scanning the horizon. Milde had already spotted a thin line of smoke against the clouds. She pointed it out, and we all stared at the distant hilltop where Urien's fort stood. We could just see it beyond the bulge of a taller peak that jutted from the woods and valleys below us.

"What do you think?" Dennis asked. "A long day's hike."

"Maybe for these kids," Dad said. "I give it two long days for we *feortinga.*"

"'Old?' Do you call me 'old'?" Dennis asked.

"Not only old," Dad replied. "An old *wind-breaker.* A *fart* in that new-fangled tongue you speak. It's a term of respect here."

Dennis laughed and switched to *Anglisc.* "Is that true, Milde? Do you respect me more for my great age?"

"Or is it the great smell?" Dad added.

"How can you two laugh?" Milde cried. "The *dry-wicce* still lives, and the mad dog with her! Your friend is lamed, your wife still captive, the longest day draws near, and you chatter on in your mumbling language, first to moan, then to argue, then to whine, and now to laugh?"

"Yes, brave woman, yes – to laugh!" Dad cried. "Forgive us for spouting our clumsy tongue, but know you that we laugh because we are still alive to do it. What else would you have us do? Tear our hair out? Beat our breasts? If we did that we would fall to the ground in despair."

"We do not all share your iron will, Milde," Dennis said. "We laugh at danger so fear will not overwhelm us. We laugh at despair so we won't be blinded by tears. We laugh to gird our hearts against a pain too great to bear!" His eyes were wet, and he rubbed them furiously. "Quick, Rædwod – why did the chicken cross the road?"

"Because Alrun called it!"

"No, you twit! To get to the cock on the other side! Josie, why do girls crave Ælfweard?"

I cut in, as disgusted as Milde. "Look, can we just get starte—?"

"Because he's an archer," Josie said, playing the straight man for him.

"Yes! And archers are armed with strong, stiff shafts!"

"No more!" Dad cried. "Your odor worsens with every word!"

"You are crazy," Milde said. "All of you."

*Not me*, I thought, *I'm with you.*

But then she turned away and stumbled to a fallen block of stonework, sitting stiffly, clenching her side. And I finally noticed that the side of her dress was dark with blood.

# *Chapter 19*

Josie cried "Milde!" and they all ran to her, smothering her with questions: what happened, where is it, does it hurt? Milde kept saying it was fine when it obviously wasn't. I hovered at the outside, worried, feeling useless. I have to admit, my first thought was, *Oh, crap! Not now, we don't have time for this!* Then Josie told me to find water and light a fire, and I put everything aside for the moment. It was a relief to have something definite to do.

Finding water was easy; the fort was a ruin, but it still had an open well near the remains of the wall. I emptied my pouch and lay on my belly to fill it. It dripped, but the waxed seams were tight enough. I hurried back, and there was Josie putting pressure on the wound. Milde's dress and undertunic were up past her waist. Dad and Dennis were working on a fire with their backs carefully turned. I stopped short, blushing.

"Just bring the water, Ed," Josie snapped.

She used her free hand to drape the front of Milde's clothes so only her right hip was showing, but just having that hint was worse. I shuffled over and gave her the dripping pouch, staring as far to the side as I could.

Milde actually laughed once, which made me feel like a kid.

"It's not too bad?" I said.

"Just a scratch," she replied.

176

"A very long scratch," Josie added. "The spear sliced her, but it isn't deep, thankfully." She slid four fingers through the slit in Milde's dress. "An inch to the left and . . ." She let the cloth fall. "I need a rag to make a bandage. Put pressure on this while I cut a strip from something. Press hard. It keeps oozing."

So I knelt beside Milde and pressed hard on the long slice in her hip. It took both hands. Her skin there was very smooth, her muscles hard. I tried to stay focused on the cut, but I couldn't help notice how the drape of her dress didn't quite cover everything, and how frayed the hem was from being cut to make a bandage for my head. This wound seemed much worse.

"You can cut a strip from the bottom of my tunic," I told Josie.

"Not while you're kneeling like that," she said. She began to slice a strip from the bottom of her cloak. "You just keep that pressure on."

I pressed harder and asked Milde, "This doesn't hurt, does it?"

"No. Wyrd has other plans for me." She sighed. "Such a big fuss for such a small thing. Your forehead is much worse. I am ashamed to be so weak."

"Weak? The way you felled that warrior with your weaving sword?"

"Dennis felled the warrior."

"After you stove in his side. Besides, I meant the first one."

"Josie had stunned him. Anyone could have done what I did. Dennis is the swordsman, not I. He has a true warrior's spirit."

"And so do you. You're well matched there."

"You are kind to say so, Eadgar. You shot well, too. The first was perfect."

What could I say to that? Killed one, missed one, and still trying to sort out how that felt. I'd done better in the tournament, trying to impress Gail Silverton. No one had died there. No bows broken.

177

Josie brought over the bandage, just a strip of cloth and a wad of wool from Milde's bag. Yeah, Milde had brought her bag, as well as Egili's. And I suddenly remembered we didn't have our little hunter any more. We didn't have horses, haversacks, cloaks. My bow. It felt like three steps back for every step forward.

Josie sent me to get more water while she wrapped Milde's wound, which was fine with me. I was suddenly very thirsty. And I needed to get away from Milde and everyone else for a minute. I drank a pouch-full, stared at the thin line of smoke at least two days away, then took a deep breath and carried another pouch-full to Josie. She drank a little but used most of it to dampen another strip of her cloak so she could clean Milde up a bit. Dad and Dennis were struggling with the fire, so I took over that job and let Dennis be the water bearer. He donated his leather helmet to the cause. It probably wasn't as clean, but it was a lot bigger. I got the fire going, small so it wouldn't smoke, and everyone gathered around to figure out what to do next.

We were in a mess. Dad kept insisting we had time, even without the horses, but I wondered how he could be so sure. There were no calendars, no clocks, and the sky was cloudy so frigging often it was next to impossible to keep track of the sun, let alone the moon and stars. I voted for moving out right away.

"We certainly can't stay here tonight," Dennis agreed. "It's too exposed. We'll need to move down into the woods and find a site that's shielded from the wind and from the view of Urien's fort. But we're not ready for a forced march. Milde and Ed should take it easy. And we'll have to forage for food."

"I'll do that," Josie said. "I know some of the plants Milde collected, and I can probably hit a hare or grouse with a stone, if I spot one."

"You've never hunted a day in your in life," I said.

Her look almost re-opened the cut over my eye, but Dad stepped in before she could lay into me.

"We have seen your skilled arm at work, Shosefina. No doubt you could hit anything that moves in this forest. But none of us should wander around alone. Who knows what might loom from the shadows: a boar, a *ðyrs*, or worse, a man. Dennis must go with you."

"Dennis is as quiet as a bulldozer with the blade down," I said. "He'll scare away every animal on this hill."

"Yes, Ed," Dennis said, "we know you're the only one here who has any experience tracking and hunting, but you have a head wound."

"It's fine," I said. "The bleeding's stopped. I can hardly feel it."

"And you no longer have a bow," he added.

"I know that!" It came out a lot sharper than I expected. I took a breath and tried again. "I'm sorry I broke my bow, and I know Josie can hit anything she aims at, but shooting is only half of hunting. The other half is finding game. I'm nothing like Uncle Alf or Egili, but I can read tracks. If I can't shoot, I can at least help Josie find something to throw her stones at. I can make sure she doesn't get lost, too."

"It make sense to me," Josie said.

Dad and Dennis looked at each other, then shrugged in unison. I wondered how they could stay so calm.

"All right," Dennis said, "but first we put out the fire and move down into the woods."

"We'll build another fire, and bigger," Dad said, "ready for your return with fine meat."

"And greens for the salad," Dennis said.

"And more meat for dessert," Dad added. "I could eat a horse."

"I hope our horses will be all right," Josie said.

"Urien's men will undoubtedly find them," Dennis said.

*Either that or the* ðyrs *will*, I thought, but I didn't say it out loud.

We moved into the woods and found a good spot in a small stand of pine and fir. On the way down, Milde spotted some greens we could eat, and she tried to convince

Dennis that she should go hunting with Josie and me. Dennis didn't say no, he just quietly asked her to please stay and help him and Dad get the fire going.

"Let your wound knit. We need you to be whole when we face Urien again. Light a fire and then you can sing a few hares right into the flames."

"Maybe Rædwod can. I am no *galdor-galere*," she muttered. No charm singer.

"You sang Egili out with a hare," I reminded her.

"Egili and I are friends," she said. "I would sing him to us now if I could."

"For that I would gladly sing with you, fair Milde," Dad said. "We all would."

We were silent a moment. Then Milde took charge, sending Dad and Dennis to find wood and clear a big circle in the thick layer of pine needles carpeting the ground.

Josie and I went hunting. We followed the hill downward toward the sound of running water. Animals need to drink. Sure enough, we saw tracks of hare, deer, grouse, and what I thought might be boar, or at least feral pig. I was glad they were the only strange set of prints. We could avoid a boar. Something like the *ðyrs* would be harder.

We followed the deer track across the brook onto on obvious animal run. Josie walked in my tracks and was really good at copying the rolling footstep that Uncle Alf had taught me. We startled a hare, which bounded off before she could pitch a stone at it, but we flushed a grouse within a dozen more steps. This time Josie was ready, and she winged it before it could lose itself in the trees. It fell in a tangle, flopping crazily. I ran over and snapped its neck. The stone had fallen right beside it, too.

"Good job!" I said, handing her the stone.

She cradled it in her palm and studied the dead bird.

"Were you frightened, Ed?" she asked.

I thought about it. I remembered my arrow striking home. My heart had been racing, but was it fear or just excitement? Or something else entirely? And what was it now?

"Not really," I said finally. "I was too angry, too upset about Mom. I guess I was afraid for her, but the way she looked – the cuts, the bruises, the dirt? Mostly I just wanted to kill Morgwydd."

She nodded. "Yeah, I kinda got that." She kept looking at the stone.

"You were afraid?" I asked.

"Yeah. After Milde killed that sentry, I suddenly thought that this could be it." She looked up at me. "You know, when we wound up on that other Earth and I tried to call home? I didn't dial the wrong number. They just didn't live there. It hit me that I had no idea where my folks lived on that world, or how to find them, or... I mean, what if they lived in Seattle? Or Hawaii? And then the sentry died and you shot the warrior and your bow broke and Urien was coming over the wall—" She swallowed. "Death or capture; either way, I would never see my mom and dad again."

A string of thoughts went through my mind: that she was adopted so she'd already lost her real parents, but I knew she didn't feel that way. That I was in the same place about Mom, that she could be dead already, because Morgwydd was crazy and we'd just made her angry. That I had already lost my dad, and the fact that he'd showed up alive didn't change a single part of the thirteen years without him.

But I didn't know how to say any of that, not without sounding stupid. And selfish. Not that what I did say was any better.

"You'll get back, Josie. I'll get you back. Trust me." Yeah, just like a bad politician.

She looked at me a minute, then smiled. "Thanks, Ed. Promise me one thing, okay?" She reached up and gently touched the bandage on my head. "Don't kill yourself over it?"

I shrugged. "Not if I can help it."

"Good." She took the dead grouse and hefted it. "This isn't big enough for all of us."

I scanned the underbrush. "Yeah. Now's when we need Egili."

"She couldn't leave him behind, trapped in his bag, Ed. He'd have starved if we didn't come back. And we didn't."

"I know."

"Milde's really mad at herself, too."

"Yeah, I noticed."

"Good. So you won't say anything, right?" She tapped my shoulder. "Besides, you're doing a great job being my bird dog. Sniff something out for me again."

"Yeah, woof."

I guess a dog's luck was with me, because I flushed out three more grouse and another hare. Josie missed twice, but we still had a pair of grouse and the hare to take back for dinner.

"Good work, Pointer. That'll do," she said as we headed back.

"Ha ha," I replied. "Please don't call me that around the others."

"All the others, or just Milde?" she asked, grinning

"All of them," I said. "Dennis would use it every chance he got, and Dad would probably make some kind of awful song out of it."

"And Milde?"

"Milde wouldn't get it. They don't have pointers here."

"They have hunting dogs," she said. "You know, Milde understands a lot more than you think."

"Meaning what?"

"She knows you're infatuated with her, Ed."

"Whoa! I'm not infatuated with her! Did you tell her I was?"

"Come on, Ed, it's obvious. The way you look at her?" She jumped across the brook.

I jumped after and grabbed her arm. "Look, I'm not infatuated with her, all right? I mean, yeah, she's really good looking, but that's not why I look— I mean, I don't stare at her. Not on purpose. It's just she reminds me of . . .

You know. Gail. I keep getting surprised by it. Besides, she's obviously too old for me."

"How old do you think she is?" Josie asked.

"I don't know. Twenty? Twenty-one?"

"She's sixteen, Ed. And she's married."

I stared at her. "No way! How do you know?"

"We talk together. It's a girl thing, but you should try it." She started walking.

I hurried after her. "Okay, okay, I'm an idiot. Sorry. Wow. I guess that explains why she couldn't carry the water for Leofrith."

"Have you been obsessing about that all this time?" Josie snapped.

"No, I—"

"Well, she *was* married, that's why she's not a virgin. But her baby was killed by the *wealcyn*, along with her husband. Her whole village was, while she was in the woods hunting for a lost lamb, and that's why she became a slave, because she had lost everything and she had to offer herself to the mercy of the neighboring chief. Who sold her when his wife got jealous."

"You mean he . . . ? She . . . ?"

"No! But it's what his wife thought. He kept staring at her, like you do."

Josie was enraged just talking about it. I was amazed. I'd never thought about why Milde was a slave. Or how Osweald managed to buy her. And I knew I should say something to her, but I never knew what to say when people were hurting. So I laid it on Josie.

"Um, tell her I'm sorry, okay?"

She wasn't having it. "Don't be a jerk, Ed. Tell her yourself."

I said I would, but I couldn't imagine how. I hadn't been afraid of Urien's warriors, but I was terrified of upsetting Milde. I mean, I'd seen her break a man's neck with a weaving sword. I'd seen her shred Osweald with just her tongue. Okay, I could deal with her anger, I guess. But what if she started crying?

# *Chapter 20*

I didn't get the chance to tell Milde I was sorry. There were opportunities. We plucked, skinned, and gutted the meal together that evening, but that didn't seem like the best time to talk about your family getting killed. I suppose I could have said something quietly just about anytime, but we were never really alone. I didn't want to embarrass her by bringing it up in front of Dad and Dennis. I knew I would have been embarrassed if it'd been me. It had happened often enough when people asked how come I didn't have a father.

I made up my mind to tell her the next morning, but it didn't turn out that way. It was a chilly night, and none of us slept easily. Only Josie and Milde had their cloaks. Dad, Dennis, and I had left ours with the horses. We made up beds of pine browse, which helped a little, but the cut on my head was aching, and I couldn't stop thinking about everything that had happened that day. It kept replaying, first Mom being cut, then the arrow hitting the warrior's face, then the slice on Milde's leg. It took me a long time to get to sleep, and when I did, I dreamed. It was one of those dreams so real you're certain it's not a dream. Even after you wake up, you think it's still happening, and then you think it's a memory. When you finally realize it was a dream, your body's still reacting, all tense, ready to run away. But it was a strange relief, too, because I didn't dream about the fighting. It was like my mind decided that was history; there were more important things now.

I dreamed I was still hunting with Josie, only we hadn't caught anything. I was searching through the trees, desperate to find something, because I didn't want to mess up and come back to Milde empty-handed. I was scrambling around on all fours, looking for tracks, scat, bits of fur, anything that would show me where the game had all got to. Josie was talking to me, only I couldn't understand her. She was pointing this way and that and making noises that I was certain would scare away the game. I tried to tell her to be quiet so I could do my job.

"If you hadn't broken your bow you wouldn't be down on your knees like that," she said. "You wouldn't need me to do your job for you."

"I know that!" I said. "Just be quiet. Everything can hear you."

And then I was afraid about what might hear her. The ðyrs. Urien's warriors. Morgwydd. They all appeared for an instant, then disappeared into the shadows under the trees, running away. Fleeing something bigger, more powerful. Much worse. My heart was pounding, and the noise was so loud that everything fled before it: deer, hares, mice, weasels, birds – all the game and everything else. The woods emptied. There was no hope of shooting anything. I was furious, raging, when I heard something rustling in the underbrush. I hissed at Josie and she finally shut up. She had a stone in her hand; I drew my *seax*, staring at the thicket where the noise was coming from. I glimpsed something moving. A nose came through, a pink nose. It was Egili.

I was so glad to see him I almost cried. My chest was bursting. He came bounding over to me, and I bent way down and we touched noses. Then he turned and hopped along an animal run I hadn't seen before. He looked back and *dooked* at me, then hopped a little farther. Josie and I followed him deeper into the woods. I don't know how far we went; the dream changed. It was darker. The woods were thicker, the shadows deeper. Then Egili stopped. He was all stretched out, one paw up, pointing like a hunting dog. I peered into the deep thicket that had suddenly appeared to block the trail. I couldn't see a thing.

I asked Josie, "What do you think?" And she said, "We can't go back now." And she was right, because the trail behind us was gone. There was nothing but forest and thicket. Egili hissed softly. I took one more step forward.

And a grouse burst from the underbrush right under Egili's nose and *whirred* away through the branches. Josie threw a stone, and it *whirred* like the grouse and hit dead on. The bird fell and the ground shook. I ran toward it, pushing through the bushes, brambles, vine, branches – everything was in my way. Josie was beside me, dragging on my arm, trying to hold me back. I was inches from the grouse, reaching, when something else bent down and picked it from the bed of leaves where it had fallen.

It was Milde at first, tall and straight, lean as a racing hound. Egili was on her shoulder. She lifted the bird and stroked its plumage. Its head hung off her palm, neck broken. Milde looked up and changed. Her hair was long and free. Her face was older, her skin more pale, her nose longer, but still beautiful. It wasn't Milde's face anymore. Or Gail's. Closer to Mom's, but not her either. It was all of them, but none of them. The woman closed her hand, and it was somehow large enough to enclose the entire grouse. When she opened it, the bird was gone. The stone was there in its place. She handed the stone to Josie, who was suddenly there beside her.

"This is hers," she said to me. "Where is yours?"

I knew she meant my bow. "I broke it," I replied. Egili hissed.

"You will need it soon," the woman told me. She beckoned. "Come."

Suddenly we were riding in a cart pulled by two white horses with long silver manes. Josie was still there, and she took my hand. The sky was clear. I could see the Plow and followed the line of its blade to the North Star.

"Tiw wields his ax tonight," the woman said, "and

Thunor his Stone." The ground shook again. "Strange that they walk together."

Then we were walking in a grove, surrounded by dark trunks and a dense canopy of soft needles. The ground was thick with them. Egili led the way, a low, sleek shape bounding ahead of us. We came to a narrow brook flowing slowly through the heart of the grove. It gave off light, as though it were reflecting the moon, though the canopy above us was black and unbroken. On the other side was a mound of gold, gleaming in the light from the stream. A massive trunk rose from the center of the mound. Propped against the trunk was a bow, strung, braced, ready. I could read the rune carved into the grip: ᛂ

*Ear.* For Eadgar. Or Death.

"Take it," the woman said.

Josie gripped my hand. Then I was alone.

I went to the edge of the brook and began to step across but the mound of gold began to shift and ripple. A golden snout pushed up, and the gold flowed away from it in a small cascade of coins and nuggets. An arrow-shaped head emerged, then a long, rippling legless body, as though the gold had become a living thing. A huge *wyrm*. It looked down at me, tongue flicking.

"That's mine," I said, pointing to the bow. "I have to have it."

"Earn it," a voice said.

The *wyrm* opened its mouth. It was fanged like a wolf. Then a light grew in the depths of its throat and burst out in a flare of blue-white fire.

The ground shook. Thunder rolled across the hills and through the woods.

I was awake, still coming out of the dream. Another flash of lightning brightened the canopy of trees. A pause, then came the thunder, not as close as it had seemed in the dream, from somewhere to the east and south, toward Urien's hill. I sat up and rubbed my eyes. I could hear Dad snoring. And Dennis. He was supposed to be on watch. It was probably my turn by then anyway. I got up quietly. The fire was almost dead, just a small, uneven mound of dull embers. I squatted by its warmth, thinking about the dream as the lightning grew fainter and less frequent and the thunder moved away.

I stayed awake till dawn, keeping a sort of half watch. I dozed but didn't dream again. When it grew light, I stoked the fire. Milde and Josie were lying side by side in their pile of pine browse. Sometime in the night, Milde had given Dennis her cloak. I admit I felt a little cheated, but who was I kidding? Dennis was the warrior; I was the jerk with the broken bow. I woke everyone up then.

We were eating the rest of the meat, me trying to think how I could get Milde alone long enough to tell her I was sorry, when Dad said, "I had a wondrous dream last night, more vivid than the one that brought me back to the North."

Everyone was absolutely silent for a moment. Then Josie asked, "What was it about?"

"Ed was in it," he said, looking at me. "And Egili and your mother, Ed. We were in the woods together, you and I, looking for a path back to Urien's fort. We were quite lost. You were searching for tracks, and there was something in the woods, something terrible and fey, coming closer. That's when Egili appeared, nose a-twitch, our ferret-boar and guide. He led us along a path that wasn't there before, till we were blocked by a wall that was also fresh-appeared. Suddenly I had my harp and began to play. Your mother's sweet voice answered from behind the wall, and the stones trembled and disappeared, an illusion. Your mother was there, waiting. She thanked me for bringing the harp. She asked you why you hadn't brought your bow."

"Then she began to lead you somewhere, didn't she," Josie said to me. "We followed her, and the dream changed. We were in a wagon, pulled by two—"

"Two snow white horse with silver manes," Dennis said. "And it wasn't exactly Alrun, either; she had changed, too.

The sky was clear, and Polaris glinted brightly high in the north."

"Tiw's star," Milde said. "Wielding his ax above the plow. We rode into a dark grove."

"Egili led the way," Josie said.

"To a brook, where a hoard of golden helms and jeweled swords appeared by a great tree," Dennis said.

"The goddess asked you a riddle, and a great *wyrm* flowed from the water," Dad said.

"And you began to fight the *wyrm*," Josie finished.

My throat was dry, my hands were cold. "Then what?" I asked.

"Didn't you dream it, too?" Josie asked.

I nodded. "But the thunder woke me."

"Thunor was jealous," Milde said. "His mother chose you, not him."

"No-no," Dad said. "Thunor was simply busy at his great task, as you are at yours, Son."

They were all looking at me. I shrugged. "Didn't anyone see the end?"

They all shook their heads, and Dad said, "It hasn't ended yet."

"Oh, come on," I said "You've been living here so long you've gone native on us. But Dennis, Josie, you don't think this is real, this dream, right? I mean, some kind of vision? Come on."

The two of them looked at each other. Dennis shrugged. "When in Rome," he said.

"This isn't Rome," I muttered.

Dad laughed, suddenly all Rædwod. "Rome no longer! The Legions have departed, taking their gods with them. This is the land of giants and *wyrms*, of gold rings and heroes and gods who still meddle in the lives of women and men, while silly *scops* caper for *briw* and mead. Live long enough and you'll get used to it, Son."

"Okay! We all dreamed the same dream and it's all going to come true! But we still don't know the ending.

Can we just get going now?"

After that, no one said anything for a while. We finished eating, put out the fire, and started walking. Dad led the way, and Dennis brought up the rear. I was second, but sometimes I walked beside Milde for a while. And I never thought to say I was sorry.

We walked steadily for hours, first down the long slope, then quickly across the open valley, then back up into the woods along the next slope. We stopped when the sun was well past noon and wolfed down the last of the grouse. My head was pounding, and Milde was really favoring her cut side, though she tried hard not to let it show. She and Josie doled out some goosefoot and sorrel they'd found at the edges of the clearings. We drank from a stream. We were all exhausted from traveling, sleeping on hard ground, the shock of the attack and our flight through Tiw's gate, the constantly gray sky. I kept thinking about the dream, about what it could mean, for us, for Mom and Uncle Alf. For me. What was I supposed to do?

Josie sat down beside me and patted the tree behind us. "This is ash, isn't it?" she asked.

"No, it's some kind of linden," I replied. "And stop reading my thoughts."

She shrugged. "We're all having the same thoughts today, Ed. Nobody is peeking into your mind."

"Easy for you to say. You didn't have the whole world stream your dream."

"Stream?" Dad said.

"On the Internet. Videos. Like TV."

Dad laughed. "TV! Woden's left eye, I haven't thought about TV for years!"

"You haven't missed much," Dennis told him.

"Oh, be quiet, you two," Josie said. "Look, Ed, we didn't see *your* dream; we all dreamed our own versions of it. Some things were different, but they all had the same point."

"I know! I need a bow!" I stood and walked off. "Well, there's no place to get one here, unless I can steal one from Urien's men, who, you may have noticed, don't seem to be in the habit of carrying them around."

"Oh, the *Norðwealas* have bows," Dad said. "They are great archers, but only for hunting. Like your uncle."

"Ælfweard is an archer," Josie said.

"In battle, he wields a spear," Dennis replied. "He's a bowman in the hunt."

"A direct descendent of Ægil is Ælfweard," Dad recited, "Whelan's kin and the finest archer in the land, offspring of *entas* and *swan-mæðga*, in the times when they still kept the company of men."

"That's really true?" Josie asked. "Alrun and Alf are descended from Whelan Smith and a swan maiden?"

I blew up. "Josie, come on! I don't need mythology, I need a bow!"

"Then make one," Dad said. "It's what Alf trained you for, isn't it?"

"Make it with what? My bare hands?" I drew my knife and *seax*. "This is what I have for tools." I hacked down a sapling. "This is what I have for wood. Too thin!" I slashed at the bark on a broad oak. "Too fat! All of it green! Dripping with sap! I need dry wood I can split. I need an ax, wedges, drawknife, scrapers."

"I have an ax," Josie said. She held it up. "Small but sharp."

"I don't have a bowstring!"

She pulled my old bowstring from her pouch, neatly coiled. "I saved it," she said.

I gaped at the string. "You saved— No!" I cried. "That's not it! I don't have time!"

"I've seen Alf rough out a bow in a day," Dennis said.

"Operative word: rough," I told him.

"Rough is better than nothing," Dad said. "You can work on it each evening."

"We don't have enough evenings – it'll still be green!"

"It'll dry while we walk. "

"It'll bend too much, follow the string."

"It doesn't have to last," Milde said quietly. "Two arrows only: Urien, then the witch."

We all looked at her, and Dad laughed.

"Gentle Milde, so beautiful, so brutal, so brutally, beautifully wise. I could swear you were Alrun's kin." He turned to me. "This is the only time we have. Go look for the right tree. We'll camp here." I tried to protest, but he held up his hand. "Go. Never refuse a goddess."

What else could I do with all four of them staring at me like that? I went.

The woods there didn't seem any different from what we'd been traveling through since we left Coria. I could tell by the size of the trees that they'd grown up from cleared land in the past seventy-five years or so. The growth was uneven; some groves were younger, some were evergreens, but mostly it was mixed hardwood, a lot like home. Oak, ash, beech. Mountain ash or something like it. Elm and maple and linden. A lot of woods can be used to make a bow. Hickory would have been nice, but I didn't see any. Ash, oak, and some kinds of elm were fine, if you could find one that wasn't bent or twisted, without too many branches, and small enough to cut with Josie's hand ax in less than a week. Four inches would have been okay, six inches better but a lot tougher to cut. I was staring at a particular ash tree – my bow had been ash – when Josie spoke from right behind me.

"Is that the one?" she asked.

I nearly jumped out of my skin. "What are you doing here?" I snapped.

"Looking for you." She gave a whistle, and Milde answered from not too far away. "We can help you chop. Oh, and you forgot this." She held up her ax and repeated her question.

"I don't know," I said. "It doesn't feel right."

"Okay, you're the bowyer. What are we looking for?"

By then Milde had arrived. She was limping, and I suggested she and Josie should go back to the camp. She pulled herself straight and gave me a look to freeze my blood. I backed down and tried to describe the perfect tree. I was sure they were going to be more trouble than worth – a lot of false alarms, wrong type of tree, too many branches, all that – but I had them fan out to either side, and we started walking in parallel along the hillside.

We didn't find anything for at least a hundred yards. Not that we didn't find any trees, but every one of them had something wrong with it. I could almost hear Uncle Alf muttering to them the way he always did, almost like he was apologizing. He would pat some of them, like they were horses or cows he wasn't going to buy, nice enough animals, just not right. I caught myself doing it on the good ones that were just too big for me to deal with, or too small now but good prospects in a year or two.

Then Josie stopped cold, pointing. "Ed, Milde, look!" she whispered. "A horse!"

# Chapter 21

It wasn't just a horse, it was a white horse. So white it almost glowed. We had walked into an old grove, with tall, broad trunks and a high canopy, low underbrush, ferns, deep shadow. It was the sort of place where you'd almost expect to see a fantasy creature. Like a unicorn. The horse filled the bill. It was small and graceful, with a silver mane; about Bil's size, though not as stocky. If it had been bigger, it would have looked just like one of the horses pulling my dream wagon. A shiver pulled at my spine. A unicorn couldn't have shocked me more.

It looked right at me, then at Josie, then Milde, then back at me. Its eyes were black as the space between the stars. It dipped its head and blew softly, the same way Bil would greet me in the morning, then it turned calmly and began to walk away. The three of us followed. It looked back once and blew again, then led us deeper into the grove.

We didn't say anything. This was too strange to talk about. I expected the scene to change at any moment, to find myself in a wagon drawn by this horse and its mate, with Josie still beside me, Milde turned into a goddess, Egili perched on her shoulder, and the stars gleaming above us. It didn't happen. We just kept following the horse through the trees.

The land climbed steadily, then leveled out in a bowl cupped by steep slopes on either side. And the trees changed. Some sort of evergreen began to replace the hardwoods; a tree with soft, flat needles that were bright green at the growing tips of the branches. The oldest needles were so dark they were almost black. Soon there were more evergreens than anything else. The forest floor was covered by a blanket of brown needles and twigs. It grew warmer. The air smelled tart, or bitter, or a little of both.

We came to a perfect ring of trees, all the same kind. That evergreen, kind of like a fir tree, but with cedar-like bark. The trees in the ring were all the same size: slender, six or eight inches across, straight. It occurred to me that they were just about the right size. But the horse kept walking, and we followed it through a gap, into the ring. There was an open space inside, roofed by branches. A larger tree stood in the center, much larger, and it had made the ring. Each of its lowest branches had grown out and down in a smooth curve that touched the ground. Where the branches touched, they had put down roots and sent up a sprout, the fairy ring of trees. I paused, amazed. But the horse kept walking and the others kept after it, so I went, too.

There was another ring outside the first one, and more beyond that, and alongside, and overlapping – a huge grove of interconnected trees, where you couldn't tell the edge of one ring from the edge of the next, as though we were walking from room to room in a massive cavern supported by living columns. As we moved through the grove, the central trees became larger and larger, the space around them wider and higher, until finally we came to centermost ring. The grandmother tree.

It was the dream tree. The goddess tree.

The trunk was broader than the three of us standing hand-to-hand with our arms held wide. It was channeled, pillared, as though several saplings had grown together and kept growing, engulfing each other, bonding for the sake of strength. It looked like bones and muscles lay just beneath the bark, tensed to bear the weight of the sky. The lowest branch was three times higher than the top of my head, and as broad as a tree itself. Layers and layers of branches and needles spread out above it, crisscrossed in a tight weave of bright and dark green, gray, brown, and red. The bark was almost the color of dried blood in some places, cocoa brown in others, wide flakes on a smooth, ruddy skin. You almost expected to see it flex and breathe.

It should have been dark in there, the canopy was so thick. But we could see clearly. The air itself seemed to carry light. The horse was bright white. Milde's hair glowed. Josie's face shone. There was a narrow brook between us and the trunk, maybe a foot or two across. The water bubbled from a spring near the far edge of the ring of trees that walled this cavern of needles. It flowed slowly in a gentle curve, past the trunk and out the other side, hardly rippling. The surface of the water gleamed, as though it were the source of the light.

Josie went close and looked in. The light turned her face bronze. She stood very still, eyes moving slightly, as though she was watching something. I went and looked, and saw a perfect reflection of the two of us, like we were insects in amber. The slowly moving water made our images shift slightly, and the pattern of branches and needles danced above our heads. But I could see through us, too: pebbles, dark sand, tiny water plants shifting in the current, and a quick flick of movement. Maybe a tadpole or some tiny water snake, there and gone.

But no source of light. It was the water itself that glowed. Josie and I looked at each other in the water. She took my hand and squeezed it.

"We're beautiful," she whispered. "Like in the dream."

I don't know how I looked, but the light showed off her beauty in a way I'd never seen before.

"There is no bow," Milde said. She was whispering, too. It was that kind of place, like being in a church, or listening to Dad's music. But she was right. Josie and I looked up, she dropped my hand, and we blinked our eyes clear and looked at the empty spot beside the goddess tree. Whatever made the light, it was bright enough to see there wasn't any pile of gold. No bow for the taking. Nothing but us and the horse, watching quietly from the other side of the brook.

Josie walked over to the wall of needles and ran her hand down one spray. "Could this be *eoh*, Ed?"

"It is," Milde replied. "Eoh."

Another shiver grabbed me. Eoh is yew. And yew is a legend to archers, at least on our world. To hear some tell it, the English warbow had been the A-bomb of its age, the only reason the English had beaten the French and the Scots, against all odds. Those warbows were made of yew.

Uncle Alf always snorted when anyone said he should make bows out of yew. It didn't grow where we lived, and there were plenty of good bow woods that did. He worked with what he could cut down himself. But he did make two yew bows. One of the re-enactors just about forced him to. The guy bought the staves himself, shipped all the way from Europe. He got two staves, because Uncle Alf said he wouldn't do it without a second one to practice on, and they each cost more than what Uncle Alf charged for most of his finished bows. He never let me touch a blade to those staves.

The first bow he made was a beauty, but he wasn't satisfied. He broke it over his knee and threw into the fire. Then he made a second that didn't look as polished but was everything a bow should be. When it was finally ready, he shot a half-dozen bulls-eyes at a hundred yards. He let me try it once. I could hardly draw it; it must have pulled 120 pounds or more. The customer had insisted on a warbow, and he got one. He could hardly draw it himself, but he was happy as a pig in mud and forked over eight hundred dollars. Uncle Alf snorted as he took the money.

"It's worthless," he told me, after the man had left. "The fool will never master it." And the rune Mom picked was ᛗ, for *dæg*. It means day, but also *doles*. Dolt.

Now I was surrounded by acres of yew trees. I kept expecting to hear thunder and wake up, but I didn't, and the weirdness should have made me quake in my boots. Instead, I was thinking it was time I starting earning my new bow.

"These trees are too big," I said. "Let's go back to the first rings."

I went out what I thought was the same way we'd come in, back through the interconnected halls to the outermost wall of drooping branches. But when I pushed through the soft needles, I walked into a shattered place. The ground was scorched, the dense floor of fallen needles still smoking. The central trunk was black, split in long furrows that showed a light-and-dark pattern of charred wood inside. Many of the drooping branches were broken at the trunk. Half of its ring of child trees had fallen, torn from jagged, splintered stumps.

"Frige's heart!" Josie exclaimed. "What happened here?"

"Thunor's stone," Milde replied. "Last night he walked here and argued with his mother. He struck at her hall in his rage."

*Maybe*, I thought, *but she had rooms to spare*. And he'd made my work much easier.

I scanned the broken ring of trees. One was smaller, just about six inches across. It was still standing, and it wasn't attached to the center tree. It had never been attached. Somehow, it had sprouted there from a seed and fought for height beneath the shadow of the ring. It was a survivor. Had been. All of its needles were brown now, sucked dry by the blast of heat that had shattered the central tree. The trees in the ring, standing or fallen, were split and parched, useless for anything but firewood. This one was still sound, and well on its way to being dry.

It didn't occur to me then how impossible that had to be: a seasoned tree right where I would find it. I just knew this was the tree I needed. Without my even asking, Josie handed me her ax. I took the first stroke and began to make my bow.

As Josie had said, the ax was small, but Dennis had

made it very sharp. I felled the tree easily. Then I measured out about seven feet and cut off the top. Step one done. I handed Josie the ax and asked her to cut some branches about three inches wide and eight inches long. While she was doing that, I took out my *seax* and carefully began to peel the bark from the trunk.

"What can I do to help you?" Milde asked.

"Start at the other end and peel the bark," I said. "Be very careful not to cut into the wood at all." She set to. Her knife was small, but she had skinned hundreds of animals in her life. This wasn't much different.

When Josie was finished cutting the branches, I took the ax and angled their ends to make a set of wedges. The final tool I needed was a heavy mallet, and there were plenty of thick branches for that. With the wedges and mallet, and Josie and Milde to brace things, I split my tree in half, and then in half again. And there were four bow staves, as rough as could be but ready for work.

We carried them back to the heart of the grove and made a camp before the goddess tree, where there was water and shelter and the white horse for company. It was getting dim, so the last thing I did was study the four staves, trying to decide which was best. Perfect was too much to expect, but I finally decided which one was the straightest, with the fewest pin knots from early branches. I lashed the other three into a tripod, to use as a brace when I shaped the good stave.

When I looked up from all that, I saw that Milde had started a fire near the brook, in a cleared space ringed with stones. I didn't think to ask where she had found the stones, because Josie appeared from the other side of the tree carrying a dead hare.

"It hopped into the ring right over there," she said, pointing. "I was digging a little slit trench for a latrine and there it was, staring at me."

"The goddess is pleased with you, Eadgar," Milde said. "You have wood now. Soon you'll have a very fine bow. She doesn't want you to go hungry."

I didn't feel hungry. I was thinking about the next steps in making the bow. I'd been whining about needing tools, but I had everything important. Uncle Alf had shown me how to make a bow with next to nothing. He'd made it clear it was part of my job: to watch, listen, copy, and learn from my own mistakes, which he was always ready to point out. This was going to be the final exam.

I ate because there was food and Josie told me to. Then I studied the stave some more, mostly by feel, getting a sense for how the wood moved beneath the surface. When it was too dim to do even that, I sat by the fire and honed the ax, *seax*, and knife, till they were sharp enough to shave with. Then we slept in the golden water-light. It didn't keep me awake, and while I slept, I worked through the making of the bow, step by step, over and over, until I could have done it in my sleep. Because I just had.

The next morning, we all woke together. I felt completely rested. I drank from the brook and went to the stave.

"Milde, I'll need a new bowstring," I said. "My old one won't be long enough. Do you have flax in your bag, or linen yarn?"

"No," she said, "only wool."

"My shirt is linen," Josie said. "We can unravel the yarn from that."

"Your people make fine, strong thread," Milde said.

So that was decided. They went behind the tree so Josie could slip her shirt off from under her gown. I whittled a piece of firewood into a handle to fit over the point of my *seax*, so I could use it as a drawknife. Then I began to shape the stave.

First it needed a good back, so I shaved the sapwood down to a single growth ring near the start of the heartwood. The pale sapwood back could take the stretch as the bow bent toward the string. The dark heartwood belly could take the compression as the bow squeezed around it. That was the beauty of yew – the heartwood and sapwood were perfectly matched to make a strong bow.

I used the *seax* to split off the outer sapwood until I was close to the ring I had decided to follow. Then I switched to my small knife, carefully shaving down from one end to the other. It was painstaking work. One nick past the ring would have weakened the bow. So I took my time. For some reason, I didn't feel rushed at all. I had three other staves in case I botched this one, but I knew I wouldn't need them if I just let my eyes and hands do their work.

When Milde and Josie came to me with a skein of linen yarn unraveled from the weave of Josie's shirt, the back was clean, and I was ready to put down my knife and show them how to lay in a bowstring. Then I took a moment to stretch and touch up the edge on my knife, picked up the ax, and began to rough down the sides. With each slice, the true figure of the wood appeared, a slow wave in the grain from end to end. I didn't cut across the ripples; that too would have weakened the bow. I let the wood follow its own path.

Finally, I used my *seax* to carve straight tapers on the belly, from the grip to the ends of the stave. Josie made me take a break then, and I was fine with that. We finished the hare and drank from the spring. I went back to the bow. I had no idea what time it was and didn't care.

What happened next was all the fine work. I shaved the belly down a little, then bent the bow to test the curve. It's called tillering, and it's the most important part of the job. You study the curve to see where it's too flat or too bent. You scrape the flat spots a tiny bit with the edge of the knife and check it again. Both ends have to curve together through a smooth arc. Only the few inches of grip stay straight, and even there the arcs have to blend smoothly. If there's the slightest kink, the bow can break. When I was learning, I broke my first bow trying to tiller it. My second bow, I scraped too much; it was so limp a baby could draw it. You have to scrape just a little, then bend the bow carefully five, seven, maybe ten times to let the wood settle into its new shape. Then check it, then scrape a little more, then tiller it again. At some point, you stop tillering on the ground and set up a jig to hold the bow. You put on a string that's too long, so the bow starts flat. Then you pull it down a couple of inches, step back, and study the curve.

And you take the bow off the jig and scrape. And tiller again.

And so it went. I used a tree in the ring as the base for my jig. There was a stub of a branch at just the right height, and a spine below it in the trunk where I could cut notches a couple of inches apart, lower and lower, each one a step to bend the bow farther. And the string was ready when I was, smooth and even, better than any I had ever made. Milde had even put a tight seizing on the center of the loose strands, like the one on my old string, to protect it from chafing in the arrow nock. It shone, and when I looked closely, I saw there were silver strands worked in with the beige linen.

"From the mane and tail of the mare," Josie said. "Milde combed them out."

I went to the mare and thanked her, thanked Milde and Josie, and went back to work.

By the end of the day, the bow was finished, as good as I could make it. It pulled somewhere around 65 pounds. I still had to flex it a few dozen times, then trim the ends and reset the nocks, but that was for tomorrow. It was too dim to keep working. I drew it to half draw and relaxed it an even fifty times, then loosened the string to half the usual brace. I drank from the stream again. Josie gave me something to eat; another hare I think. Maybe a grouse. Whatever it was, it tasted wonderful. I thanked her and Milde, and we lay down together by the stream and slept.

I dreamed of the goddess again. She stood by the great tree, lit by the flowing glow from the water, holding my bow. She tested the draw carefully, then ran her hand along the gentle wave in the edge.

"This is well done, Eadgar," she said. "You should be called *Beorhtboga*." Brightbow. She looked up at me. "But can you use it?"

"I can use it," I said, though I didn't feel as sure as I

sounded.

She looked at me long and hard. "You will get only one chance," she said finally. Then she smiled. "Watch over him, Milde. And you, Shosefina. Give him room to shoot."

They were standing on either side of me. They stepped closer, and Josie took my hand.

"We will, Mother," Milde told her. "If it means our lives, we will."

The goddess nodded. "It may mean that. I have done what I can; you will do what you can. Wyrd will decide if it is all enough."

She crossed the stream in one smooth step, took my face in both her hands. One was cool, the other warm as firelight. Then she kissed me. My eyes closed, but I could feel her fading; the touch of her hands and lips growing lighter. Then the dream changed, and the pressure returned. I was lying on my back. I put my arms around her and pulled her close, felt the press of her breasts. Her arms were bare. My heart was racing. So was hers. Her hair brushed my face as she ended the kiss and lifted her head. I opened my eyes, and the goddess was smiling, fading still. Changing. Milde was above me. We kissed. Only it wasn't Milde, it was Josie. And I wasn't sure I was dreaming, but I wasn't about to question it then. She kissed me, and I kissed her back.

Ear

# *Chapter 22*

I woke up first the next morning. We were still lying under the goddess tree, beside the brook. I could see my bow, leaning against the tripod of staves, where I had left it the evening before. It seemed like nothing had changed, except I was lying between Josie and Milde. When we'd lain down to sleep, I'd been on the end, and at least four feet away. The dream came back to me – all of it – and I realized I didn't want to be thinking about it when Josie woke up. Or Milde. Not lying there between them, with Josie's bare arm brushing my shoulder. I eased my way into a crouch and was trying to step quietly out of the center when Josie opened her eyes. She was looking right up at me, her face framed by her dark braids. She started to smile, then her brain woke up. I could almost see the dream replay in her eyes. She blushed.

Josie never blushes.

I stumbled a step or two out of the way, almost stomping on Milde's head in the process. That woke her up. She yawned, rolled onto her side, and raised up on an elbow.

"I dreamed of the goddess again," she said. "Did you?"

Josie and I glanced at each other and glanced away quickly.

"I guess I did," Josie said.

"Yeah," I muttered. "Excuse me, I've got to go use the . . . the thing. The trench."

You know, it's hard to pee when you can hear two women whispering just the other side of a big tree. Particularly when one of them starts to laugh and the other shushes her. I played it real calm and cool when I came back. I went to my bow and picked it up, drew it carefully.

"I'll only have one chance. That's what she told me," I said, and I knew that they'd know what I was talking about. There, in that grove, dreams and reality were the same thing.

"She praised your bow, Ed," Josie said.

"She praised *you*, Eadgar," Milde added. I wondered if she meant a little more than she was saying out loud, but she was serious. "We will do as she asked us. We will stand by you."

"Yes, I heard that," I replied. "Thank you."

"We'd have done it anyway," Josie said, but she still wouldn't quite meet my eyes.

"It seems we all dreamed the very same dream this time," Milde said.

I looked back at my bow. Maybe we had, but I still didn't want to talk about the last part. I drew and relaxed the bow another fifty times, then shortened it a couple of inches from both ends, reset the nocks, and drew it fifty more times. I could feel the wood taking the set and the draw lightening. It was still a few pounds heavier than my old bow, but not enough to be a problem. Of course, I wouldn't know that for sure until I shot it.

I went looking for a target and found one as soon as I pushed through the far wall of branches. One of the trees in the ring beyond had died and started to rot. The trunk was firm, but punky. About as hard as a stiff bale of hay. About shoulder width across. Perfect. I wasn't at all surprised. I whispered a thank-you to the goddess, paced off thirty yards to the opposite side of the ring, and drew an arrow from my quiver. It was the gatekey, and the arrowhead was glowing faintly. For some reason, it made me smile to think I had that much power at hand. But I wasn't about to use it for target practice, not even to test that new bow. I put it back and took another.

When I nocked the arrow and drew the bow to full draw, I could feel the wood singing through the grip. I loosed the arrow, and it flew straight and quick to the heart of the tree.

Josie and Milde cheered. My stomach knotted. I hadn't realized they were there behind me. I nocked another arrow, aimed, loosed, and just nicked the tree. The arrow disappeared into the foliage beyond it.

"Crap," I muttered. I knew I had to forget about them and just shoot. If I asked them to leave, they'd wonder what was wrong. They'd worry that I wouldn't be able to hit anything when the time came, when I really needed to.

I told myself, It's just Josie and Milde, you frigging idiot! Relax! Then I realized I'd used the goddess's name in vain. I knew she was the goddess I'd spoken to; the one in my dream. Only Frige could have kissed like that. Unless it really had been Josie. And that thought totally blew my concentration. I shot two more arrows into the branches on either side of the tree. After that, I gave in and asked Josie and Milde to leave. Well, what I said was that it was going to take me some time, and they would probably get bored so maybe they could get something ready to eat.

They both got the real message, I could tell, and it made me feel like crap. But as soon as they were gone, I put five arrows right beside the first one in the center of the tree. The bow was a dream itself, a dream to shoot. It was smooth, quick-ended, quiet. I shot ten more arrows, and never missed the trunk. Some were a little high, a little low, a few inches to the side, but it was still a fine pattern. My heart was light, even when I went to find the three that had missed. And they were right there, lying on the ground in the next ring of trees, undamaged. I guess the goddess didn't mind if I swore by her now and then, as long as I didn't swear at her.

I went back to the goddess tree and thanked her again. And there were Josie and Milde, with a tidy grouse roasting over a small fire. We ate, buried the bones, put out the fire, and were ready to go, except for one last thing.

I asked Josie if she'd cast the runes for me.

"You mean for the bow?" She sounded surprised.

"Yeah. Normally Mom would have done it, but ..." I shrugged.

She hesitated, and the look on her face made me think of myself trying to hit the bull's eye while she and Milde were watching. I'd never ever thought of her being nervous that way. But it passed quickly. She smiled at me, like I was the one doing her a favor.

"Okay, but I want you to hold the bow."

She laid out her cloth and I held out the bow. Then she put one hand over mine on the grip, closed her eyes, and cast the runes. Her hand was warm on mine, and it grew much warmer as she studied the fallen runes. She made her choices: ᚹ ᛠ ᚠ *Wyn, Ear, Feoh.*

"Joy, Death, Treasure," I said.

"Or Whelan, Eadgar, Frige," Josie said.

"Or any combination," I muttered. "What do you think?"

She shrugged. "I think we'll find out later, and when we do, we'll feel dumb that we didn't get it right off."

"Yeah, runes. Clear as mud, as usual." I admit I'd been hoping for something obvious.

I etched the three runes on the grip. Then we said goodbye to the tree and the mare and made our way out of the grove, layer by layer, until we stepped back through the very first ring of trees, right onto the footprints we'd left coming in. That's when I realized how much time had passed. All the anxiety, the hurry, the fear of missing the solstice – it burst back on me, as though I'd just woken from a dream within a dream. A three-day-long dream.

"We'd better move it," I said. "Dennis and Dad will be— I don't know what they'll be. Or even where." I led the way as fast as I could on the uneven slopes.

"They would have waited for us, Ed," Josie said. "You know they would have."

"They would have gone looking for us," I replied, "and

neither of them is worth a damn in the woods. If they're not lost, they've probably starved or died of exposure or something."

"Beorhtscyld is made of stronger stuff than that, Eadgar," Milde said, "as is Rædwod. They will be well and waiting for us."

"And they'll be mad as a wounded boar."

"Not when they see the bow," she said.

"They'll still be hungry."

"Then we'll bring back some food," Josie said. "Slow down. You're scaring the game."

"You're ganging up on me," I muttered, but Josie just punched my arm.

I had to slow down anyway, because it was hard to make out our prints in the thick duff that covered the forest floor. And I never saw any hoof prints. I was about to mention it when Josie grabbed my arm. A hare and a big ugly grouse were eyeing each other at the edge of a thicket not ten yards away. They were so intent on each other that they didn't even notice us.

"You take the grouse," Josie whispered, pulling a stone from her pouch.

I slid an arrow from my quiver, nocked it, and drew slowly. Josie cocked her arm.

"Now!" she breathed, and threw. I was just an instant behind her.

The hare dropped, kicking. The grouse exploded into the air, but my arrow grazed its rump and feathers flew. I was already reaching for a second arrow, but Josie had another stone in the air in a blink. More feathers flew, and the grouse fell right beside the hare.

"Frige provides," Milde said. She strode over and neatly snapped their necks.

I found my arrow, but the shaft had split. Frige was providing food, but maybe also a message: Learn to shoot, *doles*.

It was getting dim by the time I found our way back to the campsite. There was a little fire going, and we rushed up to it, looking around for Dad and Dennis. They came out from behind the trees, one on each side. Dennis put down his shield and sheathed his sword.

"So it is you," he said. "We were beginning to get a little worried."

"*Beginning*?" I said. "A *little* worried?" I looked at each of them. They were calm as could be. "What is this, a joke?"

"Hardly," Dennis said. "It was getting dark and we were afraid you might have gotten lost." Then his eyes went wide. "Wherever did you find that lovely bow?"

Josie, Milde, and I looked at each other. "Ed made it," Josie said. "That's why we were gone so long."

"Thunor's stones," Dennis exclaimed. "You made that in just a couple of hours?"

"We've been gone almost three days," Josie said.

Dennis looked from the bow to her, then to me, then to Milde. We all nodded. Dennis shook his head. "Now who's joking?"

"It's no joke!" Josie exclaimed. "Look at the bow!"

"All right, it's a lovely bow. But three days? It has only been a couple of hours."

"Beorhtscyld, it has been three days," Milde said. "Look, my side is healed."

She lifted the hems of her dress and tunic and showed her hip. There was no wound, not even a scar. Dennis stared, then turned and peered at my head. I pulled off the bandage, only just realizing that the cut no longer hurt. The scab was gone. My forehead was smooth.

Dad struck a chord on his harp and laughed.

Josie and I told the whole story, while Milde cleaned and cooked our dinner. Dad listened, nodding, smiling, like we were talking about a trip to the mall. Dennis had a harder time; only three hours had passed for them. It was easy for me to accept because I had the bow in my hand. My head had healed. I had not only seen the goddess in that last dream, I had felt her touch me. Before she changed. Neither Josie or I mentioned that part, but I caught Milde hiding a smile when we both fell silent at just that moment. She finished telling the story – not including the kiss – and brought it up to the present. Or back to. Whatever.

Dennis took my bow and ran his hands along the length. He touched the string Milde and Josie had made, studied the silver strands of horsehair braided into it.

"I have to believe you," he said, handing it back almost reverently. "How does it shoot?"

"Smooth, quick. The best I've ever shot," I said.

"That's saying a lot. Well, however you got it, I don't doubt we're going to need it. And your sharp eye."

"Yeah," I glanced at Milde and Josie. They knew how sharp my eye had been when they were around. For sure the goddess knew. And it was eating at me.

We left at the crack of dawn the next morning. I couldn't sit though breakfast, so we skipped it. We came to a river when the sun was high, and had to skirt the bank until we could find a ford that was more or less shielded by trees. We were coming from the northeast, from Urien's own country. There was a good chance no one would be watching in this direction. But we couldn't risk it. We kept to the trees and the hillsides as best we could.

That night, no fire. We ate leftover hare and greens that Milde had picked along the way. And she had a surprise for us: wild strawberries. They were tiny red beads in her palm, just a few for each of us. They were sharp and sweet all at once, with more flavor than a bucket of store-bought berries. She didn't eat any herself; she gave her share to Dennis. He noticed and thanked her with a poem, one of his own that he used to tell at the fairs as a blessing to a feast. It ended, "After the meat and the sweet and the mead, bless, too, the hostess and all who share the table. They are the finest and fairest portion to any meal."

↑

I had the graveyard watch that night. Nothing happened, but as soon as it was light, I snuck off to shoot a few more arrows. I chose an old wolf pine for a target and paced off twenty yards, the longest clear shot I could get in the woods. I was drawing my first arrow when Dennis showed up. I lowered my bow, hoping he was just looking for a place to pee.

"Go ahead," he said. "Don't mind me."

So I shot three arrows, and managed to hit the tree twice. I paused for a minute, trying to psych myself up – deep breath, closed eyes, all that. I was drawing the next arrow when Dad wandered over.

"Pay me no mind," he said, when I lowered the bow. "I am but a wind in the trees, a leaf on a branch, a worm in the soil. I matter not."

Right. I prayed to the goddess and raised the bow again. I hit the tree, but three feet too high if it had been a man. The next one went wide. So Dad started playing his harp, real softly.

"Don't," I said.

He bowed silently and started to leave.

"No, I didn't mean you had to go," I snapped, which isn't really what I felt.

"You should stay," Dennis said. "He has to be able to shoot straight and true no matter how many people are watching."

"Thanks, Dennis. Always looking out for me."

"It's true, though, isn't it?"

What could I say? I clenched when people were watching. But only when something else was on my mind. Some*one* else. Trying to shoot for someone else always undid me. Uncle Alf, Gail Silverton, Mom. Okay, Milde, too. Even Josie. And now I had a goddess to worry about. I didn't care about the target, I wanted to be perfect for *them*.

"I don't want a spell to help me shoot," I said. "I want to do it on my own."

"Why do you need any help?" Dad said. "Dennis tells me you're downright gifted."

I looked at Dennis.

He shrugged. "Well, you are, when you stop worrying about how you look to other people. Trust me, whether it's Marguerite or Milde, whoever is the distraction of the moment, you don't have to impress her. They both know you're a good shot. So shoot to serve her, shoot to protect her, not to woo her."

"Easy for you to say," I muttered. "Uncle Alf is your only distraction and you don't have to impress him. You're already wrapped around each other's fingers."

"A terrible metaphor, especially in the plural," Dennis replied, "and quite beside the point. I don't let the thought of him distract me. I will fight and, if it happens, die for him. And for your mother. To free them, not to impress them."

"Fine, good, you do that!" I told him. "Now, do you mind if I take a few shots? Because I need the practice, or I'm not going to free anybody."

"Just trust yourself, Ed, okay?" Then he walked away.

I watched him go, then turned to Dad. "You got anything else to say?"

"Me? I hardly know you," he replied. We were speaking English, and he sounded more sane than I'd ever heard him. "Woden knows, I wish I was as familiar with you as Dennis is, and could presume to give you advice about archery and women and other distractions." He stroked his harp once. "All I can offer is this, a little soothing music, but I won't be playing that sort of tune when the times comes for you to aim your bow and kill. Oh, no, not soothing at all. I will be your worst distraction."

"What do you mean?" I asked.

He struck another chord, this one sharp and uncomfortable. "I can't wield a sword, throw a stone, or shoot a bow. But I can play a tune that will make men stumble, and sing a charm that will make them see their fears made flesh. You'll hear that song, too, and your only defense will be that you know it's coming. But, oh, it will distract you even then."

"Well, maybe it'll take my mind off impressing anyone

except the ones I'm aiming at."

"Alf used to tell me he never aimed, he just—"

"Saw the target," I finished. "Yeah, that's what I try to do. Don't aim. Don't try to hit. Just see the target, and only the target."

"That's good advice. I couldn't do it, and that's one reason why we're here."

"Okay, Dad, you've lost me again," I said.

He sighed. "When your mother and Alf and I came through the gate that last time, trying to ambush Morgwydd and Urien, do you know what weapon I carried?"

"No."

"I brought a gun, a deer rifle. And five clips of ammunition. Much against poor Alf's wishes, mind you." He laughed bitterly. "He felt it would be dishonorable. Let me tell you, Son, war is never honorable, no matter how many honorable people it kills, or how many songs about it get sung."

"What happened?" I asked.

"I missed," he said flatly. "Oh, I scared them all right, but not enough. They kept coming. I managed to kill a few, but still not enough, and not the right one. I ran out of bullets while Urien still lived."

He paused, his one eye staring off through the trees. Then he laughed again. "You should have seen it! No one knew I was out of bullets, not even your mother and Alf. I told them to get back through the gate, that I'd hold off the enemy till the last minute. And they did hold back, until Urien himself, seeing Alrun turn and flee, bellowed in rage and ran forward, brandishing his sword, shield held before him like the prow of a ramming ship. The gate was closing, but slowly. Even then Morgwydd had some control in her voice and could weaken your mother's charm. I waited, aiming my empty gun. And at the last minute, when Urien was no more than two paces away, I shouted *bang!* Urien was so startled, he stopped dead. Half of his men threw themselves to the ground. Morgwydd stopped singing."

He took a deep breath, beaming. "It was wonderful,

that moment. I laughed at them, and the gate slammed shut behind me."

I shook my head, amazed. Proud. "That was really brave," I said.

"Oh, no-no-no. It was tremendously stupid."

"Hey, it worked."

He touched his eye patch. "In a manner of speaking. But that was then and this is now, and we are here to do whatever we can. What happened happened. What will happen is something we can't know, even were Alrun and Josie both here to cast their runes, but I think you and your bow can do much more on this world than a gun and I ever could. Don't worry about hitting targets, Son. Either you will or you won't; Wyrd will decide. But let me add that a goddess never chose to sleep with me." He winked his patch. "Perhaps she'll put in a good word for you."

# *Chapter 23*

Dad left and I shot six more arrows. Five were dead on. The last one missed the pine completely, glanced off another tree, hit a stone, and split. I told myself that five-to-one wasn't bad, but I didn't believe it. I carefully dug the good ones out of the pine and searched through the brush for the others. I found them, but I was down to twenty-one arrows, including the gatekey. I couldn't afford more practice. Dad thought I only had to hit two people, but I doubted it.

We traveled quickly that day. Even Dad finally seemed to realize that we couldn't waste another minute. He led us in a broad loop that curved through the woods to the back side of Urien's hill. By the time we reached the start of the climb it was late afternoon. We had glimpsed the smoke of a cook fire, but no other sign of life.

Dad said, "Good! Oh, this is very good. If the whole band were there, there'd be more fires, wood-cutting crews, horses tethered outside the wall, music, the smell of roasting meat. It's still the same small band. The odds favor us."

*Odds?* I thought. *Favor?* If this "small" band was more than twenty we could be really screwed. How many could Dennis handle? Or Milde, or Josie? How many would be left for me to kill in order to reach Morgwydd before she killed Mom and Uncle Alf?

We stopped to rest beside a brook that ran down the

hill in a narrow ravine. We crouched low and tried to plan in whispers. As near as we could tell, this was the stream that ran out through the wall. We could follow it upward and wait just inside the tree line until the sleepiest hours of the night. Dad said his song would have the strongest effect then, on warriors surprised from their dreams. He would create a diversion by the sag in the wall. We would go over it halfway around. And hope Mom and Alf were still being kept in the same place.

As the sun set, the moon rose behind the clouds. They glowed like a pale awning. It was midsummer's eve and by good luck or bad, or maybe Wyrd's will, we had a full moon. We could use it to find our way in the dark. Morgwydd could use it to strengthen her spells. Tomorrow at mid day – the solstice – she would work her magic, whatever it was. Unless we could stop her.

I didn't care about that. I just wanted to get Mom and Uncle Alf back home.

We made our way slowly uphill along the steam bed, slipping from shadow to shadow in the cloud-light. The walls of the ravine grew higher, the pathway darker, but it was also better cover. Soon the walls were over our heads. Then we ran out of ravine.

It didn't dead-end exactly. It stopped at a jumble of huge stones that canted together at uneven angles. They were rough and gray and crusted with lichen, except in the center, where two thick slabs leaned together to form an A-shaped gap. The mossy opening was just barely chin high, an arm-span wide at the base. The stream poured out over a ledge and hurried downhill into the shadows.

Dennis bent and peered into the gap. "It goes through. I can see light." He looked at each of us. "Through? Or up and over?"

Dad closed his eye and leaned his forehead against the stone. And waited. It felt like an hour. I almost grabbed him, but Milde stopped me. Finally, he raised his head and said, "I may be remembering a dream, but I feel we were meant to find this doorway."

"Lead us, Beorhtscyld," Milde said.

Dennis nodded. "Through it is."

"Yeah, why climb fast when you can crawl slow?" I muttered, but no one heard me.

Dennis hung his shield over his shoulder and went first, then Dad, then Milde and Josie and me. We all had to stoop. The angled stone ceiling went on for ten or twelve feet and got lower. The stones underneath were slimy, and it was all we could do to keep from sliding into the stream, which splashed us anyway. I was about to suggest we turn around, when the cave opened out and up, like a mead hall. The stream banks were flat and even, as though they'd been floored with flagstone. The walls and ceiling were damp and faintly green with moss and lichen. Light filtered in from ahead, where another gap stood like a doorway in the stone. It was truly an arch, rounded at the top, with clean edges. The light flickered softly off the surface of the stream, which trickled down a channel on the right-hand side of the doorway. The cave seemed familiar. It was the light; not moonlight at all, but the same leafy amber that glowed under the canopy of the goddess tree. Dennis went right up to the doorway and stopped dead, silhouetted by that light.

"Wow," he said, and stepped through.

We didn't have much choice but to follow.

This inner hall was even bigger, maybe twelve feet high and wide enough around to hold a large pool. And a mound of gold. Here was the pile of treasure we had all seen in our dreams: a waist-high jumble of coins, chains, bowls, plates, cups, daggers, and even two or three gleaming swords with jeweled hilts. But mostly it was chunks and shards of cut and broken gold. Heaps of it. Some was silver and some just plain, but mostly it was carved gold, embossed with scrollwork and scenes, a face here, an arm there, a boar's snout, half a tree, a bent lion, a circle of red jewels, three of them missing. As though whoever had piled it there hadn't really cared about it; just a bunch of scrap, glowing in the low, amber light from the pool.

We all moved toward it. Who wouldn't? We were hypnotized by the color, the shapes, the sparkle from each jewel and untarnished plate. Dennis stopped inches from the tumbled edge of the pile. A single small ring lay on the floor right at the point of his toe. He bent, reached down.

"Beorhtscyld, no!" Milde cried.

She was too late; he had it in his hand. "What?" he asked.

The light began to ripple and flow. The surface of the pool roiled. Water splashed over the lip of stone onto the floor of the chamber. And a creature boiled out at the edge nearest to us. It rose smoothly, shedding water, a tall, mottled, man-like thing with pebbled skin, sloped shoulders, a wide, triangular head. It crouched on the stone floor, regarding us with huge green eyes. Its pupils were dark slits. I thought at first it was the *ðyrs*, but it looked smaller, leaner, even crouching beneath that high stone ceiling.

Dennis threw the ring onto the pile and drew his sword. "What is it?" he asked.

"*Nicor*," Milde breathed. The water beast. She stepped to Dennis' sside, her weaving sword held across her chest.

"Hold, fearsome friends! You cannot blame it for being ugly," Dad said.

The beast sat back on its haunches and swung a sleek, pointed tail out of the water, draping it across its long hind feet. It made a rolling sound deep in its throat. Dad began to pluck his harp gently.

"Stop!" the beast growled, pointing at him. Its raised arm revealed a thin flap of skin from elbow to ribs. "Quiet your awful charms, *wight*. I know the sound of *galung-cræft*. Your songs have no power on me, ugly or not."

"Forgive me, proud one," Dad said, lowering his harp. "I mistook you for a *bealuwaru*, who meant us harm."

The beast made the rolling sound in its throat again. It was laughing. "Not I," it hissed. "The dweller in evil lives above, in day and night, singing songs more awful than yours. She is harm embodied, that one, but her old gods do listen to her and sing through her throat."

"They call that singing?" Dad exclaimed. "For such a crime they deserve such a throat! Though no one deserves to suffer her cruelty. The harm-hag holds my wife hostage."

The beast leaned forward on its forearms, like a cat, relaxed but ready to spring. Its shoulder blades rode high on its back, fringed with loose skin. Its belly splayed on the stone floor, swollen. Moving from the inside, as though its last dinner was still writhing in its gut. A silvery membrane flicked over its eyes and back. "Why? Can you tell me?"

"Only those evil can read evil minds," Dad replied. "The *dry-wicce* has some purpose she means to enact tomorrow midday, when the sun pauses to confront the unsmiling moon behind the shield of the earth. She plans some magic that requires my wife, and her brother."

"Sacrifice?" the beast asked.

"In the end, oh, yes. My wife is skilled in *run-cræft* and the song of living things. I fear the *dry-wicce* means to use her power to steal my wife's, but I know not how or why. Do you, great gray guard of the underground?"

The beast blinked again. "I have sensed her thoughts upon me and mine, but not their intent. Whatever it is can't be good for any but herself."

Dennis spoke, first bowing to the beast and sheathing his sword. "You are wise, water-king. We seek your leave to pass, so that we might free my friend's wife and troth-brother, and thus break the *dry-wicce's* purpose."

The beast turned its gaze toward Dennis. Milde stood taller. She didn't lower her sword or shift from Dennis's side.

"Is that why you took my ring?" the beast growled.

Dennis held out his empty hands. "It lay under my foot, wise one. Curious, I picked it up to admire its beauty. You see, though; I have returned it to your hoard."

"You are not without your own wisdom, *sweord-wight*."

"May we pass, then, cave-king? We must do what we can, before the night above becomes dawn."

The beast laughed again. "First call me rightly: queen, not king." The beast stood, revealing the huge bulge of its stomach and the smooth, low mound at its groin. It was a female, and it was pregnant. The surface of her stomach writhed as she moved

Dennis bowed again. "I am very sorry if I have offended you. I have never met one of your kin before."

"Not one of my sex, I agree," the beast replied, "and I was not offended."

"Then may we pass?" Dennis asked.

"You may try," the beast replied.

Dennis laid his hand on his sword hilt. "Must it come to that?"

I drew and nocked an arrow. The beast swiveled her gaze to me.

"Do you think you could kill me?" she asked.

"I could hurt you enough you'd regret it," I said.

"If it was me you had to fight, yes," she replied. Then she opened her mouth wide and made a sound that was half hiss and half roar.

Something answered from the passage behind her, and the *ðyrs* hulked into the chamber.

It stooped just inside the entrance, eyeing us. Its face was long and pointed, its eyes huge and green, its skin leathery and pebbled, like the water beast's. But it was bigger in every way. Its jaws bulged with bone and muscle. Boar-like tusks protruded from the corners of its mouth. Its head brushed the stone ceiling, even with its shoulders hunched. Its chest was broad and roped with muscle. Its arms hung past its knees, and ended in massive hands: blocky, almost square, with stubbed fingers. Stubs tipped with long claws.

"My mate is my shield," the waterbeast said. "Him you cannot harm, not while I live. Believe me, others have tried, time and again. For generations of your kind, we shared an old home across the sea, they and I, but you are smarter than those, I think." She inhaled deeply, taking our scent. "You have walked the road of the frost giants, beyond the marches of the Middle Earth. That interests me. I challenge you, then. Put away your iron and stone and wood; unsheathe your wits instead. If you best me, you shall all pass unharmed."

"Best you how, cave queen?" Dennis asked.

"Riddle me," she replied. "If I cannot guess, you may pass."

"And if you do guess?"

"Then I shall riddle you, and so it shall go, turn about until one loses, and dies."

"That could take all night!" I said.

"It well could," she replied.

"We don't have all night! My mother and unc—"

"Are not my concern!"

"What if we just go back the way we came?" Josie asked.

The water beast laughed. "How fast can you run? My mate loves the chase."

"I guess that means no," Josie said, in English.

"Yes, it does," the beast replied.

"There are five of us," I said. "Do we each get a chance?"

The beast nodded. "I like that challenge. Each of you may ask in turn; if any one of you can best me, all will live."

"You are most generous, hoard-keeper," Dad said. "We accept with joy. I will go first." He stroked a sweet chord and recited, "A creature came where there sat many men most wise. He had one eye and two ears, two feet and twelve hundred heads, one back and one belly, two hands, two shoulders, two arms on one neck and two sides. Now say his name."

The beast laughed. "I told you your songs were useless, one-eyed harper. Your riddle is also useless, and very weak. Do you think I know nothing of the ways of men? It is the one-eyed man selling garlic in a market." She turned her head to Dennis. "You next, swordsman."

He bowed. "As you wish, queen of caves." He stood tall

and chanted, like he was playing to a tent full of faire-goers. "Raven-black, I'm born to fly, but empty air kills me; I am bound to hard things. I travel flat ground. Oft times at my master's beck I climb on walls and trees, float upon leaves, and even walk beneath waves where the sky's eye can see me. In darkness I die. Who am I?"

"You recite well for one born to the sword," the beast said, "but you mistake the breadth of my wisdom. I have not always lived in this shadeless place. Newborn, I flew between the earth and sun and saw your riddle wing the ground beneath me. Shadow it is."

Dennis took a slow breath, and I was afraid he might draw and go for her. But he just smiled thinly and said, "You are indeed a font of knowledge."

"I'll go next," I said. I knew I was bad at riddling, but I had a crazy feeling there wasn't a thing on that Earth she didn't know, and a crazier hunch about how to stump her. There was no poetry in my riddle. I just blurted it out as it came to me. "Many men carry me, and women, too, in pouches and pants and bags and . . . and things. I make them grab and grope when I sing their favorite songs, then hug – no, kiss their cheeks as they tell me all their secrets. And nearby people frown. But I don't keep their secrets. I pass them on. The words, through the air, like tiny light-ning without light. What am I?"

The beast was silent, her face unreadable as a cat's. She stared at me for a long time. I stared back, trying not to think of the answer. I didn't dare look away, and I don't think I could have anyway. Her huge, green eyes held me. I was her mouse.

Finally she said, "You disappoint me. This is a thing of your own world, not a tool or a charm I could ever know."

"Can you answer?" Dennis asked.

"I need not even try," the beast said.

"You would make him answer riddles from your world, why can't he—?"

"He is on my world, in my home, speaking my tongue. And he will play by my rules." She stared at me again. "I will remember when it comes my turn to riddle you."

"If you get that turn," Josie said. "You haven't heard my riddle yet."

The beast swung her long face toward Josie. "I haven't, strange maiden, nor hers." She looked toward Milde. "Can you weave a riddle from your own world, loom-wife?"

Milde stood tall, like Dennis. "I would rather weave your shroud, cave beast," she replied, "but I will try." And she did a pretty good rendition of Josie's riddle about love.

When she finished, the beast nodded. "Your stern face hides a bruised heart; your riddle reveals an empty hearth."

"Is that your answer?" Dennis asked.

"No," she growled. "A long life with mate and son."

It was close enough. Dennis didn't try to argue. The beast turned back to Josie.

"It comes to you now, strange princess. Will you disappoint me as badly as did your consort? Can you leave the riddles of your own world behind?"

"You be the judge," Josie replied. "Alone on this world I see my queen, the green-eyed one, as she guards her hoard, dreams, swells, and awaits her meeting with Wyrd. In and out, up and down, side to side and straight through I watch the awe-filled lady. No one sees her as I do."

The beast blinked. After a long moment, she said, "A pile of polished gold."

"No," Josie replied. My heart raced.

"A mirror?" The beast asked.

"One answer!" Dennis cried.

"I know that, little swordsman," she hissed. "But I must hear the true answer."

"It's water, my queen," Josie said. "The mirror of the surface of your stream."

"Ah." The beast sighed. "Yes. It is. You may all pass." She turned back to Josie. "But first, dark-eyed stranger, you must kill me."

# *Chapter 24*

"What do you mean?" Josie demanded. "You couldn't answer my riddle. We won."

The beast rose to her full height. "I lost, but you have not yet won. The loser must die."

"That's crazy," Josie said. "Why?"

"That is how the challenge is won. You must kill me. If you do not, my mate will not let you pass."

I looked at the *ðyrs*, filling the way out. He was staring at Josie, unblinking.

"And when she kills you, he's just going to step aside and wave goodbye?" I asked.

She turned her green eyes on me. "Yes, he will let you leave here. He knows you have the honor. He knows it is time."

"Time for what?"

"Time for me to die." She took two gliding steps to the side of the hoard and held out her arms. Her bloated stomach writhed. "Do it now."

Josie stepped back. "I don't—"

"Do it!" the *nicor* roared, and the *ðyrs* lifted his huge hands to his ears and roared with her. The sound cut to my heart. It was rage and power, but mostly pain.

I raised my bow, drew, and loosed the arrow without thinking, desperate to stop the noise. It struck at the base of her breastbone. The broadhead point sliced through her leathery skin and the arrow plunged deep into her gut. She stopped roaring. The *ðyrs* stopped. There was no sound but the dripping of water. She sank to her haunches, arms still splayed wide.

"Ed!" Josie cried.

"Thank you, bowman," the *nicor* whispered.

Her stomach tore open, all the way to her groin, and a wriggling mass poured out onto the stone floor. Glistening, wet with blood and the remains of some shiny fluid and bits of membrane. I could make out heads and tails, impossible to count how many. Each one was a foot long, maybe two. Snake-like. Not guts, though. *Wyrms.* They were dark gold, tinged with green. Darker than their mother, but with the same green eyes. They wrapped around each other, knotting, pulling apart. Lunging. Fighting. Biting each other with tiny fangs. Tearing off chunks of flesh, eating it. Some were bigger, and they swallowed the little ones whole, head first, choking them down inch by inch, while even bigger ones tried to swallow them. They roiled and bit, spitting, hissing. One lashed against the piled gold, bringing down a small cataract of coins and scrap. It struck at the heap, attacking, biting, swallowing anything that fit into its mouth. And its mouth could open very wide. More of them came, attacking the gold and the one who had found it first and each other. Already dozens of them were gone, but the mass was no smaller. The remaining *wyrms* were swollen with their swallowed kin, and now with the gold. The little beasts grew with each mouthful. One reared up and began striking at the backs of the others. Another reared to face it, hissing. The first one spat, a shining, steaming spew that struck the challenger right in the face. It squealed and fell back, and its eyes poured from their sockets, dissolved by the spray of venom.

"I think it's time to go," Dennis said.

"Yes! Shosefina, come!" Milde cried.

I tore my gaze from the *wyrms* but Josie just kept staring. Milde and I grabbed her hands and dragged her after

Dennis.

Dad didn't move. He watched, swaying. His eye gleamed. "What a sight! Frige's sweet lips, what I wouldn't give for two eyes to see it. Who has witnessed such a thing and lived? I will tell this story, I will sing it!" He struck a loud cord and hopped in place.

I let go of Josie and ran back to grab his arm. "They'll never believe you," I said.

"I don't care," he replied, letting me drag him away. "I will sing it! I could not not sing it and still call myself *scop*."

The others were waiting just beyond the pile of gold. The *ðyrs* had sunk back against the wall of the cave, arms on its knees, head low, staring at the body of its mate. Its eyes were half closed, its mouth stretched wide in a silent cry. I glanced back and saw one of the *wyrms* slither into the gaping belly of the water beast. Another began to climb its outstretched arm, nuzzling at the crumpled fold of skin that hung from there to the ribs. It opened its mouth and began to feed. The *ðyrs* threw back its head and howled. Dennis dodged past it, squeezing against the opposite wall, only inches from the beast's angled knee. Milde went next, then Josie, then Dad. I took one last look. The *wyrms* had swarmed over their fallen mother. Her body trembled as they tore off larger and larger mouthfuls of her flesh. I swallowed bile and squeezed past the *ðyrs*, trying to shut my ears to its keening wail. It watched me pass, eyes filled with hate.

There was a short passage into a final room that stank of old garbage. The others were already leaving through another passage on the far side. I kicked through bones and slipped on something gooey, too firm to be turds, rotting meat from the smell of it. I gagged and ran faster. The next stretch was tall but narrow, hardly wide enough to fit the *ðyrs*. The light faded as we went farther in. I worried that we were heading deep into the side of the hill, but then the passage began to climb and suddenly we came back to the stream. It rushed down an uneven cascade and disappeared under a low slot that angled toward the hoard hall.

Dennis began to climb the rocks beside the stream. They were wet and treacherous, but they were the only way up. I held my bow against my side, as far from the spray as I could. The ceiling of the cave lowered and the light faded behind us. Soon, we were groping for hand-holds in near darkness. Now I was sure we were going the wrong way. The cave narrowed. The steps got higher. Dad was clutching his harp under his tunic. He slipped, but Josie and I caught him before he fell in. He hadn't even tried to catch himself.

Finally the sound of the stream changed, and the smell. We spilled out of the cave and into the night, into fresh air between the low walls of another ravine. Another few yards' scramble and we were in the woods, with the slope of the mountain rising before us.

We stopped, panting, soaked, shivering from the adrenaline rush. I couldn't get that last image out of my mind: the swarm devouring the body of the beast. The hateful stare of its mate.

But there was no time to think about it. We had to get to the wall before dawn. The trees were thick, the sky was still overcast, but the glow of the moon was well down the western sky. Dennis led us toward the top.

We stopped at the edge of the trees. Urien's fort seemed to float at the peak of the hill, black and dense. The sky and the ground were both deep gray, patched with dark hollows and holes of light. The place was dead silent. We waited a long, anxious time, watching, listening. There was no movement on the wall top, no glimmer of light beyond the sagging stones where the stream flowed out. Dennis gestured and led us around the curve of the cleared land, just inside the edge of the trees, until we spotted the broken wall top where we had first snuck a look inside. We waited again.

Everything was still but my heart was pounding, my mind racing. I remembered our first time here, how it had all gone wrong. I looked over at Milde and thought of her wound. And then of her family. Any one of us could die in the next hour.

I leaned toward her, touched her arm, and she turned sharply, frowning. My tongue stuck in my mouth, but it seemed like her frown was more a question. I swallowed and whispered, very faintly, "I'm sorry. About your baby. And your husband. I can't imagine how much it must hu —"

Her frowned deepened and she shook her head. "No. Not now." She turned away, but turned back and laid her hand on mine for just a moment. "Thank you, but now I need anger."

Then Dennis gripped my shoulder and breathed, "Go."

"Show no mercy," Milde whispered.

"For you will get none," Dennis added.

I gave Josie my bow and quiver, keeping only the one arrow – the gatekey. She leaned close and kissed my cheek.

"I'll be back for you in half an hour, tops," I told her.

"Just get them out," she replied.

Dad started to play the soft, rambling tune that could fool a watcher, and the two of us walked slowly toward the wall. It was all I could do not to stoop and scuttle as fast as I could, but Dad walked in time to his music. I forced myself to match his pace, step for step across the uneven ground.

No one called out. No spears flew to meet us. The moon didn't break through the clouds and shine like a search light from a prison tower. We reached the shadow of the wall in hardly a minute or two. My heart was pounding, my right hand was clamped around the arrow shaft. Dad changed his song, and I started to relax. After one verse, I even felt sleepy. I shook my head and bit my lip, waiting until he finished another full verse.

"Tell your mother I still love her," he whispered in English.

"She knows that, Dad," I replied.

"Tell her anyway. Now shut up and climb."

I did. It was easy enough, even with the arrow in my hand and the music trying to lull me to sleep. I stopped just below the top and peered over. The timber walkway along the inside of the wall was empty, and I started to scramble up. There was a snort. I froze. A guard was slouched in the shadow beneath the walkway.

A moment later he snorted again. And again. He was asleep and, lucky me, a snorer.

This was why I had insisted on coming in alone. Anyone else would have made enough noise to wake him up, even Josie. I blessed Dad for his music, and Uncle Alf for teaching me how to stalk game. I used every trick he taught me to slip onto the walkway and creep a dozen yards away before letting myself down to the ground inside the fort.

I went straight for the hut closest to the wall and ducked into the shadow beneath its low eaves. I was wide awake now, heart racing again. The camp was silent. I couldn't hear the guard's faint snoring or even the sound of Dad's music. I strained my ears, wondering where the other guards were, and if they were sleeping, too. I thought I heard footsteps on the other side of the fort. Then a horse whinnied softly. It was Bil, I was sure of it.

*Hush*, I begged. *Pretend I'm not here.*

I crept around the hut and across the short space to the next one. Still no sounds; even Bil stayed silent. I moved on to the next hut, and now I was at the edge of the open ground in the middle of the fort. Uncle Alf's bow shop – the hut Mom had come out of – was straight ahead of me. The moon was dipping lower, lighting the clouds all around with a silver-gray glow that made dark shadows. I listened again, staring through the tricky moon-glow at each dark doorway in the huts that ringed the center ground. Then I inspected the wall top, as much as I could see, and finally the gate. Nothing moved, but I couldn't believe the guards were all asleep. I *could* believe they were lying in wait for me, warned by some vision from Morgwydd. I stuck to the shadows, working my way around the ring of huts.

Finally I had one last gap to cross, and then I reached the broken shadows of Uncle Alf's workshop. I moved carefully, trying not to bump anything. It was only a lean-to, but he had laid it out just like his shop in the garage at home. For a moment I almost expected to find a real door in the wall of the hut, complete with a doorknob. Instead, there was a flap of hide over a rough doorway around the curved wall. I hesitated, slipped the arrow under my belt and slid it around to the back, out of the way. Then I drew my *seax*, crept to the doorway, and listened.

I heard the faintest whisper of music. Mom was humming the same tune that Dad was playing to keep the guards at the wall asleep. I lifted the flap, ducked inside, and immediately slid to the left along the wall, away from the doorway. Just like in the movies. Only, in the movies, there's never a guard sleeping against the wall. I stumbled over his legs and fell, choking on a curse. He startled awake and kicked out, still half under the spell. I came up on my knees, hampered by the arrow in my belt, but threw myself toward him, jabbing with the *seax*. It was dark, the only light a faint red glow from the remains of a fire on the hearth in the center of the hut. I cut his sleeve, but all that did was wake him up more. He fumbled with his hilt, trying get to his feet and draw his sword. I slashed the *seax* sideways and cut his hand. He cursed and sprang away. Then he was up and his sword was out, coming at me.

There was a rattle of chain and the guard jerked backward. He dropped the sword and clawed at his throat, trying desperately to shout. Uncle Alf towered behind him, hauling back on a gray, iron chain he'd slung around the guard's neck. His shackles; he'd turned them into a weapon. The guard kicked and thrashed, grunting, choking.

"Kill him!" Uncle Alf growled. "Quickly! Before he wakes someone!"

I hesitated. I'd struck at the guard in self defense, but this was different. Like murder.

The guard kicked backward and Uncle Alf almost fell. He jerked the chain. "Thunor's stones! Are you still a child?"

I jumped forward and rammed the *seax* into the man's chest. He was wearing heavy leather over thick wool. And I hit a bone. The blow jolted my hand. The guard squealed, twisting right and left. I pulled the *seax* out and stabbed again, as hard as I could. The blade slid between his ribs, but he kept twisting, and I had to lean in, prying the blade side to side beneath his ribs. Finally, I found his heart. He shook violently. His bowels let go with an awful stench. Then he went loose, hanging by his neck from the chain. Uncle Alf let the body drop.

"That's about time," he said. He leaned heavily against the wall, taking the weight off his bandaged legs. But he was standing, able to walk. That was key to our plan.

He held out his hands. "Did you bring something to open these?"

I was shaking, and not just from the effort. It's one thing to kill a man with an arrow from thirty yards away; it's another to struggle face to face, to strike again and again, to work at the knife. It was no wonder Dennis hadn't answered my question. I couldn't have answered it then. I still couldn't. But I dream that fight sometimes.

I took a deep breath and tried to sound calm. "Just my *seax*."

"Help your mother, then."

Mom. I hadn't seen her, hadn't thought of her since I'd tripped over the guard. I searched the darkness, and only found her by a faint reflection of the embers on her pale hair. A dark strip covered all of her face but her eyes, and they were closed. She had stopped humming during the fight. I hurried past the fading hearth, and her eyes opened as I reached her. They were circled with dark rings, exhausted. She was tied to the wall by thick ropes knotted to iron rings. Even her head was pinned back by the strip across her face, a wide leather strap that doubled as a gag. Morgwydd had stopped her from singing, but left one small hole for her to breathe. And to hum. The guard had paid for that oversight.

I drew my little knife and sawed at one end of the leather, hard work. It had been put on wet and shrank and hardened as it dried. I sawed and sawed until finally the strip parted and I could peel back the leather. She gasped in lungfuls of air. I started sawing at the ropes that bound her body, but she whispered, "*Lagu.*" Water.

"Here." Uncle Alf hobbled over with a bucket and a cup. I kept sawing at the ropes.

She drank three full cups, then let her head fall and rested. Uncle Alf pulled my *seax* from the dead guard, wiped it on the man's clothes, and helped me finish cutting the ropes. We let her down gently to sit with her back against the wall. I knelt in front of her.

"Thank you, Eadgar," she whispered. "That was well done."

"Yeah, well, it's done, but don't thank me till you're both back home. Can you walk?"

"Soon," she said.

"How soon?" I asked. "I have to get you out of here before dawn."

"I could walk now, slowly," she said, "but not far, not fast."

"You don't have to go far or fast. Just outside, so I have room to open the gate. I have the key." I turned and showed her the arrow in my belt.

"But where is your bow?" she said. "You must have a bow."

"Josie has it. I don't need a bow for this. I'm going to take you straight home, then come back for the others."

"Oh, Eadgar, this I did not foresee, or even imagine. You are too clever for me."

"It's Josie's idea, the best one we could come up with."

Mom shook her head. "We cannot go with Morgwydd still alive."

"We'll come back and take care of her later."

"No, it must be now, today."

"What do you mean?" I said. "With Urien and his men surrounding you?"

"Dawn brings the solstice. We cannot let her cast her spells."

"We'll come right back, only outside the walls."

"How?" Uncle Alf demanded.

"I can do it," I told him. "Dad taught me the right melody. I could bring us back right in Morgwydd's hut if I wanted to."

"Your father—"

"Hush, Brother!" Mom said. She took my hand. "Eadgar, I cannot risk leaving."

I jerked my hand free and stood. "You're crazy," I turned to Uncle Alf. "Tell her we have to get out of here now. Before Morgwydd turns you both into a blood sacrifice!"

Uncle Alf snorted, a bitter laugh. "She never listens to me, boy. You know that."

"Thunor's stones! Are you both crazy? Don't you realize—?"

"I realize she knows more about this than I ever will. I am a hunter, a bow-maker, not a *hægtesse*. If she says we must stay, then we must."

"Why?" I cried. "What's so important that you can't escape when you have the chance?"

Mom pulled herself to her feet, clinging to the wall. "I cannot say."

I almost lost it, only just managed to keep from shouting. "You mean it's like when Dad disappeared and you let me think he was dead? I'm still too young to understand? Well, you're too late. I know all about Dad now. He's waiting outside the wall, ready to come charging in if I don't get you out. He and Dennis and Josie and even Milde, who doesn't even know you. They're all ready to throw themselves at Urien's men in order to save your life. So you'd better tell me why they have to die for you, and it'd better be a good reason. Or are you going to pretend you can't talk, so you won't have to tell me anything you don't feel like saying?"

Mom reached for me again, but I stepped back. She let her hand fall.

"Eadgar, I cannot say because I do not know. The runes warn me of pain, great suffering, defeat if Morg-wydd lives this day. They hint that you must be here, with a bow. *Ear, eolh, wyn.* Eadgar, yew, joy. Every day for weeks. But they do not tell me why. Not even a hint. Go back to Josie and the others. Get your bow. But tell them this is not their fight."

"Too late, Mom. They've made it their fight. Morg-wydd didn't give them much choice. So either you come with me, or Dad starts playing a really nasty tune on that harp of his and Dennis leads the charge."

"*Doles!*" Uncle Alf growled.

"Yeah, I guess this place does that to you. I thought Dad had gone crazy, but you—"

"Hush!" Mom hissed again. "Listen!"

"What?" Uncle Alf turned to the door.

"Don't you hear it? Eadgar?"

I did hear it. Music. Dad's harp, faint but clear. A famil-iar tune: the song he'd played to drive the *ðyrs* from our campsite. Then we heard the roar of the beast itself.

# Chapter 25

The horses stamped and whinnied and began to charge around in their paddock. A rooster crowed. The *ðyrs* roared again, closer. The fort woke up.

There were shouts near the gate, replies from the huts around us, running feet. I couldn't hear Dad's music over the noise. Maybe he stopped when he realized it wasn't doing any good. I hoped he'd had the sense to run back into the trees, out of sight.

"What is it?" Uncle Alf growled.

"The *nicor*?" Mom said. "Could this be Morgwydd's weapon?"

"The nicor is dead," I said. "This is its mate, a *ðyrs*."

"It followed you?"

"She said it wouldn't, but— No, she just said it would let us leave. She never said it wouldn't come after us." I remembered the look it had given me. "It's probably hunting for me. It was Josie's riddle that won. Maybe if she'd killed it . . ." I shrugged. "What do I know?"

"You make no sense!" Uncle Alf muttered. He limped across the hut and took the dead guard's sword. "Now is when we need your bow."

"What about the one you were making?" I said. "Is it still—?"

"Urien has it."

"And Urien will be here soon to check on us, or Morgwydd will," Mom said. "Go, Eadgar, while the *Wealas* are confused and looking outward. This *ðyrs* may prove to be our ally. Go and find your bow, then wait and watch."

"Go quickly," Uncle Alf added. "Only Morgwydd kept Urien from killing you before. Now he has even less reason to love you." He toed the dead guard. "This was his son."

I suddenly felt queasy. I don't know what bothered me worse, that I'd just killed someone's son, or that the some-one was a professional warlord.

"Great," I muttered. "Just frigging wonderful."

"Careful how you use the Goddess's name," Mom said.

"Don't worry, she's on our side."

There was a sudden commotion at the wall: shouts, cries, the roaring beast.

Mom grabbed me in a fierce hug, then pushed me toward the doorway. "Go!"

The hug got me moving. I hugged her back, and even gave Uncle Alf a quick hug.

"Stay alive, damnit," I muttered. Then I hurried to the doorway and slipped past the hide.

The moon shadows had lengthened outside; the sky seemed lighter. The shouting and roaring continued. I heard a horse scream, the crack of wood splitting, and then the wild drumming of hooves as the horses broke out of their paddock and fled among the huts. It was enough to confuse anyone. But I could tell the *ðyrs* was coming from the same direction I had. I bolted in the other direc-tion, aiming for the shadows behind the next hut.

Bad choice. A guard ran right out of those shadows and nearly bowled me over. I pushed him away, grabbing for my *seax*. But it wasn't there. Uncle Alf still had it. The guard slammed his shield against me, and I stumbled back against the stone wall of the hut. He followed, shoving hard, pinning me to the stones with his shield. I tried to kick him, to shove back, to get out my little knife, but he held me off balance. His raised his sword for the blow.

Morgwydd saved me. She came around the hut with another guard, saw us, and shouted. I don't know what she said, but the sword didn't fall. It didn't go away either. The guard holding me almost froze in place. His eyes kept flicking from me to Morgwydd and back. He didn't like being noticed, I could tell. He just wanted to kill me and get over to the wall. Away from her. I'd have been happy to go with him.

The moonlight gave Morgwydd the face of a *scucca*, a shape-shifter. Her blue tattoos were black holes in her cheeks, deep grooves in her forehead. Her hair rose in a tangle of shadow and silver. Her eyes were empty, until they caught the light and flashed green as a hunting cat's. She strode over and grabbed my throat. Her fingers were thin, her nails sharp, and they dug in. She was strong and she was angry.

"You! The son! How came you back? You know your mother's charms? Answer me!"

I couldn't. Her fingers almost tore through my throat.

She laughed at my croaking gasps. "Poor little man. Afraid of pain? Afraid of me? Like your father, you come from a weak world. Good. I can use you, perhaps. When your mother pretends to be brave? She would let me kill her brother perhaps, but not you. No, she showed her fear for you the last time she opened her mouth. After such long silence, all to save you, the one she will not sacrifice. You will be my bait."

"Bait for what?" I gasped.

She smiled. Her teeth were small and yellow in the moonlight. She looked ready to bite. "For what comes after," she said. "After you, and all your clan. The beast you cannot kill or turn aside. The plague to drive you back into the sea."

"The *nicor*?"

Morgwydd shook her head. "This is no riddle, *Angle*." She twisted the word into a curse. "You will know it when you see it; then you will fear and die. All of you!"

She shouted something to her other guard, and I picked out one word: Urien. The guard hurried toward the commotion at the wall.

All the noise came back, as though Morgwydd had turned down the volume while she paused to toy with me, then turned it back up so life could go on, in all its fury. There were cries and yells coming from the wall, screams, a terrible shriek that stopped cold. A tremendous crash shook the whole fort. Rocks fell, wood splintered. A body sailed through the darkness and smashed against the hut across the center ground, sprawled onto the dirt, lay still. The guard holding me flinched, then pressed in on his shield all the harder, till I could barely breathe.

And there was the *ðyrs*, a dark bulk looming among the huts. It had broken in. Urien's men surrounded it, stabbing with their spears, hacking at its legs with their swords. And bouncing off. It brushed them aside and came toward us. The guard Morgwydd has sent for Urien screamed a battle cry and rushed into the melee. The *ðyrs* kicked him aside like a yappy dog. The warriors fell back. I saw Urien among them, bronze helmet glinting. He bellowed commands and his men split into teams. Some attacked the beast again, others raced around the huts to either side, to head off the beast before it reached the center ground. It paused at the opening and turned its head, nose raised, as though it was scenting the air. It's huge head swung toward me, and the hairs shivered on the back of my neck. It had found me. Its eyes gleamed as bright as Morgwydd's.

Morgwydd met its gaze. She stepped toward it, into the full light of the moon. Cried something in her thick, lilting tongue. The warriors stared at her. Urien hesitated, glaring, then motioned them back. The beast watched her, head lowered like a bull about to charge. Morgwydd began to sing.

The song clawed at my guts. It wasn't like the repelling charm that Dad had used to drive the *ðyrs* from our camp. I don't think it was the charm that she'd used on the little pig, either. Whatever it was, the *ðyrs* hated it. It growled and dug its fist into the thatch on the hut beside it, then wrenched a huge handful free and threw it toward us. The thatch flew in a spray, a big wad of it thudding against the lean-to roof of Uncle Alf's shop. The roof collapsed with a crash. Morgwydd only sang louder. The *ðyrs* shook its head and growled back. It took a step toward us, tried to turn aside, noticed Urien and his men and bent low, roaring. Even Urien stepped back.

The *ðyrs* turned back to us and took another step. Morgwydd held out her arms. It took another step, shuffled sideways, resisting her. But its head sank lower, its growls softer. Another step, and another, and now it was right beside Mom's hut. Morgwydd pulled off her brooch. The beast laid back its head and howled. It swung wildly at nothing, battering the air. One fist glanced the wall of Mom's hut, and the little building trembled. A stone fell loose. The roof shifted. I could hardly breathe, watching. Morgwydd raised her hand with the brooch, and the beast raised its hand above the hut. The guard holding me took half a step back.

I shoved the shield with all my strength, screaming, and the guard fell back, off balance. I lunged, knocked him over, and stumbled toward Morgwydd.

"Hey, *ðyrs!*" I shouted. "Here I am!" I waved, standing right behind her. If he was going to come to her, let him come mad. Mad enough to go right through her to get me. "I killed your lover, *ðyrs!* You want me, come get me!"

It wanted me. It lurched to its full height, eyes fixed on mine. It bellowed, the sound rising to a howl. I turned and ran.

It howled again. I glanced back and saw it coming. Morgwydd leaped aside. The guard was scrambling to his feet, and the beast went over him like a steamroller. Coming for me and only me. I dodged around the next hut.

As if she'd seen me running, Mom started singing. The song of the gatekey rose from her hut. And I thought, *Crap, I can't sing and run at the same time!* But the beast roared again and the warriors shouted, and I didn't have any choice but to try. I was panting for breath but I sang. As loud as I could. Running in time to the music. Double-time. Moonwise around the huts. Maybe the direction didn't matter; I didn't care, I just ran. The arrowhead began to glow, shining faintly from behind my head, into the corners of my eyes. I reached around back and grasped the lower end of the shaft with my right hand. The edges of the feathers scratched my palm. I couldn't pull the arrow out like that, but the arrowhead flared. I could feel the warmth at the back of my neck, see the glow on the huts as I ran by. The gate cracked open in front of me.

A warrior suddenly appeared from between the two huts on my left, trying to cut me off. The beast roared again and threw a roof pole that twirled past my head and crashed into the hut beside me. A bale's worth of loose thatch pelted my back. The warrior slashed wildly with his sword, but I was just ahead of him, at the gate, racing through – two, three, five, ten paces into the cold, glittering path between the worlds. I stopped singing, and the gate crashed closed behind me. I slowed, gasping.

A howl rose behind me, pain and rage. I glanced back, and there was the *ðyrs*, outlined by the star we had just fled, bleeding from the stump of its tail. The closing gate had chopped it off as clean as a cleaver.

And he wasn't alone. The warrior had come through, too. He was staring back at the beast, just like me, but then he turned around and his face twisted in hate. He shouted and shook his sword; a challenge, an insult, I didn't know and didn't care. I turned and ran away. Roaring, the beast came after us.

I went toward the closest star, but felt it resist right away. I veered off and ran toward the star that felt the most familiar. I reached back and gripped the arrow again, started singing. Not loud, I didn't have the wind for that, but I held the tune and mouthed the words, knowing I wouldn't have time to stop and catch my breath when I reached a world that would let me in.

I saw the gate begin to form while I was still a long way off, the glowing line that could mean my salvation, if only I could squeeze through quickly. If only I could stay far enough ahead of the warrior and the *ðyrs*. It was hard to run with my right arm twisted back to hold the arrow, hard to breathe and sing, but I tried to run faster. The bright star of the world grew bigger as I got closer. The gate lengthened. I could see three brighter spots within the glow of the world, sky iron linked to the arrow head. I focused on the closest, sang harder, felt a slight resistance disappear, a faint breeze fade. Then the gate tore open and I charged through.

Into flames. I screamed and jumped, more shocked than hurt, and sprawled onto grass in darkness lit by bright firelight. I heard a bellow from the warrior. And a roar right behind him as the *ðyrs* barged through the closing gate and into the fire. Then a chorus of screams all around me. I scrambled to my feet in a ring of frightened, fire-lit faces. With Elizabethan hats, balloon sleeves: the bright, modern costumes of a renfaire. It was the final night, the bonfire. I had really crashed the party.

The *ðyrs* howled and kicked, scattering flames and embers into the crowd. People shrieked and ran. Others quailed, frozen in fright. A few idiots – men and women both – drew their rapiers and daggers and stood their ground. The warrior stared in shock at the new threat. Then he spotted me. He made a quick slash at the nearest re-enactor, easily knocking the rapier from his hand. The fool at least had the sense to flee. I did, too.

I ran behind the vendor tents and dodged through the patch of trees toward the walkways and stalls in the main concourse. Horses whinnied and blew in the stalls beyond the grandstand as they caught scent of the *ðyrs*. People were still yelling and screaming, but I could hear the warrior's feet beating on the packed dirt of the walkways, chasing me. It was almost as if I'd been transported back to the fort. But I knew the fairgrounds, and Urien's man didn't. It was dark outside the circle of firelight. There was no moon here. There were places to hide.

I cut between two small buildings, circled back, ducked through one of the small exhibit halls, and came out on the other side. The grandstand loomed ahead of me across a short open field. I went for it. I was halfway there when the warrior spotted me, but he was several stalls and a field of grass back. I dodged around the corner of the grandstand, vaulted the railing, and scooted between a row of seats to one of the aisles. Then up to the top and out, onto the exit stairs and back down on the outside, as quietly as I could, half falling. There was a landing at the bottom, with a door beneath it, a door that led into the guts of the grandstand: bathrooms, a taproom, a kitchen, and more than one storeroom. The only light in there came from the faint glow of a microwave and an exit light inside the taproom. I banged my way through the stools and tables and into the kitchen. It was even darker there. Another door led out on the opposite side. I made for it and slipped into deep shadow. Stopped. Crouched beside the doorway, winded, trying to listen for pursuit through my panting breath, my own wild heartbeat.

Someone giggled.

I spun, banging a pot that clattered like an oil drum.

Another giggle, then a voice. "I'm over here, my little page. Did you get it?"

A girl. I knew the voice, but I couldn't put a face to it.

"Shhh!" I hissed.

Again the giggle, and a stage whisper. "Don't worry, they're all at the bonfire. It's just you and me." Her voice was slurred. She'd been drinking, but I realized who it was.

A rustle, a click, and a light came on. Her cell phone, right in my eyes but I knew it was Gail Silverton. And she knew it was me.

"Don't be shy, my Eadugar," she said, "my big little knight in shining armor."

I just gaped at her. I don't know what surprised me more; that she was talking like she'd expected me, or that she had a cell phone at the faire. Dennis would have been ripped. Then she sat up, laid the cell phone in her lap, and held out her arms. Her gown fell back off her shoulders and I forgot about Dennis. The lacings were undone down to her waist. Her skirts were a jumble around her thighs. The cell phone lit her tight belly, the underside of her breasts.

"Come on, I'm not going to bite you," she said. "I'm just thirsty again."

I didn't know what to say.

"Didn't you get it?" she asked. She pulled the front of her gown together and pouted. "You must not love your lady very much."

She was right, I didn't. I thought, *You're not the Gail I know*, but even as the thought came, I realized that I didn't really know Gail Silverton, not any of them. Yes, they were beautiful, but the little I had seen beyond that didn't really appeal to me. Except for Milde.

"Look," I began, "I'm not exactly who you—"

Someone stumbled into the taproom and pushed through the furniture toward the kitchen. I froze. Gail looked at the door with a puzzled face, then giggled again and crossed her arms over her breasts.

"Oops," she whispered, grinning, "let's hope it's not the king, or it's off with your head."

I searched madly through the gloom for some kind of weapon and snatched up the pot I'd knocked over. It was a big, deep one, with two handles. I squeezed back against the wall, pot raised, ready to crack whatever skull came through the doorway.

He started speaking out in the kitchen. "I'm back, my lady," he whispered hoarsely. And he came bowing through the doorway, holding out a bottle.

I lowered the pot, totally blown away. Despite all the Gails, I had never expected this.

It was me.

# *Chapter 26*

He – me – strode to her and fell to his knees. "My quest has not failed," he said. "I come bearing mead, my uncle's finest." He pulled out the cork and sniffed at the top. "Ah, sweet nectar of the bees!" He handed her the bottle.

Gail took it mechanically, eyes flicking from him to me and back. I'd never seen anyone look more confused. I – he didn't notice. He began to unlace his jerkin – just like my new one – babbling about how easy it had been, with everyone at the bonfire and some kind of fight or something, everyone shouting, running around, a perfect distraction.

Finally he looked up at her face. "What is it?" he said. "What's the matter?"

She shook her head. "Jesus! Am I that drunk?" She looked at me and him again. "What's going on? Did you put something in the wine? Some kind of drug or something?"

"What?" he exclaimed. "What are you—?"

She tried to pull her gown back up and clenched what she could across her breasts. "Acid or something? A rape drug?"

"No! Why would you think—?" He followed her gaze, and there I was. He looked as confused as she did.

"Who in hell are you?" he cried. "What are you doing here?"

How do you answer questions like that from yourself?

"It's a long story," I told him, "and you wouldn't believe it anyway." To Gail I said. "He didn't try to drug you; he idolizes you too much. He's a bad liar, too; you'd know."

"Wait a minute!" he said. "Where do you get off with that . . . that crap!" He lurched to his feet. "Just get out of here!" His hand fell on the pommel of a short sword hanging from his waist, a falchion, maybe one of Dennis's.

"Don't worry, I'm going. Just be quiet, okay. Close the cell phone and stay out of sight. There are some very—"

There was a noise out in the taproom.

*Frige help us*, I prayed. "Hush! The phone! Off!"

Too late. It was the warrior, and he barged across the taproom, scattering chairs and tables. I just had time to back against the wall before he charged into the small room, shield high, sword ready. He must have been half crazed by all the strangeness. He shouted something at the Eadgar he could see and raised his sword. I swung the big pot against his head.

He staggered and spun quickly, swinging blindly at the source of the pain. His sword split the pot like tin foil, tore the pieces from my hands, and nearly split my chest. I jumped back, grabbing for anything I could throw: jars, cans, a sack of onions. He took them on his shield and came toward me.

Gail woke up. She grabbed her sword – a slender rapier, still in its sheath, belt dangling – and lunged at the warrior's side. His thick leather tunic took the brunt of the blow, but he yelped and swung at her wildly. Sheath and rapier broke, flew out of her hand. He struck again, backhanded. She lurched away but his blade slit her upper arm. Blood sprayed across her gown, and my other self. He jumped in front of her, fumbling for his falchion as the warrior raised his sword again.

I yelled in *Anglisc*. "Urien's turd! Morgwydd's dog! I'm the one you want!"

It startled him enough that he paused. He looked more closely at me, then back at the other me. I stepped sideways, thinking to turn him away from the others, and bumped against a fire extinguisher hanging by the door. I jerked it from its bracket and a fire alarm began to blare. That really startled him. He looked up toward the sound, and I yanked the pin and shot a spray of chemical foam into his face.

He fell back, flailing his sword, trying to get his shield in front of the spray. I dodged the sword, kicked the shield away, and kneed him in the groin, still spraying his face. He stumbled to his knees, gagging, just as the extinguisher gave out. So I clubbed him with the canister, again and again, until he finally dropped and lay still.

I stood over him, panting. Ready to club him again. When he didn't move, I stomped on his hand as hard as I could, then took the sword from his wrecked fingers and threw it into the kitchen.

"Jesus," the other me said. "Who are you?"

I thought he might believe me now, but I didn't try to tell him. He was kneeling by Gail, gripping her arm to stop the bleeding, without much success. She was staring at nothing, shivering; in shock I guess. I drew my knife and cut a strip from the bottom of her dress, and together with my other self, wrapped the wound as tightly as we could. He took her hand and held it, and she turned her head and threw up. He used his new jerkin to wipe her chin.

"You know," I whispered, "Gail is really pretty and really brave – maybe too brave when she's drunk. I mean, I know you weren't trying to get her drunk, but I think she . . . But I think there may be somebody who actually loves you for more than Uncle Alf's mead."

"What the hell are you talking about?" he demanded.

"Josie."

"Josie?" he said. Josie who?"

"Josie Mayer. Who do you think?"

He looked at me like I was crazy. "I don't know any Josie Mayer," he said. "I don't know any Josie at all. Look, forget this Josie, we've got to help Gail."

I just stared at him. The world, his world, suddenly felt

totally wrong. Forget Josie? I couldn't imagine me without Josie.

"Never mind," I said. "Just stay here. There'll be help coming soon, what with this damn alarm. I've got to get out of here."

"But what about Gail's arm?" he said. "What about him? What if he wakes up?"

"Tie him up before he comes to. And tell the police he speaks something like Old Welsh."

"What?"

"Old Welsh. Look, just make something up. I've got to get out of here, before the *ðyrs* finds us."

"The *thoorse*? What the hell—"

"Ask Uncle Alf!" I snapped. "If you live through the night. Now shut up and lay low. And pray you don't smell like me, too."

I grabbed the bottle of mead and sprinkled it all over him and Gail and the rest of the place, then splashed it behind me as I made my way out of the taproom. He started cursing, but I didn't stay to explain. All I could do was try to protect them. And that meant I had to find the *ðyrs* and lead it back through the gate before it caught his scent. Or killed someone else. I tossed the empty bottle back into the taproom and slunk quickly down the dim hallway to the other exit, so the *ðyrs* would have a clear trail to follow.

It was a good thing I did. As I reached the doorway, I glanced back, and there was the beast, lit by the red exit sign inside the taproom. It was turned half sideways, bent low, snuffling at the linoleum floor. It barely fit through the narrow hallway. The light glinted off its tusks. I swallowed hard. It looked huge. Quietly, I reached behind me and pulled the arrow from beneath my belt. Gripping it tightly in my sweaty hand, I began to sing the song of the gatekey.

The *ðyrs* must have had a bloodhound's nose. It looked up, saw me, and snarled. I turned and ran out onto the field.

The alarm was still blaring and sirens wailed in the distance. The arrowhead was already glowing. I didn't sprint. I went fast enough to get some distance from the exit, but slow enough to keep my breath and sing clearly. When the beast reached the doorway, it howled and rushed at me, still bent over, almost galloping on all fours, claws tearing chunks of sod from the mowed field. I curved away, moonwise. The gate began to form in front of me. I sang faster, wishing Mom and Dad where there to help, fighting hard not to flee in panic. There would be time for that later. I lowered the arrowhead, and the gate began to open. Cold poured through the widening slit in the night.

Then someone yelled, "Stop!"

It was the cop, Officer Quincy or his version on this planet. Drawing his gun. Running across the field toward me. I couldn't warn him; I didn't dare stop singing. But he wasn't yelling at me; he'd seen the *ðyrs* and was trying to draw it away. The beast ignored him. It wanted me. The cop stopped, took aim, and fired.

The *ðyrs* didn't even slow down. It snorted and slapped its shoulder, as if it was swatting a fly. The cop fired again, and now the beast slowed, swatting again. It saw the cop, saw the flash of his next shot, and slapped at its head, roaring in pain. That drew the beast all right. It charged the cop, swatting the next shots like it was fighting a swarm of bees. Its last swat was a roundhouse blow that knocked the cop fifteen feet away. Gun, hat, and shoes went four directions. Poor Quincy landed in a heap, bent almost in half.

Just as the gate opened wide. I could see the cold road, the black darker than night, the millions of stars. The way out of there. I stood at the entrance, cold washing around me, singing, holding the gate open while the arrow vibrated in my palm. Waiting until the beast turned, roared again, and came at me.

I jogged through the gate, still singing, still holding it open, watching behind till I could see the *ðyrs* on the other side, silhouetted in the opening. It took one step through, and I stopped singing. I lowered the arrowhead. The gate hovered open a moment longer and slammed shut.

I had waited a moment too long. The beast howled in pain, but only its arm had been caught by the closing gate. And it, of all things, wasn't chopped clean off. The slit held it. The arm seemed to end at nothing, just a faint ridge of black at the shoulder. Blood seeped around the edges. The beast howled and danced, jerking against the trap. I didn't know how long it would hold him and I didn't wait to find out. I took off running, singing again, racing toward my mother's world.

I hadn't gone a dozen steps when I heard the beast cry out in agony. I looked back, and it was kneeling before the star that was so much like my own. Its right arm was gone. Blood leaked from its torn shoulder. But it was watching me, and it staggered to its feet, snarling. It clamped its left hand over the wound and lurched after me. I was so tired from all the running, but at least I knew I could outrun it now. I kept jogging, kept singing. I saw the star and it grew closer, brighter, widening far faster than each step should have taken me. I pointed the arrowhead, paused and squinted into the glare. There were the points of light, there was Morgwydd's green ring. I aimed just to its right. The slit appeared, grew into a gate, opened before me. I stepped through.

But I had missed. I was halfway down the mountain, beside the stream, at the mouth of the ravine.

I was still singing, though. The gate was still open. I could go back through, adjust my aim, and come out at the top. Dawn had broken, but the sun hadn't topped the horizon. I still had a little time. I turned back to the gateway. And there was the *ðyrs*, stepping through, silent now, stalking me.

I shut up and jumped back. The gate closed with a crash. But the beast was through, and too frigging close for comfort. Time to panic.

I managed not to, but I turned and ran like I had, up

the ravine, which I knew would get steeper and rougher and narrower, harder and harder for the one-armed *ðyrs* to manage. Maybe it would fall. Maybe it would bleed to death in just a few steps. Maybe not, but if I could make it to the cave, it would have to crawl, and then I'd be all right. I hoped.

It didn't bleed to death. It may have fallen once or twice; I didn't look back to check – I would have fallen myself if I'd tried. I didn't have to look back. I could hear it growling and moaning behind me. It was still there when I reached the mouth of the cave. I splashed madly into the stream and squeezed through the low, slanted opening. I was on my hands and knees by the time I reached the chamber inside. I paused for a second to catch my breath. My heart was pounding, but I could still hear the beast moaning over the sound of the stream. I peered back. The opening was completely blocked by the huge bulk of the beast. Inch by inch, it was forcing its way through.

"Thunor's stones!" I yelled. "Don't you know when to quit?"

It snarled and inched forward, grasping with its one hand. One set of claws was more than enough.

I swore again and ran for the next doorway. It was still lit from within by the leafy amber glow of the goddess light. I paused, but there was silence inside, near as I could tell over the sound of the water. The light rippled with the movement of the stream. I crept through and pressed back against the stone wall, watching for snakes.

There was only one left alive. No trace of the others or their mother. The thing was twenty feet long at least, and four feet wide, draped across the remains of the hoard, still eating. Still growing. Not a snake now, truly a *wyrm*. A dragon. Its head was low and broad, like its mother's, but much longer. As I watched, its mouth opened wider than my body. A spew of not flame but steaming venom sluiced out onto the small jumble of gold and silver and weapons left from the huge pile. The metal boiled and shifted, softening. And the *wyrm* began to eat it, all but the iron blades of the swords and daggers. They blackened and pitted, shedding their gold hilts and jeweled pommels into the *wyrm's* maw.

I slid right, toward the stream, thinking I could slip in and make my way to the other end of the chamber. But as soon as my foot touched the water, the light rippled and flickered on every surface of the cave. The wyrm stopped eating. It raised its head and scanned the room. Its huge green eyes found me.

# *Chapter 27*

I froze, but the *wyrm* had seen me. Its eyes gleamed. Its head rose on a tapered neck, mouth opening. Fangs lined its jaws, top and bottom. Flaps of skin twitched along its back, and it started toward me, a biting stench simmering from deep in its throat.

Then the *ðyrs* lurched through the doorway, reaching for me with its remaining hand. I stumbled back into the water, holding out the arrow like a sword, my only defense. The *ðyrs* roared and swung its claws at my head.

The *wyrm* struck at the *ðyrs*.

I dove into the water.

The stream was shallow, and I slammed onto the stone bed with enough force to knock the wind out of me. I got in one kick, then had to surface. I pushed my head above the water, tried to breathe in, to restart my lungs. The *ðyrs* was screaming. I went under again and pulled myself along a few more feet, but I had no air, no energy to drive my muscles. The arrow slipped from my right hand, and I only just caught it by one white feather as the current twirled it around and tried to snatch it downstream. I came up gasping, finally able to breathe again.

The *ðyrs* was still screaming. The *wrym* had it by the wounded shoulder, but the *ðyrs* still had one arm, and it was nine feet tall and muscled like an ox. It beat at the *wyrm's* head, clawed at its eyes with its free hand, raked its neck with its feet. The *wyrm* twisted, trying to wrap a coil

253

around the *ðyrs*. It had no legs, no claws, but its long fangs were thrust deep into the body of the struggling *ðyrs*. And it had venom. Its neck swelled. The bulge rippled upward under its gleaming scales, and burning fluid poured out around the *ðyrs's* body. The *ðyrs* shrieked.

I couldn't watch any more. I pulled myself out of the water and ran for the far side of the chamber, though the doorway that led out and up, past the cascading stream, slipping on the wet rocks, cracking my shins, tearing my free hand in a mad scramble to get out and away and back into the open air. I ran, stumbling in the dim light; ran all the way out of the ravine and fell to my knees beneath the trees, gasping in the cool, fragrant air, fighting down dry heaves. It was dead silent outside. No breeze, no cries from above or below. Not even a birdcall. But the light was brighter. The sky to the east showed the edge of dawn. I heaved myself to my feet, still panting, and began to climb the hill as quickly and quietly as I could.

It seemed to stretch endlessly upward, an unbroken slope of trees, brush, and rough ground. Finally I glimpsed the wall and stumbled to the edge of the clearing. I leaned against a tree to catch my breath, peering from behind the trunk. There was a guard on the wall top where the stream came through, another guard maybe a hundred feet along toward the gate, and another the same distance the other way. I slipped through the trees toward the low place where I'd gone over, but the top of the wall there was a wreck, a wide vee of earth and timber torn down and scattered in a jumble on the ground around it. One of Urien's men stood on either side, and a third right in the middle. The *ðyrs* had really screwed up our plan. It and my stubborn mother. Getting in wasn't going to be easy. I had to find the others, get my bow from Josie.

Josie. My heart skipped when I remembered what my other self had said.

I slipped deeper into the woods and tried to guess where they would have gone. Assuming they hadn't been captured.

A glimpse of white flitted at the edge of my vision. I spun, backed against the tree, holding out the arrow. I drew my little knife.

*Dook dook.*

Egili came bounding toward me, eyes bright. I almost laughed in relief. I knelt, dropping the arrow and knife so I could catch him in my arms.

"Hush, little friend," I whispered. He scrambled up my chest and touched his pink nose to mine. I squeezed him till he squirmed out of my grasp and plopped back to the ground. At once, he bounded away, then paused to look back at me, waiting. I heard Dad's harp, sounding almost like a distant hail through the trees. I picked up the arrow, sheathed my knife, scooped up Egili, and hurried toward the sound.

They were tucked in a copse of beech saplings: Dad, Dennis, Milde. But no Josie. Egili squirmed free and scampered down my legs and over to Milde, *dooking* happily. Dad stopped playing. Milde hugged Egili, but she was smiling at me.

"A happy return," she said, I think to both of us.

"Meager words for such joy," Dad said. He threw his arms around me, banging my back hard with his harp, and squeezed me so tightly I couldn't lift my arms to hug him back.

"Thanks," I muttered. "Where's Josie? Is she okay?"

Dad let me go, beaming. "She is indeed. She keeps high watch on the death-hag and her lackeys. And, I doubt not, spares more than half an eye for you."

"She's alone? Where?"

"Up that tree," Dennis said, pointing toward the top of a tall oak. "Don't worry, your bow's safe. They'd have to go through us to get it." That didn't really make me feel any better.

"What of the beast?" Milde asked.

"Dead," I said. I gave them an edited version, mostly about the *ðyrs*. I didn't want Josie ever to hear that she wasn't on that other world.

255

"I knew you would come back," Milde said. "You are too quick for any *Wylisc* dog."

"What about the *wyrm*?" Dennis asked. "Do you think the *ðyrs* might have killed it?"

I shook my head. "Not a chance."

"Let's hope it's enough of a snake that it likes to sleep a few days between meals."

"At least until we're through here," I agreed. "What's the plan now? It looks like the whole wall is lined with guards."

"Not so many," Milde said. "The *ðyrs* killed a handful. It was wonderful."

"The enemy of my enemy," Dad said, smiling grimly.

"But we'll never surprise them now," I said. "And Mom and Uncle Alf are still in there. Mom wouldn't come. She insisted she had to be there when Morgwydd started casting her spells, or whatever she's going to do. And me; Mom says I have to be there."

"Why?" Dennis asked.

"She doesn't know. She thought maybe the *nicor* or the *ðyrs* had something to do with it, but they're dead, so maybe we're all just wasting our lives." I threw up my hands. "It's all in the runes with her, and you know how clear they can be. *Ear, eolh, wyn.* That's what they keep showing her."

"Eadgar, yew, joy," Dad said.

"Or death, bow, Whelan, or who knows what combination!" I slapped the nearest tree angrily. "I need my bow. I can take out a few of the guards, then we go in."

"Not yet," Dad said. "If Alrun says wait, we wait."

"Till when?" I demanded. "Till Morgwydd sticks a silver knife in her throat?"

"Till she gives us a sign," he said.

"How's she going to that when we're out here and she's hidden behind that wall?"

Dad struck a quiet chord on his harp. "We'll know," he said. And he was smiling, like a smug nun bragging about her faith.

"Woden's frigging eye! Are you completely blind!" I would have said a lot more but Josie came down the tree. She rushed over and threw her arms around me, then stepped back quickly, before I had time to hug her back. Milde, Dad, and Dennis were all grinning.

"Ed's right," Josie said. "We need to get inside now. They're setting up stakes by the well." All the grins disappeared. "Urien just came out of Morgwydd's hut and ordered two of his men to start digging holes. When they started to plant the first pair of stakes, I figured they were for Alrun and Alf. We have to get closer now."

"We're not going to do that without killing everyone inside," I said. "Not in daylight. They're all wide awake and on the alert."

"Oh, we can get some of us in," Dad said, "with the right diversion." He stroked an ugly chord that made Egili hiss. Dennis put him in his pouch and slung it over his shoulder.

"You'll hear us coming, with a warband at our back," Dad explained. He was still playing, and I could almost see the mass of horses and tall spears. "Wait till Urien's men leave their posts, and don't be surprised by anything you hear or see, now or later."

He and Dennis snuck off through the trees.

Josie held out my bow and quiver. I slid the gatekey into the quiver, then squeezed her hand for just a moment, trying to come up with a thank-you that meant as much as I felt. I couldn't find any words, but she squeezed back and it was good. I put on the quiver, took the bow and braced the bowstring, and was ready as I could be.

We moved to the edge of the woods and waited. It seemed for hours, though it couldn't have been more than fifteen minutes. Finally we heard a faint sound in the distance. Not music, but horses, a lot of them, coming up the path from the road. The warriors turned toward the sound. A low cloud of dust rose beyond the gate, and one of the warriors there called out. The men on the wall dropped from view or hurried along the scaffold toward the gate. All but one: the warrior stationed in front of us at the broken gap in the wall. He turned away, craning his neck to see between the huts, but he didn't go.

"*Cwead!*" Milde muttered. Crap. "You will have to shoot him, Eadgar."

I'd been worrying about the same thing. But there was no other way. I nocked an arrow.

"Would you like us not to watch?" Josie asked quietly.

"No, that'd just make it worse," I told her. "I can either do it or I can't."

I drew and loosed quickly, not daring to think about it, and the arrow went true. The warrior stumbled forward, back arching as the shaft drove through his leather armor. He fell out of sight without a sound, and I didn't have time to worry about how I felt.

Milde was already racing across the open ground, weaving sword drawn. Josie was right behind her, ax in hand. Milde hurtled the wall and Josie vaulted it. They were inside before I even reached the ditch. I heard a moan, a thud, then silence. I peered over just in time to see Milde slit the man's throat. His head was already dented and bloody. Josie was scanning the huts and lanes, making sure no one had seen or heard us. Keeping her back to Milde's work.

I stepped over the broken wall and joined them. Milde wiped and sheathed her knife and I nocked another arrow. Then she and Josie dragged the body around the hut and out of sight inside, while I kept watch. Milde went back for his spear and tossed it in with the body. We could still hear the horses and see the dust. And now there was the sound of men shouting in *Anglisc*. Then Urien's voice, shouting in his own language. We slipped behind the next hut just as two warriors hurried along the scaffolding on the other side of the fort, back to cover the rear. If they'd looked our way, they would have seen us easily through the gaps between the huts. But they didn't, and they were on the opposite side from where we'd come in. They didn't notice the missing guard. As soon as they were out of sight, the three of us scooted around the hut and in through the doorway, dropping the flap behind us. We were one row of huts away from the center ground, with a clear view of the well, Morgwydd's basin, and three tall stakes sticking head-high from the packed dirt. Within easy striking distance.

We were just in time. Morgwydd began to sing. Harsh and high, almost a screech, in a tune full of twisted notes that made your heart wince. Milde dropped her sword and covered her ears. My stomach turned queasy. Josie closed her eyes and began to hum a sweeter tune, some lullaby that made Morgwydd's voice easier to bear. After the first verse, Milde joined in. I swallowed hard and kept down the bile.

When Morgwydd finally stopped, the sound of horses had stopped, too. There were more shouts from the gate, angry commands from Urien. Morgwydd cut him off. They argued for a moment. Peeking from behind the flap, we could see the cloud of dust had disappeared. Dad's distraction had failed.

More guards were moving back along the wall. Then Morgwydd and Urien came into sight in the center ground, followed by seven or eight warriors. One began to light a fire by Morgwydd's basin, and two others began to fill the basin from the well. The rest followed Urien out of sight. They came back a few minutes later, dragging Mom.

She was gagged again, but this time with just a cloth. An ugly new bruise colored her left cheek. Her wrists were tied, her feet hobbled with a short length of rope. They tied her to a post with leather straps wrapped around her body and went back for Uncle Alf. Morgwydd came over to Mom. She drew her knife and slid the blunt edge softly along Mom's throat, held the point by her left ear, smiling.

"Silence until I tell you, hag. Say one word before, and I will geld and gut your brother while he still breathes. Then I will slit your throat. Understand?"

Mom nodded. Morgwydd laughed and cut off the gag.

Then Urien appeared, leading Uncle Alf by a noose

around the neck, like a choke-chain on a dog. Two pairs of warriors held his arms out straight to the sides with ropes bound to his wrists. A fourth man followed, holding another tight rope around his neck. Uncle Alf shuffled slowly between them, favoring the wounds at the back of his knees. They began to tie him between the other two stakes, arms bound wide, neck held from both sides. He stared straight ahead, ignoring everything around him

There were more shouts from the gate, and four more warriors came into view. Two of them were supporting the third, who hung between them, feet dragging. Blood covered his side, and one arm ended in a bloody knot of cloth crudely bound at the wrist. Urien waited grimly till they reached him, then began snapping questions. His voice wasn't loud, but the force of his anger made the warriors hunch. The leader held out Dennis's leather cap and my heart sank. Milde drew in her breath. But the warrior gave an answer Urien didn't like. His voice rose with more angry questions. The leader gestured, pointed, shook his head. I gave up trying to guess what had happened, but I was certain Dennis and Dad had escaped. The cap was all the warriors had managed to capture, at the cost of one very wounded man. Maybe more.

Urien turned from the leader and stepped to the wounded man, lifting his head by the chin. He said something quiet and let the man's head drop, then gave an order to the two on either side, pointing right toward our hut. They mumbled a reply and began to come our way. I nocked an arrow, Josie pulled out a stone.

Morgwydd stopped them, called them back. She sounded even more angry than Urien. She made them drag the wounded man over to face her, right beside the basin. It was filled, the fire burning well, the sun shining clearly two hands high above the wall. She asked the man another question. He struggled to lift his head, to answer. Everyone else was dead silent, but I could hardly hear him. She put her hand on his head and began to sing, slowly at first, softly. Not sweetly – her voice was never sweet – but almost gently. Almost a lullaby. The warrior closed his eyes, and his head sagged to his chest, lolling to the side. Still singing, Morgwydd raised her slender knife, and slit the warrior's throat with one smooth swipe.

His eyes flew open. He tried to speak but couldn't. Blood ran down his neck. The warriors holding him stood stiff as poles, staring straight ahead, trying not to show the fear in their eyes. Morgwydd grabbed the front of the bloody tunic and pulled them all forward, made them bend their dying comrade over the basin to catch his last blood in the silver water.

She never stopped singing, she just changed the tune. Her voice grew harsh again, normal. It rose, dragging across our ears like fingernails. She pushed the dead man away, and the others dragged him off quickly, almost running out of sight. Morgwydd stood where she was, staring into the basin, singing, wailing. That other voice joined her, horribly off key, twisting her lips, knotting her throat, pouring out of her mouth like vomit. The sound was a curse, damning everyone who heard.

I wanted to cower back in the shadows of the hut, wrap the filthy blankets around my head, stuff wax into my ears. But I couldn't step away from the doorway, couldn't tear my eyes from the thin view beyond the door flap. My feet wanted to get closer, to step outside, to go to her and give myself into her hands. Josie moaned and leaned toward the opening. I dropped the arrow and grabbed Josie's hand. Milde took her other hand, and we held her still. And she held us, while Morgwydd kept singing, louder and louder, beyond the strength of a human throat. Warriors cried out and covered their ears. They jumped from the wall and came to the center of the fort. The horses whinnied and reared, kicking the rails of their paddock. Still Morgwydd sang. The sound echoed off the walls, wailed from the surrounding hills. Trees on the hillside bent. The ground shook. Stones cracked and rattled downhill.

And in that chaos, the *wyrm* rose from the trees and into the sky directly below the midsummer sun.

# *Chapter 28*

The *wyrm* flew on three pairs of wings that beat in a smooth wave down the length of its back. A small fourth pair flared from its tail, like flukes on a dolphin. Its long body flashed in the sunlight, as though the gold and jewels it had eaten had dissolved into its skin and turned into scales. It spiraled high, rippling across the ball of the sun, then soared toward us, like some giant, airborne eel, with brilliant, seeking eyes.

For a moment no one moved, stuck in place by awe and terror both. Even Morgwydd stopped singing. But it wasn't fear that held her; it was joy. She raced to Mom's side.

"It comes now, hag!" she cried. "The dragon your gods sent to spoil our land. Sing to it in the tongue it knows. Call it to me, teach me its name. Give me the charm to bind it."

Mom laughed. "You are mad to think I have that craft. No one – man, woman, or god – speaks a tongue the night-walkers will obey. They are *mærc-stapan*, beasts of the empty marches; they go where they will."

Morgwydd grabbed Mom's hair and jerked her ear close. "Sing! Make it mine, or your brother will be its first meal on this land, and you the next."

Mom watched the oncoming *wyrm*. "You are more than mad to think I would give one as you such power over the world, *Wylisca*."

Morgwydd twisted the hair in her fist. "You lie! Sing! Sing or die!"

"Sing your own song," Mom gasped. "You called it, you tame it."

"I will," Morgwydd hissed, and she slammed Mom's head against the stake.

I grabbed up the dropped arrow and pushed past the door flap. Josie followed, clutching my shoulder.

"Ed, no! Wait for Alrun's signal!"

"Yes," Milde said, "we must wait." She stood at my other side.

I gritted my teeth and waited, arrow nocked, but not a single person noticed us. By then, the *wyrm* was above the wall. Before Morgwydd could open her mouth, it was overhead, passing her, swooping straight for the horses. They shrieked in terror and broke down the rails, charging the gate. The warriors there cried out and fled behind the huts. Urien ran from his own hut, raising a heavy, dark bow. The bow Uncle Alf had made for him, for just this moment.

Morgwydd stepped in front of Urien "No!" she cried. "He will be mine!" She began to sing.

Her harsh voice rose over the chaos of stampeding horses and yelling men. It doubled and then tripled, sounding chords no single throat could shape. Milde groaned. Josie clutched my arm. I could feel her shaking, and began to tremble myself. Because Morgwydd's face had changed. Had doubled. Morgwydd was there, but also some other, glaring from behind the tattooed spirals and lines. A hard-edged, white face, like bone, or stone on an altar, carved in a cruel shriek. A god's face, but vaguely female; a goddess. Brigantia maybe, or a demon hag from whatever kind of hell Morgwydd prayed to.

The *wyrm* heard the song. It turned from the horses and looped in a wide, rippling curve back toward us. It hovered a moment, staring down at Morgwydd and who-ever or whatever possessed her. Its eyes glinted. It settled almost gently on the packed dirt beside the well, its tail extending down the lane toward the gate. Its wings folded against its back as it slithered closer, lifting its head as it came. It stopped at Morgwydd's basin, head cocked almost like a dog's, studying her, eye to eye. Morgwydd sang on, unflinching, meeting its steady gaze with her own, and the other face smiled. Slowly, she lifted her right hand, unhooked her brooch, spread open the pin. The *wyrm* watched. Morgwydd dragged the pin across her scarred breast, and blood dripped into the basin. The *wyrm's* nostrils flared. Its gaze seemed to sharpen; interested, but inhuman. It lowered its head toward her, nodding in time to her horrible song. A sound flowed from the depth of its chest, deep, quiet, more like a hum in my own chest. Like a giant cat was purring. Its eyes began to close.

Mom lifted her head and sang a single piercing note.

The *wyrm* heard it. It jerked upright, swinging its head. But Mom had fallen silent. And Morgwydd was still singing. The *wyrm* turned back to her. It rose higher on its long neck, curving its body like a spring.

Urien realized what it was doing. He raised the dark bow again, drew, and loosed the arrow. It flew low, just glancing the belly of the rising *wyrm*. The beast hissed and came faster.

Urien cursed and nocked a second arrow. He drew the string to his chin, sighted, then drew it farther, back to his ear. And the bow shattered. Urien stumbled to one knee in a shower of broken wood. Uncle Alf roared with laughter. Morgwydd's song faltered.

The *wyrm* struck. Its head moved fast as an arrow, driven by the spring of its long body. Its mouth closed over Morgwydd's head and chest and clamped around her waist. It drew back, lifting her easily from the ground. Her legs kicked. Her right hand clawed the side of its snout, still clutching the brooch, then fell to the ground, severed at the wrist. The *wyrm* tipped its head and bit again and again, pulling her in. Its throat bulged and rippled downward, and Morgwydd was gone.

Urien struggled to his feet, screaming in rage. He drew

his sword and faced the *wyrm*. It ignored him. It drew in on itself, curling into tight loops, peering back at the gate, the milling horses. I wondered if it would ever stop eating. Urien ran toward it, sword raised in both hands, and hammered the blade down on its flank just behind the front wings. The sword struck sparks and bounced off the thick scales. The *wyrm's* head swung back like a whip, striking Urien with the side of its snout, still smeared with Morgwydd's blood. Urien went sprawling. Uncle Alf laughed again.

"The *Anglisc wyrm* is more than a match for any *Wylisc hund*!" he crowed. "We will all die, Urien, but you can be next! Go gloriously! Fight! Strike again!"

Urien would have. He pulled himself to his feet and found his sword. But the *wyrm* wasn't interested. The horses were all it wanted. Urien shouted commands, and a few brave warriors formed up in a ragged line across the lane. The *wyrm* raised its wings and launched itself into the air, as if it were striking upward. Wings out flat, it soared over the men and landed among the horses. They screamed and bucked, scattering in terror. All but one, a small one, that stood its ground, and reared, striking at the *wyrm's* snout with its hooves. It was Bil. I drew and loosed the arrow, but the *wyrm* reared and the arrow flew beneath its muzzle to smash against the wall. The *wyrm* struck, catching Bil in its jaws. Bil growled – that's the only word for the sound he made – Bill growled and kicked and bit, never once giving in. The spearmen ran forward and hurled their weapons, but the spears did no more damage than Urien's sword. They bounced off the scales and fell to the ground. The *wyrm's* skin just twitched, and it slid away, shaking poor Bil in its jaws. The scaffolding along the wall crashed down in sections as the *wyrm* passed beneath it, out of sight beyond the huts. The warriors ran for their fallen spears and looked to Urien. They had no idea how to deal with the beast.

Then the gates shook and shook again and burst open. In came a giant, flanked by a dwarf with a silver bow and a great, white boar as tall as a man. The giant towered in the gateway as horns sounded and drums beat. Mom greeted him with a song, and he seemed to grow even taller. He strode into the fort, brandishing a massive iron hammer and bearing a bright red shield adorned with a writhing portrait of a winged *wyrm* circling a golden peak. The dwarf and boar followed. They moved like gods. Like Thunor and Woðr and Frige's boar, Hildeswin. It was too much for the warriors. Half of them fled toward the other side of the fort. The rest retreated toward us down the lane.

Urien had started to go after the *wyrm*. Now he turned back to rally his men. One of them charged Thunor, sword raised. The god side-stepped lightly, turned the blade with his shield, and brought his hammer down on the man's head, splitting it with one blow.

"It is Beorhtscyld!" Milde cried.

The illusion dimmed for me as soon as she named him. Thunor was Dennis, with his sword and shield. Dad was the dwarf, the silver bow his harp, and he played a song of rage and power and fear. Made more terrible by Mom's singing.

"That's our sign," I said, and I drew and loosed an arrow at Urien.

He stepped forward and the arrow sang past his shoulder to strike a warrior beyond him. Urien spun, crouching, and recognized me. Rage filled his face. I drew another arrow. Josie threw a stone, but it was a long toss and Urien took it easily on his shield. He started to come toward us, but Dennis roared Urien's name in the voice of a god, a voice Urien couldn't ignore. He yelled a command, pointing at us with his sword, then turned to face Dennis. Two of his warriors left the others and came at us. Grateful, probably. Better us than face a god, right?

They underestimated Josie. I drew and aimed, Josie raised her ax. The warriors ran at us, stooped over, making themselves as small and protected as they could get behind two-foot-wide shields. Josie ran sideways a few steps, forcing one of them to turn toward her. Josie made him my easy target. She was my strength, not a distraction. I shot the warrior in the heart, neatly under his shield arm, and he sprawled in the dirt.

The other sprinted at me while I was unarmed, and Josie threw her ax. It spun toward him, struck his shield, and nearly split it. But didn't go through. He stumbled and kept coming. Right at me, ignoring Milde. She cut downward with her weaving sword, striking his arm so hard his sword spun to the ground. He yelled in shock and pain. As he tripped and staggered, she swung a back-hand swipe across the bridge of his nose. He fell at my feet and she hit him again. My strength.

I looked up just as Urien struck at Dennis, sword on shield, both striking and dancing and striking again. The white boar bounded among the other warriors. They struck and stabbed but could never hit him. There was nothing there but air, unless you knew what to look for and where. The boar was Egili, our small, insanely bold ferret. Their swords and spears whipped harmlessly over his head. But they were beginning to realize something wasn't right. They were staring harder, stepping back, thinking. I gave them something else to think about.

The dwarf appeared to be shooting his bow, so I added real arrows. I took down three and wounded another in the arm, and they never caught on. But I also missed one, and just barely grazed another. And I couldn't afford to do that. I was running out of arrows.

I nocked and drew again, and Josie said, "Shoot Urien! Take out the leader!"

But Dennis was in the way and Dad was behind him. And suddenly the boar broke free of the melee and bounded up the lane toward Mom. One of the warriors had come around the huts and was going for Uncle Alf. Josie threw a stone first; I shot a second later. She hit him, brought him up short, and my arrow passed between him and his shield. I nocked another, but Josie and Milde were racing toward him, blocking my aim. This warrior wasn't as big a fool as the others had been. He waited, spear and shield ready. Then Egili ran up his back, hissing like a snake. The man screamed and spun, reaching behind, flailing wildly with the shaft of his spear. Egili flew off and landed hard, but he'd earned me a clear shot, and I took the warrior in the chest.

Josie reclaimed her ax from the fallen shield and ran to Mom. She attacked the leather straps, chopping through the lot in three quick strokes. Milde ran to Uncle Alf, drawing her knife to cut his bonds, neck first, then the wrists. He almost fell when the first arm came free, but caught himself. Milde wedged herself under his shoulder and sawed at the rope on the other wrist. I stayed where I was. With the boar gone, Urien's men were rallying, circling toward him and Dennis. I killed one, missed another but wounded a third beyond him. The rest looked for cover. Mom, finally free, turned to face the fight and sang louder. Thunor appeared to grow and, for a moment, Urien fell back. Dennis taunted him.

"You cannot stand against me, Urien, son of Cynfarch. I have come from the Hall of Heroes with your name on my weapon. It will drink your blood before the sun peaks the sky."

It worked on Urien's men. They hung back, out of sight and out of the fight. But not Urien. He didn't answer Dennis in words; he came at him harder with his sword.

Now Dennis fell back and side-stepped. Urien lunged past, almost tripping. Dennis's riposte fell on Urien's shield. Then they were at it again, and I still didn't dare shoot for fear of hitting Dennis. Or Dad, who was behind Urien now, still playing, still singing, holding the illusion together with only Mom's help. Urien must have guessed about the music. He landed a massive blow on Dennis's shield, then jumped back, spun, and swung his sword at Dad.

The harp shattered in a final, twisted chord. Shards of wood tore from Dad's hands. He fell backward, twisting, arms flailing. Hit the ground face down. Silent.

Time stopped again, like it had for the *wyrm*. Mom's voice faltered, then died. Dad was dad again, no dwarf. And Dennis was Dennis, no god. He leaped at Urien, cursing in *Anglisc*, beating him back, away from Dad. Mom ran up the lane toward them. Josie and Milde and I took off after her.

The remaining warriors ran from cover to help their chief. I stopped and hit the first one in the leg, the second in the side. But two reached Dennis. He fell back, holding them off only because they crowded Urien and got in each other's way. I aimed again, but another warrior came at me from around the nearest hut. I turned, trying to shift my aim. He cut left and right, getting closer. I loosed the arrow, but he dodged and it missed him completely. He came straight at me while I fumbled for another arrow. He was too close. What I needed was a sword. Or Josie and Milde. But they were running with Mom.

A spear flew past my shoulder, punched through the warrior's shield and into his breast. He fell at my feet. I stared at him, then looked behind. Uncle Alf was limping toward me as fast as he could.

"The spear!" he bellowed. "Give me the spear!"

I dropped my bow and grabbed the shaft, yanking and twisting to free the spear head. The warrior screamed once, then vomited blood and died as the spear tore lose. By then Uncle Alf had reached me. He grabbed the spear with a nod and headed for Dennis, using it like a staff. Not nearly as hobbled as he'd pretended. There was no time for thanks. I swallowed hard, picked up my bow, and ran after him, drawing another arrow.

I shot it and hit the inside of Urien's shield. It startled him and he jumped back and Dennis went at him. But one of the others swung from the side, catching Dennis's shield on the center boss. The iron rang. The wood cracked and the red shield split. Without even a pause, Dennis threw it at the warrior's face and drew his long *seax*. He spun, he slashed, he turned their blows and tangled them up in their own weapons. Urien struggled with the arrow in his shield, trying to keep it out of his face. Another warrior appeared from behind the huts. I stopped and shot him.

When I looked back, Dennis was bleeding. Uncle Alf planted his feet and heaved his spear, bellowing Dennis's name. Dennis leaped aside and the spear went past him, into the body of one of the warriors. Dennis lunged, jabbing at Urien's face with the *seax*, then brought his sword down. Urien's helmet tore off, ringing like a bell. He staggered to one knee. But before Dennis could kill him, the other warrior charged in between, bulling Dennis back with his shield, stabbing around it with his sword.

Josie and Mom reached Dad, but Milde had stopped to pick up a fallen spear and throw it high to Uncle Alf. He caught it neatly and plowed on. Dennis broke off and ran to meet him. They embraced. Dennis was bleeding from cuts on both arms, limping slightly on one leg. But not about to give up.

And I finally had a clear shot at Urien. I nocked, loosed, and missed. Cursing, I nocked another arrow, drew back, and realized it was the gatekey. Our only way home. I put it back and pulled out another arrow. But by then Urien and his man had raced by me. And another had appeared from somewhere to join them. And a fourth came around the hut, lunging at me with his spear. I threw myself back and slammed against the wall of the hut. He spun and came at me again. Then Milde was there, deflecting his blow and slashing back upward to catch him under the chin. His head snapped back and he fell.

Urien and his men were forcing Dad and Uncle Alf back to the center ground, almost to the basin. Urien led the way, growling as he wielded his sword, blow after blow. The others tried to circle around to the sides. Dennis and Uncle Alf stood back to back, holding them off. I missed Urien again, wounding one of the warriors instead. Uncle Alf finished him with a swiping slash of the spear. Dennis stabbed another under his shield. But Urien brought down his sword and caught Dennis's blade. Dennis cried out as the grip tore loose. He pulled back, shaking his empty hand. Urien drove forward, raising his blade for another stroke.

Uncle Alf threw himself in the way, falling at Urien's feet, tripping him. Urien's blow went wild. And Dennis lunged in with his *seax*, to bury the blade in Urien's neck.

Urien stood a second, blood oozing round the blade, then fell across Uncle Alf, wrenching the *seax* from Dennis's grip. The last warrior took it all in: Urien dead, Uncle Alf pinned, Dennis disarmed. I shouted and fumbled for another arrow, Milde screamed and ran toward them. The warrior glanced at us, then turned back, raising his sword.

Only to find himself face to face with the *wyrm*, as it glided silently from behind Morgwydd's hut.

# *Chapter 29*

The warrior took one look and ran. The *wyrm* watched him, head lifting on its slender neck. Dennis turned and saw the great head rising above him.

"Beorhtscyld, stand still!" Milde cried.

But Dennis bent and began to heave Urien's body off of Uncle Alf. His right hand refused to grip. He had to jerk and drag with just his left.

"Flee!" Uncle Alf said. "Go! Get away!"

Dennis stayed, straining to move Urien's dead weight. The *wyrm* noticed him. Its gaze turned from the fleeing warrior. Its mouth opened and its neck began to swell.

"Run, Dennis!" I screamed.

He ran to the side, away from Uncle Alf. Not away from the *wyrm*. But he didn't keep running. He stopped, snatched up a fallen spear left-handed, and then went straight for the *wyrm*. Right at it, with the spear wedged under his elbow, as the bulge rippled up the thing's neck. Dennis rammed the point of the spear deep into the *wyrm's* open mouth, into the soft flesh of its tongue. The *wyrm* heaved backwards, swinging its head from side to side. Dennis went flying, ten feet or more. But somehow he held onto the spear. He pulled himself up and faced the *wyrm*, set his feet, waiting, and when it turned back to him, when it had him fixed in its gaze, Dennis threw the spear with all the might he could find in his left arm. Just as the bulge reached the back of the *wyrm's* mouth. Venom spewed out, engulfed the spear, and sprayed all over Dennis.

Uncle Alf roared. He heaved Urien's body to the side and stumbled on all fours to Morgwydd's basin. He hit it like a football tackle, hurling it over, spilling the water across the dirt at Dennis. Dennis fell, swept off his feet by water and venom and pain. The *wyrm* recoiled a moment. Another bulge grew at the base of its neck. Uncle Alf heaved the basin onto its edge and jerked it off the ground. Staggering under the weight, he managed three steps, then fell to his knees and lunged, planting the basin in front of Dennis, curling up against him, braced against the next fountain of venom. He screamed when it came.

Milde cried Frige's name and ran toward the *wyrm*, sword raised.

"Milde, no!" Josie shrieked. She was just behind me, with Mom, helping Dad stumble along between them. Blood streaked his face. His arm hung crookedly. Josie was pressing a bloody wad of cloth to his shoulder.

"Shoot him, Son," he said.

I looked back. The *wyrm* had seen Milde. It was turning toward her.

*What good will that do?* I wondered.

"It's why the goddess helped you make the bow," Dad said. "She did her part, now do yours. You'll either kill it or you won't. That choice falls to Wyrd."

"Can you call it?" I asked. "Can you bring it closer?"

Immediately Mom began to sing. Her voice rang clearly across the center ground and echoed off the walls. The *wyrm* paused. Dad joined in. His voice was weak, but the *wyrm* lifted its gaze toward us. Josie ran forward a few steps and hurled her ax as hard as she could. It spun toward the *wyrm* in a high arc. The *wyrm* saw it, watched it falling, then curled neatly out of its way and lifted its head again. Its terrible eyes locked on us. I only had one arrow left: the gatekey. I nocked it and lifted my bow. Josie waved her arms, jumped up and down. She didn't know the words to

Mom's song, but she sang the melody in nonsense sounds, *la-loo-lay* to call a *wyrm*. As mad as Rædwod ever was.

The *wyrm* coiled back on itself. Its wings unfolded and it lunged into the air, soaring toward us, mouth open to show its rows of teeth.

I drew and waited. Watching it come. Watching only the *wyrm*. Seeing only its face, only its huge, green eyes. Only one eye.

I loosed, and the arrow went true, straight into the slit of its eye. The sky iron head sliced the eye open. The heavy pile punched through the bone at the back of the socket. The arrow buried itself all the way to the fletching.

The *wyrm* lurched, head whipping, wings beating wildly, out of sync. But its weight carried it forward. I watched, astounded. One arrow should never have done such damage. Never. That's all I could think as the *wyrm* fell toward me.

Josie wrenched me out of its path. Its forewings knocked all of us flat as it crashed to the ground where I'd been standing. It rolled and twisted, nearly on top of us, beating its own head against the ground, smashing the nearest hut. Finally it settled, cold and broken beside us.

"Frige's sweet breast, that hurt," Dad moaned.

"Dennis!" Josie cried.

She and I scrambled to our feet and ran toward the basin. Uncle Alf was on his knees with Dennis's head cradled in his lap. Milde was with them, a hand on Uncle Alf's shoulder, the other on Dennis's breast. Egili appeared from behind them, climbed slowly onto Milde's knee, staring at Dennis, nose twitching frantically. We knelt with them.

Dennis was a mess. Still alive, but his skin was blistered and peeling from his face. His clothes were half rotted, and the skin beneath was blistering, too. His left hand was half bone. His wounds were bleeding, and there was no loose skin to close them with. His eyes were open. I don't think he could shut them, and I'm not sure how much he could see. I choked back a sob that was half bile. Uncle Alf shook, weeping. Tears ran down his cheeks and fell on Dennis's face.

"Don't cry for me, dear one," Dennis said. We could hardly hear him. "Wyrd offered me glory. I humbly accepted. Well, maybe not *humbly*." He tried to smile, but his lips were cracked and bleeding.

Josie began to weep. "Alrun, can't you do something? Milde? There has to be something, a charm, an herb. A song?"

Mom wiped her eyes and shook her head. "Even if there were, there is no time."

"Wait!" Josie cried. "We can take him back! To a hospital!" She jumped up and grabbed my arm, pulling me up with her. "Ed, quick, the arrow! Sing the song. Quick!"

"I don't have it," I told her. "It was my last arrow."

"Your last—" She looked back at the fallen *wyrm*. "Oh, no. No! You couldn't! We need it! I'll get it out!" She ran to the *wyrm*.

I ran after her. "Josie, no! Don't touch it!"

She didn't listen. She plunged her hand into its punctured eye, gasping when she touched the bloody fluid in the bottom of the socket. I ran up and grabbed her arm, but she was already pulling back. She had the end of the arrow clenched in her fist and was jerking on it.

"Don't," I said, taking her hand. The touch stung my palm. "You'll break the shaft."

She stopped jerking and began working it more slowly, turning it, angling it. Suddenly it let go, and I was afraid the head had pulled off inside the *wyrm's* skull. I was half right; the shaft was soft and punky, and the lashing broke just as she lifted it free. She caught the falling arrowhead before it hit the ground, grimacing as the coating of blood and slime stung her other hand.

"The well," I said. "Wash your hands. Quickly."

We hurried to the well, Josie cradling the leaf-shaped arrowhead as though it were a cracked egg. She held it under the water, swishing hard, rinsing it and her hands. I rinsed my own hands, too, but they still stung as though

I'd grabbed a nettle. The venom clung to my skin. To the arrowhead, too. It was corroding. Not even the sky iron was immune. I took it from her, rubbed it gently under the water, and patted it dry on my shirt.

Josie looked terrified. "Will it work?" she asked.

"Sure. Of course," I replied. "Don't worry, I'll get you all home."

We hurried back to the others, but Dennis wouldn't be moved.

"Nothing can stop this," he whispered. "You go, fair Shosefina, Queen of Speona. Go, all of you, while you can. One escaped us."

It was obvious Uncle Alf wasn't going. He knelt, hunched like a boulder, weeping. Milde, too, not weeping but there, to wait with Dennis till he passed. We all stayed. He asked for water once, and managed to choke down a sip. His breathing became so faint I kept thinking he had just died, but when I looked at his eyes, they were still shining.

Then he said, so faintly, "Sing. Please, sing."

Dad began it, softly, the song Milde had sung to Egili. *"Ne wearð wæl mare æfre gieta folces gefylled beforan þissum sweordes ecgum . . ."*

Never before this were more men slain by the sword's edge.

He used a different tune, not a lullaby. More like a hymn, I guess. Praise and thanks and glory, wrapped around sadness. Mom joined him, and their two voices woke memories. I wanted to sing with them, but I couldn't have choked out a single word, even if I'd known the song. Josie was choked up, too. I took her hand, and she almost broke mine squeezing back. Even Milde was weeping now, though she did sing, clear and strong, never once taking her eyes from Dennis's face. The music swelled and rang from the walls of the fort, even louder than the song that had captured the *wyrm*.

When they finished, Dennis had died. So quietly, I don't think anyone noticed, except maybe Egili, who

buried his face in a fold of Milde's gown. And probably
Uncle Alf, but he had let the song finish. He caressed Dennis's cheek, while Josie went into one of the huts and came
out with a blanket. He watched silently while Josie, Milde,
and I wrapped Dennis in it, and Mom and Dad stood
behind him, touching his shoulders. Then he heaved
himself to his feet, and went to wash his hands and knees
and all the other places that stung from the *wyrm's* venom.
The rest of us washed, too. And then we got ready to leave.

Because Dennis was right: one had escaped us. Maybe
on horseback. And not all of the fallen warriors were dead.
Even wounded, they were a threat. I was ready to open the
sky gate and go home, but Uncle Alf said no, Dennis had
promised to return the horses to Regenswig if we succeeded. None of us even tried to argue with him. Milde and I
went to find the horses, while Mom bound Dad's wounds
and Josie looked for food. The horses were all huddled
together just inside the gate, more than enough for the six
of us. We took the ones we knew and a couple more mares
that seemed calm enough for Josie and me. I would rather
have ridden out on Bil. Ridden beside Dennis. But that was
not their fate.

We laid Dennis's body across the mare he had ridden.
We saddled the stallion for Uncle Alf and called him, and
he came with a sheaf of arrows for me. The ones that had
missed, but the others as well. He'd pulled them out, and
made sure the wounded were dead.

"Take them," he said. "You are our protection now."

"You have a spear and a *seax*," I pointed out. He had
found his own spear somewhere and pulled Dennis *seax*
from Urien's neck.

"If Wyrd wills it I will use them, lame as I am," he said.
"With these, you will give me time to get off my horse and
find a place to stand where I won't fall over at the first
touch." He paused a moment, then said, "You shot well. It
was good. Now help me onto that tall horse."

It took Milde and me both. Josie and Mom helped
Dad, and Mom got up behind him, because he couldn't

really handle the reins with his bad arm. Then we rode out the front gate, around the fort, and carefully down the steep back side. Toward Regensburg. Dad had said Coria, but I said no, the Roman road wasn't any safer now. And Leofrith was in Regensburg. Maybe she could do something for Uncle Alf. And for Dad, so he could hold a harp again.

"I'll hold a harp again, if I have to do it with my teeth!" he exclaimed.

"You need to be able to sing, too," I said. "You have to sing Dennis's song."

"Oh, I won't need a harp for that. Oh, no. I will have your mother to sing with me."

"You will, husband," Mom said, hugging him from behind. "I will not let you go again."

"I won't let you let me," he replied. He craned his neck to kiss her, then yelped when he twisted his broken arm in the process. "Well, maybe Leofrith could be of some help. I need to hold you more than I need to hold a harp. Frige's lips!"

"What is it?" she cried. "Did I hurt you?"

"No! I can't wink my eye with this broken thing! To Leofrith!"

We rode till it was too dark for Uncle Alf to see the way, and Dad was almost falling from the saddle despite Mom's support. We camped without a fire, ate cold food, and stood watches. Then we mounted at dawn and rode long hours again. But we stopped in the daylight, in an open meadow beside a stream, shielded by hills.

"Here," Uncle Alf said. "Gather wood, all you can."

We built a pyre from fallen branches and deadwood we cut down with Josie's ax. It was harder work than it had been in the Goddess's grove, but we took turns, and it felt good. It was twilight before we had a big enough pile. We laid Dennis's body on the pyre, broken shield on his breast, sword by his side. We left him wrapped in the blanket. None of us wanted to see his face so damaged again.

Uncle Alf stayed dry-eyed this time. He lit the pyre all around, leaning on Milde so he could move quickly. Dad recited again from Beowulf's ending. Then Mom sang, and Milde sang, and Josie, and me, one after the other, offering what we could. Even Uncle Alf sang, and Dennis had been right: he couldn't carry a tune in a bucket. But it didn't matter. His voice was strong, he sang of heroes and glory, and Dennis would have cheered.

I sang the song of the gatekey. I thought maybe it would help Dennis pass through to whatever Earth claimed him now. And now's when I should tell how a shooting star arched past Tiw's star, right through the Ax, or thunder boomed, or a pair of white horses appeared at the edge of the trees. None of that happened.

What happened was that Egili came out of his pouch, where he'd been hiding since we'd left the fort. He climbed up Milde's gown and lay down across her shoulder. And watched. And suddenly he lifted his head and stared deep into the fire, neck arched, body tense as a drawn bow. His gaze turned upward then, slowly, like he was watching something rising in the smoke and embers. Something heavier, moving more slowly, but still . . . Rising. And after a minute of watching, higher and higher, while we all watched him, Egili lowered his head and relaxed and fell asleep.

We tended the fire all night, pushing in the half-burned lengths, cutting more by torchlight, hot and sweaty while we worked, hot on the front and cold on the back while we kept watch by the fire. By dawn, there was nothing left but a pile of smoking ashes and the bits of iron and brass from Dennis's gear.

Uncle Alf and Milde used sticks to scrape most of the ashes and smaller pieces of metal into a clay pot they'd brought from the fort. Milde used her weaving sword to prod the larger pieces of metal – the iron boss and brass *wyrm* from his shield, the blade of his sword – out of the ashes, so she could douse them with water until they were cool enough to wrap in her cloak and tie behind her saddle. Uncle Alf carried the pot. We rode over the height of land where we had been ambushed hardly a week before. We didn't stop; the place felt wrong. And there was still enough time in the day to get well past our first campsite. But not quite enough to make it to Regensburg. We camped one more night. I went hunting with Josie. We bagged two hares and a grouse between us, and when we got back, Egili happily lit into the best parts.

While the meat was cooking, I braced my bow string again and reached into my pouch for the piece of beeswax I always carried. My hand brushed the arrowhead. I had wrapped it in a bit of cloth and put it there to keep it safe. Now, as I rummaged for the wax, the cloth fell apart like it was rotted. The side of my hand brushed the tip of the arrowhead, crumpling the iron like tinfoil.

My chest knotted. I dropped the bow and held the pouch wide open, carefully reached in and brought out the half-wrapped arrowhead in the cradle of my palm. The cloth *was* rotted, and fell apart as I lifted it. The arrowhead was rotting, too.

Wyn

# Chapter 30

"Dad? Mom?" I called. I must have sounded terrified, because everyone dropped what they were doing and ran over.

"Frige's heart," Milde muttered, looking into my cupped hand. The sky-iron was pitted, its waving pattern etched, like it had been lying at the bottom of the ocean for years. The vanes on the leaf-shaped blade were thin and fragile, the tip completely gone, broken off when I'd bumped it. Even the heavy pile looked ancient. There was no sign of the runes.

"What happened?" Josie cried.

"Did you wash it?" Mom asked.

Obviously not well enough. And I realized the scrape on my hand was stinging. The venom could still burn my skin, still eat away at the iron. And now I noticed that the knees on Uncle Alf's pants were torn and rotting, and thin spots showed all over his tunic where the venom had spattered him, despite the rinsing he'd given them after Dennis died.

I looked at Josie's face and remembered what she'd said; about how she'd felt on the first wrong Earth, when she realized she might never see her parents again. How I'd felt when Dad had disappeared.

"Mom, Dad." I said. "I need to get Josie home."

"No," Josie said. "It's all right." She stared at my hands,

at the crumpled arrowhead. "We're stuck, okay. It's not the worst place to be." She could barely get the words out.

"No! We are not stuck," Dad said. "Not while we can sing. Hurry! Alrun, Ælfweard, Milde, all! Take hands while there's still some sky-iron left in that cursed thing!"

I closed my right hand gently over the arrowhead to shield it as much as I could, then held out my left hand to Josie. She came back to life and laid her hand in mine. Mom took her other hand, and Dad took Mom's as best he could with his wounded hand. He held out the other to Milde. To Uncle Alf.

"Come!" he said. "Leave the horses, leave all but what you value most. This trip on the star road will make the others seem like a stroll on a sunny day!"

They both hung back. Uncle Alf bent stiffly and picked up my bow. I had completely forgotten it. He studied it closely, stroked it. But he wouldn't look at us.

"This is what I value most," he said. "This world is what I value next. I would have both."

Mom let go of Dad and Josie and went to him. "The choice is yours, Brother," she said. "I know you have never been happy in our new home." She threw her arms around his neck and held him tightly for a few moments. He freed an arm and hugged her back.

Josie let go of me and went to Milde. "You're staying, too, aren't you."

Milde nodded. "What I saw of your world – or that one so like it – has no place for one like me. It smelled wrong. Things moved too quickly. The goddess I love is here."

"The Goddess loves you, too," I said. *And so do I,* I thought. *But not as much as Josie. Not enough to trap her here.* "Take care of Uncle Ælfweard, all right?"

She managed a smile. "As much as he will let me. I can never be his Dennis."

"But you can be much indeed!" Dad said. "I have known Ælfweard in younger days. He loves beauty. He loves strength even more. I have even known him to love women. Only Wyrd knows how you two will fare, dear, sweet, brave, gentle Milde, but I know he will gladly accept your care if you wish to give it. You need only remain as you are: tough and bold and keen as a spear head, true as a well shot arrow, supple as one of his bows."

"As one of Eadgar's bows," she said, glancing at Uncle Alf, who was still holding my bow. He glowered. But he also blushed. The first time in his life, as far as I knew.

Mom laughed, but there were tears in her eyes. "Get him to Leofrith. She knows charms that will ease the hurt in his legs, and time may ease the hurt in his heart. Quickly now! Enough leave-takings or we may not be able to go."

Milde pulled Egili's pouch off her shoulder and handed it to Mom, then turned and called him. He came bounding from his meal, leaped for her skirts, and didn't stop until he perched on her shoulder. Milde pulled him down into her arms, squeezed him tight enough to make him hiss, then held him out to Mom.

Mom handed back the pouch. "He was Dennis's pet, not mine," she said. "Now he will be yours."

"Pet?" Dad exclaimed. "That one? Never! Egili is very much his own ferret!"

Milde took the pouch, quickly hugged Josie, gave me another smile, and went to stand by Uncle Alf. Dad, Mom, Josie, and I took hands. Then I began to sing.

Mom and Dad and Josie joined in. But it was as hard as it had been the very first time. Even harder. Nothing happened at first, nothing at all. So I began to walk the pattern, pulling the others behind me. Sunwise thrice and moonwise back. Walking got harder, loose sand, deep water. And the arrowhead didn't get heavier, it got lighter, thinner, as though the charm was sucking the sky iron from its guts. I pushed my cupped hand ahead of me and sang louder. As the verse ended, a feeble light began to show between my curled fingers. On the next turn, the sky in front of me began to waver. A slit began to form, the faintest line of darker blue against the backdrop of tree and hill and sky. I fixed my eyes on it, till it was the only thing I could see, and sang till the song was the only thing I heard.

The slit slowly tore open, two feet, four feet, finally taller than me. Not wide, but wide enough. I turned sideways and squeezed through.

It was cold, aching cold. And black, the thousand, thousand stars dim and wavering. I flinched, but I kept pulling, squeezing Josie's hand so hard my own hand hurt. She seemed to stick for a moment. Her voice faltered. I could barely hear Mom and Dad. I was singing as loudly as I could, but even my own voice seemed thin. I had to drag them through after me, just heave as hard as I could and keep heaving until we lurched free and I felt the gate snap shut. I didn't dare stop then to rest. Tendrils of . . . mist? Fog? Something gray and ghostly swirled around my legs, dragging at my clothes, my feet, as though it had hands and wanted to hold us back, to keep us there with it. I wondered if this was what Josie had meant about fog that first time we'd walked there. No wonder she'd been shaking when we'd finally come out at Ad Gefrin. I was shaking.

But I kept singing and kept walking, and the arrowhead kept glowing, pulsing a little brighter whenever I walked the right path, dimming if I strayed. I sang into the cold, against the clutching mist. Josie's voice helped me, faint as it was. Mom and Dad were a constant harmony I could only feel. A wind came up behind us, and I thanked Tiw and Frige and kept walking, searching for home.

A familiar star appeared in the distance, so faint only a weak pulse from the arrowhead convinced me it was the one I wanted. There were others beside it, but I couldn't even turn toward them. I was slogging, forcing my way forward, despite Josie pushing me, helping with all her strength.

The star slowly drew nearer. That's how it seemed, as though we were walking in place and the star had to come to us. My throat was raw, my voice hoarse, the arrowhead lighter, drained by the power of the charm we were forcing through it. But the star drew closer and closer, step by step, till I could reach out and touch it, holding the remains of the arrowhead in front of us as gently as I could without crushing it. Even so one of its blades flaked off and disappeared in the swirling mist.

I touched what was left to the star, leaned in, and pushed. And sang. And cried, I realized. Tears fell on my hand, onto the arrowhead.

*Open*, I prayed. *Open for us.*

The slit appeared, thin as a strand of Mom's hair. I pushed harder, squeezed a little more volume from my waning voice. I could hear Josie's voice, too, suddenly strong. Never stopping, as the slit lengthened and widened, till we could squeeze through. Barely. Just in time. I pulled her past me, and she pulled Mom and Mom pulled Dad, unwinding through the slit till I was the only one left outside, but still holding Josie's hand.

My fingers almost slipped free then, but Josie dug in her nails, let go of Mom and took me with both hands to drag me through. The slit snapped shut, slicing off the back of my boot and a thin flap of flesh from my heel.

We fell to the ground, gasping. Josie was weeping. I was too tired to weep. I opened my hand and flakes of rust trickled out. That was all. The arrowhead was gone.

"It's all right, Josie," I said. I wrapped my arms around her. "It's all right. You're home."

"Home." Dad was weeping, too. His voice cracked. "Home!" he cried, and then bellowed it as loud as he could: "*Home!*"

He began to dance, still holding Mom's hand, pulling her around on the grass with him. It was dark, the moon was setting, and I could make out the grandstand against the sky, a few of the smaller buildings to the side. A jet flashed high overhead, blinking red and green among the faded stars. The air stank of gasoline and diesel and the gods knew what else. Whatever gods were left to know on this world.

Yeah, we were home. Josie and I lay side by side on the grass, our hands still clenched together. Mom and Dad danced around us, singing silly children's rhymes in *Anglisc*.

"All right, what's going on over there?" a voice called. A flashlight's bright eye wobbled toward us in the hand of a striding silhouette. I recognized the voice: Officer Quincy. And we had a lot of explaining to do.

I started to laugh. Josie, too. I laughed and laughed, and Josie laughed with me, while Mom and Dad danced and poor Officer Quincy stood there, shaking his head at the four idiots who had appeared out of nowhere on his shift. We laughed because we couldn't help it. Because we were home. Because we were still alive to do it.

# Coming Next: The Bell Cannon

## From Chapter 12

*So far . . . It's September, 1878. Ewan Gilmore, a cabin steward on the steamship* Isle of Lewis, *is traveling as a passenger in order to act as a secret bodyguard for Professor Jakub Skovajsa. Skovajsa and his daughter have been forced to leave the U.S. after a mysterious but deadly accident. Rumor has it that the professor was building an unimaginably powerful weapon for the Army, but a trial run had killed at least a dozen people, including two Senators and Skovajsa's own wife. The press has vilified the professor, death threats have come from many directions, and no other steamship line would take him aboard. Now Ewan's task is to keep him alive. On the second night of the passage, Ewan discovers a murdered passenger in the Ladies cabin above the saloon – a man who, from the rear, looked very much like Professor Skovajsa. Ewan's suspicions fall on one of his cabin mates, a young man named Derek Reid, who spends most of his time in the company of the professor.*

Alone now in the cabin with sleeping Derek, Ewan studied the young man's boyish face. If Derek was plotting something against the professor, it certainly didn't show in sleep. His valise, on the other hand, might yield more. It was tucked under the berth.

Ewan knelt and carefully slid it out. Derek had left the

buckles undone, and the latch was unlocked. It opened with a loud *snap* when Ewan pressed the catch. He froze, but Derek didn't move. Ewan slowly lifted the lid. Two poetry books lay on top of the clothes, next to a shaving kit and a small flannel bag that turned out to hold a second pair of shoes. A pocket inside the lid held a writing set, papers covered with scribbled poems, and a thin leather wallet with a few small bills and a draft on a Kentucky bank for fifty dollars more – hardly enough to tour the Continent.

Unless he had means to get more. Someone to slip him cash when he needed it. An accomplice. A master.

Ewan dug through the clothing: shirts, handkerchiefs, trousers, underthings, socks, and finally felt, beneath it all, the rasp of very coarse cloth. A burlap sack. Hiding a rough jacket, with trousers to match. And squashed between the sack and the bottom of the valise was a battered, wide-brimmed hat.

The memory clicked on like an electric light: Coming up from steerage. A man at the saloon hatchway. A thick immigrant accent. A glimpse of blonde hair beneath his hat. This hat.

Ewan sat back on his heels. If he'd needed more proof that Derek was a stowaway, he had it now. But it still didn't prove that Derek was stalking the professor. Or had murdered the reverend. It still seemed so unlikely. Ewan finished ransacking the valise but found nothing more that could be called evidence. He stood and checked Derek's jacket and overcoat, too, draped atop the spare upper berth. They held nothing more than a handkerchief and a thin pair of gloves. That left the trousers, but Derek was wearing them.

Ewan carefully tidied the contents of the valise, shut the lid, and slid it back under the berth. He studied Derek's sleeping form one last time. Finally, he leaned over and slowly, carefully, slid his hand under Derek's pillow.

Nothing there.

Derek's eyes fluttered. He drew in a deep, wet breath and rolled onto his side. Ewan slipped his hand out, stepped back, and turned around, grabbing at his tie and shrugging off his coat. Derek sighed and went quiet.

Ewan let out his own slow, sigh of relief and tip-toed over to Keane's berth, where the much labeled valise was lying right on top, unlatched, with the end of a necktie sticking out from under the lid. Ewan opened it and began searching inside. Clothes, colored scarves, packets of playing cards, a slender wand, a pair of phony roses, a paper-mâché thumb, a Chinese puzzle box. Ewan shook the box and tried to figure out the trick, but it wouldn't open. He muttered a curse and tucked it back in with the rest of the gear, trying to arrange it the way he'd found it, making sure to leave the end of the necktie sticking out.

When he turned away, Derek was watching him with bleary, puzzled eyes.

Ewan smiled. "Woke up, did you? You were thrashing about there so much I was sure a bad dream had swallowed you whole. Sorry if I disturbed you. Just getting into bed here. Don't mind me, I'll be quiet as a mouse." He forced himself to stop babbling and started getting undressed.

Derek grunted and rolled onto his side, still facing Ewan. He closed his eyes, but Ewan could tell he didn't fall right back to sleep. Ewan turned off the light, crawled into his berth, and lay still, listening. After a minute, he shifted and tried to breathe more slowly, feigning sleep. He almost did fall asleep. Derek's next movement brought him back from the edge of the abyss.

Ewan forced himself to lie still and keep his breathing slow and steady. He kept his eyes closed, trying to see with his ears. Derek slid out from between the sheets. His feet landed softly on the deck. His valise whispered out from under the berth. Clicked open. Clothes shifted. The lid clicked shut. Then more stealthy movements: Derek getting dressed! Ewan stiffened and Derek froze.

Ewan snorted, swallowed, and went still again. After a

long few minutes, Derek finished dressing. The door clicked open, admitting a brief gleam of light, and shut again. Ewan counted to fifteen, then threw off the covers and hurried to listen at the door. Nothing. Maybe Derek had just gone to the head, but maybe not. Ewan wasn't going to wait to find out. He pulled on his clothes, grabbed his hat, and slipped out into the companionway. It was empty. So were the heads and the baths. Ewan hurried forward, listening for voices behind the cabin doors. He paused a second at the silent stairs, then decided to check the saloon first. It was empty, too – odd, because Keane was still out and about. Ewan wondered if he and Derek had planned to meet. If so, it would have to be in the smoking cabin.

Ewan hurried up the companionway and paused to check the ladies cabin first. A chill went down his neck as he shuffled into the dark room, half expecting to trip over another body. But the cabin was empty. With a foolish surge of relief, Ewan went out on deck.

He found the ship mantled in fog. The horn sounded just as Ewan stepped out, and he realized he'd been hearing it belowdecks the whole time. He'd been so focused on Derek's movements that he hadn't even noticed the deep-throated moan. The sounds of the sea and the wake were muffled, too. There was part of a moon somewhere up in the sky, but the drifting fog hoarded light. The ship's running lights glowed dimly, red and green orbs of gauze. The side of the deckhouse was dark gray velvet. The lifeboats hovered like distant clouds. The rail was all but invisible.

Ewan stood a moment to let his eyes and ears adjust. He started aft, toward the smoking cabin, then heard something behind him, footsteps maybe. He turned, peering into the gloom. He went forward. His footsteps tapped dully on the damp planks. The horn sounded again. Ewan passed the end of the deckhouse. He could just make out the engine room skylights beside him and the bulk of the funnel, looming overhead. He took one more step, when an arm looped around his neck and jerked him backward, choking off his startled cry.

\* \* \* \* \*

Vermont author Dean Whitlock writes fantasy and science fiction for young and not-so-young adults. His stories have appeared in Asimov's, Fantasy & Science Fiction, and Aboriginal SF, as well as in anthologies in the United States and abroad. His first two YA fantasy novels were originally published by Clarion Books, but now he publishes independently under the Boatman Press imprint. In 2019, His novel *Finn's Clock* was awarded First Place in the Young Adult category for the 7th Annual Writer's Digest Self-Published Ebook Awards. An Air Force brat, Dean has lived in a dozen states and three foreign countries, a life of travel that gave him plenty of time to read in the car and now enriches his writing. You can find out more about Dean and his upcoming new titles and reprints at www.deanwhitlock.com.

↑

*This book would not have been possible without the help and knowledge of several special people:*

Jessica Buster, my creative and poetic Anglo-Saxon translator.

David Huggins, an Anglo-Saxon and Viking warrior.

Erica Layton, who showed me how to spin wool with a bobbin and introduced me to . . .

Rebecca Crane, a traditional weaver who knows how the Medieval Anglo-Saxons did it.

Cynric, an SCA archer who critiqued the first draft of the crucial opening chapters.

Pierre-Alexandre Sicart, who made the final, careful edit (and translates my stories into French).

Robert Goodrich, the late Lord Robert of Panther Vale, who gave me my first archery lesson and showed me how to make arrows and bowstrings.